SPIRIT
AND DUST

ALSO BY ROSEMARY CLEMENT-MOORE

Brimstone

Highway to Hell

The Splendor Falls

Texas Gothic

SPIRIT
AND DUST

ROSEMARY CLEMENT-MOORE

Delacorte Press

Text copyright © 2013 by Rosemary Clement-Moore
Jacket art: photograph of girl © 2013 by Elena Zanotti; lettering © 2013 by Mikhail/Shutterstock with manipulations by Hothouse Designs; back cover art © 2013 by David M. Schrader/Shutterstock

All rights reserved. Published in the United States by Delacorte Press, an imprint of Random House Children's Books, a division of Random House, Inc., New York.

Delacorte Press is a registered trademark and the colophon is a trademark of Random House, Inc.

Visit us on the Web! randomhouse.com/teens

Educators and librarians, for a variety of teaching tools, visit us at RHTeachersLibrarians.com

Library of Congress Cataloging-in-Publication Data
Clement-Moore, Rosemary
Spirit and dust / Rosemary Clement-Moore. — 1st ed.
p. cm.
ISBN 978-0-385-74080-7 (hardcover : alk. paper) —
ISBN 978-0-375-98970-4 (glb : alk. paper) — ISBN 978-0-375-98271-2 (ebook)
[1. Ghosts—Fiction] I. Title.
PZ7.C59117Spi 2013
[Fic]—dc23
2012034696

The text of this book is set in 14-point Vendetta Light.
Book design by Angela Carlino

Printed in the United States of America

10 9 8 7 6 5 4 3 2 1

First Edition

Random House Children's Books supports the First Amendment and celebrates the right to read.

I HAVE BEEN BLESSED WITH A CIRCLE OF FRIENDS
WHO RIVAL THE GOODNIGHTS IN LOYALTY, LOVE,
AND ECCENTRICITY, IF NOT IN NUMBER.

GIRLS, THIS BOOK IS FOR YOU.

SPIRIT
AND DUST

1

THE LOCAL COPS kept staring at me. I couldn't decide if it was the plaid miniskirt in subarctic temperatures, or the fact that they'd never seen anyone talk to the dead before.

At the moment, I was mostly shivering, but that had more to do with the gray Minnesota afternoon than residual psychic energy, though there was that, too.

"What do you see?" asked Agent Taylor, my FBI handler and the reason—other than the dead man—that I was there.

I had to swallow before I could speak. I like to pretend I'm all *Daisy Goodnight, kick-ass teen psychic*, when really most of the time I'm all *Please don't let me puke in front of the FBI.*

The medical examiner had carted off the body of the man I was supposed to read, and a daylong drizzle had washed away any physical traces from the sidewalk. But an afterimage—one that only I could See—remained where he'd fallen, the vivid imprint of his violent death stamped into the intangible fabric of reality.

It wasn't a pretty sight. I mean, the guy hadn't been pretty even before someone had shot him in the head.

"One guy. Big, bruiser type." I gestured to the curb. "Shot here, in the back of the head with a small-caliber pistol, I think." Psychic traces of him smeared the sidewalk and grass beyond. Unlike bloodstains, they couldn't be rinsed away by the rain. "Bruiser definitely died here, but it looks like maybe he was dragged out of sight, around the back of this building."

Chief Logan, the local guy in charge, exchanged looks with Agent Taylor and his partner, Agent Gerard, but I already knew I was right. Not because I was Daisy Goodnight, kick-ass psychic for the FBI, but because the death was so recent that the details were way more clear than I needed.

Standard procedure was to let me read a murder site cold, with no prior information. And boy, was I reading this one cold. Like, icicles-on-my-belly-ring cold.

Four hours earlier I'd been in Texas—freshman chemistry lab, to be precise, trying not to blow myself up before I'd even finished my first college semester—when I'd gotten a 911 text from my uncle Sam. By which I mean Uncle Sam in the person of Agent Taylor. I'd given a cover-story excuse to my professor—because the feds are a little weird about the whole psychic-

2

consultant thing—then headed outside, where a big black sedan waited for me on the street.

"Hey, Agent Tasty," I'd said, when I saw Agent Taylor waiting beside the car. I liked Taylor, and not just because he was young and really hot for a buttoned-up guy with a G-man haircut and a newly minted FBI badge. I sort of *like* liked him, but we worked together and I was still three months shy of legal age, so it stayed within the boundaries of "sort of." None of which kept me from noticing that he did not skimp on the FBI physical training program.

"Watch it, Jailbait," he replied, like he always did. Then he sized up my outfit, which was perfectly adequate for a sunny San Antonio autumn day. "I hope you brought a sweater."

I hadn't. And his partner, Agent Gerard, stick even farther up his butt than normal, had refused to stop by my dorm for a jacket.

An hour later, the three of us—Taylor, Gerard, and I—were on a plane to the Midwestern tundra. Their haste made me uneasy, and not just because they'd whisked me off to hot chocolate country in my iced tea clothes. The feds like to exhaust all other avenues of investigation before they call in a psychic. Even me. Which made me wonder why I was risking hypothermia while I looked for clues on the mean streets of Elk Butt, Minnesota.

The college town was picturesque—dead-guy psychic slide show notwithstanding. Its biggest claim to fame, other than two liberal arts colleges, was that Jesse James botched a bank robbery there.

Taylor had briefed me on that much before we'd pulled up in front of a redbrick building on the Charleston College campus,

3

where bright yellow crime-scene tape held back students who were taking pictures with their phones. It was a girls' dorm, surrounded by lawn and overlooking a small lake in back. Not exactly the low-rent education district.

Bruiser did *not* look like a college student capped on the way to sociology class. He looked like a thug, his spirit traces felt vile, and worst of all, the freshness of his death had slammed me as soon as I'd climbed out of the car.

Agent Taylor and I had been called to a scene this fresh just that past summer, out in the desert, west of Sonora. One kid killed, another missing, the state troopers determined to find any clue, and fast. As soon as I'd gotten my feet on the ground, I'd known the little girl was dead, but it had taken me all afternoon and half of a heatstroke to find her body.

That had been a bad one.

"Hey, Daisy." Agent Taylor's voice yanked me out of memory. "What do you hear?"

He wasn't really asking what the dead were saying. Nothing in his tone—only our code question—gave any hint that he could tell I'd taken a mental step offside. He'd suggested the code when he'd figured out I wouldn't ask for help in front of other officers—especially Agent Gerard.

What do you hear? Was I that transparent, or was he thinking of the Texas desert, too?

"Nothing but the rain," I said, the proper response for "Don't worry, I still have both hands on the wheel." I mean, what was a little ghost brains on the sidewalk?

Agent Gerard, hands on his hips, showing the butt of his sidearm in his shoulder holster, said, "Can we get this dog and pony show on the road before it ends up on the effing Tweet-book?"

He was right, which annoyed me. I had questions, but the whole reason I was there was to get answers the way only I could.

Ignoring the audience of students and cops, I blew into my icy hands, then crouched to lay my palm on the pavement where Bruiser had fallen. Over time, the imprint of his death would fade, but now it was a clear, sharp buzz of connection that raced up my arm like a hit to the funny bone.

Panic and prayer. Not much. Not long. Just *Oh God.* A milli-second of petition but no contrition. And then nothing.

"He didn't see it coming," I said, the image vivid on my closed eyelids. "I don't get any kind of anxiety or fear. It seems like he was just minding his own business—whatever that was—when *blammo.* Out of nowhere."

What *was* kind of weird was that for such a clear death im-print, there was barely a trace of Bruiser's actual spirit, something I would expect only from a much older site.

"Anything else?" asked Chief Logan.

The question confirmed my hunch that there was more going on than just a dead thug on a college campus, but I forced myself to focus and search deeper and wider for any other recent psychic events strong enough to stick.

"No one else was killed. At least, not here." I stood and shook imaginary cobwebs off my hand. I wished I could shake off my dread as easily, but the threads of suspicion had knit together too tightly. "There's someone missing, isn't there? A girl from this dorm?"

"We'll ask the questions," snapped Agent Gerard, making Taylor visibly grind his teeth. Before they could argue, Chief Logan overrode them both.

"The victim," he said, nodding to the sidewalk, "was the driver for a girl named Alexis Maguire. Yes, she is a student here, and yes, she is missing."

"Okay," I said, but I was trying to convince myself. *It's okay. She's not definitely dead. It's not like the little girl in Texas.*

Taylor had taken a small step closer, as if worried I was going to faint, which I was absolutely not going to do. I was Daisy "Talks to the Dead" Goodnight, and freaking out wouldn't help anyone.

"Okay," I said again, with more conviction. "Let's go *hablo* dead guy."

2

I'VE BEEN READING spirit remnants since I was a kid. "I see dead people." The whole shebang.

Because I was raised by a family of witches and psychics, I never thought I was crazy, though I did have some unpleasant moments on school field trips to battlegrounds of the Texas Revolution. I don't think they'll ever let me back into the Alamo.

My gift does tend to isolate me from the living. One, I suppose I seem a little weird—I mean, aside from my wardrobe choices. And two . . . Well, everyone wants to know if there's something left of us when we die, but most people are a little afraid of the answer.

I'd stepped off the pavement and was following the psychic smears on the grass—the trail of Bruiser's dragged body. I moved with purpose, Taylor scrambling to catch up, Gerard and Logan trailing behind as we rounded the building to the stretch leading to the small lake. There was crime-scene tape there, too, but the area must have been searched for trace evidence already, since no one stopped me from crossing it.

"Why are we headed back here?" asked Taylor, a logical question. I'd just said that I wanted to talk to the victim's shade, and usually I did that where someone died, or while holding something of theirs.

"Because he's not there," I said, jabbing a thumb back to where Bruiser had met his end. "There's the imprint of his death, but not enough of his spirit for me to talk to. The remnant must be where his body was hidden."

Only it wasn't. Which was weird. And when I say something is weird, it is *seriously* weird.

I stopped in the middle of the lawn between the dorm and the little lake. I could picture coeds sunning themselves there on a much warmer day. I didn't have to picture Bruiser's body, poorly hidden by a clump of bushes, because I could See him there with my extra senses. But with a death this new, I expected Bruiser's remnant to be standing there like something out of the Haunted Mansion, or at least a mist or shade I could draw out for a chat.

He couldn't have moved on already, because there were still shreds and tatters of his spirit wisping around the site.

Taylor had nearly run me over when I'd halted so quickly.

8

"What's wrong?" he asked. "You're not going Basingstoke on me, are you?"

That was our code for "batten down the hatches," and it shook me out of my befuddlement.

"I haven't even *done* anything yet," I said, because Gerard and Logan hadn't caught up. "I'm not *that* big a wimp."

He glanced toward the older men and lowered his voice. "Well, I don't know what you're Seeing. It's not . . . You don't See *her*, do you?"

Then I felt like a total heel, because when he'd asked me if I was going Basingstoke, he must have been imagining the worst. I mean, he'd been in that Texas desert, too.

There was no sign of a murdered college girl, but before I let either of us be relieved about that, I said, "Give me a second so I can be sure."

With my eyes closed, the spirit traces of Bruiser were bright, vile yellow scraps of fog, eddying closer to me. I ignored them for the moment, ignored Gerard and Logan coming up to us, ignored the damp and cold seeping through my sneakers.

I perceive the spirit world through the five senses already wired into my brain, plus the emotions we all have. I've learned to dial the volume up or down on the psychic impressions—the visit to the Alamo taught me the importance of *that* skill—but mostly it's like seeing in color. I just *do* it.

Harder to describe is how I interact with that layer of reality. I pictured my psychic self as a sort of ghost me living in my skin, part force field, part sensory array. When I sought out spirits, remnant traces of human souls, I imagined my psyche rushing with my blood out into the smallest capillaries of my skin to my pores, where it could mesh with the energies around me.

That was what I did in the wet grass behind the girls' dorm in Elk Butt, Minnesota, searching for any sign of a murdered girl.

Nothing. A relief, but not in any way an end to my worry.

I opened my eyes and looked at Taylor. Gerard and Logan had joined us. "What's the girl's name again?" I asked.

"Alexis Maguire," said Taylor. "She's a senior, in her last year."

"I don't get any hint that she was killed here," I told them. "But if you give me something of hers, I can tell you for sure if she's still alive."

Chief Logan nodded slowly. I didn't know what he really thought of the psychic stuff, but he seemed to like my professionalism. Which was why I worked so hard at it. "We can do that."

Then I gestured to the image half hidden in the bushes, even though they couldn't see it. "You said Bruiser over there is the driver for the missing girl? Is that some kind of code for 'bodyguard'? Because this guy looks more like a WWF wrestler than a chauffeur."

"Driver *and* bodyguard," said Logan. "Her father is a rich, powerful man."

Money and enemies. So, the girl came from a political or crime family. And going by my sense of Bruiser, I was thinking crime. I was thinking *enforcer*.

"How long was his body hidden?" I asked, trying to figure

out the weirdness of his spirit traces—not to mention the time-table for the missing girl.

Logan was obliging with answers. "All night. We know that the driver was supposed to take the girl into the city to go club-bing. She never showed up, but her friends didn't think anything about it until she didn't come to class this morning. A search turned up the body shortly after that."

So Alexis was the type of girl likely to ditch the club scene but rarely miss class. Not exactly the stereotype of a mafia princess.

"Okay," I said, rubbing my hands together, getting blood and psyche flowing. "Let's see what Bruiser has to say."

I crossed the short distance to where his body had lain for twelve hours or so. The grass had been trampled by the crime techs, but the ground was soft from the misty rain. I squatted and dug my hand into the dirt where blood and brains had seeped from the hole in Bruiser's skull. Since he'd been moved there after the fact, there wasn't more than a trace, but gray matter always made the best connection.

It should have taken just a fraction of willpower to bring him into focus, like tuning in to the right radio station. But nothing about this remnant was behaving normally.

Normally the death imprint and the actual spirit of a person are closely linked this early in the game. The spirit moves on quickly; the remnant—what most people call a ghost—erodes and fades unless something keeps it here.

This spirit was in tatters, something that usually happened with time. But the shreds were strong with personality, which

I only Saw with the newly dead or remnants kept vivid by the memories of the living.

The wisps tangled around me, creeping over my skin, crawling up my sleeves and down my collar. I grabbed the threads and knit them together, exerting my will on the frayed—no, torn—edges until they started to mesh.

What could tear apart a ghost?

Suddenly it was done, and the shade of Bruiser stood in front of me—big and brawny, shadowed by his sins and screaming like the hounds of hell were after him.

My psyche was the bungee cord holding him together, and his terror earthquaked across that link with a discordant screech. Instinct said to let go, but I clamped down tighter, gripping the reins on Bruiser's visceral panic.

"Stop it!" I shouted over the scream in my head. The agents jumped; they couldn't see or hear Bruiser. I was just a long-legged, red-haired college freshman squatting in the soggy ground, yelling at the air.

"No one is going to hurt you," I said, my voice less shouty but still pitched high with effort. I didn't have to speak aloud, but *thinking* at him was too much work. My psyche, that invisible ghost of myself, staggered under the effort of keeping the shade knit together. If my attention slipped, he started to dissolve back into bilious fog and discordant screaming.

Seriously. Weird.

A tattered remnant should have been too weak to pull apart once I brought it together. And, yeah, with murder victims, panic was normal sometimes. But this was extreme. I didn't like to admit there was anything ghost-related I hadn't seen before. But this was something ghost-related I had never seen before.

Finally, the shade stopped yelling. He looked around, bug-eyed with terror, jerking with surprise when he saw me.

"Who are you?" Bruiser demanded. "What's happening?"

"I'm here to help you." It wasn't a lie. He could be the vilest vile thing on the planet, but it went against my principles to let a spirit suffer on this side of eternity.

Bruiser was dressed as he had been when he died, in a dark suit and white shirt, jacket bulging over his muscles and a pretty obvious shoulder holster. The shade's hand jerked toward his weapon when he noticed Taylor beside me and Chief Logan and Agent Gerard behind him. "What about them? Cops? I didn't do anything."

"They don't care about you," I told him with authority. You have to let freaked-out spirits know you're in charge. "We just want to ask you some questions."

"What's he saying?" demanded Gerard, who clearly believed enough to boss me around while I was doing my job. "What happened to the girl?"

"Give her a chance," said Taylor. Then, to the confused Chief Logan, he explained, "We can't see or hear what Daisy sees and hears. Whether the ghosts see or hear us depends on the type. Also, she says murder victims are sometimes a little discomposed by the event."

"Scrambled in the head" was what I'd actually said.

Bruiser watched Taylor with a deepening scowl. "What's he talking about? What murder victim?"

"Focus on me," I told the shade as he started to blur and waver. "Tell me what happened when you arrived at the dorm to pick up Alexis."

His ugly face twisted in concentration. "It was my night to babysit the little princess. I texted her that I was waiting. When she came down, all tarted up for the club, I got out to open the door."

With the returning memories came more of his personality, and it wasn't a nice one. Hollow eyes raked over me. "She used to give me the same stare you're giving me right now. I'm in big trouble if the little tease is dead, but I won't miss her and her snooty looks."

The agents were waiting expectantly, so I ignored that comment. For the others I said aloud, "So, you got out of the car to open the door for Alexis. What happened then?"

The shade's face went blank. His eyes darted, looking for clues or answers. "I don't know. How did I get here?"

Gerard ran out of patience. "Ask him who took Alexis Maguire. Was he in league with them?"

"No!" said Bruiser, who could hear the question perfectly well. "It's my ass if anything happens to that little bitch. I'm not crossing Devlin Maguire for anything less than a private island and an army to protect it."

"He says no," I relayed.

"Could he be lying?" asked Chief Logan.

"No," I said. "Spirits can't lie." They can misinterpret or misremember, but they can't state an untruth.

14

"What do you mean, 'spirits'?" demanded Bruiser, with way more insight than I'd have expected. "You mean *me*?"

Crap. Panic started to pull at him again, and I shook with the psychic strain of holding his shade together, my muscles burning as if they supported all his weight.

"Tell me what happened after you opened the door for Alexis," I repeated, now that he was facing his end.

"Blackness," said Bruiser, panting with fear, even though he had no lungs. "Snarling. And the black dog."

"Dog?" I asked, totally confused. "What black dog?"

"What black dog?" echoed Taylor. Faintly I heard him ask Chief Logan, "There wasn't any kind of dog bite on the victim?"

I lost the chief's answer in the rising wail of Bruiser, the thug becoming one big terror-stricken tremor. "Ripping and tearing." Then his gaze latched on to mine with a flare of hope. "You! You can send me where the dog can't rip me up."

His *certainty* about that rocked me as much as his desperation. I was already on my knees in the wet grass or my legs might have failed me. "How do you know?"

"I just do."

He wasn't lying. Somewhere in his scrambled mind, something told him I could help him, even if he didn't know how.

Distantly, I registered the men talking behind me. "She doesn't look so good," said Chief Logan.

"She hasn't given us anything useful yet," snapped Gerard. "Why do I put up with this malarkey if it doesn't get us anywhere?"

Then Taylor, crouched beside me, his voice reaching through the cold net of psyche that tied me to Bruiser. "Come on, Jailbait. It's time to wrap this up."

"Okay," I said, through chattering teeth. When had my lips gone numb? I was barely upright. But I couldn't leave the job unfinished.

Calling open the Veil wasn't difficult. A whisper from me and it shivered into my view, ready to put things in their proper place. Our world was for the living. The dead belonged . . . somewhere else.

The threshold between here and eternity was only a waver in the air, like a curtain of liquid mercury. But Bruiser shrank away from it. "What is that?"

Whatever's next, I told him silently. That was as much as I knew. I could See the Veil, but not what was beyond it. "It's what you wanted. To get away from the black dog."

Maybe. It was an empty promise when I didn't know what he was talking about.

"I don't want to go." He swung around, pulling his gun from its holster and pointing it at me. "You can't make me go."

Probably not, but whatever lay beyond was happy to reach out and pull him in. I couldn't See that, either, but Bruiser could, and his screams raked my bones.

I loosed my hold on him, my strength giving out. He dropped into the next world like a pebble into a pond. The Veil shimmered with a promised glimpse into a place outside the walls of time and space, lingered until the moment when my curiosity became a longing ache, then vanished.

It was always that way. I could almost hear a whisper. *There's something stupendous here, but not for you. Not yet.*

But this time ... *this* time, in the closing shudder in the surface tension between *there* and *here*, I thought I saw a shape. Something that might have been the inky silhouette of a lean, feral-looking dog.

That was all I got, a corner-of-the-eye impossibility. Then the recoil of all that effort to hold Bruiser together slammed a ball-peen hammer of a headache right between my eyes.

"Basingstoke," I gasped.

But not in time for Taylor to catch me before I face-planted into the Minnesota mud.

3

"REALLY," I TOLD Taylor for the fiftieth time, "I'm fine."

I admit, I might have been more convincing if I weren't sitting in Alexis Maguire's desk chair with my head between my knees.

On the plus side, I'd known as soon as I stepped into her dorm room that she wasn't dead. I was less certain *I* wasn't dying a slow death by migraine.

Taylor twisted the top off a bottle of Coke and handed it to me. "It's not usually this bad."

I finished half the soda in three long gulps, then held the cold plastic to my pounding temple. It was my second bottle. He'd had the first waiting for me as soon as he'd picked me up from the mud behind the dorm.

"It's not usually this hard." I didn't mind admitting that to Taylor, since Agent Gerard was on the other side of the room with Chief Logan and his two detectives. The older officers had their heads together, maybe debating whether to take my word that Alexis was still alive, maybe debating whether to take me to the funny farm.

My cousin Amy swears there is some Goodnight charm that protects us from men in white coats, so I wasn't worried about the second possibility. But I would be monumentally pissed if I'd gotten this headache just to have the police dismiss the few clues I could give them.

Goodnights and law enforcement go way back. Supposedly, one of my ancestors consulted on the Jack the Ripper case, though maybe that's not a ringing endorsement. My track record for solving cases was a lot better.

Not that you'd know it, from the way Gerard bitched about working with a psychic. When he came to San Antonio he got Taylor as a partner, which meant he got me. Until this trip, he'd talked to me as little as possible.

Of course, back when Agent Taylor and I first met, he hadn't known what to make of me, either. He was straight out of the academy, and he'd inherited me from his predecessor. *I'd* inherited the gig from my late aunt Diantha, and though I'd done a good bit of work for the local and state police, I was still earning my cred with the FBI.

Our very first case together, Taylor and I were stuck in the car on a ride to a crime scene in the Rio Grande valley. That was nearly a year ago, back when Aunt Pet still rode along with us. She'd been my legal guardian until a judge awarded me emancipation at seventeen so that I could do my civic duty without her having to take off from her job every time someone died or disappeared in the South Texas desert.

"So... forgive me if this is a rude question," Taylor had begun. There was no radio reception and the only sound in the car was the click of Aunt Pet's laptop keys as she worked in the backseat.

"Born this way," I answered. I didn't need to read minds—which I *can't* do—to know what rude question he wanted to ask. I'd only been surprised it had taken him so long.

"Just born psychic?" he'd asked. "Not hit by lightning or something?"

"Nope." I leaned forward to search for a radio station. *Any* radio station. "No brain fever, no head trauma, no near-death experience."

"No traumatic death of a loved one?"

I sat back and gave him the stink eye. He *had* to know about my parents. There was no way the details of their murder hadn't been passed along in office gossip.

"Look," I said. "If we're going to work together, let's get a few things straight. I won't do any of that TV-psychic flimflammery and you won't ask me trick questions. Not about a read, not about my family, not about me. *Capisce?*"

He glanced my way for a moment, clearly reassessing me. "Okay. So what *about* your parents?"

I sighed and sank into the seat. "They died when I was three. I only remember them as ghosts."

"And your aunt Diantha solved their murder." He stated it as a fact, not a question.

"Well, mostly she nagged the police until they searched Farley Driscoll's vacation house for evidence that he tampered with my parents' car." Driscoll had been my father's business partner, and none of his high-priced lawyers could keep him out of jail once the evidence started mounting up. You do *not* mess with the Goodnights.

"So your whole family is psychic?" Taylor asked.

"Yep. Well, psychic or magic."

"Huh," he said in a noncommittal way.

Here's what I've discovered in seventeen and three-quarters years as a Goodnight and a psychic: One, people can rationalize a helluva lot when it comes to explaining the inexplicable. And two, there's not a hard line between believers and skeptics. People tend to pick and choose what they'll swallow.

For whatever reason, Agent Taylor had only ever questioned *why* and *how*, never *if*. And after a few successes, he'd started bringing me in on more cases, and reopening cold ones, until we both started making a name for ourselves.

Which, I suppose, might be another reason that Agent Gerard, for all his bitching, had never refused to work with us.

It was the sight of Agent Gerard standing in the middle of all the girliness of Alexis's room that brought me back to the present. He was frowning at a bulletin board filled with party pics

21

and ticket stubs, and behind him was a window overlooking the little lake.

"I wonder why the killer didn't drag Bruiser's body the rest of the way to the lake and throw him in," I said. "It would have delayed discovery of the murder and washed away trace evidence."

Taylor followed my gaze and my train of thought. "Maybe that was the plan, but he was interrupted and had to make do with the bushes."

That made sense. I imagined grabbing a girl from in front of her dorm meant time constraints.

No one had said "kidnapped" yet, but it was what everyone was thinking. I didn't need to read minds to know that. I just had to look around her room.

Her dorm was about twice the size of mine, and she had it all to herself. Most of it was standard issue—desk, chair, bed, bookcases, worn carpet, and industrial beige paint. Some of it was upgrade—a minifridge and a microwave and a pair of retro beanbag chairs.

The mess was not standard. The police had found it ransacked—books thrown from their shelves, drawers turned out of the desk and bureau, heaps of clothes and papers under snowdrifts of polystyrene from the gutted chairs.

I risked a cerebral explosion by bending over to pick up a textbook from beside my foot. It was literally Greek to me.

"What is Alexis studying?" I asked, turning the book right side up. It didn't make a difference, except for the pictures.

I'd asked it loud enough to get the attention of Gerard and

the detectives across the room. Chief Logan answered. "Classical languages, I think."

I would have raised my eyebrows, but my head hurt too bad. "You mean, like Greek and Latin? That kind of classical? How's that going to be useful in a crime family?"

"How did you know—" Gerard began, then cut himself off with an unvoiced curse. Taylor coughed to cover a laugh, and I was very careful not to look smug.

"Bruiser didn't look like he made a living driving Miss Daisy," I said. Putting the heavy book on the desk, I saw something else. "Her laptop is missing."

"We noticed that, too," said the chief. Then he indicated the mess with a tilt of his head. "Can your, um, sight or whatever tell why someone trashed the place? The computer would have been easy to find, so that wasn't what they were looking for."

I shook my head carefully. "I only read remnants of the dead. All I can tell you is they weren't zombies." Chief Logan, a sober, trim man in his forties, gave a start of alarm, and I allowed myself a weak smile. "There's no such thing," I assured him. "The inside might hang around sometimes, but the outside is just dust."

As for my limitations—which I was feeling keenly just then—I knew that Alexis was alive because of what I *didn't* feel. I sat at her desk and rifled through her stuff without a whiff of reaction from the spirit world. Remnants really don't like you messing with their stuff.

And someone had definitely messed with Alexis's things. Too bad the dorm didn't have a resident ghost, like the houses at Hogwarts. Then I could just ask *it* what the thieves were after.

Taylor voiced another question I'd been contemplating. "So, still no word on a ransom demand?"

Logan glanced at one of his detectives, who shook his head. "Her father says there hasn't been any call."

"Maybe he's lying," I offered. "You know, like they do in the movies, when the kidnapper says, 'Don't call the cops.'"

"This isn't a movie, Peanut," said Gerard, not bothering to hide his scorn. "It's a serious criminal investigation. Why don't you sit quietly until we have something else for you to Ouija or whatever it is you do?"

I didn't think it was possible for my head to hurt any worse, but a hot pulse of humiliated anger proved me wrong. "I don't *Ouija* things, Agent Gerard. I read the remnants of energy that linger after death. Especially violent and unexpected death."

"Not that it was any help here," he said. "What was all that black dog business? Was she kidnapped to be raised by wolves?"

"Spirits get confused. You might be confused, too, if your brains got scrambled by a bullet."

"That's enough, you two," snapped Taylor, and as awful as it was to have Gerard dismiss me like a kid, it was ten times worse having Taylor scold me like one.

"Daisy brought up a valid point," Taylor continued, not that I still didn't want to crawl into the deflated remains of the beanbag chair and die. "If anyone would think he could handle this solo, it's Devlin Maguire. He has reason not to want the police poking into his business."

"Maybe he knows the person behind this," said Gerard. "Criminal roads from all over the country run back to him, but no one has been able to sew up the connection. Maybe the girl's kidnapping is our chance."

An awkward silence rocked everyone back on their heels a moment. Then Taylor, with soft-voiced intensity, said, "There's a girl's life at stake. The important thing is finding her."

He did *not* say "It's not about your career, asshole." At least, not aloud. I'm not sure I'd have had that kind of willpower.

"Of course," said Gerard, with cover-my-ass bluster. He turned to Logan. "We'll leave your office to finish the investigation on the murder here, and Taylor and I will hook up with the Minneapolis field office on this kidnapping. Even if Maguire won't cooperate, we can talk to him, put a tap on his phone. . . ."

Taylor listened with his jaw twitching, but didn't contradict his partner, just added, "I think they've already requested a warrant for that."

"Then we should get a move on," said Gerard.

Finally, we agreed on something.

The clock was ticking, and not just for Alexis. My window of usefulness was closing. Sugar and caffeine had pushed back the nausea and the crimson haze of my headache, but I figured I had thirty, maybe forty minutes of coherence before the migraine stomped me flat.

4

WE EXITED THE dormitory and a camera flash drove a spike into my eye.

My knees buckled as the headache blossomed to full force. Taylor caught me under one arm and Gerard under the other, hustling me through a small crowd of reporters bristling with cameras, microrecorders, and questions.

"Are you the agents in charge?"

"Any leads on who killed Dev Maguire's henchman?"

"Or the whereabouts of Miss Maguire or her body?"

"Does Mr. Maguire know you've hired a psychic to find his daughter?"

Taylor took up the rear guard, offering them nothing but "No comment at this time" while his partner shoved me into the backseat of the black SUV waiting by the curb.

"Effing reporters," growled Gerard as he slammed my door. He might as well have been slamming it on my head.

"How the hell did they find out about her?" the agent demanded, once he and Taylor had climbed into the front and closed out the reporters.

"Pretty coed goes missing?" said Taylor, buckling his seat belt. "It was going to splash, even without a whale like Maguire involved."

"No. I mean *her*." Gerard stabbed his thumb toward me, sitting innocently in the backseat, trying not to be sick.

"Chill." Taylor sounded like he'd reached the end of his patience about five snarky comments ago, and I was glad those hadn't come from me. "It's not her fault college students like to Tweet. Hell, she's probably got a fan page on Facebook by now."

Gerard chilled. He went positively frosty and flexed his hands on the steering wheel like he was picturing them around someone's neck. "I swear, rookie, if little Miss Ghostbuster blows this investigation for me, I'm going to make sure she—and *you*—are sidelined until monkeys fly out of my ass."

Taylor spoke low and grim, reminding me why I wanted to stay on his good side. "You know, Gerard, the Minneapolis field office didn't ask for us. They asked for Daisy. You wouldn't even be here if it weren't for her. Maybe you'd better think about what's best for the case instead of what's best for your career."

Just a guess, but this wasn't going to make Gerard like me

any better. He slammed the SUV into gear and pulled out from in front of the dorm so fast my head bounced on the back of the seat. Fireworks exploded and my stomach flipped over.

I must have made a sound, because Taylor turned to look at me. "Hang tight, Daisy. We're headed to one of the precincts in Minneapolis. We'll base out of there, and you can get some rest in the ready room."

A swig from my latest bottle of Coke helped me sound half normal as I said, "You should take me with you if you're going to see Maguire."

"How do you propose we explain you?" sneered Gerard, eyes on the road. He wasn't even pretending to be nice now that we were in private. "Junior Miss Marple, goth edition?"

That might have been funny if he weren't such an ass. "He's going to know about me from the six o'clock news anyway. And crime boss or not, he's a dad. Parents will try anything to find their kids."

Taylor and I had searched for enough children to know. It only took one.

With his arm hooked over the seat back, Taylor studied me. From his skeptical frown, I figured I must look as bad as I felt. "No offense, Daisy, but are you going to be good for anything? You look like you're about to hurl."

"Do *not* throw up in this car," snapped Gerard. "We'll be responsible for having it cleaned."

Just when I thought I couldn't hate him any more than I already did.

· · ·

We arrived at a police station in Minneapolis, where we—meaning the agents—were liaising with the local PD and meeting someone from the FBI field office. I was hazy on the details, and Taylor didn't introduce me to anyone before he strong-armed me into an office, sat me on a sagging sofa, and made sure there was an empty trash can within easy reach. I would have protested, but the fluorescent lights sent signals to the hammers inside my skull. A dark office was only sensible.

"An hour," I told Taylor as I flopped over on the couch. It smelled like shoe polish, stale coffee, and cop eighteen hours into a twenty-four-hour shift. "That's all I need. It will take that long, at least, to get the search warrant for Maguire's house, right?"

"Longer," he assured me, with a glance at his watch, "since they'll have to drag a judge away from his dinner."

The thought of dinner made me glad for the trash can. "I'm sorry," I moaned, my cheek sticking to the pleather sofa.

"Why?" Taylor crouched to eye level, which would have helped if I could see straight. Just then he had four dark-blue eyes and two square jaws. Not quite as handsome as the usual number. The expression on his face made up for it. "The fact that you can't locate Alexis is a good thing, right?"

"Yeah," I said. It meant she was alive. "But all that stuff about the black dog. And Bruiser. It was so *weird*. And worse, it was useless." I closed my eyes because they were starting to sting and I didn't want to cry in front of him. "I wish my head would stop hurting so I could *think*."

After a quiet moment, Taylor picked up my legs, which were hanging off the couch, and put them properly up beside the rest of me. Then he covered me with a scratchy blanket that smelled like gunpowder. His hand clasped my shoulder before slipping away. "Get some rest, kiddo. There's nothing to do right now anyway."

Ugh. Kiddo. That was nearly as nauseating as the migraine and the sofa smell.

Someone shook me awake about five seconds later. It was a young woman with short blond hair and too much makeup for a uniformed cop. But then, I couldn't quite focus on her face, so maybe I was wrong.

She shoved a bottle of Coke under my nose. "Here. He said you'd need this."

I took it automatically and sat up to crack the seal on the plastic cap. "Agent Taylor sent you?" The soda was cold, and so was the air when my blanket slid off.

"Yeah," she said. "I'm assigned to take you to a hotel to get some sleep."

I choked midswallow and wiped at my chin. "That is *not* the plan. The plan is I sleep here until the warrants come through."

"What good are you when you can't even drink properly, kid?" She stood, then hooked a hand under my arm and pulled me to my feet. "Come on. The motel is close and a lot more comfortable than this. I'll come get you when those warrants are done."

I wanted to be stubborn and tough things out. I also knew I'd recover faster in comfort and proper darkness. So I knocked back another slug of soda and followed the uniformed woman out of the office and down a hall. Either we were traveling very fast or my brain was moving very slowly, because it seemed like we were far away from the noise of the squad room by the time I wondered if I should text Taylor and remind him to take me with him to call on Maguire.

"What are you looking for?" asked the uniform, when she saw me digging in my backpack.

Earphones, lab notebook, e-reader, but no sweater. I had to start packing better. "My phone." I couldn't seem to put my fingers on that, either. And it wasn't a big bag.

"I'm sure it's in there somewhere," she said as we neared a bar-locked door at the end of the hall.

I didn't like that answer. I didn't like that she wore so much makeup. I mean, I can rock the black eyeliner, too. But I wasn't wearing the badge of the Minnesota PD.

"So, what do you hear?" I asked, in a conversational tone. If Taylor really had sent her, she'd give me the no-worries response.

"That they're hoping to have those warrants in a few hours." The officer didn't miss a beat as she straight-armed the door and held it open to the frigid night. "Now come on. I'm letting all the cold air in."

This? Was not good.

She saw in my face the instant I decided I wasn't going anywhere. And *holy cats,* that chick moved fast. In a flash she snagged my arm, yanking me off-balance so I stumbled out into the cold.

The icy air sliced through the fog in my head, but too late. The door slammed and latched closed, and I was standing on a sidewalk, not in a squad car bay, and in front of me was not a black-and-white cruiser but a big black sedan.

This was *also* not good.

The young man who leaned on the fender straightened when he saw us. He looked about eight feet tall, and as he stepped forward he practically *vibrated* with purpose, all of it narrowed in on me.

I did the only thing possible: I ignored the red haze of the migraine and ran.

Tall Guy grabbed me by the shoulders, but I realized it wasn't to catch me because I was running, but to catch me because I was falling. The haze was taking over, blossoming in crimson over my vision, closing in black from the edges until the last thing, the very last thing I saw was a pair of hazel-green eyes, swimming with ghosts.

5

I WOKE FACEDOWN in a drool-soaked pillow.

There were worse puddles to wake up in, I suppose, but I didn't want to think about that. I just wanted to lie there, absolutely still, until I was certain that nothing was going to kill me. Not my migraine, not Agent Gerard, not whoever had snatched me off the curb.

Imminent death seemed unlikely. I was tucked under a fluffy quilt, sprawled on a bed that was more comfortable than the one in my dorm room. When I cracked an eyelid to take a peek, I glimpsed a nicely decorated room, with a reassuring absence of white slavers and crack whores.

A quick inventory under the covers revealed no amateur sutures, so I didn't seem to be missing a kidney. Just my clothes.

Not all of them. I still had my underwear on, thank God. Good thing I listened to Aunt Pet and put on clean ones every morning.

I was due an almighty freak-out. I mean, my family is unconventional to say the least, what with teen psychics and mad scientists and kitchen witches. But kidnapping was out of the ordinary, even for a Goodnight.

First things first, though. I'd spotted an adjoining bathroom, and I had to pee like a racehorse.

Once I had taken care of business, I put off panic and took stock of the bathroom in case I needed to make a last stand. An inventory of the medicine cabinet turned up a disposable razor, a bottle of mouthwash, a toothbrush in a cellophane wrapper, and assorted travel-sized toiletries. Ones with French names, so I knew they were *très* expensive. And on the back of the bathroom door was a bathrobe. It was like I'd been kidnapped and dumped at the Four Seasons.

I put on the bathrobe rather than wander around in my skivvies, then used the mouthwash to rinse the taste of stale cola and migraine off my tongue. Only after I swished and spat did it occur to me that the mouthwash might be drugged. Wouldn't *that* just pull the handle on this crapper of a day.

I sat down heavily on the closed toilet lid and tried to figure out what had happened. A dark car pulling up in front of me, hands hustling me toward it. An embarrassingly short scuffle, then...unconsciousness.

Had I been taken by the same people who had snatched Alexis Maguire? What were the odds it was some random grab? Maybe not zilch, but close.

How long before Agent Taylor missed me? If he thought I was still sleeping off the post-mojo migraine, he wouldn't bother me until the warrants were approved. As for my thirty-six cousins and aunts, we have a kind of radar for when one of us is in trouble, but I tripped it so regularly, no one would really worry until I didn't check in.

Phone. I remembered looking for my phone in my small backpack. I charged out of the bathroom, intent on finding my stuff. Instead I found a man coming in the other door.

I screamed, and he did, too. I scrambled for a weapon, but only turned up an ornamental wooden duck from the top of the dresser. I cocked it back, ready to let fly if the guy took one step toward me.

He didn't. He just stood in the doorway recovering his dignity, and said in a pained voice, "Please don't do that. That decoy is an antique."

That pretty much defused my fight-or-flight response. And I couldn't exactly picture this tidy, gray-haired man jumping me in any case. He was way too . . . *dapper*.

He was also carrying my clothes, neatly folded, and he put them on the table near the door, without making any sudden moves. "Your clothes have been cleaned and pressed. I was just going to slip them in here. We were expecting you to be unconscious for a bit longer."

"Who is 'we'?" I demanded. "And where am I?"

35

"I'll let them know you're awake," he said, taking hold of the door handle. "Can I get you anything, Miss Goodnight? A sandwich? Cup of coffee?"

I lowered my arm, realizing the futility of menacing anyone with a duck. "I would really like an appetizer of 'what's going on' with a heaping portion of 'get the hell out of Dodge.'"

"I'm afraid that's not on the menu, miss."

With a sigh, I put the decoy back on the dresser. "I'll just take a cup of coffee, then."

Jeeves nodded and closed the door behind him. I heard the solid click of a lock but hurried to try the knob anyway.

No dice. Next I ran to the window and flung back the curtain. I was on the second floor of a huge house. Like, mansion huge. It was dark outside, but I saw no other house lights close by. An estate, then. Was Alexis somewhere here, too? Was one of Maguire's crime-boss rivals behind this? What could they possibly want with *me*?

It didn't matter. I wasn't going to just sit there in that comfy bathrobe waiting for someone to make me an offer I couldn't refuse.

I grabbed my clothes and got dressed. The shirt and skirt were still warm, and I pulled my socks on over my goose pimples, missing the robe already. A quick search turned up my sneakers, but not my backpack. I was just lacing up the former when I heard footsteps in the hall outside.

The panic I'd been putting off had me hard in its teeth. What if it wasn't Jeeves? What if they'd sent someone like Bruiser to get me?

I snatched up a vase, dumped out the cut-flower arrangement, and jumped behind the door. It opened without hesitation, and I didn't hesitate to attack.

The guy who came in was considerably taller than Jeeves. The vase glanced off the back of his skull and smashed on his shoulders. He hit the deck and didn't get up as a dark wetness soaked his blue dress shirt.

Sweet Saint Gertrude, I'd killed him.

No. It was only the water from the vase. The guy sprawled on the floor was better-looking than Jeeves and *considerably* younger. Like maybe twenty-one. Twenty-two at the outside limit. They'd sent an *intern* to collect me.

I hadn't thought as far as what I'd do next, but running seemed smart. I burst out of the Four Seasons prison cell into a wide hallway with a high ceiling and hardwood floors, polished smooth and dust-free. The walls were painted a warm, sandy color, and there was art. Real art. I thought I recognized a Remington landscape, and at a glance, it didn't look like a print.

Alexis might be in the building somewhere, but there was no convenient clue where I could find her. Just the endless *House Beautiful* hallway. The sound of big, heavy somebodies approaching from the left, however, was a pretty big hint I should run the other way, so I did.

That hall dead-ended at another one, and I picked a direction at random, feeling like a rat in a *Lifestyles of the Rich and Infamous* maze. The corridor made another turn, and *dude,* this place was *huge.*

A billiard room. A den or library. Then an invitingly dark

room, which turned out to be a freaking movie theater. I dove behind a row of cushy chairs, holding my breath until I heard two linebackers go by.

This was not a good plan. The house was too big to randomly search for Alexis. I couldn't even find the stairs. But if I did, and I managed to get out, I could bring back help.

I crept to the door, and after a quick check of the hall, doubled back the way I'd come, running as quietly as possible. Except when I rounded the maze corner back to that first hall, there was a wet and cranky henchman intern in my way.

He raised his hands in the international gesture for *halt right there.* He may have actually said "Stop!" but I had escape ringing in my ears, so I accelerated to ramming speed.

He probably had fifty pounds on me, mostly height and shoulders, but I had inertia and surprise on my side. I knocked him out of my way and kept going.

But now I'd pissed him off, and he was fast, with really long legs, even longer than mine. Before I got to the end of the hall with its glimpse (finally!) of stairs, he grabbed me from behind, arms wrapped around mine.

"Calm down," he said in my ear. "I don't want to hurt—"

The rest was just a grunt of pain as I slammed my elbow— and I have really pointy elbows—into his ribs. He doubled over with a wheeze but still had a grip on me, so I kicked him in the instep and he let go.

But only for a second. The bastard even *limped* fast.

He grabbed me again, but our feet tangled up and we tumbled forward. I braced for impact, and for all that *guy* to come down and snap me like a twig, but at the last instant, he twisted to take the brunt of the crash onto the hardwood floor. It knocked the wind out of him, but he was a *tough* bastard, so as I squirmed out of his hold I kneed him in the groin just to make sure he stayed down.

I have really pointy knees, too.

Bruised and breathless, I left him in a groaning heap on the floor and ran for the stairs. On my way down I met Jeeves on his way up, my cup of coffee on a tiny tray in his left hand.

"Sorry," I said, breezing past. "Can't stay for refreshments."

The butler didn't say anything. He just grabbed my hand as I went by, and with some twist of physics, mechanics, or magic, I was suddenly pinned to the wall, my arm twisted up behind me, utterly unable to move.

Jeeves hadn't even spilled the coffee. "I apologize, Miss Goodnight," he said with unflappable courtesy. "Hell out of Dodge isn't on the self-service menu, either."

Reinforcements arrived, cutting off all exits. They were the expected gorilla types, rather than the dapper man who had me tasting wallpaper.

"Thanks, Bertram." It was the intern. I recognized his wheeze. He'd hauled himself up from the floor and limped over to join us. "I'll take it from here."

"Are you quite sure, Mr. Carson?" I could almost hear the butler raise an eyebrow.

I could *totally* hear the grinding of Mr. Carson's teeth. "Yes. You can let her go."

Bertram did, and I turned around, flexing my arm and

viewing the butler with new respect. Poker-faced, he held out the tray to me. "Your coffee, Miss Goodnight."

I took it. Frankly, I was afraid to piss him off.

"Mr. Maguire wants to see you," said Mr. Carson a little impatiently, probably because I made him wait while I added cream from the tiny pitcher and stirred with the tiny spoon.

And then the name made it to my brain, and I dropped the spoon onto the tray with a clatter. "Hold on a sec. You mean Alexis Maguire's father? That Mr. Maguire?"

"Yes," said the intern. "That one."

After the initial surprise, the new information sank in. It was almost a relief, because I could imagine what *he* wanted, just not why he'd gone through this much trouble to talk to me. All he had to do was ask, and I'd tell him Alexis was alive. Somewhere.

I turned to Mr. Carson, planning to say just that, but paused when I got my first good look at him.

My first impression didn't lie. Young. Twenty-one-ish. Younger than Agent Taylor, and almost as tasty. And *tall*. I'm five foot ten, and I had to tilt my head to look at him. His hair was brown, still wet, and standing up all over. His eyes were a dusky green—no, hazel—and I'd last seen them in the Minnesota cold, just before everything went dark.

"*You!*" I exclaimed, with all the melodrama his offense deserved. "You're the one who *whammied* me behind the police station."

He didn't look chagrined or apologetic. He looked annoyed. "I did not whammy you anywhere. You passed out without my

40

doing anything to you. Which is more than I can say for what you did to me."

"You *kidnapped* me! I'd say *that's* something."

Bertram gave a wordless warning and held the tray under my wildly gesturing cup. Carson—I refused to give him a "Mr."—just stared me down, unfazed. Then he turned, signaling the goon squad to make sure I followed along.

"Come on. You don't want to keep the big man waiting."

6

MAGUIRE'S INNER SANCTUM loomed ahead like the gates of Mordor, except with fewer orcs. Just one man sitting guard outside the double doors. He'd stood when we came into the office foyer, and he and Carson exchanged nods.

"The boss is expecting us," said Carson, and the guard straightened his jacket before tapping on the door. I knew from my FBI associates that jackets never fell quite right over a shoulder holster.

I reached automatically for the psychic lay of the land. Some people do a tactical assessment, counting exits and potential threats. I read the room for remnants, telling me who to watch out for, which way lay danger.

So far there hadn't been any spirit resonance worth mentioning, but that wasn't weird for a semipublic part of a house. I got a bit of a buzz off the door guardian, like maybe a loved one lost, and the goons behind me carried the whiff of violence and threat, but not *actual* death. That was good, I guess.

But these rooms where Maguire did business? Unnervingly blank. It was as if all the psychic fingerprints in the place had been wiped clean.

It seriously bothered me, because I didn't know what it meant. I was in enough of a jam without there being something *weird* about it. The knots in my stomach had knots, and I was only a little ashamed to admit that I really wanted Taylor to show up and handle this. I wouldn't even have minded Agent Gerard. I was plenty proud, but I was even more worried that I was in way over my head.

"It will be all right." I looked up, startled by Carson's low voice in my ear. He stood close, maybe in case I decided to bolt again. His eyes had gone grayer. A trick of the light, but the color matched the steel in his voice.

He might believe his words, but I didn't. "How?" I asked. "It's already not all right. I have a whammied head and bruises to prove it."

A thread of regret laced his tone. "I am really sorry about that." After a beat, he offered, "If it makes you feel better, I think you cracked my ribs."

"It helps." Not much, but a little.

The corner of his mouth tightened, either in a flinch or a microscopic smile. It softened his face, and I remembered how when we fell in the hall upstairs, he twisted to hit the ground first, cushioning my fall. I mean, kidnapped was kidnapped, but still . . . there was that.

The guard at the door gestured for us to go in, and Carson took my arm, his grip firm. "Just do as the man says," he told me. "Don't antagonize him and you'll be fine."

Threat or reassurance? Both, I was thinking, plus a small plea for me not to say anything stupid.

Gosh, it was like he knew me or something.

"Let's do this thing," I said, and shook off his hand to stroll into Mordor on my own power.

Easy to say. But as soon as I crossed the threshold, a powerful, undefinable . . . *something* hit me in the psychic solar plexus. It zapped the strength from my knees, and a bright, blinding haze washed my vision. Panic came next—there could be a tiger in the room and I wouldn't even know it.

Then Carson touched my arm again, and the physical touch grounded me. Still shaking, but only on the inside, I was able to dial back my *other* senses and see the man standing behind the desk.

There was the tiger in the room.

Devlin Maguire was a big man. Big in presence, and tall and broad in an oak tree sort of way. The office was supersized to accommodate him, everything from the ceiling-high bookshelves to the massive oil painting on the wall (Napoléon Bonaparte in Egypt—very subtle).

His desk was a mahogany acre of real estate, his leather desk chair a throne. He was on the phone, and I hadn't even noticed. "Here's what's going to happen," he said calmly into the receiver. "You're going to have that information in my in-box in one hour, and I am going to keep your helpfulness to me a secret from your boss at Homeland Security." And after a pause, "Yes. I thought you might."

Yeah. Whatever the poor guy on the other line had promised, I bet I might, too, in his shoes.

Wait. I *was* in his shoes.

Finishing the call, Maguire turned with an air of moving on to the next thing. Which was me. "So, this is the FBI psychic." He came around the desk and looked me up and down. "You are not at all what I expected."

I shrugged. "I get that a lot."

He smiled slightly, though it didn't reach his eyes. "I'll bet you do."

"I'm sorry about your daughter," I said, because it was true. "You must be very worried."

My sincerity seemed to surprise him, but he merely nodded acknowledgment and got down to business. Half sitting on the desk, his fingers laced loosely as they rested on his thigh, he said, "I'm sure you can guess, Alexis is the reason you are here."

"Yeah, about that," I said, with a bravado that made Carson

give my arm a gentle warning squeeze. "You couldn't have just sent a limo?"

"Sit down, Miss Goodnight." Mr. Maguire gestured, very civilly, to one of the chairs in front of the desk. I didn't want to sit, but my cousin Amy always says "Pick your battles," so I sat.

This chair was enormous, too, and it swallowed me. I'm sure that wasn't calculated to intimidate his visitors or anything. Carson had moved closer to his boss's right hand, which I didn't think was by accident, either, symbolically speaking.

Maguire continued as if this were a perfectly normal meeting. "I'm sorry that you were inconvenienced, and that the misunderstanding led to such unpleasantness. But I need your assistance. *Without* the interference of the FBI."

I didn't need a map as to why he didn't want the feds up in his business. Whereas anything I Saw, psychically speaking, was inadmissible in court. "I'm not sure how I can help you, Mr. Maguire," I said politely, since we were pretending this was all normal. "Your daughter isn't dead."

He seemed unsurprised. "That's good to know, since I received a ransom demand earlier today."

"I knew it!" I slapped the leather of the chair arm. "I *totally* called it."

Maguire merely raised a brow. "I can see I made the right choice bringing you in to find Alexis before anything bad happens to her."

My elation drained away. "Except what I do is kind of specialized. I can't get any kind of read on the living."

"Can't?" asked Maguire, then after a beat, "Or won't?"

46

He was studying me as if I was a peculiar specimen. Which, granted, I am. But there was something weighted about his gaze and the significant pause between words.

"Can't," I stated firmly. The truth was close enough that I felt no guilt leaving exceptions off my résumé. I can read a man's dying thoughts from the change that was in his pocket when the bus hit him. But trying to read the impressions of the living is like trying to answer a cell-phone call in an elevator at the bottom of the Grand Canyon.

What I was really leaving out, though, was how much the dead told me about the living. Like how the radioactive concentration of remnant energy in this room should make a normal person twitchy over time, yet there was Maguire, calm as could be. The man had iron will and Teflon nerves, and I was *so* screwed if he didn't believe that my abilities were of no use to him.

"Miss Goodnight—may I call you Daisy?" He took my agreement as a given, speaking with a we're-all-friends-here candor that let me know exactly how much we were *not* friends. "I'm giving you the opportunity to be completely honest with me. If I find out you haven't, I'm not going to be happy."

"Look," I said, brazening this out. "It's not a straightforward thing. We're talking about the inexplicable forces of the universe here. Not the rules for *Donkey Kong* or something."

Carson coughed like he was covering up a laugh. Maguire glanced at him, more calculating than curious, and the younger man sobered up quickly.

Maguire turned back to me, shifting topics suddenly. "Are you hungry? I can have sandwiches brought in."

I wanted to say no, because I didn't think I could swallow past the lump in my throat. But my stomach didn't know how screwed we were and gave a loud growl. "I'll take that as a yes," he said, and pulled out his BlackBerry to fire off a text.

"Mr. Maguire," I began as he sent in his Quiznos order or whatever. "I'm willing to see if I can sense traces of someone—alive or dead—on Alexis's belongings. But I can't promise anything."

"Oh, I think you will." He looked up from the BlackBerry with a basalt stare—cold, black, and smooth. "It's just a matter of finding the right motivation."

The knot of fear in my chest, the one I was trying to pretend wasn't there, looped even tighter. I glanced at Carson, who had promised things would be all right. His gaze was on the floor, and a muscle in his jaw flexed rhythmically but unhelpfully. If he was trying to send me a message, I was out of luck, because I'd never learned Morse Code for Assholes.

The door opened and I flinched. So much for my cool bravado.

I recognized the woman who entered, even though she'd changed from the police uniform into a leather jacket and Union Jack T-shirt. Her platinum hair was cut short and spiky and her makeup was all black eyeliner. She looked like a punk-rock pixie.

"This is Lauren," said Maguire as the blonde took her place beside him. "It was her suggestion we bring you in, when her attempts to locate Alexis by magic met a dead end."

I blinked, because it sounded like he just said he had a witch on the payroll, which was unexpected, even to me. But that did explain how this Lauren person could have walked into the police station and out again with me in tow. I wouldn't have felt an illusion- or misdirection-type spell because that's not my thing.

Oh man. Like getting kidnapped and strong-armed by a *normal* crime organization wasn't bad enough? I was in *so* far over my head I couldn't even see daylight.

I'm a psychic. Sensing remnants and spirit traces is more about who I am than something I do. But magic? All I knew about magic came from watching the witches in my family, and I wasn't sure how that compared. Goodnight spells were very low-key, nothing flashy, except when my cousin Phin was involved.

I bet that Maguire wanted a lot of flash from his witch. And from her complacent smile, I imagined he got it.

Carson, when I glanced at him, didn't seem fazed by talk of magic. He didn't seem much of anything, because he hid his feelings well. This time, though, he met my eye, and I remembered him telling me, just do what Maguire says and everything will be okay.

So I put on a face like I was riding the wave and not drowning in it. "What spells have you tried so far?" I asked Lauren, just one professional to another.

She didn't give me the same courtesy. "This and that." She sounded bored, or maybe like she was humoring me. "Divination, location spell … and a little misdirection to hide your disappearance from your FBI boyfriend. He thinks you're tucked safely in a cot at the office, sleeping off your headache." She looked smug, because she was proud of her spellcraft, or maybe she was just a bitch. "In case you were wondering."

I *hadn't* been wondering. I'd been *sure* Taylor would be looking for me soon. The bottom dropped out of my bravado, leaving an empty, sick hole where I'd kept the comforting thought of rescue. But I was on my own. A glance at Carson showed he had gone inscrutable again, avoiding my gaze. He might not wish any harm on me, but that didn't make him my ally.

"Here's what is going to happen," said Maguire, sounding chillingly certain that I would comply. "I think you can do far more for me than you let on. You will follow the clues leading to Alexis. Think of it like a treasure hunt. But you *will* take this on. And you will give me your oath, three times."

I gripped the arms of the chair. A triple oath was a binding promise. You couldn't break it by your own actions. It was one of the most basic spells, and I bet it came in hella handy as a mob boss.

"And if I don't promise more than once?" I asked.

Maguire picked up a phone from the desk. *My* phone. With a few taps, he scrolled through my pictures. "You have a lovely family, Miss Goodnight. Lots of young cousins, lots of talented aunts. If you won't work with me, I will work through *them* until I find one who'll do the job." He set the phone on his desk, propped so I could see the screen and the snap of my cousins and me at Aunt Hyacinth's farm, our arms linked, faces flushed with laughter and summer heat.

"And please believe me, Daisy," Maguire added in that same velvet tone, "the inconvenience of that will fray my temper in ways you do not want to imagine."

The room had grown icier, and it wasn't just the coldness of his gaze holding mine. Remnants whispered wordless warnings in my ear, as frightened for me as I was for my family.

Anything he could do to me was insignificant next to the idea that someone I loved might be hurt or killed because of my refusal. The idea turned everything inside me dark and heavy, filling a noxious pool in the pit of my stomach.

"I'll do it," I said, my voice steady only because I forced it to be that way. The triple vow seemed unimportant when I was already bound by my fear that I would fail—fail Alexis, my family, my duty... everything.

Maguire smiled, as if I'd said something funny. "I know you will."

"But without the binding oath," I added, because redundant didn't mean harmless.

He didn't seem surprised or impressed by my rebellion. "I'm afraid it's my way or the highway. Stand up," he said, gesturing Lauren and Carson forward as well.

"Is this really necessary?" asked Carson. "She has plenty of incentive not to renege on the deal."

Understatement of the century. But Maguire hauled me out of the chair and pushed me toward Carson. "Let's just say I want no errors in judgment along the way."

Carson steadied me when I stumbled and kept his hands on my shoulders, standing behind me so we both faced Maguire. It was probably a good thing. I wasn't going to run, but my knees were high-diving-board shaky and might not hold me up.

My cousins and I played with this type of binding spell—geas was the old-fashioned term—as kids, the Goodnight version of a triple-dog-dare. Nothing really mattered but the words and the intent. That was it. But the *witch's* intent as she pulled a red silk cord from the pocket of her leather jacket and held out her hand for mine made me shrink back.

"What's that for?" I asked. "No one in *my* family needs props."

Lauren raised a thin brow. "But I know the value of a sense of ceremony." She grabbed my hand and put it in Maguire's waiting one.

The moment we touched, I felt the weight of the remnants that clung to him. Shreds of lives he'd ruined or taken. Frayed tatters of crimson rage and purple grief and black mourning. They hung from him like the chains on Marley's Ghost, except Maguire didn't seem to regret his, or even acknowledge their existence. I felt them, though, like a stone on my chest.

All that haunting pressure didn't even include the brightness that had staggered me when I'd come in. That was not attached to Maguire. It was anchored to something else, but it was *focused* on him. And, I realized with a start, on Carson as well.

A remnant? It had to be, or I wouldn't sense it. Too strong to be just one, yet too uniform in texture not to be the same psychic substance. I had never felt anything like it, and curiosity pulled me further into my other Sight. I wondered what on earth that fierce glow could be.

Maguire's fingers tightened painfully on mine, snapping the thread of my question, yanking me back to the physical world and my current problem.

Lauren wrapped the cord around our linked hands, and I understood what she'd meant by "a sense of ceremony." Symbols had power. The smooth scarlet against my skin elevated the very simple spell from kid stuff to something resonant and far-reaching.

I'd never felt magic at work before, but I was sure I felt it then—Lauren's intent, racing along the points of our triangle.

"Your promise," said Maguire, straightening his coat with his free hand.

I grit my teeth, still fighting coercion. "I promise to do everything in my power—"

"Not good enough," said Maguire, almost carelessly, though I wasn't fooled. "You're a Texan. Where's that 'Remember the Alamo' spirit?"

"Yeah, that didn't work out so well for them."

"Then you'll have to do better."

Impasse. I could not clever my way out of this situation.

When I went too long without speaking, Maguire sighed, then grabbed my chin in his free hand, forcing me to meet his gaze. "Repeat after me, Daisy Goodnight," he said, letting me glimpse beneath his veneer of civility. "Because the lives of the people you love best are at stake."

My eyes stung, but crying would help no one, so I shoved the tears down, hard. Carson's fingers tightened on my shoulders, and he was tense with some inner struggle of his own.

"Now," said Maguire, "I, Daisy Goodnight, will follow the trail of Alexis Meredith Maguire and find her without delay."

"I promise," I said, feeling the geas start to take hold. The vow had to be spoken only once, then agreed to. "I promise. I promise."

With the third oath, the slipknot of the spell drew tight. It was a yoke on my psyche and a hot pavement under my feet, and it would press at me until I did what I had sworn.

The thing that happened next, I couldn't explain. A buzzing, like the hum of feedback from a loudspeaker, filled my skull, pushing out everything else. It crackled like static and lit my nerves—and then Lauren slipped the cord from our hands and the psychic sound vanished, leaving only clear, crisp fury.

"If you touch *any* of my family . . ." I spat the words at Maguire, still clasping his hand, and I was just *full* of intent. "If you even go near them, I swear I will find a way to curse you all the way to the Veil and push you through. I promise this. I pro—"

Carson clapped a hand over my mouth before I could complete the vow. *Now* I struggled, and he wrapped an arm around my waist, pulling me up against him with my elbows tucked against me and my legs unable to do anything but flail uselessly.

Maguire waved the three of us toward the door. "Get on with it. Tell me when you know something."

"Yes, sir," said Carson, then grunted as my foot found his shin. He adjusted his grip, tucked me under his arm, and marched to the office door.

7

"ASSHOLE," I GROWLED as soon as we were out of the office. Lauren trailed after us, making choked sounds that I realized were laughter.

"I told you not to antagonize him," said Carson, setting me onto my feet and slamming the door behind us.

"I wasn't talking about *him*," I snapped, and made sure my clothes were covering all the parts of me they were supposed to. My emotions needed some sorting, too. As much as I hated being manhandled, Carson had kept me from doing something really stupid.

Maguire scared the crap out of me. When I blinked, I could

See the glow of his remnant debt stamped on the dark of my eye-lids. A man with a conscience would buckle under that weight. Maguire had none, and that gave a concrete reality to his threats.

So what did I do? Threaten him back. It was insanely stupid, but it was the only defense I had left.

Laughter made me jump. The guard from the door and the two gorillas who'd escorted Carson and me were clustered around a smartphone, paying no attention to us at all.

"Play it again!" said the guard, and the goon with the phone tapped the screen. "Look at her go! Like a red-haired gazelle, that one." I couldn't see the video, but I could guess they were watching the farce of my escape attempt. Their cackles when I hit Carson and the groans of sympathy when I kneed him were a giveaway.

"Something funny, Murphy?" asked Carson. A rhetorical question, because *clearly,* it was hilarious.

The goon squad sobered, but Murphy, the guard from the door, didn't bother to hide his grin, even when he said, "No, sir." Then he gestured to a cloth-covered tray on a console table tucked against the wall. "Bertram brought this up for your guest."

Lauren went over and lifted the napkin to reveal a toasted sandwich, an avalanche of potato chips, and a pickle spear. "Do gazelles eat turkey sandwiches?"

Not voluntarily, but I was running on four Cokes and a long-gone snack pack of pretzels from the plane. I snatched up the sandwich before she had a chance to do anything witchy to it. *"You,"* I said with as much dark venom as I could muster over my growling stomach, "are going to be *so sorry.*"

She took a handful of potato chips. "You know that thing about magic coming back on you three times is a myth, right?"

"Not where my family is concerned. If anything bad happens to me because of this, the Goodnights will bring the rain. So pack an umbrella."

Carson grabbed the napkin and handed it to me. "Walk and eat. I want you to get a read on Alexis's room, see if there are any clues."

The thought of Alexis made the gourmet turkey and bread about as appetizing as a boot-leather-and-cardboard sandwich, but I wolfed it down anyway. It wasn't bravado, it was biology. I needed food if I was going to be good for anything.

I followed the platinum cockscomb of Lauren's spiked hair down another of the house's hallways into another wing of the building. That made three. I'd lost track of the number of corridors.

Carson had fallen into step beside me. Not crowding, but within arm's length. He wasn't taking any chances.

"I don't know where you think I'm going to go," I said around a mouthful of sandwich. My aunts would be appalled. "I don't think I could find my way out of here with a GPS and a team of Army Rangers."

He shot me a sideways look, and I noticed the darkening bruise on his cheekbone, corresponding to the lump on my head. "I'm not going to underestimate you twice. You just threatened to shove Devlin Maguire into the afterlife."

I shrugged to hide a shudder. "I was very angry." I was *still* angry, which was unusual. Mostly it's all explosion, no simmer with me, which I hate because I've known too many dead people not to have learned where hotheadedness gets you.

But as hunger receded, I still had a knot in my gut—the slow burn of outrage turning into a coiled spring of tension, telling me to move, act, swing for the bleachers.

Unless it wasn't anger, but something else.

I slowed my steps, wondering what would happen. If I was just pissed, then nothing. But as soon as I started dragging my feet, my muscles tensed and my heart pounded and my chest tightened with term-paper-due-tomorrow tension.

I wasn't just pissed. I was *bound.*

Son of a witch.

Whatever *I* knew, so did the geas. Turning away from Alexis's room with no other plan would not find the missing girl. The spell gave my subconscious power over me, like OCD dialed up to eleven.

"What's wrong?" asked Carson, with a sharpness I didn't understand.

"Seriously?" Stopping to look at him wasn't difficult. Clearly my subconscious knew the value of venting. "I am *ensorcelled.* Bound by magic to find Alexis or die trying. Which, by the way, I would have done for free, if your boss had asked politely."

His shoulders shifted as if he were trying to ease an itch of guilt. It was a small movement, but I was used to reading the slightest inflection in a remnant. Reading this Carson guy was sort of the same. "Then what's the problem?" he asked.

"The problem," I said, "is I don't *know* what problems this will make. Is it going to cloud my judgment? What if I can't find her? What if I *die*—"

Oh God.

It was a prayer, not a curse. If I died, would I still be bound to Devlin Maguire? If I got stuck here because of the oath, who would cut my spirit free? I didn't know anyone else who could do what I did.

Carson had reached out like he wanted to steady me, but I leveled a glare that made him wisely draw his hand back.

"If I die and get stuck here," I swore coldly, "I'm going to chew myself loose from your boss and make your life a living hell until you find someone to free me."

If I hadn't been glaring at him, I would have missed his flinch, a neuron flash of pain like the dart of a fish beneath a sheet of ice. "That's not going to happen," he said. "Lauren said the spell is harmless in the long term, and I'm not going to let you get hurt in the meantime."

"Dude." I rolled my eyes. "Did you tell yourself that before or after you kidnapped me from the back of the police station?" Without waiting for an answer, I set off purposefully after Lauren—or rather, the corner she'd disappeared around.

"Trust me," Carson said, easily matching my pace. "I wasn't nuts about doing that even before I knew what a pain in the butt you were going to be."

Weirdly, I sort of believed he hadn't thought I'd come to harm. Not that it let him off the hook. "Did you dump me in the trunk, or just toss me in the backseat with a blanket over my head?"

"You should thank me for springing you from testosterone

central." He defrosted a little as the argument turned superficial. "Your junior G-man must be half dead not to realize how short that skirt is."

I refused to blush, even though my strides down the hall sort of emphasized his point. "The skirt is standard issue. My legs are too long."

"Oh, I disagree," he said, in a matter-of-fact way that wasn't matter-of-fact at all. It sounded like approval. Young, handsome Mr. Carson approval. I suspected he was just trading one mask for another, but even I'm susceptible to flattery.

Then he added in a bland tone, "Your knees are a little bony, though."

They absolutely were not. Unless, I guess, they were making an impact on a delicate area.

I pursed my lips to hold back a vengeful smile. That was mere prudence. The geas had nothing to say about inappropriate banter with the enemy.

Lauren waited for Carson and me at an open door, arms folded, brows pitched at a scornful angle. "Don't let the mortal peril of our friend hurry you kids up or anything."

As much as I disliked Lauren—which was a lot—I still felt a little guilty for wasting time on a purely selfish freak-out. Duress or not, the important thing was finding the girl. Okay, maybe this was anything but a normal day. But it was my job to put my psyche on the line for a lost soul. Alexis was no different just because she still had a body attached to hers.

So I squared my shoulders and blew past Lauren into Alexis's room. It was actually more of a suite, professionally decorated in the violet and green of a pansy patch, but other than the size of the room—and the flat-screen TV on the wall—it wasn't ostentatious. Maybe because there were so many books.

Lauren and Carson came in and closed the door. They were an odd pair—the witch, with her vintage punk clothes, and the… whatever Carson was, with his stoic face and haunted eyes. They conferred in soft voices while I made a circuit of the room, running my hand over dustless tables and fluffed pillows. Picking up traces of the living was like getting a radio station at the very edge of my reception, but sometimes it was easier when the signal was boosted by a big event or strong emotion—the same kinds of things that make remnants of the dead stick around.

I didn't get anything like that from Alexis's room, just the faint static of daily living, as if she hadn't been there in a while. There was a stronger energy attached to some childhood books and mementos on a shelf and a hot spot near the desk where Lauren leaned, arms folded, watching me. Alexis must have invested a lot of time and emotional effort there. I guess you don't study Latin and Greek if you don't like putting in the hours.

There was also a curio case holding trinkets she must have collected. I reached for one, a small human figure carved from reddish stone, and Lauren's voice stopped me. "Careful. Those are old and delicate. And possibly cursed."

"Then shouldn't they be in a museum?" I asked, even though I was pretty sure the piece was fake, maybe a gift-shop replica. If it had been truly old, let alone cursed, I was close enough that I would have been able to tell without touching it. "There are laws about importing artifacts, aren't there?"

Lauren rolled her eyes, and I remembered who I was talking to. Mafia staff witch.

"Is this important for finding Alexis?" asked Carson. He leaned against a bookcase, arms folded, but his vibe wasn't relaxed. More like he was hanging back, observing.

"I don't *know* what's important yet." I tried to think like Agent Taylor had taught me. Focus on the victim. Her path had to have crossed the kidnapper's somehow. By knowing her habits and haunts, so to speak, eventually I would see the intersection. "Tell me about Alexis. She seems like a bit of a nerd."

"Being smart doesn't automatically make you a nerd," said Lauren. Which I guess was true. Alexis had been heading out for a night of partying when she'd disappeared.

"She *is* pretty brilliant," said Carson. "But yeah, I think she's too cosmopolitan to be called a nerd. I think it was shopping in Rome with her mom that first got her interested in the classical world—ancient Greece, Rome, Egypt."

Since I doubted Roman gladiators had kidnapped her, I switched directions with my next question. "How much magic are we dealing with?" I asked. "Are there magical protections around the property? Wards on Alexis's dorm room? Tracking charms sewn into her underwear?"

"Can't you tell?" Lauren asked—about half real question and half taunt.

"I keep telling you guys," I snapped, to cover how naive and outgunned I felt. "I read remnants of the dead. Magic isn't my thing. Mary Poppins could have grabbed Alexis and I wouldn't know it."

Carson allowed himself a small smile. "There is a long list of people who would want to stick it to Devlin Maguire. But Mary Poppins isn't on it."

"Lord Voldemort, then?" What I really wondered was, if Maguire had an arcane arsenal, what did the kidnappers have in *their* bag of tricks?

Lauren heaved a sigh. "Magic one-oh-one, Red. This isn't Harry Potter. There are protection charms here and on the dorm room, of course. Tracking charms are a great idea in theory, but huge power drains. Expensive—magically speaking—to maintain when a GPS chip in her phone works just as well. *Most* of the time," she added, preempting my next question.

That part I got. My cousin Phin *loved* to give me lectures in Magic 101, and now I wished I'd paid more attention. But I did remember that the major impediment to big, flashy magic was the impractical amount of energy required to make something go against its nature. Magic worked on probabilities and enhanced inclinations. That was why fireballs and flying carpets were fantasy.

At least, that was what I had thought until now. Maybe it really was just a matter of getting enough power. But power had to come from somewhere.

Dude, magical theory was a mental labyrinth and I didn't have a map. So I focused instead on the current problem.

"You said that Alexis was hidden from your locator spell," I said to Lauren, confirming what she'd said in Maguire's office. "Do you think the spell was blocked somehow?"

She didn't have to think about it. "Less blocked, more like scrambled."

I worked that through. "So someone could be doing it deliberately. Like a radar scrambler."

She pointed at me like a game show host. "Ding! Give the girl a toaster."

"Look, you." She was seriously pissing me off. Worse, her bad vibes were majorly interfering with my mojo. That's not just an excuse fake psychics use. "You don't *want* me to be more useful than this," I told her, "because it would mean someone is dead. Which I can arrange, if you keep mouthing off."

She laughed, then pretended she hadn't meant to. "I'm sorry, kid. You're about as intimidating as a hissing kitten."

"Lauren," said Carson, without moving from his lean against the bookcase, "back off or go away. And you, Sunshine, calm down."

Has anyone in the history of the planet actually calmed down when someone said "calm down"? All it did was turn up the gas under the teakettle of my temper.

"Why doesn't Maguire just pay the stupid ransom?" I demanded. "I mean, what are they asking for? His left kidney?"

Carson debated a moment and glanced at Lauren, who gave him a "your call" sort of shrug. "Because it's not money they want," he finally said. "It's a thing. And he doesn't have it."

"Why doesn't he just go get it?" I asked, slightly more calm, but much more confused. "Or send somebody. He seems pretty good at that." The two of them exchanged another look. *"Hey,"* I said, at the end of my rope with them. "Stop with the secret eyeball communication. I'm *standing right here.*"

Carson sighed and reluctantly confessed, "Because we don't know exactly what it is."

I eyed him suspiciously, but he didn't *look* like he was joking. "That doesn't make any sense. Are you supposed to just *guess?*"

He didn't laugh. "What the kidnappers said was, 'Bring us the Oosterhouse Jackal.' But no one here has heard of it."

"Did you Google it?" I asked, because that's what I would do.

Lauren slapped her forehead. "Oh my gosh, Carson! Why didn't we think of that? Google! What a genius idea!"

Carson straightened and jerked a thumb toward the door. "Out, Lauren. Now."

I expected an argument, or some more eye rolling. Instead, she indulged him, calling, "Don't let her beat you up again," before she closed the door behind her.

At least Carson seemed as annoyed by that as I was. So we agreed on something.

The room seemed smaller somehow, once he'd taken charge. He had a trick of fading out when he was with Maguire and Lauren, standing still and contained, as if he were just the muscle, waiting for orders. It would be easy to underestimate him. Maybe that was why he did it.

But now he was all business. "Yes, of course we did an

Internet search for the Oosterhouse Jackal. Nothing useful came up, but Maguire has people on it."

I was sure he did. Scary people without the restrictions of, oh, say, jurisprudence or civil liberties. My job was to follow the clues to Alexis. That was what I'd sworn to do.

But something kept nagging at me. I mulled over what it might be as I went back to the curio case, looking at the stuff Alexis had collected, picking up the figurine Lauren had warned me away from. It actually did look old, even felt that way to the touch. But to my other senses it was oddly . . . inert. At any rate, it was not cursed from the tomb.

When I turned, Carson was watching me, as if curious when the show would start. "I still don't get it," I said, fidgeting with the carved stone. "Why would the kidnappers ask for something that Maguire doesn't have, or even have access to?"

"Lauren and I have a theory," he said. "We think *Alexis* knows what it is or where to find it. So maybe the kidnappers assumed the boss does, too."

"Her dorm room was totally trashed," I said. "It could be they were looking there for this jackal thing. Whatever it is."

He took the stone figurine from my hand and placed it with care back on the shelf. "She wouldn't keep anything valuable in her dorm. It's too unprotected."

No argument there. But his point did spin up a new idea. "*This* place," I said, meaning Castle Maguire, "is like a freaking fort. When was Alexis last home? Could she have hidden something here?"

"About a week ago," he answered. "The mansion *would* be a safe place to keep something secure from outsiders. We thought of that, and Lauren did her divination thing. There's no sign of anything on the property."

"Yeah, but if you don't know exactly what the Jackal is, any kind of locating spell would be only slightly better than guessing." I knew that much, because it was usually the same for psychics.

I'd also caught his qualifier—safe from outsiders. Where would Alexis keep something she didn't want *Maguire* to know about?

"Is there a picture of Alexis somewhere? Maybe a photo album?" I wanted to get a better image of her physically to see if that helped at all.

Carson nodded to a wall that separated the sitting part of the suite from the bedroom part. It held a decorator-perfect arrangement of frames, but when I went closer I saw that the shots were mostly candid: teenage Alexis with glasses and braces, slightly older Alexis with straight white teeth, arms around her girlfriends, all of them wearing school uniforms a lot like the one I'd worn to Our Lady of Perpetual Snobbery in San Antonio. There was Alexis in front of the Eiffel Tower and the Louvre, on the ski slopes of the Alps, in front of the British Museum and the Trevi Fountain.

The only picture with her father was also the only formal portrait, one of those where they try to make it look unposed and natural but it just ends up looking like a magazine photo of a happy family. Maybe it *was* a magazine shoot. In any case, Alexis and her father didn't look miserable, but their body language was almost businesslike.

Contrast that with the one picture of Alexis with Carson. He wore a tux—and wore it really well—and they leaned into each other, grinning cheekily at the photographer. The photo couldn't be very old, but the carefree guy in the photo seemed a lifetime of experience from the young man standing nearby, watching me with folded arms.

I pointed to the picture. "Did someone put a happy spell on your prom tuxedo or what?"

He allowed himself a shadow of that smile. "Alexis's first sorority formal, our freshman year. She went to an all-girls high school and hadn't dated much until then, and she was wary of asking a stranger."

Yeah, I could see where having Devlin Maguire as a dad would impede romance, with the bodyguards and all. So who was Carson to her? He would have been too young to be Maguire's employee then. He still looked too young now.

"How long have you known Alexis?" I asked, moving to the nightstand to poke around. The *something* was still nagging at me. Something besides curiosity about Carson.

His answer was unobliging. "A while."

"Since you started college?" I asked, undeterred.

"Since before." He obviously knew I was fishing for information on more than just Alexis, and he gave me a grudging morsel. "Maguire sent me to school."

I paused in my drawer rifling. "Is *that* why you work for him?"

He smiled slightly, but the humor in it was bitter. I'd hit a nerve. "That would be the simplest answer." It was also clearly the only one I was going to get. "Are you finding anything?" he asked. "Or just pretending to look while you give me the third degree?"

"Trust me," I said, tough, like I was some badass ghost interrogator. "If I give you the third degree, you'll know it."

I shut the bureau drawer. This room was neat as a pin, cleaned regularly, and totally unhelpful on a psychic level. What I needed was a dead person.

"There aren't any pictures of Alexis's mom," I said, suddenly noticing. "Where is she?"

"Gone," said Carson.

"As in dead?" I asked, maybe a little too hopefully.

The corner of his mouth turned up at my tone. "As in remarried and living in Europe."

"What about a grandparent or an aunt or uncle?" I asked. "Someone she was close to, who might check in on her from the beyond now and then?"

"Her maternal grandmother." He must have followed my line of reasoning, and anticipation sparked in his eyes, though he kept it tightly reined in. I suspected Carson kept everything tightly reined in. "Lex—Alexis, I mean—always spoke of her fondly."

"Excellent. Grandmothers are the worst busybodies." I rubbed my hands together, shifting into higher gear. I pretty much *never* reined anything in. "Does Alexis have something of hers? Anything intimate or personal should do."

"How should I know what's intimate or personal to her?" asked Carson.

"Dude, you were her backup date. Obviously you're close." I had been actively ignoring the "dead" part of the spectrum, so as not to overshadow the "live" part that I didn't See very well. Now I refocused and scanned the room intently for some hint of remnant.

"What do girls inherit from their grandmothers?" I asked. "China. Knickknacks ... How about jewelry?"

Carson, jolted by the suggestion, turned toward a painting on the wall. As soon as I focused on it, I felt a faint psychic hum. A wall safe, maybe?

We nearly raced each other to it. Sure enough, Carson swung the frame from the wall to reveal a safe with a keypad lock, and the *something* went from nagging to unrelenting.

"It's been there all along, but I've been trying to focus on Alexis." I felt like an idiot. "We've wasted so much time. The jackal might be in there right now!"

Carson shook his head and started keying in a number. "I already looked. There's nothing in here but jewelry. But maybe there's something for you to read...."

He glanced down at me, breaking off when he saw my narrow-eyed stare. So he didn't know where Alexis kept her intimate stuff, but he knew the combination to her safe? "There's a master code," he explained, correctly interpreting my suspicion. "The boss gave it to me this morning so I could search."

So I was right. The mansion was not the place to keep something hidden from Maguire. Alexis would know that. Carson would, too. But whose side was he on? He was obviously loyal—maybe *obedient* would be a better word—to the boss. On the other hand, he didn't seem happy about that. So maybe there was nothing obvious here at all.

I pushed that thought aside as Carson opened the safe door and pulled out a velvet-lined tray full of sparkle. I had never seen so many gemstones up close. The fire inside them was downright hypnotic.

But the stones weren't what called to me. It was a pile of pearls. Their glow was softer, like warm, pale skin. And more, they seemed to hum, raising gooseflesh on my arms as I dipped my fingers into the tray and pulled them free into a long, perfectly matched strand. The necklace *sang* with impatient intensity.

"It's about time," chided a voice, coming from everywhere and nowhere. "I've been waiting an age for you to get to me, young lady."

8

THE SHADE OF Alexis's grandmama was head-to-toe haute couture, from pearls to little black dress to classic pumps. Her brown hair was swept up à la Audrey Hepburn, and I was sure she could have breakfasted at Tiffany's in her day.

She looked down her nose at me and sniffed. "Stop gaping, dear girl, and show some manners. It's bad enough your generation goes around uncovered half the time."

I closed my mouth and smoothed the pleats in my skirt before I could stop myself. I'd gone to Catholic school for twelve years. When a woman in black says jump, I don't wait to ask how high.

The apparition didn't surprise me, but the strength and

suddenness of it did. I figured I'd have to coax the threads of personality from the necklace into something coherent. But this shade was very sharp, as if fed daily by memory.

Carson had startled when I did, but he seemed to be following my gaze rather than sighting on his own. "Can you see her?" I asked him.

He shook his head and reached out, as if testing the wind. "It's not as cold as I thought it would be." The ghost gave his hand a scathing look, and he pulled it back as if she'd stung him. "I take that back. Brrr."

"Let me do the talking," I said. "And keep your hands to yourself." Remnants needed careful handling. They couldn't always be reasoned with like a whole living person because they didn't have whole-person logic. Sometimes they were a snapshot of a moment in time. Sometimes they were a hodgepodge of steps in their life's journey.

Like the woman in front of me. She seemed to be in her late twenties—a lot of shades appeared the way they had at a favorite time of life—but she had all the imperiousness of an elderly society matron.

"What do you mean you were waiting on me?" I asked.

She made an impatient noise. "I heard your voices. I haven't been able to rest since Alexis was last here. I knew something was wrong, and now the two of you are here, poking around like a pair of common thieves...."

I hurried to reassure her. "We're not here to steal anything, Mrs...."

My leading pause hung empty. She assessed me for a long

moment before finally filling it. "Mrs. James Hardwicke the Third. You may call me Mrs. Hardwicke."

"Right." Mrs. Hardwicke was kind of fascinating. She'd obviously had a *very* clear self-image in life, which had carried over into death.

"Is it Lex's grandmother?" Carson asked me. "What is she saying?"

The matron shot him a look. "If you're going to grope a lady, young man, you might at least address her directly."

We'd wasted so much time already, I shouldn't have wasted more being amused by that. "She says you should apologize for groping her."

To my surprise, Carson blushed. "I beg your pardon, ma'am. It was inadvertent."

"Humph," she said, giving him a quick inspection. He was a bit rumpled from our tussle, and he had the barest hint of God-knows-what-o'clock shadow along his jaw. His short brown hair stood up all over, and his trousers had no hint of a crease.

"When Alexis was last here," I pressed Mrs. Hardwicke, "what made you worry about her?"

"Her demeanor, of course. She was very anxious. A grandmother can tell these things."

"Anything else?" I asked. Had Alexis known someone was after her, or this jackal thing? "Did she do something unusual? Leave anything behind?"

"Nothing but the key," said Mrs. Hardwicke, as if this should be obvious.

"The key?" I echoed, half for Carson's benefit.

"What key?" he asked, still holding the tray of jewelry like a plate of canapés.

Alexis's grandmother sighed. "The key she put into the safe, of course. That was the last time I saw her."

I elbowed Carson aside and peered into the eye-level safe. There were two shelves. The jewelry had come from the lower one, and the upper one was empty.

"There's nothing," said Carson. "I looked." He set down the tray and peered over my shoulder. In another situation, his breath on my ear would have been very distracting.

"You're blocking the light," I said, though really I just needed him to step away so I could concentrate. There *was* something. My psyche caught the whiff of dirt and ash and the hollow sound of metal and stone. I needed both hands, so I looped the strand of pearls around my neck. Then I reached into the safe, feeling along the shelves and sides.

I tapped on the back and it rang hollow. With a press of my fingers, a panel slid away, and a cold piece of metal fell into my hand. The psychic vibration ran up my arm like a live current and knocked me backward into Carson, who caught me around the waist as the object fell to the carpet with a heavy *thunk*.

"Honestly," said Mrs. Hardwicke, tutting in disapproval, "the way you girls throw yourselves into a man's arms these days. No finesse."

With a little groan, I struggled to get my feet under me. "Next time I'll try for a dignified swoon."

"What was that?" Carson asked, steadying me until I stopped wobbling.

I gestured to the floor. There lay an old-fashioned key, about five inches long including the sturdy filigree on the end. "Alexis hid that. It must be important."

"No, I mean that jolt you got," he said, still hovering. "Are you okay?"

"Fine." Waving off his concern, I crouched to retrieve the key but first had to work up the nerve to touch it again.

"Let me," said Carson, grabbing it before I could. He held it up to catch the lamplight on its dull bronze surface. "I'm guessing this has got some ghostly kick to it?"

Mrs. Hardwicke's shade peered over our shoulders, a very human move. "Well, it should," she said. "It's the key to a mausoleum."

I turned to her in surprise. "How do you know?"

She sniffed, and went to her "foolish mortals" tone. "Because it's the key to *my* mausoleum, of course."

Long-standing remnants could be awfully pragmatic about their state of being. It made a nice but startling change from the recently dead wig-out by Bruiser's shade.

"What now?" Carson asked, sounding frustrated with the one-sided conversation.

I blinked him into focus and he raised his brows to reiterate his impatience. Ingrate.

"You are very pushy." I stalled, because knowledge was gold and I was still processing this nugget. "*Agent Taylor* never rushes me while I work."

He gave a satisfying twitch of annoyance, then held up the key between us. "What. Is. This?"

Alexis had hidden the key from everyone—including Maguire. That was important. So whatever the key opened—the mausoleum—had to be important, too.

"What sort of girl-detective game are you playing, young lady?" demanded Mrs. Hardwicke as the silence lengthened. Her aura was keen and protective. "I've seen *this* young man"—she nodded at Carson—"with Alexis. But who are *you*?"

Behind Carson was the picture from the sorority dance, and I saw that Alexis was wearing the pearls. That explained how Mrs. Hardwicke had seen him—she seemed to be tied to the jewelry. Otherwise she would have called to me as soon as I entered the room.

"I'm here to help Alexis," I told Mrs. Hardwicke. That was the rock-bottom truth. There was no debate about whose side I was on. Maguire had bound me, but Alexis was my priority.

Where did Carson fit into that? He was still waiting for me to answer him about the key. Where was *his* loyalty?

Before I could answer him, something caught his attention. If a guy could prick up his ears like a dog, Carson would have alerted like a Doberman pinscher.

With startling speed, he palmed the key and shoved the tray of jewelry into my hands. "Stow that and close the safe," he ordered in a murmur, then stepped around me, heading across the suite just as the door flew open.

"The cavalry is here." Lauren's voice carried around the bookcase that hid me, and the safe, from view. "Time for Elvis to leave the building."

9

I COULDN'T EXPLAIN why I jumped to do what Carson said, except that I trusted Lauren less than I trusted him. Blocked from her view, I whisked the velvet-lined tray into the safe. I started to put the pearls back as well, but Mrs. Hardwicke's voice stopped me.

"Take me with you."

What? I asked her silently, my hand poised at the back of my neck. *Why?*

"I know what you are," she said, in a weird mix of plea and direct order. "You must help Alexis. I can help you do that."

From the other side of the suite I heard Carson say to Lauren, "It took them longer than I thought to get a warrant."

He meant the FBI, and a lightning strike of hope lit my heart. Agent Taylor—the cavalry—was on his way.

I closed the safe and swung the painting to cover it, my brain running double time. If Lauren's spell was working, Taylor still thought I was asleep on that smelly couch in the office. I needed to give him some kind of heads-up. Not for myself, but for my family. If anything happened to me, he would have to protect them from Maguire.

Could I leave him a clue and get my message across? Taylor hadn't ever shown any sign of ESP, but he had instincts that were almost as good. While I had the chance, I unlooped the pearls from around my neck and unfastened the chain I was wearing in the same movement. The pearls I slipped into my skirt pocket, feeling Grandmama Hardwicke fade to a bare psychic stirring. My own necklace and pendant I hid in my hand, just as Lauren called to me.

"Stop stalling, Red," she snapped. "If you haven't found anything by now, you're not going to."

I dropped the necklace—Saint Gertrude's medal gleaming up at me—beside the bureau and hoped the detectives were thorough in their search. Then I hurried toward the door before Lauren or Carson came looking for me.

"Where are we going?" I asked warily. Maguire needed to stash me while the FBI was there, and I did not put it past him to have a dungeon.

"Out," said Carson, giving me a nudge.

I followed Lauren into the hall. Carson lagged behind, and I hoped he still had the mausoleum key. Surely he would know it was important even if I hadn't yet told him why.

"You two are going to check Alexis's dorm room again," Lauren told me. "Just don't get caught. You can't find Alexis if you're in federal custody."

"Thank you, Captain Obvious," said Carson, sliding out of the bedroom and closing the door firmly. Lauren gave him a talk-to-the-hand wave and disappeared to tend to her own duties, which worried me for Taylor's sake. She'd better not put another spell on him.

Carson, meanwhile, took my arm and hustled me toward a back staircase, which led down to an enormous kitchen. Bertram was waiting with two coats and a set of keys. "It's got a full tank," said the butler, "and a six-pack of soda in the back, as you requested."

"Thanks, Bertram." Carson pocketed the car keys and slipped into one of the coats. He grabbed the second one, and when I didn't move fast enough, wrapped it around me and shoved me toward the back door.

We froze at a sound from the front of the house—one of the goons answering the door, then the familiar murmur of Agent Taylor's voice and the harder crack of Gerard's demand.

I drew a breath to yell to him. Drew it, held it, my tongue making the *T* in *Taylor*. Then the geas jerked on my leash with boot-to-the-chest force. My shout came out as nothing but air and a grunting wheeze.

80

Black fireworks splashed over my vision as I tried to make my diaphragm work, to pull breath back into my lungs. I grabbed at a wall to keep from falling over, but it turned out to be Carson. "Daisy?" he asked, sounding genuinely alarmed.

This was why Maguire had bound me to a task I would have done freely. I couldn't call out to the agents because they would stop me from looking for Alexis. If Taylor didn't ship me back to Texas for my safety, Gerard would arrest me for interfering with a federal investigation.

By accident I staggered toward the door, and the iron band around my chest loosened. I took another step and was able to gasp, "Let's go."

Carson didn't argue, just ushered me out. The biting cold of the Minnesota night snatched away the breath I'd just caught. I stumbled into the garage with Carson, wrestled my arms into the sleeves of the coat, and fell into the passenger seat of a sedan as soon as he unlocked it.

"A Taurus?" I asked as he started the engine. There were four other cars in the garage and all of them were more ... well, more *everything* than the beige Ford.

"We're going for unremarkable." He hit a button on the remote clipped to the visor and the garage lights went dark. "What would *you* pick?"

Not the one that looked like a car from *Tron*, I guess. He was right; blah was better.

Another button, and the door in front of us lifted. Headlights off, Carson pulled out of the garage and crept the car along the unlit drive as it curved through the surrounding woods. I could see the front of the house through the trees, and the two uniformed officers posted there, leaning against a squad car, watching for anyone sneaking away. Like us.

I could have jumped out of the car and made a run for it, or rolled down the window and shouted to the cops. But the memory of the geas's donkey-kick in the kitchen kept me still and silent, sunk low in the seat.

Once we'd reached some distance from the house, Carson put his foot down and the Taurus slipped along the dark drive like a moon shadow. It wasn't until we'd reached the county road and turned onto it, free and clear, that the knot in my chest finally loosened.

I sat up and looked out the window, realizing how bright the night really was. Full moon, beige car... "How did those officers not see us?"

Carson turned on the headlights and settled into a more comfortable position behind the wheel. I could make out his silhouette, and he seemed to debate his answer before admitting, "That was a little sleight of hand on my part."

He said it so calmly that it took a second for me to realize what he meant. "Hang on," I said, rearranging my brain to fit in this new information. "You do magic, too?"

Another pause, another debate. I'd assumed it was a yes-or-no question. "Not spells or anything like Lauren does," he explained, sounding almost sheepish. "It's more like a talent."

Okay, I didn't even know where to put that in my file cabinet of supernatural information. "You mean like Jedi mind powers? 'This is not the Taurus you're looking for'? That kind of talent?"

"Not exactly." He was definitely looking sorry he'd admitted anything. "Not mind powers."

"Does Maguire know about this?" I asked, gnawing on the question like a dog on a bone, trying to get to the marrow of it. Or maybe just of him. I had to know how much to trust him.

I could see his knuckles flex on the steering wheel. "This has nothing to do with finding Alexis. Let's stick to our job."

"How about *this*, then." I didn't like unknowns, especially where they intersected with me. "Maguire has his normal resources, his criminal ones, plus you and Lauren, the Wonder Twins. Why do you need me?"

He let slip a millisecond of uncertainty before answering. "The boss is one for covering all bases. Maguire saw you on the news, and it was too good an opportunity to waste."

"So he sent you to pick me up like a loaf of bread from the market." I sank into my seat, not even bothering to get indignant over well-trod indignities.

"What the boss wants, he gets."

After the guillotine finality of that statement, we drove the next mile in silence. I spent the time trying to sort out my tangled thoughts. God knew what Carson was thinking. But after a few minutes he broke the quiet. "Can I ask *you* a question?"

I sighed and answered, "I was born this way."

"That explains a lot, but it wasn't my question." We'd reached a state highway, and cruising speed. "Who is St. Gertrude?"

I fought a wary fidget and played it cool. "The patron saint of the recently dead. And of people afraid of mice, oddly enough. Apparently she had a lot of cats."

My worry was justified. Carson reached under his coat into his shirt pocket and pulled out my necklace, Saint Gertrude's medal dangling in the dashboard light. "Then you might miss this."

It was too dim to make out the saintly nun in her habit, cat cradled in her arms. But I imagined her scowling in disapproval, not because I'd blown the chance to send Taylor a message, but because I'd almost forgotten whose side Carson was on.

I snatched the pendant from his fingers, furious with him and me both. "Jackass."

A muscle flexed in his jaw, but I didn't know him well enough to know what that meant. I found out an instant later, when he swerved onto the shoulder, stopped the car, and twisted in the seat. Suddenly he was in my space, with a hand on the dash and another on the headrest, beside my ear. He moved so fast I hadn't even seen him unbuckle his seat belt. I drew back against the passenger door. It didn't occur to me to open it; I was that sure he'd stop me if I tried. But really it was the leashed anger in his gaze that trapped me there.

"Yeah," he said. "I am a jackass. But let me tell you about the guy I work for. If your Agent Taylor interferes with the boss's plan—any of his plans, but especially any involving Alexis—Maguire will make him wish he'd never been born."

Hearing their names in Carson's whipcord threat raised their specters in the cold darkness of the desolate road. My pulse beat so hard that it was difficult to swallow, but I had to before I could speak. With courage as thin as my breath, I challenged, "If you mean a long swim in the river, just say so."

"The big man doesn't kill people very often. He just makes

them wish they were dead." Bitterness honed the razor edge of his voice. "At the very least, he will make sure your boy loses his career before it even starts."

I got his point. Maguire needed me alive and cooperative. But Taylor was expendable, and I had put him in danger by trying to leave him a clue. Worse, Maguire would add him to the list of ways to punish me if I pissed him off.

I have a big family. It's a long list. Carson couldn't have struck closer to my heart if he tried. I started to think maybe I should be worried about how well he aimed.

Warm air poured from the car vents, but my insides were icy. "If he's such a bad man," I asked, "what does that make you for working for him?"

I'd shot blind, but scored a hit as well. The specters in his gaze flinched, though he didn't move for a long moment. Then, wordlessly, he took the necklace from my hand and fastened it around my neck.

He clasped the chain over my hair, getting it on the first try, before I even thought of protesting the invasion of my space. Before I thought *anything*, other than that he smelled really nice for an apprentice criminal.

When he sat back, he was cool and in control. "It makes me a bad man who doesn't want anything bad to happen to you." Mood shifting, he turned and put the sedan in gear. "So let's get to work."

That was the best idea I'd heard all night. I exhaled my own tension, happy to have a goal. Or the idea of a goal, since I didn't know what to do next.

"I didn't read anything at Alexis's dorm," I said, dropping the oval pendant under my shirt while Carson pulled back onto the empty state highway. And when I say empty, I mean *empty*. I'd seen no other cars while we were stopped. "Her bodyguard didn't have much useful to say. He was escorting her out to the car to take her to a party and"—I didn't go into detail, just made a fake gun with my fingers and a pistol-shot noise—"that's all she wrote."

Carson drove like he knew where he was headed. "I don't know why Walters—that's the bodyguard—was driving her last night. He was taken off that duty after Alexis complained about him. I always figured he would go down in a bar brawl if the coke didn't rot his brain first." He glanced at me with chagrin. "Not that I'd wish a bullet on anyone."

I didn't think he would. There was iron determination under his surface calm, but no stone-cold killer. And no accusing remnants, either. Whatever haunted him was figurative.

"Any chance Walters was in on it and got double-crossed?" Carson asked. He might not be stone cold, but he was pragmatic.

"No," I answered. "His surprise was genuine."

"He couldn't have been lying? Walters wasn't exactly a stand-up human being."

I shook my head, then realized he was looking at the road. "Trust me; deception was *not* the last thing on his mind."

And yet I was sure I was missing something really obvious. It nagged at me, and I sifted through all the pieces of the long, confusing day trying to find it.

Think, Daisy. What would Taylor do? The investigators would go through the mountain of paper and avalanche of books in Alexis's dorm room, looking for clues. They would interview her dorm mates and friends and review video from the security cameras.

What could *I* do that they couldn't?

I could talk to the dead.

"I am an idiot," I said, and reached into my pocket for Mrs. Hardwicke's pearls.

"Yes, you are," agreed her shade, from the general vicinity of the backseat. Though she had no physical form, she sat in prim disapproval. "You should never agree to ride in an automobile with a boy you just met."

Well, she had *that* right.

"What's going on?" asked Carson, looking from me to the rearview mirror and relaxing slightly when he saw nothing there. "Is Grandma back?"

"Grandma?" she echoed, and the temperature in the car plummeted. "I *beg* your pardon?"

"I'll take that as a yes," he murmured, turning up the heater.

"Be nice," I said. "We need her. And the key in your pocket. It *is* in your pocket, right?"

He took one hand off the wheel and dug into his trousers, pulling out the heavy antique. "Are you finally going to tell me what this is?"

"It's a clue." I braced myself before I took it from him. The metal was warm from his body, a living energy that dampened the graveyard's effect. "I don't know where Alexis *is*, but we can go where she's been."

Carson glanced at me, the blue glow of the dashboard lights giving him a faux ghostly aura. "And where is that?"

"The Hardwicke mausoleum." I glanced at the shade in the backseat. "You can give us directions to it, right?"

"Of course I can," she said. "I visited Spring Creek regularly to pay my respects to Mr. Hardwicke."

"Is that the name of the town?" I asked. "Spring Creek?"

"I know where Spring Creek is," Carson told me, checking the rearview mirror again. "But a mausoleum . . . That's where they inter the dead. Are you up for that, Sunshine?"

"Don't call me that." I was Daisy Goodnight, kick-ass speaker for the dead. I would not be overwhelmed by this situation. "If I'm not up for it, then who is?"

That didn't sound quite as kick-ass as I would have liked, but the statement stood. Maybe this was what I was meant to do. No one else would have gotten the inside info from Mrs. Hardwicke on what the key unlocked.

I held the key up between us. "Alexis hid this, so it's important. We should see why. Maybe we'll find the jackal in the crypt, or some clue to what Alexis was involved in, or why someone would want to kidnap her."

"Okay, okay." Carson slowed the car, safely this time. "I'm convinced. Spring Creek, Minnesota, here we come."

He was serious. Serious enough to execute a tidy U-turn in the middle of the empty highway. "That's it? No argument why we should continue with the search-the-dorm-again plan?"

"That was a lousy plan. This is better." He glanced over, letting me see a trace of wry humor. "Besides, you're the go-to girl when it comes to dead things. I'd be a fool not to take your advice. I'm not a nice guy, but I'm also not a fool."

Mrs. Hardwicke gave a snort from the backseat, but I didn't see any reason to spoil the moment by passing that on.

10

I WAS REALLY not dressed for breaking into a graveyard.

Spring Creek, Minnesota, was a small town about an hour from the Twin Cities, and the cemetery lay on the outskirts. We'd parked in the lane in back of the place and crept through grass that crunched with frost to reach the perimeter.

I shivered in my borrowed coat and gazed up at the fence that Carson expected me to climb—brick and iron, and about nine feet tall. The moon was still bright enough to see the points on top of the bars. Were people in Minnesota that desperate to call on their dearly departed outside of visiting hours?

"Can't you just pick the lock on the front gate?" I whispered, even though we were the only people within miles. But voices carried, and I didn't want to accidentally wake the dead.

Carson didn't deny that lock picking was in his skill set. "The front gate is too obvious. There are probably security cameras. And I'm not sure we weren't followed."

"You think we were followed?" The only thing worse than the people I *knew* would cause trouble—Maguire's goons, Taylor and Gerard, any local police officers or security guards—were the nameless, faceless "others" who had kidnapped a young woman and shot her bodyguard in cold blood.

"I took precautions," Carson assured me. "But I'm not a hundred percent certain." He crouched and offered his linked hands like a step. "Come on. I'll boost you up."

I eyed the spikes on top of the fence—dull and mostly for show, but still *spikes*. Then I eyed Carson, judging the estimated levels of sight line (his) and hemline (mine). "You have got to be kidding."

"What?" There was a challenge there. "You were never a cheerleader?"

A ridiculous question, and from his glance at my Hello Kitty skull T-shirt, he knew it.

"Were *you*?" I doubted it. One, I couldn't imagine that interning for a crime overlord left much time for the NCAA. Two, he wasn't pretty enough. He wore clean-cut like a disguise, but there was a no-time-for-nonsense intensity to his gaze and an older-than-he-should-be hardness to his jaw, as if he'd had to toughen up in a hurry.

Again with the challenging lift of his brow. "You don't believe I spend my Saturdays cheering the Gophers to victory?"

My snort fogged in the cold. "You'd have to manage to *be* cheerful first."

Then the corner of his mouth quirked up—not as far as *cheer,* but just a hint of shared humor and a slash of handsome guy-dimple.

Sainted Mary Magdalene. If my lungs weren't half frozen, my breath would have whooshed right out of me.

No, he was not pretty. He was worse. Devilish.

There was a bodiless sigh from the darkness. "I would greatly appreciate it if you two stopped flirting and got on with this unseemly business."

Mrs. Hardwicke, our ghostly chaperone, was still along for the ride. She faded out when I didn't give her my attention, but she always managed to pop back in when she had something to say.

"Fine," I said. At Carson's bemused look, I explained, "Mrs. Hardwicke is impatient." No reason to mention the flirting part. At least I couldn't blush with ice in my veins. I put my toe in his clasped hands and warned, "Do *not* look up my skirt."

"Eyes down," he promised soberly. "Scout's honor."

I only cared on principle. I rebelled in a lot of ways, but indecent underwear wasn't one of them. I'd talked to one too many shades who'd died embarrassed because of not listening to their mothers on that score.

I grabbed the bars of the fence for balance. On Carson's count, I jumped while he lifted me like I weighed nothing. Somehow I managed not to skewer myself on the pointy top, then got a toe up on the horizontal rail, eased over, and dropped to the other side.

Carson, as far as I could tell, just vaulted across. Maybe he really was a Jedi.

"Which way?" he asked, blowing into his cupped hands.

"Give me a sec." I flexed my own fingers to get the blood going, and with it, the intangible me. I pushed my psyche out like a sixth-sense radar net and got my bearings.

The graves around us were relatively new. Here and there the soft echoes of souls lingered, damped by the earth. Later, as dust returned to dust, the last remnant traces on this side of the Veil would unravel and vanish.

"Is this weird for you?" asked Carson. "Being in a graveyard?"

It was my turn to raise a brow. "Weird compared with what? Talking to Alexis's dead grandmother in the backseat of a Ford Taurus?"

He gave me that point. "When you put it that way..."

I tucked my hands into the coat pockets, wrapping my right hand around the mausoleum key. An electric tingle washed over me, carrying subtle information, like flavors I could taste but had no words to describe.

"The remnants here"—I gestured around us—"are all sleeping. Proper burials are like that. Most spirits have someplace better to hang out. What's left are the memories of loved ones visiting. They blend together, and it's kind of pretty, actually."

It was more like an abstract watercolor than a patchwork quilt. But with the key in my hand, I could sense which part of the psychic finger-painting we needed. Like called to like, and key called to lock.

Through the graveyard came the soft sound of metal on metal. I jumped and Carson did, too, but there was no way to tell where the noise had come from.

"You heard that, right?" I whispered, unsure and scared, despite all my big talk about the sleeping dead. In searching the dark, we'd ended up back-to-back, so nothing could sneak up on us through the silver-iced headstones and the black moon shadows beneath.

"Yeah." His low answer vibrated through my shoulder blades. "But it could be a mile or more away. Sound carries at night."

"Okay." I made a tight fist around the key in my pocket. "But let's hurry anyway."

He swept out an arm, inviting me to take the lead. "Lay on, Macduff."

Dude. He'd just quoted Shakespeare and given me the reins of this crazy train. It was a good thing I had more important things to figure out than the mystery of this guy. He was *so* much more than just the hired muscle.

I led the way through neat rows of modern marble headstones on to where the markers got more worn and more eclectic and uneven. There were a few small crypts, but we were headed to a sandstone building with marble accents and topiary guardians beside the door. A miniature mansion for the dead.

I stopped a few feet away, checking the place out with my other senses. Carson's vitality made a distracting gravity well in the spiritual landscape. I adjusted for his presence like a pilot adjusts for wind speed. That wasn't just me being girly. I had to do the same thing with Taylor, but I was used to him. Working with him was like a preset on my psychic radio.

"Hand me the key," Carson said, before I could get too worried about Taylor and what was happening back at the Maguire mansion. I gave Carson the key as ordered, happy to let him take the lead in the tomb-robbing part. At the door he took a small flashlight from his coat pocket and used it to find the keyhole. Turning the key took some effort, but it finally gave way with a loud clunk of the tumblers.

The door opened smoothly. I held my breath as a swirl of air rushed in, pulling the dead leaves around our feet with it. But nothing deathly wafted out, and I allowed myself a sigh.

"At least it doesn't look like Dracula is buried here," Carson said, echoing my relief. I peered over his shoulder as he passed the flashlight beam over the vaults, which were sealed with smooth stone and marked with the names of those resting inside. The chamber smelled of metal polish and cold marble, with a whiff of classic floral perfume that said our Mrs. Hardwicke was around. It was clean, but felt echoing and empty, even to my remnant senses. Everyone there was long gone or sleeping deeply.

I slid around Carson and went in, my footsteps ringing. He followed my movements with the flashlight. The walls weren't all marble—there was a stained-glass window at one end of the building, and another over the door.

"What are we looking for?" Carson asked.

A good question. "Something that doesn't belong here, I guess."

95

The beam swept over the marked crypts. Big family. Old mausoleum. *Lots* of crypts. Carson voiced what I was thinking. "Where do we start? I'm not breaking into a grave unless absolutely necessary. I didn't bring a sledgehammer."

"Give me a minute." Alexis's grandmother was just a faint glow in the shadows of the chamber, but the misty aura took on her familiar shape as I gave her my attention.

"Do you know when Alexis was last here?" I asked her. Was it too much to hope that Alexis had been wearing Mrs. Hardwicke's pearls when there? *If* she'd been there. I was beginning to doubt the genius of this plan.

Disappointment laced her tone. "The last time I was here with Alexis, I was alive and she was just a child. In *my* day, people visited their dearly departed. I brought flowers for Mr. Hardwicke twice a month."

She nodded at a marble-sealed crypt, about head high. The marker read JAMES HARDWICKE III. BELOVED HUSBAND AND FATHER. There was a brass sconce next to it—I thought it was some sort of lamp. There were more, spaced evenly between the vaults. Then I realized they were empty vases for flowers.

Mrs. Hardwicke sniffed her disapproval. "I think it's clear that no one has been here in quite some time."

I pressed her for useful information. "Did Alexis say anything when she hid the key in the safe? Did you sense her thoughts, like if she might have hidden something here?"

"No." Her image turned watery, weakening. "I want to help Alexis, but this is more difficult than I thought."

I realized I was the only thing keeping her coherent and

aware. When I relaxed my psychic hold, she dissolved into a sigh of fog, but I could still feel her hanging about in a formless sort of way.

"What did she say?" asked Carson, sounding edgy, or maybe just uneasy. I mean, standing in the dark among the dead might get to some people.

"She doesn't know when Alexis was last here," I said. "Which only means that Alexis wasn't wearing the necklace when she visited. We're back to square one."

"What about . . . ?" He gestured with the flashlight toward the vaults that held the remains of Alexis's maternal ancestors.

I took a deep breath just *contemplating* the heavy lifting it would take to get anything coherent from the scraps of memory that lingered there. Could I do it without getting my hands on at least one set of physical remains?

"There's not much here to work with," I told him. "Before I try to pull off a miracle, let's look for signs of any disturbance, like if she hid something. You check the physical, I'll cover the psychic."

"Got it." Carson began a systematic study of the marble-fronted crypts, running his hands and the flashlight over the seals and the ledges in front. That left me in the semidarkness, but I didn't need light to read the spirits in the place and know they were undisturbed and unhelpful.

I ended up standing where Mrs. Hardwicke had disappeared. In front of me were two side-by-side crypts. Mr. Hardwicke III was in one. The other engraving said ALEXANDRA HATTERSLEY HARDWICKE, BELOVED WIFE AND MOTHER.

This was nuts. How could a girl like Alexis hide anything in one of the vaults? Even if it was unoccupied and unsealed, opening it would be a task for a heavy-lifting crew.

Then why come here? I put myself in her shoes, like I did with the remnants too old and tattered to read properly. She must have felt this was a secure place. She came here with her grandmother—maybe there were happy associations. They brought flowers....

Bingo! The answer was staring me in the face. Or rather, I was staring right at it—the empty brass vase right above eye level, between Mr. and Mrs. James Hardwicke III.

"Carson, come here!" The vase would definitely hide something small dropped inside. I could reach the lip but not down into it. "Give me another boost, will you?"

He saw what I was up to and handed me the flashlight, then offered his linked hands as he had outside the cemetery wall. I stepped into them, grabbing his shoulder for balance.

He had nice, solid shoulders, and he took my weight without a quiver. I was only up long enough to get my hand in the vase and grab the object inside. I gave a soft whoop of triumph and Carson let me back down, then moved closer to see as I aimed the flashlight onto the treasure in my palm.

It was a plastic mummy, about three inches long, wrapped in white bandages, ready for the sarcophagus. Or maybe to come awake and start shuffling after Boris Karloff, I don't know.

"That's definitely not a jackal," I said, not sure what to think. I was flummoxed.

Carson took it from my hand. "Doesn't look like it's been here that long. Maybe some visiting kid left his toy?"

"A kid couldn't have put it in that vase, it's too high."

"Is that writing on it?" He twisted the plastic figure in the beam of the flashlight. "I think it's an *o* and an *i*."

Puzzle pieces were lining up in my head. Alexis, studying the classical worlds, like ancient Rome and Greece, from which it was just a short mental hop across the Mediterranean Sea to Egypt.

Ancient Egypt, with its mummies and tombs and elaborate burial rituals and pantheon of animal-headed deities.

"Carson"—I grabbed his arm in excitement—"it's got to be a clue. Do you know who the ancient Egyptian god of mummification was? Anubis. The *jackal-headed* god."

I saw him connecting the dots, too. "So you're thinking this is related to the Oosterhouse Jackal?"

"If Alexis left this here," I said, "it's too much of a coincidence—"

That was as far as I got before Mrs. Hardwicke appeared so suddenly and so brightly that I shrieked and dropped the flashlight. Carson caught it before it hit the ground.

"Someone is coming," said the shade, her form shivering with urgency and emotion. "And I've seen one of them before, with Alexis."

"*One* of them?" I asked, and Carson looked at me sharply. I kept my gaze on Mrs. Hardwicke. "How many are there?"

"Three," she warned. "And they know you're here."

11

"THEY MUST HAVE followed us," Carson said when I told him we were about to have visitors. "Let's go." He shoved the plastic mummy into his pocket and doused the light, leaving us in the gravestone-cold darkness of the mausoleum.

I didn't immediately fall into step. "Just close the door and lock it," I hissed. "We have the only key."

"Are you sure about that?" He grabbed my hand. "Besides, I'm not a lock-myself-in-a-room-with-one-exit kind of guy."

He had a point, so I went with him.

The doorway was full of moonlight. Carson stopped at the

edge, pressing against the wall, and I did the same. "How far away are they?" he asked.

Mrs. Hardwicke's shade had drifted with us. "Just down the hill," she answered, and I relayed that in a whisper.

"Stay low and keep to the shadows," he murmured, and slipped outside. I followed, grabbing the heavy door on my way and closing it carefully, silently, behind us.

Not quite silently enough.

"Did you hear something?" asked a voice from just down the hill. *Way* closer than I expected.

"Let's pick up the pace," said his companion, and the crunch of shoes on frozen grass sped up.

Carson shoved me out of sight behind an aboveground crypt. I hit the dirt with a grunt, then gave another one as he landed on top of me.

"This is getting to be a bad habit," I wheezed.

"You're not much of an escape artist," he whispered, his breath tickling the back of my neck. "Now shut up."

The ground was really cold and hard and Carson was hot and heavy, which might be nice in some circumstances, but not just then. I moved so that whatever was digging into my hip dug into a less sensitive place. I thought it was the flashlight, but I wasn't quite sure. It only just then occurred to me to wonder if Carson was armed.

"Hold still and think *camouflage*," he whispered as the footsteps came closer. I could feel them through the ground. We were hidden from the guys' approach, but one glance to the side and they'd see us.

Mrs. Hardwicke appeared, but all I could see was a pair of gorgeous suede pumps a few inches from my nose. "This is really quite disgraceful, young lady."

I ignored that, less worried about propriety and more concerned with dying stacked like a deck of playing cards. *Do you recognize these guys?* I asked her silently. *Do you know their names?*

"Not their names," she said. "They're in some sort of brotherhood."

Brotherhood? Like ... monks?

"More like a fraternal order." It was strange to hear the granite confidence of Mrs. Hardwicke's tone crumble with worry. "I don't like them. They made Alexis nervous." Then she said, "Here they come."

My tension must have warned Carson, because he tightened his arm around me. My heart gave a girly sort of flutter at the protective gesture before I was distracted by the sensation of something settling lightly over us, a net of static that played across my nerves like the electric tingle of a ghostly remnant.

"There's no sign of anyone," said one of the guys. He sounded youngish—not high school young, but not hardened, either. Maybe twenties? "You really think she told them where to find it?"

"She" must be Alexis, and "them" must be her father, maybe Carson. Now if the guy would just say what "it" was, then lying on the freezing ground would be totally worth the frostbite. But his pal was all business. "Shut up. Team Maguire must be around somewhere."

Carson tensed, and I heard the first guy say, "Stop looking around like that. You're giving me the creeps."

How were they not seeing us? From the sound of their voices, they were right alongside our hiding place.

"You'll have worse than the creeps if they've been here and gone. We need all the pieces, or nothing will be any good. Not the Jackal, not the girl . . . She'll be useless."

"Shhh," said his buddy, on the steps to the mausoleum. "The door's unlocked."

I heard it swing open, and their footfalls going inside. But in my head was the menace of that simple statement: *She'll be useless.* Expendable.

Carson exhaled as if he'd been holding his breath the whole time. The odd tingling feeling evaporated and the toes of Mrs. Hardwicke's shoes wavered in front of me.

"Goodness," she said, sounding shaken. "I thought for sure you would be caught."

Had Carson done another Jedi mind trick? Sleight of hand, he'd called it when we were leaving the mansion.

He didn't give me time to ask. "Let's go," he whispered, rolling to his feet and pulling me with him. Part of me said, *Yes, let's run,* and another part said, *No, wait!* There was something I was forgetting. Only two guys had passed us. I hadn't told Carson there were three.

The third guy came into sight just as we jumped up from behind the crypt. The moon was like a spotlight, and there was nothing to do but freeze.

The guy was young, like the others had sounded. He wore

a knit cap with a University of Minnesota logo, and brotherhood or not, he did look like a fraternity guy. He also looked as shocked to see us leap out of the shadows as we were to be seen.

The other two came out of the mausoleum behind us. "They're not here," the burly guy in the lead started, then broke off when I swung around, putting my back to Carson's.

Carson squeezed my hand then let go. "Cover your eyes," he said.

"What? Why—?"

An instant later I heard the flashlight smash to the ground. I clapped my hand over my eyes and squeezed them shut as light flared, reddening the edges of my fingers.

Then there was darkness, and a lot of cursing and yelling. When I dropped my hand, I saw the guy in the hat blinking blindly in the moonlight.

"Get them!" he shouted, but all Thugs One and Two could do was snatch at the spots filling their ruined night vision.

"Run!" said Carson, like I wasn't already moving.

I took off through the headstones, saving my questions for later. That flare had been *way* more than a flashlight beam. Just then I was grateful for the head start and the advantage of being able to see by moonlight.

Carson followed on my heels as I weaved through the rows of stone markers. I remembered the way back to the car, and I could navigate the watercolor psychic landscape without relying on the path.

Thugs One and Two and the Cat in the Hat had gotten

themselves together, and I heard them galumphing after us. We reached the fence and I started over it with zero finesse, jumping to catch the top rail. And then I just hung there like I was trying to do a chin-up in the worst gym class ever.

Carson put a hand on my butt and shoved. Honestly, I'd seen more action since meeting him than I had in all of high school. I got my leg up and leveraged the rest of me to the top, just as the three hooligans came sliding down the icy grass of the graveyard hill.

Carson scrambled over and dropped to the other side. I tried to do the same, but the collar of my coat caught on one of the spikes. I tumbled from my perch and braced to hit the frozen ground from a nine-foot drop but instead jerked to a stop, half choked by the coat and hung out like a rag doll on a clothesline.

"Ditch the coat!" Carson said, his eyes on the hoodlums closing fast. I unzipped and wriggled out of the parka, then stumbled and hit the ground.

Something slithered from around my neck and dropped into the grass. The Hardwicke pearls. "Leave it," said Carson, and only the sight of the three guys clambering up the fence convinced me to listen to him.

We raced to where we'd left the Taurus on the darkened lane. Momentum slammed me against the passenger door, and as I fumbled for the handle, Mrs. Hardwicke appeared beside me.

A desperate cold came with her, so intense that I wheezed with it. "You have to get away," she said, her hollow eyes all icy burning. "Get away and help Alexis."

"I will," I swore, as solemnly as I'd sworn the oath to Maguire.

Behind her—no, *through* her—I could see the last thug, the guy in the hat, pick something up from the grass. Mrs. Hardwicke's pearl necklace.

Carson started the car. Then the door banged me in the hip as he leaned over and opened it from inside. "Get in!" he snapped. "There's no time for a tea party with Grandma!"

Mrs. Hardwicke's glow brightened with gratitude. "Thank—"

Then she vanished. Not from sight, from *existence*.

How was that possible? I cranked up the psychic infrared to search for her, forgetting everything else.

"Daisy Goodnight!" Carson's voice shook me to bedrock level. "Get in this car right now!"

I dove into the car and slammed the door as Carson gunned the engine and peeled onto the pavement. "Buckle up!" he yelled as the Taurus fishtailed and clipped a tree trunk close to the narrow lane.

I twisted to look behind us. Thug One and Thug Two ran for another car parked nearby. But their buddy stood in the middle of the road, both hands raised, palms up, Mrs. Hardwicke's pearls catching the light as they dangled from his fingers. I didn't know what he was about to drop on us, but it wasn't going to be puppies and Christmas.

"Duck!" I yelled, and did. Carson stomped on the gas and hunkered down behind the wheel as the rear window exploded inward. I wrapped my arms over my head as the car was filled with chunks of safety glass, frigid air, and the scent of Chanel No. 5.

12

"WHAT THE *HELL* just happened?" I had to shout over the noise, since we were speeding down a country road in a car that was totally missing its rear window. All that was left was a frame of pixelated safety glass. I craned my neck to look into the backseat but saw nothing that could have caused the damage.

Carson clenched the steering wheel at ten and two, a smattering of cuts on his white knuckles. There was one on his cheek, too, blood seeping in a slow trickle. "Just hang on, will you?"

"I will *not* just hang on," I said, frustration and freak-out making me shrill. "Someone just Lord Voldemorted the back end of our car! I want to know what was that flash of light and where did Mrs. Hardwicke go and, *seriously*, does *everyone* in Minnesota have superpowers?"

He ignored that and adjusted his grip on the wheel. "I mean buckle your seat belt, Sunshine. We've got someone tailing us."

Sweet Saint Frances of Rome. I yanked the strap across my lap and fumbled it into the clasp just as Carson gunned the car through a yellow light to take a hard left turn from the right-hand lane. The engine whined and the tires squealed, and I may have made a couple of those sounds myself as I grabbed the door handle and braced for who knew what.

We straightened out and shot down a deserted state highway. I risked letting go long enough to look back, where a pair of headlights made the same turn we had, ignoring the red light and gaining on the straightaway.

"Are they still there?" asked Carson.

"Yep." The wind through the missing window whipped my hair around my face and I gathered it the best I could. "Why are you heading into town?" I asked, alarmed to see the lights of the outskirts of Spring Creek.

"Quickest way to the interstate," he said, never taking his eyes off the road. "I'm going to try to shake them on the way. Hang on."

No argument from me this time. I sank into my seat as he punched the engine. It was just like a movie, except I couldn't picture James Bond in a Ford Taurus. Carson took a turn without braking, miraculously not hitting the car illegally parked within twenty feet of the intersection. Another immediate left and we were in a dark warren of side streets. I hoped he knew where he was going, because I was totally lost.

And I was getting carsick, which never seemed to happen in heist movies, either.

"Will you lose all respect for me if I hurl?" I said.

He didn't spare me a glance. "Roll down the window, because we're not stopping."

I didn't dare move that far. Plus, if we flipped, I wanted all my parts inside the vehicle. So I battened down the hatches and breathed deep of the icy air coming in the back window.

Two more turns and we emerged onto the access road of the interstate. Carson took the ramp at an insane speed and we shot onto the highway like a shell from a cannon. He wove between two eighteen-wheelers, then slid into the gap between two more semis on overnight runs.

Only then did he glance at me. "Still need to stop?"

We were tucked so tight between the trucks I was surprised we didn't have to buy them drinks first. "More than ever, if you don't keep your eyes on the road."

Incredibly, he smiled at that, then got back to business. "We're going to have to ditch this car," he said after checking the rearview mirror.

"You're the boss." I didn't know anything about eluding kidnappers or police. I only knew ghosts. I was missing the graveyard, not to mention my law-abiding life. Though really, I'd settle for solid, unmoving ground just then.

"Who's St. Frances of Rome?" Carson asked, after a glance at my face, which must have looked as bad as I felt.

Had I said that aloud? "Patron saint of automobile drivers."

That got a half laugh. "Appropriate, the way they drive there." He cut the headlights and the dashboard console went dark, though we were still bathed in the light of the semi behind us. "You might have another quick word with her. We haven't quite lost them yet."

There was an unlit turnoff ahead. It didn't rate being called an exit. We slowed only enough for the truck behind us to ride our bumper, then slipped down the ramp at full speed. The service road plummeted out of sight and into shadow. Carson drove with calm intent, like a runner in the zone, a thrumming tension in his body as he hauled on the wheel and put the car into a skidding turn.

I prepared for death, wondering if then I would be able to talk to the living like I talked to ghosts now. But incredibly, we slid between the columns of the overpass and came to an abrupt stop before the drop-off into a drainage culvert. The engine subsided to an idle, and the car filled with the sound of our breathing. Overhead, the eighteen-wheelers rumbled like thunder across the vaulted ceiling of our concrete sanctuary.

I fumbled the door open and staggered to the culvert, where the turkey sandwich made a return appearance. I almost never eat meat. I would almost certainly never eat turkey again.

Carson killed the dome light. A moment later he was crouched beside me, making sure I didn't tumble into the ditch while I heaved. Finally I half fell to a seat on the concrete, gasping and mortified. Wordlessly, Carson cracked the seal on a bottle of Coke and offered it to me.

It was something Agent Taylor had done a million times, and my throat clenched over sudden tears. I hoped he was all right. I hoped Alexis was all right. I felt swamped by responsibility, for them, for my family, even for Mrs. Hardwicke. The stress of it welled up until I thought I might puke again.

"This was just supposed to be a routine reading." I let anger force the words past the choking weakness. "Find a body, point the finger, go home to Texas."

"I know," Carson said, his voice deep and rumbly, with something that sounded like real regret. He took off his coat and draped it over my shoulders. "Drink your soda."

I took a swig, swished it around, and let the carbonated burn chase away the taste of deli mustard and fear. That left only anger with no target. "I was *not* supposed to end up freezing my ass off in a remake of *Harry Potter* meets *The Italian Job* by way of *Fargo*."

"Fargo is in North Dakota."

"I don't need a flipping geography lesson!"

He made a shushing gesture. In the dark of the underpass, I couldn't see much of his face, but I suspected he was trying not to laugh. "You watch too many movies."

I restrained myself from dumping my Coke over his head. "Says the guy with *getaway driver* on his résumé. And just what was that with the light show back there? What else are you packing?"

"What else am I *packing*?" he echoed. "Have we gone back to the forties?"

"I know your buddies at the compound were armed. How do I know what *you've* got in your pants?" He choked, and so did I, for different reasons. "Pockets!" I corrected, not that it stopped his laughter or my incendiary blush. Hello, Dr. Freud, my name is Daisy.

He stood, outlined by the moonlight. Deliberately, he unloaded his trouser pockets—plastic mummy, cell phone, and wallet, handing each to me before turning out his pockets and holding his arms to his sides.

"Want to frisk me?" he said. "I don't mind."

He'd just handed me his phone. Did that make him trusting or complacent? If I managed to not give it back, who could I call? I could at least *try* to see what the geas would allow. So I got to my feet and slipped my arms into the coat before handing him the wallet and mummy, hoping he wouldn't notice that the phone went into the jacket pocket. "I'll pass, thanks."

He shrugged and stowed his stuff without looking at it. "Just trying to be fair. I've gotten a few inappropriate handfuls this evening, so I thought I'd offer."

"Tit for tat, I think they call that."

That was on purpose, to distract him from the missing phone, but the surprise in his chuff of laughter made me grin. There was an intimacy in laughing *with* someone, turning the ridiculous exchange into something warmer, something shared. Something closer to flirting.

Sweet Saint Gertrude, what was I doing? I couldn't flirt with him. I didn't even know if Carson was his first or last name. It didn't matter, because he was an employee of a criminal enterprise and I was an FBI consultant and, oh yeah, technically kidnapped and probably in the throes of some kind of Stockholm syndrome.

I cleared my throat and worked to unweave what had become a *moment* between us. "No big deal. I gave you the benefit of the doubt that any groping was unintentional and expedient."

He caught one edge of the coat I wore—*his* coat—then the other, and pulled me a step closer, knitting the spell tighter. "I appreciate that. When I grope a girl, I don't want to leave any doubt that it's on purpose."

"That's good," I said, way more breathlessly than I liked. Stupid Stockholm syndrome. "Expedient groping isn't nice for anyone."

His hold on the coat was very light, but I was caught by the sharpening speculation in his gaze. Forget firearms, that was a lethal weapon right there. Especially paired with the devilish curve of his mouth. "Are you ever at a loss for words, Daisy Goodnight?"

"Well," I said, heady with the thought of winning this battle, "I did get a perfect verbal score on the SAT."

"That explains it." He trailed his fingers to my shoulders, then down my arms. His breath was warm on my cheek, stirring my hair as he leaned in. "You are good at verbal scoring."

Oh my God, was he going to kiss me? That was so inappropriate. I'd have to tell him that afterward.

Instead he just whispered, "But not much good at picking pockets." He stepped back, holding the cell phone up between us. "Nice try, though."

Ass.

"Come on," he said. While I sputtered and fumed, he changed gears as if this was all in a day's work. "It's two exits back to civilization."

He started down the dark service road, abandoning the Taurus. "Are we just going to leave the car?" I asked. Who just *leaves* a whole car?

"It's too easy to identify," he said, clearly expecting me to follow him. "Button up so you don't freeze to death."

"What about you?" I fell into step beside him. "Aren't you cold?" He wore only a pair of dress pants and the same blue button-down shirt I'd soaked when I coshed him over the head with the flower vase about a decade ago.

"I have the nobility of my intentions to keep me warm." He also had his hands in his pockets and his eyes on the distant lights of one of the last outposts of sub-suburban Minnesota.

"How about a plan?" I asked. "Do you have one of those?"

"Yes." He counted off on his fingers. "One, don't get killed. Two, don't get shanghaied by the same people who grabbed Alexis."

"Yeah. Them." The fraternity of the invisible baseball bat. "We should have demanded they show us Alexis, to make sure she's okay."

"That would have been counter to item two," said Carson. "Maguire will deal with proof of ... of that."

He was going to say proof of life. Evidence that Alexis was still alive. Obviously he watched movies, too.

"I'm worried about Mrs. Hardwicke," I said, which was not

114

as random as it seemed. My subconscious was still gnawing on the smashed rear window and the timing of the shade vanishing.

Carson glanced at me. "Lex's grandmother? Why?"

"There was something weird about the way she disappeared. Remnants can fade over time, or move on or dissipate. They don't ever just ... poof."

That got me a longer study before he suggested, "Maybe she bailed? Or something happened when you dropped the necklace?"

"Possibly," I conceded. "Except ... kidding aside, I'm pretty good at this. And I'm sure of what I felt. I just don't know what it means."

He thought that over while we walked on in silence. Or maybe he was thinking something entirely different. But he was unmistakably contemplative, and I gave myself props for reading that much.

Our goal seemed to be a brightly lit truck stop. I was thinking wishfully about greasy doughnuts and bad coffee when Carson asked, in a tone I couldn't read at all, "Why do you call them remnants and not ghosts?"

I chewed over how to explain. Psychics and mediums had certain common terminology, but all the ones I knew—in my family and those I'd met working with law enforcement—had their own methods of visualization. It wasn't exactly an objective experience.

"What most people call ghosts," I said, "aren't like you see in movies, a whole person and personality. Most of them are just impressions or traces. Like a snapshot of a particular moment, or a looped recording of an event. Sometimes it's nothing but an emotional resonance, like when you get a sad or creepy feeling somewhere."

"But you talked to Mrs. Hardwicke like a real person," he said, and I could sense that he wasn't just making casual conversation, and this wasn't just about Alexis's grandmother. "You wouldn't be worried about her if she was just some kind of . . . psychic looped video."

"This is the bit that's hard to explain." We were almost to the truck stop, and I wanted to get this out while darkness softened cynicism and lowered barriers. "A remnant is just a piece—but it's a piece of a *soul*. And a soul can't be sliced and diced, so the whole is present in the part."

He stopped, looking bewildered, and his gaze dropped to Saint Gertrude's medal around my neck. "Is this a Catholic thing?"

"No." This was a thing I'd sensed in my gut long before I donned my first plaid skirt and oxford shirt. It annoyed me when people slapped a label on something that *literally* transcended time and space.

"Think of it like DNA. If I cut myself and leave a blood trail, my whole DNA is in each drop, even though it's only one part of me."

"So where's the rest of the soul?" he asked. "Heaven, hell . . . somewhere in between?"

I get this question a lot, from the desperate, the fearful, the grieving. . . . I usually get a handle on the reasons people ask. I didn't have a handle on Carson. I didn't think my grasp was long enough to reach that deep.

"I don't know," I said, which is not something I admit very often. "I do know that most remnants, unless they have a reason to stay, are happy to go."

That wasn't entirely true. I thought about the ghost that had started my day—my yesterday, really. But something in the intensity of Carson's question made it impossible to tell him how complicated it could be.

"What do you mean, a reason to stay?"

I shrugged and started walking again. "Bits of spirit cling to things like fingerprints sometimes. But if we're talking a cognitive-type shade—well, there's unfinished business or some traumatic event. Some remnants get stuck in a rut and don't know the rest of them has moved on. And sometimes someone leaves a piece of themselves behind voluntarily. My uncle Burt, for instance. He's not leaving my aunt Hyacinth until she kicks off and can come with him."

"Very sweet," said Carson, trying for cynicism and not quite making it.

"Lots of ghosts like to pop in now and then to check in on their loved ones, or hang out in their favorite—"

"Haunts?"

I rolled my eyes and gave him that one.

His mood lightened to its usual . . . whatever it was. I'd been wrong to call it stoicism. That implied a lack of emotion, whereas Carson's demeanor allowed humor and irritation and a few other things that had distracted me when I should have stayed on task. But I was on to him now.

"Carson," I said as we reached the edge of the neon island around the truck stop. He turned, wary at my preparatory tone. I pushed my wind-tangled hair behind my ears and squinted up at him. "Have you lost someone close to you?"

"Why do you ask?" His cheeks were bright red with cold. "Do I have someone checking up on me?"

I shook my head gently. I admit I can be abrasive with the living. But I know how to be kind with the grieving. And bone-deep instinct told me that Carson, despite the careful casualness of his tone, had lost someone important to him. "I don't sense anyone around you. But I can look more closely if you want."

There was a nanosecond when he thought about it. And then we'd moved on. "Don't bother." He hooked a hand under my arm and hurried us into the outpost of transportation and commerce. "Come on. I'm freezing and you're starving. I've been listening to your stomach growl for the past ten minutes."

Nice. I'd been expounding on the metaphysical mysteries of the universe and that was all he noticed?

Except I wasn't fooled. His demeanor was only a part of the whole. The Carson he let people see was just a remnant, with his soul hidden in an unknown beyond.

13

AT THE TRUCK stop, three twenty-dollar bills convinced the driver of an eighteen-wheeler to give us a lift to the next town on his route. The guy looked us over—Carson in his button-down and muddy trousers, two a.m. shadow on his jaw and a cut on his cheek, me swimming in his coat, my striped socks up over my knees, my Converse sneakers covered in skulls. We looked one shotgun away from a Kentucky wedding, but the trucker pocketed the money and didn't ask any questions.

I had *plenty* of questions—like where were we headed and why had Carson turned off his phone instead of calling for a getaway car that didn't smell like chewing tobacco and cardboard-pine-tree air freshener. I assumed it was part of the plan where we didn't get killed or shanghaied, except that I'd always been told that was exactly what to expect if you were foolish enough to get in a car with a stranger.

But true to his word, at the outskirts of the next town, the trucker dropped us in an acre of parking lot that conveniently connected a Denny's, a La Quinta Inn, and a twenty-four-hour Walmart. For those times when you're roaming the tundra and have a three a.m. need for a new set of snow tires.

"Come on," said Carson as the semi pulled away. The fog of his breath gave him an unearned halo under the streetlamps. He left it behind as he grabbed my hand and hustled for the restaurant and out of the cold.

I was rounding third on a Grand Slam breakfast and sliding home into the second helping of pancakes I'd requested instead of bacon. Carson eyed the rapidly disappearing stack with what I decided to interpret as awestruck wonder.

"You're obviously feeling better."

"My amazing powers require a lot of sustenance," I said between bites. "I figure I'd better top off the tank for whatever comes next. Which, by the way, we should probably discuss. You can start with why you turned off your phone instead of calling for a pickup, or getaway car, or agent extraction, or whatever term you people prefer."

" 'You people'?"

"Don't make me say 'mobsters' in the middle of a Denny's."

He glanced around the restaurant, which was virtually empty. The waitress had left a carafe of coffee when she'd dropped off our order, and we hadn't seen her since. "No one's listening."

"Good." I shoveled another bite of pancakes into my mouth. "Because I want to talk about magic."

"And I want you to tell me everything Alexis's grandmother said about the guys who showed up at the cemetery."

"There's not much." I stacked my plates and pushed them to the side. "She recognized at least one of them as someone Alexis knew. Maybe they met at a sorority party, which would explain why Alexis had on the pearls. Mrs. Hardwicke said the boys were in some kind of fraternity."

"Fraternity," echoed Carson, his tone hard to read. I was going with *disbelief.*

"She actually said 'brotherhood,' which sounds more ominous. I mean, if I was going to form a kidnapping and magic club, I'd go with that over 'frat house.'"

"Are you taking this seriously?" he asked, and I didn't have any trouble with *that* tone. I answered it as it deserved.

"Uh, yeah. Dude put an invisible fastball through the back window of a Ford Taurus. Also, Mrs. Hardwicke said she didn't like them. They made her nervous. I guess for a reason. Kidnapping Maguire's daughter? I mean, just writing the ransom note would take a pair of titanium cojones."

It had been hard to really get a look at the three guys in the cemetery, what with the dark and the running for our lives and stuff. But my fleeting impression had been that they were young

121

and would pass for college pranksters if not for a tangible air of menace.

"I joke because they scare me," I said soberly. "I think they did something to Mrs. Hardwicke's shade. And the remnants of Bruiser—I mean Walters—were . . . they weren't right. I thought maybe it was the bullet to the brain that scrambled his head, but now I'm not sure."

Carson took that in, expression neutral. "What else would it be?"

"I don't know yet. I'm still figuring it out."

He turned to look out the window. I watched his profile, not expecting to read much, and not disappointed. But my mind kept turning the puzzle pieces, and suddenly some of them clicked. Carson's smile in the photograph with Alexis, the fact he called her Lex and seemed comfortable in her room and around her stuff.

I'd wondered about it before, but now it *mattered*. It didn't make finding her any more important than a moment ago. It just made it more . . . just *more*.

"Are you and Alexis . . . um . . . close?" I asked, going for tactful and just managing awkward. "Romantically, I mean."

He glanced at me, and whatever he read in my face softened the grim lines of his. "Not like that. She's like a sister to me."

"That's pretty close." I fiddled with my coffee cup. Living people were much more complicated than shades. "I'm sorry you thought I wasn't taking this seriously."

My apology took him by surprise, but he internalized it quickly. "It's okay," he said. "Now I know. Sarcastic equals scared."

"Well, sometimes sarcastic just equals sarcastic."

I didn't like this subject. He didn't need to know that about me. I turned back to important things, like our graveyard adventure. "Why do you think those guys followed us? It seems weird that kidnappers would ask for a ransom and then go looking for it themselves."

He considered the question. "Did you hear what they said at the cemetery? They thought Alexis had told us where to find something. Maybe they thought following us would let them bypass Maguire. No messy ransom exchange."

I shuddered. It was one thing to talk about this stuff, another to think about what it meant. Jump us, grab the Jackal, problem solved.

"Only the Jackal wasn't there," I said, turning away from dire could-have-beens. "At least they talked about Alexis in the present tense. If they didn't find what they were looking for, she *will* be useless to them. So she's still okay."

Carson studied me for a moment, more unreadable than usual. "For someone so fond of skulls and black nail polish, you're actually quite an optimist."

"Don't be insulting." I put my clasped hands on the table in front of me, ready to move on. "Now. What can you tell me about the blown-out car window?"

Carson reached to refill his coffee mug. "That I seriously doubt Geico is going to cover replacing it."

I snatched the carafe away, holding it hostage. "Enough, Carson. No more caffeine until I get answers."

"Daisy, it's four in the morning," he said, utterly reasonable.

"If you want *coherent* answers, you'd better let me have that coffee-pot." I set it down, then waited while he filled my mug, then his. He pushed the sugar and creamer toward me, and said, "Why do I need to explain this to you? Your family are witches, right?"

"Hedge witches. Herbs, potions, that sort of thing. Nothing like . . ." I mimed a big *pow*. "But *you* didn't seem surprised by that."

His brow arched. "Trust me. I was plenty surprised when that meathead blew out the safety glass."

"But you weren't surprised that he *could*."

"No." He might be laying his cards on the table, but he was obviously going to do it one at a time.

"Could *you* blow out a window?"

"Maybe," he admitted. "Under the right circumstances. The problem is the power it would take. A light flare from a flashlight, for example, doesn't have a lot of resistance. Kinetic force would be a lot harder."

"So is what you do a spell?" I asked, wondering if it was more like what Phin practiced, or like my innate ability with spirits. "Or a talent?"

He considered his answer. "I think it's more like a talent for a certain type of spell, if that makes sense. Lauren—who would know—describes it as magic, but I've always just done it, like you and your spirits." He paused. "I haven't always understood what it was I was doing, though, and it takes understanding to do anything useful."

I could relate to that, too. Sensing spirit energy was one thing. Actively using that sense had taken time to learn.

"Are you and Lauren the only ones on the Maguire staff who can do magic? Or is it some kind of job requirement?"

Carson shrugged. "Unless someone has some ESP they're not telling us about, Lauren and I are the only employees with any, uh, special skills."

"That makes sense." I was relieved crime magic wasn't a whole new fad. "I guess if you had a psychic on staff, you wouldn't need me."

A thought struck me. Not from the blue, but from inside my head, as if it had been waiting for me to get around to it and run out of patience.

"What?" asked Carson, because I'm so transparent.

"I don't know." The thought didn't come with helpful context. "It is kind of weird that someone like Maguire couldn't have gotten his hands on a psychic better at finding live people."

Carson topped off his coffee mug. "It's not that weird. You were close by, bona fide, and easily controllable."

"Easily controllable?" I echoed, because I was also easily insulted.

He raised his hands, fending me off. "I'm just thinking like Maguire. You have a large family that you love."

Well, he had a point, even if I didn't like it. "That's probably the first time in my life I've been called *convenient*," I grumbled.

"I wouldn't go that far," said Carson. But he turned more serious as he studied me, as if I'd raised some question for him, too. "How many people can do what you do? Out of curiosity."

Okay, it's true I like to imagine myself a badass psychic, and I don't see the point of false modesty when my skills can help someone. But I don't let on that I'm a little freaky, even for a freak. I've met mediums and people who do psychometry or who read auras—which is sort of like what I do with spirits. But all in one package is unusual. And the Veil…? I've learned not to talk about that at all.

"It's not *what* I can do," I finally answered, in an I'm-going-to-be-perfectly-honest-with-you tone that wasn't perfectly honest. "It's how well."

Carson rolled his eyes. Distraction objective achieved. I held out my hand. "Give me the doohickey from the mausoleum. Not even I am good enough to raise the spirit of a plastic mummy. But you never know what may have hitched a ride."

He took the toy out of his pocket and dropped it into my palm. I hadn't felt anything from it in the cemetery, and a longer, calmer read confirmed that there were no remnant traces attached. But as I rubbed my thumb over the molded ridges of the bandages, I noticed something else. A crack. The mummy's head and shoulders were the cap to the USB end of a flash drive.

I may have squealed a little bit when I showed it to Carson. "Look! I told you it was important!"

He took it from me and examined it. "Yeah, but we won't know how until we get it plugged into a computer."

"Don't harsh my vibe, dude." The geas sang along with my excitement. I was doing what Maguire had tasked me to do: follow the clues to Alexis.

There was some writing on the back of the mummy. I could see why Carson hadn't been able to read it with the flashlight. A lot of the black ink had rubbed off. I could read half the letters;

126

my memory filled in the rest. "This is from the Oriental Institute of the University of Chicago."

"Is that important?" he asked.

Yes, said my instincts.

"Maybe," I said aloud. "It's another coincidence." Not that a flash drive shaped like a mummy came from a museum specializing in artifacts from Egypt and points East. But that something related to Alexis was related to me.

The waitress came around to collect our plates and ask if we wanted anything else. After she'd left the check, Carson said simply, "Explain."

I sat forward, elbows on the table. "Alexis is studying classics, right? Latin, Greek, birth-of-civilization stuff. Egyptology isn't the same thing, but they're not worlds apart. Then there's this." I held up the mummy flash drive, currently headless, and rattled off the links in my logic chain. "So we've got the ancient world, this Egyptian mummy, which relates to Anubis, the jackal-headed god of mummification, which makes me think of the *Oosterhouse* Jackal."

Carson didn't seem as amazed by my reasoning as I thought he should be. "It does seem like a coincidence of jackals," he admitted, and took the flash drive from me again. "Do you think this has the information we need to find the Oosterhouse one?"

"Alexis hid *something* that those brotherhood creeps wanted."

"But we're not sure it's the brotherhood that kidnapped her," said Carson, and I couldn't tell if he was playing devil's advocate or what. "They may be a second party looking for the Jackal."

"A second party looking for something that the Internet has never heard of? What are the odds?"

He gave me a look that said what are the odds that a crime boss would have a witch on staff to help him kidnap a teen FBI psychic to look for his kidnapped daughter. Or some other unlikely scenario. "Let's keep an open mind," he said aloud. "I agree the brotherhood is connected, just not how."

"Okay." Drumming my fingers, I tried to decide how much to tell him about the encounter with the bodyguard-driver, and how to phrase it so I didn't sound crazy. "Here's another coincidence. Alexis's driver—well, his remnant—said something weird about a black dog. Maybe it was something he saw when he died, or something his spirit saw, I don't know. But a jackal and a dog might look the same. Not that Anubis would terrorize a spirit. He was supposed to be the protector of the dead...."

I trailed off at Carson's expression of flat-out disbelief. "You're not seriously suggesting an ancient Egyptian god has shown up in Minnesota," he said.

"Of course not," I scoffed, because that was ridiculous. "Who would come to Minnesota in the winter if they could help it?"

Carson gave me one of his studying looks. "You're being flippant again."

He'd figured me out. Flippant equaled freaked. And Bruiser's shade had me freaked. So had the disappearance of Mrs. Hardwicke. Someone, or something, was messing with the spirit world.

I turned to the last thing I had to offer, putting the head back on the mummy and holding it so the logo showed. "Then there's this. The Oriental Institute is a research organization and museum of Near East history. It's one of the top places for Egyptologists to study, and it's been around for ages. My great-great-aunt went on a few of their expeditions in the nineteen twenties. She's kind of a family legend."

His brows arched. "Did she raise a mummy?"

"Not exactly." Let's just say I wasn't the first Goodnight to get in over her head with the dead. "But the Oriental Institute is another tie to ancient Egypt, and we know Alexis has been there."

Carson took the flash drive from me, holding it up as if to look the mummy in the eye. "You think the Oosterhouse Jackal is there? Or maybe something that will lead to it?"

Did I? The evidence was awfully circumstantial, as Taylor would tell me. Psychic evidence wasn't admissible; my job was to find links between random-seeming things, which would then point the way to hard evidence. I wished I could offer Carson hard evidence, but all I had was my gut feeling.

"I think our best bet is to follow Alexis's footsteps. If she was looking for this Oosterhouse Jackal, then backtracking may lead to her kidnappers." I spread my hands, open palmed, on the table. "It's just a hunch. But I *am* psychic."

Carson didn't seem to need more than that. He grabbed the check and pocketed the flash drive. "Let's go. We can be in Chicago in five and a half hours." Then he glanced at me and changed his mind. "Six, if we stop to get you some less conspicuous clothes."

14

WE SPRINTED ACROSS the acre of parking lot to the Walmart, not slowing down until we reached the air lock of shelter between inner and outer doors, beside the shopping carts and stacks of shoppers' guides. I breathed on my hands and stuck them under my arms. "How does anyone live through the winter here?"

Carson laughed. The longer we were away from the Maguire complex, the easier that seemed to happen. "This isn't winter. It's autumn." He took out his wallet and handed me a thick wad of bills. "Get a change of clothes and whatever else you want."

"Holy cats!" I stuffed the money into my pockets like contraband. "What is it you think I'm going to need? A mink coat?"

"It doesn't have to be mink. When you're done, meet me out front."

"What are *you* going to do?" I asked, mentally wrestling with pockets full of cash and freedom.

"I'm going to go buy a toothbrush, and then I'm going to get us some transportation."

"Where are you going to do that at this hour? Are you even old enough to rent a car?"

He stared at me like he couldn't believe I'd just said that, and after the mental lightbulb snapped on, I couldn't believe I had either.

"Oh my God! You're going to *steal* one?"

Fortunately, I had not said this nearly as loud as it sounded in my head, which was very loud indeed, since it was accompanied by police sirens and clanging prison doors.

Carson gave me a long, patronizing look. "Would you prefer to walk to Chicago?"

"You can't call Maguire to send one of his fifteen cars for us?"

He hesitated as if considering it, then said slowly, "I don't think that's a good idea. Maguire's giving me a long leash on this, but it's still a leash."

I thought about Maguire behind his square mile of desk, surveying his kingdom, with armed guards and, for all I knew, flying monkeys at his command. If Carson had some reason he wanted to stay under the boss's radar, I was okay with that.

I wasn't okay with stealing, but we needed a car, and the binding promise muzzled my objection. I stood there wrestling my conscience for so long that Carson's expression softened in sympathy.

"Here," he said, taking the coat from my shoulders and sending me into the store with a little shove. "Fifteen minutes. Shop fast."

I had fifteen minutes and four hundred dollars. Carson had given me a lot of rope with which to hang myself. Did he trust me to come back, or did he trust the geas?

Fulfilling my vow was nonnegotiable, but I had some choice about how to go about it, as long as my subconscious believed it would work. Telling the security guard who watched me load my handbasket with toothpaste and clean underwear at three a.m. that I'd been kidnapped? Spiking pulse—and common sense—nixed that idea.

I could go out the back door and find a taxi or a phone. I could call Agent Taylor. I could share with him everything I knew, and give evidence against Maguire in exchange for immunity on my crimes so far.

Then he'd ship me back to Texas by Express Mail. The geas would put me in the bughouse and Maguire would take revenge on my family, or Taylor, and that would finish me off.

But most important, with me in jail or exile, the FBI would have no psychic on the job. Alexis's best chance was for me to do what I was doing—throw in my lot with Carson and follow her trail. We had to get to her, or get to the jackal, before the kidnappers did.

"Are you all right, miss?"

My dilemma had brought me to a halt by a counter full of accessories. The clerk behind it was a doughy-looking woman wearing a blue smock and a name tag that said DORIS. In my distracted state, it took me a moment to realize she was not wholly *there*.

"I'm fine," I assured her. Especially compared with someone stuck for eternity as a greeter at Walmart. I think that's what Sister Michaela called purgatory.

"Can I help you find something?"

I sighed, wishing it were that easy. "Do you have something that will help me rescue a girl from kidnappers who might also possibly be a fraternity of wizards?"

Doris cocked her head, pondering my problem. "Maybe something from the hunting and outdoors department?"

Very tempting. "I have to find her first. The only things I have to go on are a hunch and a plastic mummy flash drive."

"A flash drive?" she asked, blinking behind cat-eye glasses. "Would that be in camera equipment?"

"It's a computer . . ." I eyed her seventies shag hairdo and went with, ". . . thingy."

"Oh, we have computers," said Doris happily. "Aisle thirty-two. Cutest little netbooks for surfing that World Wide Web."

That would teach me to judge a shade by her hairstyle.

"Thanks, Doris." Her faded form had sharpened at the edges while we'd talked. How long had she been asking "Can I help you?" and getting no answer? I made a point of telling her, "You've been a real help."

She beamed, literally brightening with her smile. "You're welcome! Have a nice day!"

Grabbing my shopping basket, I hurried to the aisle I wanted. I didn't linger over my choices, just snagged the cheapest netbook that would serve. My fifteen minutes was almost up, but as I headed for the front of the store, a thought slowed me down. How long *had* Doris been greeting people who couldn't hear her?

I went back to Accessories. Doris's shade still stood behind the counter, still smiling, still in the loop that had been her life.

"Hello!" she said, starting from the beginning. "Welcome to Walmart! Can I help you find something?"

"Would you like to go home, Doris?" It was hard not to speak to her like a child. That was sort of what she was. A lost lamb, all habit, no home.

Her eyes were pale, in a face that hadn't seen sunlight in years, expression numbed by endless, mindless repetition. And that was *before* she died. The pattern was slow to break, but finally comprehension sparked, like light in a curtained window of a vacant house.

"You mean my shift is over?"

"Yes." I set down my shopping basket, glancing at the big clock at the front of the store. This crossing would have to be quick and dirty.

I pictured my psyche rushing to my skin like a blush, pulsing with my heartbeat—not fast and frantic like when the geas had hold of me, but a strong and powerful song. The air around me hummed an echo, and the Veil appeared in front of us like a beaded curtain of glass.

Doris gasped. "My dogs! They've been waiting for me all this time I've been at work. They must be so hungry!" She took a step forward—through the counter, feeling the pull of the next world.

I *loved* this part. It made everything else worthwhile. "Your dogs are going to be really happy to see you," I said with a grin. "Ditch the apron and go, Doris."

Pulling off the smock, she let it fall into nothingness and ran through the mercury beads that gated her eternity. As she disappeared, I caught a whiff of candle wax and a strain of Conway Twitty.

She didn't say thank you. They never did. They were too excited about what was ahead to think about what was behind, and that was all the thanks I needed.

The Veil blurred and softened to a silk ripple, and I reached with my psyche to close it, to still its vibrations like damping a ringing bell.

But I stopped when I glimpsed a black figure on the other side, like a stalking shadow on a moonlit curtain.

Free me, Daughter of the Jackal.

The words whispered through my head as the Veil closed.

My ears rang. My *head* rang. Nothing had ever spoken through the Veil before. Eternity was hidden from the living. That was the rule.

At least, that was *my* rule, because I'd never seen anything different. I was ninety-nine percent convinced I'd imagined this in some sort of stress-and-magic-induced waking fever dream.

The other one percent was certain I shouldn't be certain of anything.

I made for the checkout on shaking legs and paid for my stuff. I'd barely stepped outside when a late-model Mazda sports sedan zoomed up to the curb.

"Get in," Carson said through the open passenger window. I could tell he was pissed because he was so careful not to *look* that way.

I popped open the door and jumped in. Carson hit the gas as soon as my foot left the pavement, trusting me to get the door closed before we were up to speed.

"What part of 'fifteen minutes' was hard to understand?" he asked with icy calm. "The part where I was idling around the corner in a stolen vehicle?"

"Sorry," I said. But some emotion must have laced my voice, because he spared me a glance as he pulled onto the service road to the interstate.

"What happened?" he asked. "Are you okay? Did you have trouble with a guard?"

"No. Something with a remnant." I shivered in spite of myself. Remnants saw things beyond the Veil. I did not. Ever. Until tonight.

"Is that why you didn't manage to buy a coat?" He leaned over to turn up the heater.

His tone ignited my temper, burning off the shivers. "I didn't manage to buy a coat," I said, reaching into one of the bags and yanking out the netbook in its box, "because I was blowing my cash on a way to look at that flash drive. Ingrate."

He smiled and turned his gaze to the road. "That's better."

"I should have just taken the money and run," I grumbled. "How did you know I wouldn't?"

When he glanced at me again, he summed me all up, and it was somehow not smug, just droll. "I don't know, Gertrude. You tell me."

Obviously I didn't have to. I reached up to touch my medal. Symbol or saint, I'd picked her for a reason.

And Carson was right. There'd never been any question what I'd do. It was what I always did. I found lost souls and brought them home. I had to do the same for Alexis, no matter what it took.

15

WE STOPPED ONCE in Wisconsin to switch drivers, then again near Rockford just before the sun came up. I grabbed my Walmart bag and used the restroom of the Starbucks to wash up and change into the clothes I bought.

When I came out and looked for Carson, I almost didn't recognize him. He was at a table, poking around on the netbook, wearing a T-shirt and hoodie and a pair of rectangular dark-rimmed glasses, his hair spiked and messy with damp. He actually *looked* like a college student, harmless and sort of adorable.

I set the bag with my stuff in one of the chairs. "If you're wearing skinny jeans, I refuse to be seen with you."

He looked up, then had to take off the glasses to see me properly. "You're one to talk. We both had the same idea."

Right. I'd gone for hipster camouflage, too—jeans, layered T-shirts, skinny scarf draped around my neck—but I'd kept my studded accessories and skull-covered sneakers.

Carson held up a twenty-dollar bill. "Grab something to eat while I look up directions to the Institute."

"Don't look at the flash drive without me," I warned, and accepted his acknowledging wave as a promise.

I returned to the table with an egg sandwich, a fruit cup, a muffin, and a venti nonfat latte. Carson didn't comment on my breakfast, just slid over to make room so we could both see the ten-inch computer screen.

"Wait," I said, putting my hand on his when he went to plug the mummy flash drive into the port. "If whatever is on here sends us straight back to Minnesota, I don't want you to say I told you so."

"But I didn't tell you so," he said, confused. "I had no problem following your hunch."

"I know." I let go of his wrist. "Which is just going to make me feel worse if we've crossed state lines in a stolen car for nothing."

Rather than offer empty reassurance, Carson just plugged in the drive, and I held my breath.

This memory device is password protected.

Crap. I would rather have listened to "I told you so" all the way back to Minneapolis.

Carson reached for his coffee and contemplated the empty password box and flashing cursor. "Any ideas?"

"Does she have a pet? A favorite color? A favorite movie?"

He started typing things in—birth date, favorite actor, mother's maiden name—with no luck at all. Finally he rubbed his eyes and closed the netbook. "It's okay," he said, when he saw my disappointment. "We're not any further behind than we were before. We can be in Chicago by the time the museum opens."

Jeez. It really was that early. I felt like I'd lived a week since heading for class yesterday morning.

A few hours later, we left our stolen car in a park-and-ride lot and caught the commuter train into Chicago, then switched to the subway. I played it cool, copying Carson and trying not to look too freaked out by the close quarters in the train car.

"Not a fan of closed spaces?" he asked as we bounced along the underground track. When I cut him a glance, he nodded at my hands, white-knuckled on the metal pole. I guess I wasn't fooling anyone.

"It's not the space. It's the people." I loosened my death grip, no pun intended. "The psychic baggage gets a little overwhelming, all packed in here like this."

"Almost there," he said, sympathetic. Then he hooked his elbow around the pole, took out his wallet, pulled out a card, and handed it to me. "Here. You might need this."

"A Starbucks gift card?"

I didn't think that was funny, but he laughed. "Are you *always* hungry?"

"Dude. It takes a lot of calories to run this much psychic genius."

"I'm sure it does." He tapped the card. "Lauren gave me this for you. This looks like whatever the viewer expects it to look like. You might need ID."

I looked again and found nothing but a credit-card-sized piece of blank white plastic. I tried not to look as impressed as I was. "Do you know how many college students would give their eyeteeth for one of these?"

He flashed a grin that said he knew very well. "Don't bother listing it on eBay. It's only good for a day or so, and it won't pass a hard inspection. Oh, and don't try to buy any Starbucks with it. It doesn't work on credit-card machines."

I turned the card between my fingers. It must have taken a lot of magical mojo to make, even with the limitations. Lauren might rub me the wrong way, but she was one seriously kick-ass witch.

"How did your boss find her? I mean, is there a listing on Monster.com for witches for hire?"

Carson shrugged. "He has a lot of resources. I think her actual job title is 'arcane adviser.'"

He had deadpan down to an art, that was for sure. "So, what's *your* title?" I asked.

"Court jester," he answered, with funereal gravity.

"No, really." We stood holding on to the same subway pole, our shoulders brushing with the movement of the train. Close enough that we didn't have to raise our voices over the noise of the rails. There was a peculiar sort of privacy in the crowd.

"Really," he echoed, lightening his tone but sticking to his script. "I'm the king's fool."

I studied him with a bit of a squint, trying to bring him into focus, figuratively speaking. "I think you're wise enough to play one. I'm really out on a limb here with you, and I don't even know if Carson is your first or last name."

He gave in with a sigh, his eyes on the sign over my shoulder, displaying the next subway stop. "I'm management in training. Don't ask me more than that."

"Why not?"

The train came to a halt, and I almost missed his answer in the shuffle of riders to the door. ".Because I don't want you to think even worse of me than you do. Come on. This is our stop."

He caught my arm so we wouldn't get separated in the jostle on the platform. I was glad to let him steer while I processed what he'd said. That he cared about my opinion. That he was at least ambivalent about his role in the Maguire organization. He seemed to dislike, maybe even hate Maguire. It was a safe bet he didn't work for the man by choice. But what hold did the big boss have over him? It couldn't be as simple as college tuition.

Maybe that was wishful thinking, only why would I wish that? I didn't like morally ambivalent bad boys. I liked good guys—like rookie FBI agents open-minded enough to take on cold cases with a teenage psychic. But as we emerged into the biting Chicago wind and I glanced at Carson's Roman coin profile, I wondered why I *didn't* think worse of him than I did.

The Oriental Institute was located on the University of Chicago campus. It didn't look Near *or* Far Eastern, but totally Western, with gables and ivied stone walls and Art Deco accents. .

We arrived minutes after the posted opening time. On the front steps, I paused like I was studying the carved panel above the doors.

"What's wrong?" asked Carson.

"Nothing." I was just getting ready to enter a building with a millennium or two of history inside it. "Museums can be tricky. Just reel me in if I start talking to mummies or singing ancient Sumerian drinking songs."

"Awesome. A floor show." He pulled open the heavy front door and gestured me in with a flourish. "I'll look forward to that."

The building felt of age and academia, and I found myself treading lightly, like in a library. Only the smiling volunteer behind the info desk convinced me we weren't trespassing.

"Are you students at the university?" she asked, handing us a brochure map of the place. "Or visiting from out of town?"

Carson gave her our prearranged cover story. We'd decided we couldn't be students in the Egyptology department, because they probably all knew each other. "We have this crazy sketching assignment for one of our classes. It's sort of like a scavenger hunt."

The volunteer gave a sympathetic nod and a glance at our clothes. "Ah. Art students."

"Our art history teacher's a little bit of a head case," Carson said, with just the right mix of drama and indifference to fit the stereotype. He was scary good at this. "We're supposed to sketch something called the Oosterhouse Jackal."

The woman's frown seemed genuine. "I've never heard of any pieces called that."

"Any jackals you can think of?" asked Carson, with a hint of that devilish grin.

She smiled back like she couldn't help it. I rolled my eyes for the same reason. "Down that hall and to the right is the Egyptian gallery," she said, pointing to a pair of double doors leading off the foyer. "I'm sure there are plenty of jackals represented there."

"Thanks," said Carson. "One more question." He took out his phone and pulled up a picture of Alexis. "This is the girl we're trying to beat to the prize. Has she been in here recently?"

The lady looked carefully at the photo, then shook her head. "I've never seen her. But I only work here on Thursdays."

Carson thanked her again, and she waved us on, wishing us luck.

I'd already started down the hall, drawn by the ginormous carving at the end of the gallery. It covered most of the wall—a winged bull with a man's head. Assyrian, maybe? The distinction was probably important to someone who knew it.

There were no individual shades or remnants that I could sense. But the carefully curated artifacts saturated the air with history, bearing ancient witness to births and deaths and dynasties. My head was full of snatches of sound and color—Iron Age forges and sun-saturated desert.

"Hey, Sunshine." A hand waved in front of my eyes. "Twenty-first century calling."

I blinked myself back to the world as it was—high ceilings and climate-controlled cabinets and an almighty crick in my neck from staring up at a seventeen-foot-tall statue of a pharaoh.

I looked around, surprised to find that I'd gone from ancient Iran to ancient Egypt without noticing.

"Boy," said Carson. "You were not kidding about museums being tricky."

"I warned you," I told him, like it was his fault I'd gotten lost in time. Narrowing my focus, I circled the gallery and gingerly poked around with my extra senses, checking the room for any psychic hot spots. "Do you see anything...jackal-y?"

"You tell me."

I didn't understand what he meant until I looked with my eyes instead of my Sight, going from one limestone-encased cabinet to another, scanning the artifacts on display.

"Wow. There are a shit-ton of jackals in Egyptian art."

"Hardly surprising," said a stranger's voice. I whirled. Carson turned calmly, as if he'd seen the guy approaching. The young man went on, "The jackal-headed, or sometimes dog-headed, god Anubis played a vital role in funeral rituals and afterlife beliefs."

He seemed nonthreatening, speaking with a sort of friendly condescension, as if he couldn't quite help himself. He looked way too young to be wearing a tweed blazer with patches on the elbows. Whatever look he'd been aiming for, all he hit was nerdy.

"Do you work here?" Carson asked. Silly question—dressed like that, where else would the guy work?

"I'm in the graduate program. Sarah—the volunteer at the front desk—told me you're looking for something called... What was it?"

"The Oosterhouse Jackal." I watched him for a reaction to the name. "We're supposed to sketch it for art class."

"I don't know about a jackal," he said, without any artifice that I could tell. "But there was a Professor Oosterhouse here during the nineteen twenties and thirties. Could that be related?"

"Maybe," I said, a lot more "Here's hoping" than "Eureka."

He gestured to the exit. "Let's go up to the research library and see if there's any information in the archives."

Carson didn't move right away, but this seemed like an excellent plan, so when Elbow Patches led the way out of the gallery, I followed him and Carson followed me.

"I don't trust him," he murmured, when Elbows was far enough ahead not to hear. "Why is he being so helpful?"

"It's a *research institute*," I whispered back. "This place exists to help people find stuff out."

Carson stared at the back of Elbow Patches' head like he could see into his skull. "He was looking at you funny."

"People always look at me funny."

He made a noncommittal sound. I let him stay on his guard. One of us should be wary, I figured, even of a nerd with a slightly rabbity smile.

We went up a flight of stairs and down a hallway lined with office doors, finally reaching the reading room of the archives. Elbows opened the door for me and I had to hold back a squeal of delight. It looked like something out of Hogwarts.

There were rows of tables, shelves along the walls and more toward the end of the long room. The ceiling was vaulted, buttressed with oaken arches, and intricately painted. At the end of the room was a window with a lotus flower design filling the room with morning light.

Faint wisps of remnants eddied through the room like snatches of mist. Students at the desks. A tweed-suited librarian shelving books. None of them paid the living any attention—even me. They were merely impressions of the past, going about their business.

Elbow Patches led the way to a computer. "We'll check here first and hope we get lucky. The Institute has so many documents and books that it's an ongoing project getting the older stuff into the database."

Carson hung back, arms folded, so I made nice. "That sleek computer looks almost out of place. I'd expect a cabinet with drawers of manila cards and a librarian with a rubber stamp."

"Oh, we have that, too," said Elbows. "The card catalog, I mean. But people log in from all over the world looking for specific papers, maps, and things. Stuff you can't find anywhere else." He finished typing into the search box, and a block of text rolled up the screen. "Here we go. Carl Oosterhouse, German-born archaeologist. Born 1887, died 1941. Expeditions to Egypt in 1924, 1926, 1930, 19—well, about seven in all."

He'd reached the end of the short biographical paragraph. "Is that it?" I asked, disappointed even though I wasn't sure what I'd expected. "I don't suppose it says where he was buried."

Elbows checked. A lot of people might think that was a weird question. But not, apparently, an Egyptologist. "It just says he died at sea. The circumstances aren't listed." He turned back to me, explaining, "He's not one of our better-known faculty. I've only heard of him because I've run across his work in the archives."

I waited for him to go on, but when he didn't, I prompted, "What kind of work? Articles and stuff?"

"Oh." He shook himself and returned his gaze to the computer screen. Carson was right. Elbows *had* been looking at me funny. "Journal articles, yes. And we should have his field notes from his Institute-funded expeditions. Upper Nile valley, 1931, lower Nile valley—"

Carson interrupted the recitation. "Would the field notes say what sort of things he found on his expeditions?"

Elbows looked from me to Carson and back again. "What kind of project did you say you were working on? You must really want a good grade."

"It's more of a prize, actually." I nudged Carson to get out his phone. "We've got competition. I don't suppose you've seen this girl around here?"

Carson showed him the picture of Alexis. Elbows glanced at it, then looked closer. "I've met her. She came to an event for prospective graduate students. I think she was there with one of my classmates."

Without visibly changing his posture, Carson seemed to go on high alert. "What's his name?" Carson asked.

"Michael Johnson. He's a first-year."

"Is he here today?"

Elbows shifted uncomfortably. The way Carson was firing questions at him, I would squirm, too. "I haven't seen him." He gestured at the computer. "Do you want me to print out the call numbers for those journals?"

"Yes, thank you," I said, extra nice to make up for Carson. "We really appreciate your help."

Elbows turned quickly to the keyboard, but his ears went pink, giving away his blush. I grabbed Carson's arm and pulled him to one of the tables.

"Now we have a name," I whispered. "Have you ever heard of this Michael Johnson?"

Carson frowned. "I didn't even know that Alexis was thinking of going to graduate school."

"What else is she going to do with a degree in Latin and Greek?" I glanced over to make sure Elbows was still at the computer. "I think we should call Agent Taylor and give him the name."

That left Carson speechless for a whole second. "You think *we* should call the FBI? Is that a royal we, Sunshine? Because I'm not doing that."

"Don't be stubborn." I hissed, like we were arguing over whose turn it was to pick up the check. "Taylor can look this guy up, trace his movements. The feds have resources we don't."

"If I want resources," he said, "I'll call my boss."

Someone cleared his throat before I could answer, and we both looked up. Elbow Patches stood nearby, holding a huge stack of books.

"That was quick," I said, changing gears and hoping he hadn't heard anything. I jumped to help him put the heavy volumes on the table. "Are these actually *from* the nineteen thirties?"

"Or bound facsimiles. That's why getting everything online is an ongoing process." He seemed pleased that I was impressed. Then he said, "I've been trying to think where I've seen you before."

Poor guy. That was the best line he could come up with? Carson, out of the grad student's view but directly in mine, rolled his eyes. "Maybe around campus?" I suggested, because it might not be so funny if he'd somehow seen me on the news from Minneapolis.

"Oh, I figured it out," said Elbows. "Here, look."

He laid a book on the table. I caught a glance at the cover before he opened it. *Female Pioneers in Archaeology.* He turned to a grainy black-and-white picture of a tall, slim woman in a desert setting. She wore jodhpurs, riding boots, a dark jacket, and a don't-mess-with-me attitude. The caption underneath said *Professor Ivy Goodnight, Thebes, Egypt, 1932.*

I didn't quite gasp, but only because I stopped myself. I knew every inch of that photo from the family albums at home. The Goodnight lineage isn't lacking for pioneers who don't make the history books. Magical contributions to society are either secret or rationalized. But Aunt Ivy had managed to do something marvelous by normal standards as well as secret, supernatural ones.

I slid the book closer. "This is my great-aunt. Do we really look that much alike?"

Carson leaned over my shoulder to look, his breath tickling my ear. "It's a strong resemblance."

Elbows shrugged. "Compare enough representations of pharaohs, you start to see family traits. Bone structure, supraorbital process, zygomatic arches…" He trailed off into awkward silence, his gaze sliding away from Carson's. "Not that I was staring. Dr. Goodnight features in the archives because of her work, and … Er, well, I'll let you get down to business, then."

He scurried off, which unfortunately made him look even more rabbity than before. I winced in sympathy and turned on Carson. "You want to be a little less cranky with the guy helping us out?" I asked. "There's a saying about flies and honey."

Carson pulled the top book off the stack and sat down with it. "I don't trust anyone that helpful. And he's got no reason to be so interested in your zygomatic arches."

"It means cheekbones." But I blushed anyway. "Medical examiners talk the same way."

"He was way too interested in all of you." Maybe he was being protective (and maybe I got stupid girly flutters at the thought), but more likely it was plain old suspicion.

I slid into a chair across the corner from him. "Not everyone is working an angle, you know."

"No." He didn't lift his eyes from the index of the book in front of him. "I *don't* know."

That? Was really, really sad.

You would think that with what I do—talking to the dead, solving murders—I would be more cynical. But in bringing them justice, or at least rest, I was adding to the ledger of good in the universe. And I knew how many people were striving to do the same.

I pulled the book with Aunt Ivy's picture closer and turned the page to a photograph of her working on the excavation of the massive stone pharaoh I'd seen downstairs. Aunt Ivy had always been my hero because of how she'd made her mark in two worlds, but I hadn't realized until that moment how much it would mean to me to be in her old stomping ground.

Hang on. I was about to have a moment of brilliance dulled only by the fact I was a moron for not having thought of it a lot sooner.

"Carson," I said, sliding the book toward him, "I know how to get more information on Oosterhouse, and maybe this Jackal of his."

He studied Ivy and the excavation and put the pieces together quickly. "You think there might be a remnant of your aunt attached to the statue downstairs?"

"Yeah." I made sure my voice was low and Elbows was nowhere near. "The problem is, I didn't feel anything when I was there before. Which means that I'm going to have to get my hands on the thing."

He followed my meaning there, too. "So you need to worry about an alarm."

"Maybe, maybe not. No one could steal that without heavy-lifting equipment. I'm more worried about security cameras. I'm sure someone would have something to say about my copping a feel on the pharaoh."

Carson tapped his thumbs on the table, looking around as if searching for something to MacGyver into a solution. "Okay," he said after a moment. "I can give you a minute or two, I think. But we'll have to split up."

"What are you going to do?" The last time we'd parted company, he'd stolen a car. Splitting up made me nervous.

"Something with the electricity or the camera feed, I imagine." He stood and closed the book. "I'm making this up as I go along."

"Then how will I know when it's safe to do my thing?"

"Give me ten minutes, then go."

"I don't have a watch."

"How do you not have a watch?"

"I always use my phone, but someone stole it."

He calmly unfastened his wristwatch, fiddled with it, then took out his phone and set a timer with the clock app. "Ten minutes from ... now."

He started the timer as the second hand on the watch hit twelve. I put out my hand for the phone, but he handed me the watch instead. Obviously he didn't trust me that much after all.

"I'm going to the restroom," he announced, stacking up the books. "Meet you downstairs?"

"Sure," I said, playing my part. "I'll just put away these journals and be there in a jiffy."

Jiffy earned me an eye roll. But he sauntered off like he knew where he was going. I waited until he was out of sight, then dashed over to one of the catalog computers to see if I could access the Internet proper, but no luck. Then I remembered all the offices we'd passed on the walk from downstairs. I rebelliously ignored the sign telling me to reshelve all materials and hurried—trying not to look like I was hurrying—out and down the hall.

I felt slightly guilty for what I planned to do with my ten minutes, but the geas wasn't weighing in on the subject, so I squashed my conscience and ducked into the first empty office I came to.

The tiny room was its own archaeological excavation, with layer upon layer of books, papers, maps, sketches, more books, and in the middle of it all, a desk with a fairly ancient computer, big enough to hide me from the door.

I woke it with a tap on the keyboard, checked Carson's watch, then opened a browser window and my web mail account. I had a hundred sixty-seven new messages, all from family members. I guess the Goodnight Alarm System was operational.

I skipped all those and started a new message to Agent Taylor. It was going to have to be short, no time for sweet.

Check out Michael Johnson, grad student at U. of Chicago. Alexis's boyfriend? Ex-boyfriend? I have a feeling. I hesitated a second, then added: *Trust me. —D.*

There wasn't time to do more than click *Send* and close the browser window. I needed to be downstairs and in position in six minutes and seventeen seconds.

I checked the hall before I headed for the stairwell. I was almost there when I heard my name, at a very un-librarylike volume.

"Miss Goodnight!" I turned to see Elbow Patches hurrying toward me, a lock of blond hair falling into his eyes. My first thought was, *Crap, I'm going to get into trouble for not reshelving my materials.* My next was, *Crap, he knows my last name.* And now everyone on this floor knew I was here, too.

He was holding out a book, open to a detailed line drawing. The pages were aged, but not worn; it wasn't a book that had seen much use. "I found this," he said, excitedly. "It's the field notes of Dr. Oosterhouse's last expedition. Do you think this could be what you're looking for?"

I took the slim volume from him to look closer, because the sketch was of a jackal-headed man, with an Egyptian collar and skirt. The notations underneath said that it was made of lacquer over wood, with gold leaf and enamel details. I didn't get any kind of psychic rush, but hope was its own kind of adrenaline. "It could be. I must have missed this in the display downstairs."

"Oh, it's not downstairs. I looked it up by the catalog number." He reached across to tap a number under the drawing. "It's out on loan."

I checked the watch. Four minutes and twenty-something seconds. "Where? Please don't say Australia."

He chuckled longer than that deserved, being as my desperation was no joke. "No. Not so far as that. Just St. Louis. The St. Louis Art Museum."

Despite the ticking watch, I wanted to express my gratitude to Elbows. "Thank you," I said, giving him back the book. "You've gone beyond the call of duty."

He blushed. "I'm an archivist in a very specialized museum. I don't get to show off very often."

As he took the book from me, something slipped from the pages. We both bent to grab it and nearly bumped heads. He got flustered, and I got the manila card that had fallen to the tile floor. At first I thought it was the catalog card, but when I turned it over I saw, drawn in what looked like Sharpie, an ear. Vaguely anatomical, definitely recognizable.

"That's an odd sort of bookmark," said Elbows.

Yes, it was. I had no sense for magic, but I had two brain cells to rub together and a bad feeling about this. If it was some kind of spell, what else would an ear mean but that someone was listening?

So much to think about, but the clock in my head was ticking. I ripped the card in half, hoping it would break the spell, then turned again to Elbows. "Can you look up who last checked out this book?"

"Well, you can't check out books from the archives," he said, sending that lead into a nosedive. Then he added, "But I can probably see who last pulled it up in the catalog."

"That would be *so great.*" Maybe I laid it on a little thick, but my gratitude was very real. Spell or not, whoever last looked up Oosterhouse and his Jackal could be the best lead for finding Alexis.

It would be even more awesome if he could go look that up *quickly* so I could get downstairs in the next two minutes and fifty-seven seconds. When the silence stretched to awkward, I pointed toward the stairs. "I'll be right back. I just need to, um…"

"Oh!" He blushed again, and I was happy to let him assume whatever kept him from asking for details. "I'll just be in the…" He sidled back the other way.

"Awesome."

The instant his back was turned, I hurried down the steps, with the pieces of the manila card still in my hand. I put the scraps in my pocket as I reached the ground floor, and not-quite-ran toward the Egyptian gallery. I reached it with a minute to spare...

...and no privacy. The gallery was full of people. I mean, not packed, but inconveniently occupied. It had to be some kind of tour or class, because a docent was giving a talk around a sarcophagus and showing no signs of moving on.

Whatever Carson was going to do was going to happen in twenty seconds. Short of yelling "Fire," I didn't know how to get the group out of there. The mummy inside the sarcophagus might be quietly sleeping, but the guide was going to have plenty to say if I stepped over the low velvet cordon to put my hands on King Tut.

I was still racking my brain when the lights went out, plunging the gallery into pitch-black, holy-crap-I'm-in-the-dark-with-a-mummy darkness.

"Everyone hold still," the docent ordered. "We don't want you crashing into anything in the dark."

Forget that. The faint remnant traces on the artifacts in the cases mapped out the room for me as I ran for the majestic sentry at the other end of the room. But I'd forgotten about the ankle-high cordon. I tripped with an almighty clatter of the brass stanchions, fell flat on my face, and only dumb luck kept me from concussing myself on the basalt pedestal.

"I said don't move!" shouted the docent.

"I'm okay," I yelled back, worried someone would come check on me. But I was not okay. I had to make contact before the lights came back on.

The stone was cool under my hands, and the hieroglyphs carved into the base were rough under my fingers. I called into the past, not as far as the ancient artists with their chisels but a hundred years back, in the psychic equivalent of a shout from the rooftop. *Ivy Goodnight, if there's any trace of you here, please answer.*

Silence.

Aunt Ivy, I need your help!

All I got were approaching footsteps and the bobbing glow of flashlights.

Hope collapsed under the crushing weight of failure, and I dropped my head onto the floor with the rest of me. What now? This was the one thing I could do—talk to the dead. If this didn't work, what good was I to Alexis?

There was the lead I'd emailed to Taylor. Michael Johnson. And the fact that Alexis had been here with him. And the clue of the ear card. And the jackal statue that was in the St. Louis museum. And the flash drive we hadn't yet unlocked.

There were all those things, waiting for me to get up off the floor.

There was also a pair of worn leather boots right in front of my nose. Sand-dusted boots that I could see perfectly well in the pitch-dark, what-did-I-summon blackness.

16

"YOU RANG?" SAID the shade standing over me. My eyes traveled up her boots, her jodhpurs, and her really great jacket and scarf and found her looking back down at me, one red brow wryly cocked.

This was not how I wanted to meet my idol. I jumped to my feet, but they were still tangled in the cordon, so I just managed to make a lot of noise. "Stop moving!" shouted the docent, and from the dark someone else called, "We'll be right there. Stay put until the lights come back on."

"Who are you?" Aunt Ivy asked. She looked as she did in our family photo—late twenties, totally confident. Not nearly as surprised to see me as you might expect. She took in my red hair and amended, "The better question might be *when* are you? And where are we?"

No wonder I'd had to call so hard. The trace of her must have been faded almost to nothing. It figured a Goodnight wouldn't stick around anywhere she didn't want to.

I'm Daisy. Even without the audience I would have spoken silently to her, because it was quicker that way—the speed of thought, literally. *Your great-great... Well, it doesn't matter how many because I'm in trouble and I need to know anything you can tell me about something called the Oosterhouse Jackal.*

"I don't know what that is." Before I could curse, silently *or* aloud, she continued. "I know a Professor Oosterhouse. He is— was—faculty here." She rubbed her forehead, a very *living* sort of gesture. "Sorry. My times and tenses are all messed up."

Don't sweat it. That happens. What could you expect when your past and present and future had all already happened?

She sweated it anyway, as if she sensed my urgency. Her shade flickered with the effort of pulling her memories together, but as I poured more of myself into the psychic link between us, she steadied.

"There *was* something about him," she said, "and *jackal* is sticking in my mind. He left the Institute in the early thirties, under a dark cloud."

That would be the nineteen thirties. I added together the timeline with the professor's German last name and made a wild guess. *Was he a Nazi sympathizer?*

"Not at all," she said, and that seemed to spark a connection. "I was away when he left, but I came back to wild stories that he'd started a cult and swore he'd found something that would defeat the Third Reich."

My mind went off in some very insane, very Indiana Jones directions. *Like a weapon?*

A face-melting *Lost Ark* kind of weapon? The idea shook me down to my curled-in-horror toes.

"I don't know. Bollocks!" The air went crisp at her frustrated curse. "I only remember gossip I heard when I came back, and that's just bits and pieces in my head."

It's okay, I assured her. Except that the security guard with the flashlight had finally gotten around to us. As the beam cut across the gallery I curled up in the shadow of the statue, where the guard would miss me until he'd helped the others.

Tell me all the gossip, I urged Ivy. *His bio in the archives says nothing about when or why he left.*

She spoke fast as the guard went by. "Officially, it was hushed up, but the rumor was he went batty. Got loony ideas based on a translation he'd made of the Book of the Dead."

I knew what that was. I'd be pretty sucky at my job if I didn't. It was an instruction manual for how to mummify the body and prepare the soul for its journey into the afterlife. There was no definitive edition because the process and the rituals changed across dynasties.

Ivy went on in a rush. I could see the tumble of memories coming back to her now. "Oosterhouse said he had found a version written by an ancient cult who believed in the magical power of the soul after death. But there was no proof of such a book—not that I could find, and believe me, I looked."

Of course she would. A Goodnight couldn't let that sort of thing go uninvestigated. *So you don't know if it was genuine magic or just the professor being fanciful?*

"*Fanciful* is not a word I would apply to Dr. Oosterhouse." She frowned. "He didn't voice theories of which he was uncertain. They say—*said*—the professor tried to re-form this cult among the students. A sort of secret society."

My heart went graveyard cold. *Like a brotherhood?*

"Yes! That's what it was called. The Brotherhood of the Black…" She paused with a little quake of realization, and I *knew* what she was going to say.

Jackal, I whispered.

Suddenly I was squinting in the glare of a flashlight. "Are you okay, young lady?" asked the security guard behind it.

Ivy's shade paced to my right, talking angrily to herself. "Why didn't I remember that as soon as you said the Oosterhouse Jackal? What a ninny I am!"

"It's fine," I said—aloud. "You're just a shade."

My great-great-aunt drew herself to her full height. "I am Professor Ivy Goodnight. I am not *just* anything."

The guard moved the light out of my eyes, and I could see him looking at me like *I* was the ninny. "Did you hit your head when you fell?"

"No, no," I assured him. "I'm fine."

I wasn't fine. I was trying not to follow Ivy with my eyes and trying not to freak out at the possibility that *my* brotherhood—the window-smashing, magic-throwing brotherhood from the cemetery—was related to Ivy's Brotherhood of the Black Jackal.

I hadn't realized I'd been thinking so loud until Aunt Ivy's shade flitted to my side, her face tight with worry. "The one thing I do know for certain is that the Brotherhood was real. This Oosterhouse Jackal could well be the thing that the professor believed would stop Germany's march across Europe."

Her urgency made my head spin, and it was starting to chill the air. The guard was watching me—no, he was saying something, and I hadn't answered, and now he was reaching for his radio to call an ambulance and I couldn't let that happen.

"Sorry," I told him, and got to my feet on my own power. "I have a phobia about the dark, you see. That's why I ran and tripped." I didn't have to fake a shiver; Ivy's words had iced my veins.

The lights came back on suddenly, and I gave the skeptical guard an exaggerated reaction. "Oh thank God! I'll be all right now."

He reached for my arm. "Let's just get you out to the lobby and make sure."

If he took me away from the pharaoh, he took me away from Ivy. I panicked, and Ivy did, too.

"Listen to me," she said. Words and images and emotions came like falling stars from her mind to mine. Sand and heat, dust and danger. Cold metal tanks and hot furnace fires. "If this

163

jackal is Oosterhouse's weapon, and the Brotherhood holds the secret, you cannot let them reach it. You cannot let *anyone* reach it. You have to get to it first, Daisy."

"Okay," I said as the guard led me away. I trailed my hand on the statue as long as possible, and Ivy kept pace with me. "Okay," I said again, because there were enough *non*magical face-melting weapons in the world. And once more, because I couldn't think of any single person who should have that much power. "Okay."

That was two triple vows. Rescue the girl, save the world. *Lucky thing I'm a Goodnight.*

"You *are* a Goodnight," said Ivy, quickly, because we were losing touch. "Remember you're never alone."

I thought about the five hundred sixty-seven emails in my web mail in-box by now. I was never alone in spirit, but I felt so far away in actuality. How could any of my family help me here?

The guard held my arm like fragile china, walking me out. My eyes finally focused on the physical world, and I saw Carson running toward us. His footfalls hurt my head.

"Are you okay?" He took my shoulders and bent to look into my eyes. He was absolutely not putting on a show. I must look like crap. "What happened?"

"It was dark." I said, bolstering my white lie to the guard. "And I have a migraine coming on." That excused a lot of things, including a hasty exit. It also was true. I felt it rumbling toward me like a mudslide down a mountain.

Carson took charge, thanking the guard, sliding his arm around me, ushering me out the door. We were outside in record time.

He pushed something into my hand. "Sunglasses. Put them on."

"Thanks," I said, fumbling them into place. Even the overcast sky beat on my eyeballs.

The tide of students hurrying to class flowed around us as we blocked the sidewalk. It was windy and damp and weird to think it was still mid-morning. I checked Carson's watch and realized the lights in the museum had been out for just a few minutes. I'd been on psychic time while talking with Ivy.

"What happened?" Carson asked. He looked ready to catch me if I started to sway. "Did you reach her?"

"Yes. That's why the headache. They're not all as easy as Mrs. Hardwicke." The ghost-talking itself wasn't hard, but pulling the shade out of slumber and helping her piece her memory together left me shaking. And, oh yeah, so did the realization that we were up against someone—or some*ones*—willing to commit kidnapping and murder to get their hands on a magical artifact strong enough to stop an army.

"Daisy." Carson's voice—firm, steady, just the right amount of bossy—called me back to the present. "You're about five steps ahead of me right now. Tell me what's next."

"Next," I said, making myself sound a whole lot stronger than I felt, "I need an ocean of Coca-Cola and a ride to St. Louis."

17

WE MADE GOOD time down the interstate, in our second stolen car of the day. I was so worried about losing the lead on Alexis, so worried about getting to the jackal ahead of anyone else, that one more auto theft didn't seem that big a deal.

I had thought the headache might be the result of the sextuplet of promises duking it out in my subconscious, but at some point I'd felt one geas knit seamlessly to the other. Alexis's life came first. But as the clues came together I was convinced that the trail of the Jackal paralleled the trail of Alexis's kidnappers.

Three Cokes and a thirty-minute nap had banished the migraine by the time we got out of the Chicago traffic. On the open road, Carson drove fast, but not obnoxiously so.

The low-slung bucket seat of the muscle car made me feel like I was reclining on the pavement. "If you showed up at my house in this car," I said, "my aunt would never let me go out with you."

Carson glanced at me, then back at the road. "Does she have something against muscle cars?"

"No. Just Corvettes. I think a guy with a Corvette broke her heart once."

I unfolded—again—the note that Carson had given me from Elbows. "From your boyfriend," he'd said, once we'd boosted our ride. Elbows apologized for not finding a name, just that the query looking for the field notes of Oosterhouse's expedition had come from someone with an OI student ID. It kept this Michael Johnson guy in the running.

"Let's talk about this," said Carson, picking up the torn pieces of the card with the ear from the car's cupholder. I'd shown them to him when I'd caught him up on my adventures, and he'd confirmed that it was an eavesdropping spell he'd seen before. My cousin Phin would call it representational magic. Apparently the Maguire operation called it convenient and electronically un-detectable.

"You think the same guys who kidnapped Alexis are respon-sible for this *and* for the attack in the cemetery?"

"There's magic involved in all three things." I counted them off on my fingers. "The kidnapping, the attack, and the ear spell.

Either it's all one group or the Midwest is overrun by roving gangs of magicians."

He actually considered that possibility, then discarded it. "And you think they're related to the Brotherhood of the Black Jackal that your aunt told you about?"

"They have the Institute in common, and it's hard to ignore the jackal-y theme." I turned in my seat to face him, the better to make my case. I'd take a hazy theory over clueless stumbling any day. "This is what I think. Oosterhouse's secret society ... say it's less Dead Egyptians Society and more Magic Fastball Club. And the guys we met in the cemetery somehow found out about it and revived the tradition."

He looked doubtful. "So a bunch of students stumble across a reference to Oosterhouse in their studies and start experimenting with magic?"

I shrugged. "Why not? Half my dorm mates are experimenting with something or another."

He slid me a curious glance, then looked back at the road. "What are you experimenting with?"

"A life of crime." I didn't want to think about school right now. Especially midterms on Monday—and the fact that I hadn't studied for them.

Carson ventured his own theory. "Maybe this Brotherhood never really died out. Just went deeper underground."

"Aunt Ivy did say the one thing she was sure of was that the Brotherhood did exist. And that we had to stop them from getting the Jackal."

He let that sink in while he passed a slow-moving minivan.

"Did she specifically say that it was some kind of weapon of mass destruction? Maybe it's just power, not inherently good *or* bad."

"Don't give me that 'magical artifacts don't kill people, people kill people' business," I said. "You can pry my Goodnight Farms magical bath products out of my cold dead fingers, but I'm one hundred percent in favor of Nazi-face-melting artifacts control."

An awkward pause sucked the air out of the car. I was actually relieved when Carson called me out. "Are you seriously going to turn this into a debate about the Second Amendment?"

It *was* ridiculous, considering him, organized crime management in training, and considering me, unpaid psychic consultant for the FBI. But I pretended it wasn't. "I'm from Texas. *Everything* is about the right to bear arms. It's kind of annoying, no matter which side you're on."

I caught him smiling at that before he turned serious again. "What about this Book of the Dead that your aunt couldn't find?"

"I don't know." I closed my eyes, trying to recall exactly what the guys had said at the mausoleum. "In the graveyard, the Brotherhood was looking for something, but it wasn't the Jackal. They said if they couldn't find it, the Jackal wouldn't matter, and Alexis would be useless. Maybe they're still looking for the book."

He took the flash drive out of his pocket and handed it to me. "Do you think there's a clue to the book on there?"

I looked into the mummy's nonexistent eyes, then back at Carson. "I'm sorry. I can only talk to the real dead, not the plastic kind."

"Cute. But maybe Alexis found a clue in her studies—the ancient world seems to be the connecting thread. She knows about magic, so she might look at information differently from other students. Some link that's been missed for eighty-odd years."

"Eighty years is a long time." Also, what were the odds she found something my aunt couldn't?

"Alexis is genius smart. She was on college week on *Jeopardy!*" He glanced at me. "Maybe she knew these guys, but when she found out what the jackal was, she refused to give them information about it."

The theory held together loosely, but there were still a lot of unraveling threads.

"Did you really not know she was thinking of going to grad school at the Institute?" I asked.

"No. She didn't tell me." Carson had his game face on, but he couldn't quite hide that her silence bothered him. A lot. "Maybe she thought I would tell Maguire."

I left that thread alone. We drove in silence, Carson passing another car at faster-than-posted speed. I assumed he knew what he was doing, because we couldn't afford to get pulled over. There was almost certainly an APB out for me, or him, or both of us by now.

"So what did the Brotherhood overhear?" he finally asked.

It took me a second to rewind as far as the eavesdropping spell. "That the jackal—or *a* jackal—is in St. Louis. Which, since the spell was in the book, they knew already. Now they just know we know."

Carson was quiet another long moment. "Did Tweed Jacket call you by your name?"

Oh yeah. Now they knew that, too.

"Just my last name."

Whatever he was thinking made him flex his hands on the wheel. I tried to let it pass, but all I could imagine was my family caught between the Maguire operation and the Brotherhood of the Magical Jackasses. I hoped Saint Gertrude had reinforcements, because it was going to take a truckload of angels to protect my nearest and dearest.

"What?" I demanded. "What are you thinking?"

Another eternity went by before he let me know. "We've been wondering why they asked Maguire to get the jackal, when they know more about it than we do. Maybe they need his resources. Especially if this is a group of students."

"And Maguire has lots of resources," I said, not seeing what that had to do with me.

"Money, magic, and muscle," Carson agreed. "But by killing Alexis's bodyguard and kidnapping her, the kidnappers made sure we got one more thing: a psychic who could talk to the dead."

I shivered despite the warm air blowing through the vents. "How could they have known about me?"

"There's this new invention called the Internet."

I didn't give that the answer it deserved because he was driving. "How did they know Maguire would grab me?"

Carson had an answer for that, too. "It's not a secret that Maguire likes things his own way. But even if you'd stuck with the FBI, you'd be on Alexis's trail."

I stared at him, my brain stalling on the implications of that theory. "But *why*?"

"That, Sunshine, is the face-melting question." He looked

at me—held my eyes with a sober intensity that made my heart race in a way that had nothing to do with him taking his eyes off the road at eighty bajillion miles an hour. "Maybe I should drop you off at the next police station. You can call your junior G-man from there."

That was *so* not an option. I was way past any magical compulsion now. This was all me.

"Maybe you should shut up and put your eyes on the road," I said.

Carson almost smiled, and as he turned his gaze back to the highway, he moved his hand like he would take mine, squeeze it, say we were in this together.

Instead, he just reached for the radio and turned up the volume on some vintage Kings of Leon.

St. Louis's Forest Park was home to the zoo, a couple of museums, a theater, some sculptures, a greenhouse, and lots of winding paths. The lanes were full of strollers and joggers and the air was crisp and the afternoon sun set fire to the autumn leaves. It was exactly what fall should be, except for the part where lives were at stake.

"Maybe the museum will have a café," I said, stretching five hours of driving out of my back as we walked through the parking lot.

Carson gave me a look, sort of droll, sort of disbelieving. "What happened to the milk shake and french fries you ate two hours ago?"

"That was two hours ago." Thinking about food helped me not think about kidnappers and killers.

Our destination was a large Art Deco building, set on a hill that swept steeply down to a lawn and an ornamental lake. I was already viewing it anxiously, hoping the jackal was there, praying the Brotherhood was not. The knot in my gut made another tight loop when I saw the banner fluttering across the museum's facade.

THE ART OF POMPEII.

Great. Just to make absolutely sure this situation sucked as much as it could.

"What's wrong?" Carson asked when I didn't immediately follow him up the steps.

"Freaking Pompeii. That's what's wrong."

He didn't ask. Maybe it was self-explanatory. Artifacts of large-scale death are a pretty obvious problem for me. "Let's just go in, reconnoiter, look for any clues. We're not sure the jackal that's here is the *actual* Jackal."

"Okay," I said, pushing aside my nerves. *Some* of my nerves.

"Just stay under the radar," he said. "I'm sure by now there's an APB out on a giraffe-legged goth member of the Weasley family."

"*Gazelle,*" I corrected him. Like I could play it cool with that much adrenaline zipping through my system.

"If any cops look at you cross-eyed, nudge me, and I'll do my thing."

"Anything else, Jedi Master?"

"Yes. Assume there are security cameras and don't strike up

any conversations with people no one else can see. Try to look like we're just a couple of normal people out on a date or something."

How the hell was I not going to think about all those things? Did he not realize how much stuff was in my brain *all the time*?

But I just said, "Sure. Life-and-death situations make great first dates."

"Think of it this way," he said, grabbing the door handle and giving it an effortless pull. "It's better than a graveyard."

Inside, the lobby was a soaring marble vault, all curves and columns and clean lines. The soft voices of patrons sang in the barrel arch of the ceiling. Admission was free, but Carson put some money in the donation box. I knew he was keeping our cover, but it didn't *feel* contrived. I supposed he was a civic-minded and generous crime trainee.

"Where do you want to start?" he asked.

A sign warned that the museum would close in an hour. "We don't have much time." I looked for some clue to the layout of the place. Sculptures and bronzes stood sentry in the main hall, keeping the ancient and pre-Renaissance art from mingling with the post-Enlightenment stuff. I glimpsed a hall of white marble statues and nodded. "Let's try this way."

We passed a security guard, and I slipped my hand into Carson's, entwining our fingers. He shot me a startled glance, and I said, "We're on a date, remember? That was your idea."

He glanced, almost imperceptibly, over my shoulder, then smiled. "One of my better ones." He bent his head close to mine, murmuring into the space behind my ear, "Security camera in the corner."

When he straightened, it took me two swallows before I could get my voice to work. "You better not be making that up," I said, covering flusterment with a whitewash of grumpy. "Or I'll kick your ass when this is over."

He didn't grin, but there was a devilish gleam in his eye and he kept hold of my hand as we passed a row of Roman statuary. "You already kicked my ass when this started."

I gave the cracked marble figures the once-over for any psychic hot spots or auras, playing it cool, like the scratch of his chin on my neck didn't dress me up in goose bumps. "That wasn't your ass."

He laughed, a surprised guffaw that drew stares and a "Shhh" from the docent in the corner. Which made *me* laugh, which earned a basilisk glare, which made it harder to smother the hysteria and, jeez, maybe I was punch-drunk from lack of sleep and too much soda.

"Nice job if you get us kicked out," said Carson, no longer laughing as he hustled me into the next room.

I was still giggling, which made it that much further to crash when I sputtered out, like a jet reaching max altitude.

The dusty weight of death pressed down on me like a ton of ash. Old and communal, preserved and petrified, it filled up my lungs, coated my throat, and choked off my breath.

Carson caught me around the waist when my knees buckled. He didn't ask what was wrong, just, "What do you need?"

I needed to get my defenses in place. I needed all my concentration to push the force field of my psyche out, holding back the echoes of the crushing weight of rebel earth, the staggering impact of thousands of simultaneous deaths preserved by the very cataclysm that had killed them.

This was what flirting got me. I'd known the exhibit was there, but I'd blundered in unprepared anyway. I couldn't blame anyone but myself.

"Daisy." Carson gave me a shake, sounding honest-to-God worried. "Are you in there?"

"Yeah," I wheezed. I'd gotten my feet literally and figuratively back under me.

The room had been set up like a Roman villa, to showcase the art in the mosaics and statuary. The pieces were all in excellent shape, but the scale of death they'd witnessed had soaked into the stone, so the fractures and patches showed on the psychic surface. On small platforms around the room were plaster casts made from the hardened ash molds of the dead, preserved where they fell when the volcano erupted. They were part of the whole display, like Mother Nature's grisly art.

"Come on," Carson said, steering me toward a rear exit. There was a sign that pointed to the restrooms, and in the empty hallway he propped me up against the wall and asked, "What just happened?"

"Stupid Pompeii." I pushed off from the wall and staggered to the water fountain. My throat felt like I'd lived through the pyroclastic cloud.

He followed me, standing by until I finished my slurping gulps. "Daisy... I mean, what did you do? I *felt* that."

That got my attention, and I straightened, wiping a drop of water from my lip with a shaking hand. "What do you mean? You felt the remnants?"

"No. Maybe. I don't know." He grabbed my hand and held it up between us. "When you choked and doubled over, holding on to you was like holding on to a live wire. I thought my heart was going to stop. And then I felt like I could breathe fire."

I stared at him, wide-eyed, over our clasped hands. "What does that mean?"

"I have no idea."

Maybe not, but he was thinking something. I could see the wheels turning down deep, where he kept the whole of himself from public view.

"Do you feel anything now?" I asked, and by Saint Gertrude's many cats, I swear I only meant anything magical. I mean, *literally* magical. I did not mean, Do you feel how close we're standing, or the way my arm is pressed against your chest and yours against mine? I most especially didn't mean, Do you feel how *my* heart is going to stop if you pull me any closer?

"No," he said, with a slow smile that addressed all the things I hadn't meant but sort of did. "You're a live wire, Daisy Good-night. But whatever happened is gone."

I was saved from having to think of a reply—or think at all—by an announcement over the loudspeaker that the museum would be closing in thirty minutes.

"We'd better hurry," he said. But he hesitated just an instant before dropping my hand.

We dropped our pretense, too, half running back to the Ancient Cultures wing, through Greece, which was full of beautiful urns and pottery but contained nothing even vaguely jackal-y. "Where the hell is Egypt?"

"In Northern Africa," said Carson. And he thought *I* didn't take things seriously. At the juncture of halls, he glanced in both directions, then said with authority, "That way."

We went through Mesopotamia, where a stone carving held the spirit echo of a mason. Art was like that, full of shades that had etched bits of themselves into rock or painted bits of their souls onto canvas, fed by the reverent awe of the museum visitors.

I didn't have time for awe. I caught the ghostly essence of frankincense and myrrh and a whisper that quickened my pace, a hum that sang in my skull and down my spine. Death was my resonant frequency, and something beyond the next arched doorway was playing my tune.

I expected a ghost, but there were two. One was an Egyptian woman, complete with elaborately dressed black hair and exotic makeup. Her clothes were obvious finery, and a heavy bejeweled necklace covered more of her chest than her linen dress did. Her kohl-lined eyes stared in wide dismay at the other ghost, a middle-aged security guard with a crew cut and a thick neck, who looked every bit as surprised as she did.

Maybe because he was standing over his own body, which lay on the floor, blood spreading into a scarlet Rorschach blot across the white marble tile.

18

CARSON STUMBLED TO a stop in the doorway, and the name that burst out of his lips was either profanity or invocation, and I didn't think he was very religious. Either way, it kicked me out of my shock and into action.

I skidded to my knees beside the guard and searched for a wound, more by touch than by sight. Reaching under his stocky body I found a tear in the soaked polyester of his shirt, and under that, a small, stiletto-sized hole below his ribs. Blood seeped hot over my fingers, and I pressed upward until it stopped.

"Don't—" warned Carson, too late. I knew I wasn't supposed to touch anything, but I knew dead, and I knew mostly dead, and this was the latter. What I didn't know was if I could keep one from turning into the other.

"Get help," I ordered, then sank into my psychic senses. Everything *physical* retreated to a shadowed fog, and everything *spirit* sharpened to cutting clarity. I could see the pale rope of psyche running from the man's chest to his shade, standing over his own body. When I placed my hand next to it, to better apply pressure to his wound, a tingle crawled up my arms, like I held an alternating current between them. My skin burned with the life and deathness of it.

"Why aren't the alarms going off?" The dazed question came from the ghost of the guard. He was in shock, but he had a vibrancy about him that I'd never seen in a remnant.

Because he wasn't a remnant. He was *whole*. I was looking at a soul, and the psychic thread that tethered him to his body.

For a moment I couldn't breathe. The current between my hands, the glowing thread that ran between my fingers, wasn't the ghost of a man, but the life of one.

"He only just left," said the shade of the Egyptian woman, in a pragmatic sort of voice that drew me back to earth.

"Who did?" I asked, trying to reorient myself.

She looked at me impatiently. She was much younger than I'd first thought. My age, maybe, and strikingly beautiful. "The man who did this—and took the stone jackal."

The jackal. I didn't think I had room for any more "Oh hell no" inside of me. But I was wrong.

With an effort, I blinked my psychic senses into the background and focused on the empty pedestal nearby, the glass case lifted off and set aside. The guard's question had been a good one. Why *wasn't* the alarm going off?

And here was another: Why was I seeing some kind of connection between the man's spirit and the empty display? It was murky and hard to sharpen with *any* of my senses, and I couldn't make heads or tails out of it.

Then I felt something I did recognize, a familiar vibration humming on my skin, singing through my psyche. For the first time in memory, my heart didn't sing along with it.

"No you don't," I growled to the powers of the universe. Because it always helps to order the Almighty around when you're already neck deep in alligators.

The guard stared at the curtain of air, wavering like a heat mirage on hot summer asphalt, and a spark of interest penetrated his numb shock. "What's that?"

The Veil, shimmering between worlds, waited with neutral, eternal patience while I *literally* held this guy's life in my hands.

"*No,*" I ordered him. "Do *not* go there."

"But I see my mom." He lifted a hand with a childish wave. "Hi, Mom!"

"Not yet." I tried to sound commanding and not pleading, but pretty much failed. "The EMTs will be here soon. You'll have plenty more days to walk these halls telling people to step back from the paintings."

The Egyptian girl gave a delicate snort. "If you wish him to stay, you might offer better temptation than that."

"Look!" said the guard as the pulse of his blood under my fingers stumbled. "There's my dog!"

181

"That is *not* playing fair." I ground my teeth on the bit of my determination and pressed more firmly on the wound so not a drop more blood would escape. "Dogs and moms are not fair!"

Cleopatra walked around us both, kicking out her linen skirts with fancy gold- and jewel-covered sandals. "Are you some sort of priestess? You have a funny way of talking to your god."

"That's what Sister Michaela always told me."

She made a tutting sound. "I think perhaps you aren't very good at this. His soul is fading."

"What?" My vision wavered, and I dredged up the effort to bring the guard into sharper focus. It was more than difficult. His image was washed out, like a photo left to fade in the sun.

"Let him go," said Cleo, not quite an order, "while his soul is still strong enough to make the journey to the afterlife."

I didn't want her to be right, but I could feel the electric current fizzle and spark. If anyone could recognize the end of life and the beginning of death, it should be me. But I didn't want to lose. I wanted to grab hold of this ghost—this *soul*—and tie it to his body so he couldn't die.

I could hear, out of the fog of reality, the pounding of running feet on the marble floor. Just a moment longer. I couldn't let him slip when help was so close.

Death wasn't my enemy. But the jerkwad who thought it was his to hand out on a whim—*he* was going to get a kick into the next world when I caught up with him.

Carson was back, crouching beside me. "The guards are coming, and they're on the phone with nine-one-one."

"Okay," I said tightly, startled by how little time must have gone by since he left. "Do you think, with your superpower, you could use my energy or whatever to give this guy a boost so he'll make it long enough for the EMTs to get here?"

I couldn't look away from the ghosts, but based on the jolt of tension where Carson's shoulder pressed against mine, the idea must have shocked him. His voice, though, was level and businesslike. "I could try, but I don't know what that would do to you."

"Look at the floor," I said. "That's lifeblood there. It's the total opposite of my thing, but even *I* can feel the energy in it. If you could use even a *little* of it..."

"Yeah. Okay. I've got it."

Most people would take a deep breath before diving in. Carson just slid in close, getting one hand down where the blood was freshest and warmest and putting his other on the guard's chest. I felt a tug of friction, like something pulling against the cat's cradle of invisible string between me, the ghost, the Veil, and his body.

"Over his heart," said Cleopatra, watching with clinical interest. "That is where the soul resides."

It was also what pumped the blood to the brain and the lungs, so I relayed the message. "Over his—"

"I heard you," said Carson, and adjusted his hand up and slightly left. He'd heard *her*, which was interesting, but not something I could analyze just then. The tingle of friction became a burn, as if a binding rope were dragging across my arms where

183

they held the guard's soul to his body. Whatever Carson was doing, it was working, but something was pulling the spirit in another direction, and it wasn't the Veil.

"His heart is beating stronger," said Carson, effort in his voice. "I think maybe—"

The Veil shimmered closed, its hum ceasing without flourish. An instant later, the guard's image vanished and I felt him snap back into his body like a rubber band.

And in the very *same* instant, which I couldn't dismiss as coincidence, but couldn't explain, either, the alarm began to wail.

For two people who wanted to stay under the radar, Carson and I had been spectacularly unsuccessful.

The museum staff poured though the doorway, the vanguard pulling up short at the amount of blood and the waxy pallor of the man on the floor. But when I said, "He's still breathing," the woman in front dropped the wholly inadequate-looking first-aid kit, pulled on some latex gloves, and told me to get out of the way.

I yielded my spot, but not until she'd gotten her own hand on the trickling wound in the man's back. Then Carson helped me to my feet—adding bloody handprints to the gory blotches already staining my shirt. My jeans were soaked from the knees down, and I looked like I'd stabbed the guy myself.

"Do not move," said another guard, pointing to me and Carson. "The cops are going to want to talk to you."

Someone had turned off the alarm, and now I could hear sirens. The familiar choke hold of the geas hardly registered in the grappling sea of knots twisting up in my chest.

"Priestess!" Cleo appeared in the archway, shouting. "The thief is this way!"

I don't know what possessed me—desperation, vengeance, or the certainty I couldn't really get in any deeper. I got my gazelle on and shot for the door, leaping over the circle of first-aid workers around the fallen guard and slingshotting out of Egypt and into the Mesopotamian Hall.

Shouts of surprise burst out behind me, and an instant later Carson did the same, hard on my heels.

The Egyptian girl had popped to the next junction, and I sprinted past winged figures, stone seraphim watching our footrace through the climate-controlled sterility of their exile.

In the main hall of the Ancient World wing, I saw a blur of a figure, heard Cleo calling, "That's him!"

And then, at the *end* of the hall, blocking the way out, two police officers, guns drawn.

"Stop! Police!"

The thief cut right, between the marble-draped goddesses that marked the hall into Rome. Shoes squeaking on slick tile, I made an abrupt turn, too, into the hallway to the restrooms. Carson caught up with me there, grabbing my arm and stopping my headlong rush.

"Come on," I said, pointing toward the door we'd come through earlier. "We can cut him off in Pompeii."

He pushed me behind him and took the lead. "Stay back and let me handle this."

185

There was no time to argue about misplaced chivalry. Plus, it wasn't misplaced. The guy had a knife, and considering his employer, Carson was surely better suited to handle that than I was.

But like hell was I staying in the hall. I shored up my defenses against the death echoes of Mount Vesuvius and ran after Carson, into the exhibit.

The thief was coming in the other way. He drew up, panting, in the center of the reconstructed villa, surrounded by the plaster casts of the volcano's victims. He made a weird double image to my senses, like I was seeing him with my physical and psychic vision and they didn't quite match up. Maybe because in his corduroy trousers and unfashionable sweater and dark-rimmed glasses he looked like a coffeehouse slacker and not a stiletto-wielding art-museum robber.

He had a fat messenger bag over his shoulder, and I guessed the artifact he'd stolen was in there, because his hands were empty. But his face was full of smirk. "Too slow, Team Maguire," he taunted. "Better step it up."

Carson surprised me with the outrage in his voice and the clenched fists at his side. "You nearly killed someone, asshole!"

"But you saved him, so boohoo," drawled the thief. "That was really impressive, by the way."

There was a weird dynamic here, though I didn't always trust my read on the living. This guy knew who we were, and something about Carson's accusation had a personal edge to it, like maybe he knew who the guy was, too.

"You two work well together," said Smirky McSlackerson. "Too bad you don't work a little faster."

186

The sneer just made everything that much worse, picturing this guy grabbing Alexis, stabbing the guard, all with that superior smile on his face. Throw in my fury at myself that we hadn't gotten here first and a whole lot of pissed-off in general, and it was a good thing that Carson stood a protective step in front of me.

"Look, asshole," I said, trying and failing to get around the arm Carson put up to stop me. "Tell us where Alexis is. You have the Jackal. You don't need her."

McSlackerson blinked, as if the suggestion surprised him, and then he laughed. "This isn't the Black Jackal. I'm just here collecting the pieces we need to get it. And that's all I'm going to tell you of my fiendish plan, Supergirl. I've been monologuing long enough."

Right on cue, two of St. Louis's finest burst into the room behind the thief, weapons drawn, shouting, "Freeze!"

I'd never stared down a real gun barrel before. This day was just full of new and unpleasant experiences.

Carson relaxed his shoulders, the way he did when he was anxious or pissed and was pushing it back where it wouldn't interfere. He looked perfectly cool as he held his empty—and very bloody—hands out to his sides. I copied him, right down to the blood, which couldn't possibly make us look harmless.

"Turn around slowly," one of the cops barked at McSlackerson. "Hands where we can see them."

The thief smiled—an I-love-it-when-a-plan-comes-together smile—and raised his arms to his sides. As he turned, his hand crossed the plane of one of the exhibits, and he flexed his fingers over a plaster cast of a volcano victim, like he was testing the temperature. I did that move so often, my fingers twitched like *I* was the one feeling for spirit traces.

That was what he was doing. I had no time to think *why* before the world—both my worlds—went sideways.

Since we'd come in, I'd been braced against the echoes of thousands of hot, smothering deaths. I was not prepared for the groaning shift of the psychic air pressure, like a volcanic cone crumbling in on itself. I staggered, as if I'd been leaning against a wall that suddenly just...vanished.

Which was impossible, because two millennia of psychic energy didn't just *go away.*

Carson tensed, too, and I knew something *bad* was going to happen. When it did, that seemed impossible, too. The thief pushed his empty hand toward the cops. A wall of acrid wind blasted them into the next room. Over the roar in my ears I heard the crash of bodies and a second later, the crack and thunder of toppling stone. They'd hit the statues, any one of which was heavy enough to crush a man's skull.

I moved instinctively to help—somehow, anyhow—but Carson caught me around the waist, pulling me tight against him as McSlackerson swung around, his smile cracking the layer of ash on his face. Between his hands he gathered the ghost of a pyroclastic cloud, and all six of my senses said it was *totally* possible we were going to die.

Carson wrapped himself around me, my back against his chest, and yelled in my ear, "Make like the Millennium Falcon, Sunshine, and do *not* drop those deflector shields!"

At the first blast of heat, I pushed all I had left into my

force field. What McSlackerson threw at us wasn't psychic but physical—intangible energy turned into magical heat and wind. My defenses should have been useless. But I felt the moment when Carson mirrored what the other guy had done, transforming my psychic defenses into something invisible but solid.

Everywhere we touched was an electric zing, an icy burn that pulled a helpless gasp from my throat. The grit-laced gale scoured the floor around our untouched island. It ripped tiles from the mosaic and fired them like bullets into the plasterboard walls of the exhibit. Pillars toppled and paperboard markers scorched around the edges.

This was not the best time to discover the limits of my resources. Deep inside, I shuddered like a sputtering engine, and the muscles of my legs trembled as I braced with Carson against the wind that pounded our shield. He felt it, too, and took more of my weight, but he couldn't hold us both up and he couldn't hold the defenses at all if I didn't give him something to work with.

I thought the ash cloud was darkening around us, but I realized it was my vision. Sparkles came next, and I felt weirdly like my head was floating away from my body, and not on purpose. I clung to consciousness with ten fingernails, but I was on the steep slope over the chasm of oblivion.

"Stay with me, Daisy," said Carson against my ear. I felt it more than heard it, rumbling through my skin where we touched. "He's almost tapped out."

So was I. The smell of sulfur and choke of ash rushed in and I slid bonelessly out of Carson's grip. Dying was such a rotten way to learn I wasn't nearly the badass I thought I was.

19

"PRIESTESS! WAKE UP." The words banged my aching skull like the clapper of a bell. "You're in terrible danger!"

It was reassuring to hear a voice. Less reassuring that it was the ghost of the Egyptian girl, because that didn't mean I wasn't dead. Especially since I seemed to be dangling from someone's shoulders in a fireman's carry.

Cleo trotted alongside the guy currently carting me like a sack of potatoes through Ancient Greece. A guy who was *not* Carson.

"Do something, Priestess! I cannot touch this brigand!"

She tried grabbing his arm and jumping in his way, but he literally walked through her.

Some hunch snagged a memory, the image of the guy in the cemetery holding Mrs. Hardwicke's necklace as she vanished, and the half-formed idea made me warn Cleo away.

"Don't." My voice was just a croak, hoarse from the grit of the ash storm. "Don't touch him."

The guy adjusted my weight on his shoulders by giving me a toss. I landed hard, knocking the air from my lungs and rattling my brain. "Don't worry about your boyfriend, sweetheart. You just get your breath back. We've got a job for you."

He patted me on the ass, and I saw red. I mean, *more* red—beyond the haze of blood rushing to my pounding head. I had a one-abduction-per-twenty-four-hours policy, and this yahoo was over the limit.

Finally, a benefit to being tall besides reaching the top shelf at the supermarket: leverage. I punched him in the kidney—or where I guessed something vulnerable and extremely painful like a kidney would be—and when he cursed and twisted, I let all my weight slide backward. He had to drop me or go down, too.

This was going to hurt.

I curled my arm over my head and tucked my shoulder so that I rolled when I hit the floor. And I kept rolling, all the way to my feet, because the guy was coming after me. I was numb where my hip and shoulder had smacked the marble tile, but at least everything moved.

I don't think the guy had a plan B. He charged at me, and I grabbed a priceless Greek vase and smashed him over the head with it. He crashed to the floor and went limp.

That's vases, two; kidnappers, zero.

I checked—quickly—to make sure he was still breathing. And then I checked—not so quickly—his face and my memory. This was not the thief, McSlackerson. This was someone else. I thought he might have been in the cemetery, but I couldn't be sure.

Cleo popped up beside me, and I jumped—which made every muscle in my body protest. The parts where I hit the floor weren't so numb anymore.

"That was thrilling!" she cried. "You fight like an Amazon."

"Thank you," I wheezed, holding my ribs.

I staggered back through the door to Pompeii like a freshman at her first keg party. After all that sound and fury, I'd expected total devastation, but from what I could tell through the hazy curtain of dust, the damage to the exhibit was cosmetic. There were no piles of ash, no fire, no incinerated bodies.

No Carson.

I remembered him calling my name, his hands tangling in my hair as he kept my head from hitting the floor when I'd gone limp in the volcano attack. After that, there was just the murky twilight of unconsciousness.

"Where's my friend?" I asked Cleo. Adrenaline hadn't dismissed my headache but sent it to sit in the corner. "How long was I out?"

"Moments only," she said, bouncing with excitement. "When you fainted, the magician laid you down so gently, and then he turned on the thief like a *lion*. The knave took one look and fled, and your magician pursued."

"He just left me here to get hauled off like yesterday's trash?"

"That ruffian"—she jerked a thumb toward the unconscious guy in Greece—"was not here then. It was like he stepped out of the air after the other two left. But you can catch them if you hurry."

With her urging me on, I did hurry, into the main hall where I tried to get my bearings. I couldn't believe no one was investigating why the police hadn't arrived downstairs, or wondering about the almighty racket.

"This way!" said the Egyptian girl. "Through the hall of the bearded old white men."

That narrowed it down to just about all of Western Civilization. I had to cross the big, open space to get there, but a bang and clatter from the front doors sent me diving for cover behind a nude statue with a conveniently large ... pedestal. A squad of EMTs ran by, their bright yellow stretcher garish in the monochrome decorum of marble and bronze.

It gave me a chance to catch my breath. This ache was different than the usual rebound migraine. I felt stripped and raw, and drained like an old car battery. My thighs shook like I'd run a marathon.

Worse, I couldn't seem to bring my second Sight into focus. In the pale light of the hall, Cleo looked translucent, like a hologram. The vibrancy that had earlier colored the museum, the pieces of their souls that the artists put into their work, none of it sang to my extra senses.

Was this what *normal* felt like?

"Something is wrong," I said, trying, and failing, to keep a lid on rising panic. "I can barely See you. And I can't feel any echoes or remnants."

She gave me a pitying look. "Do you think power is inexhaustible? You are a very formidable priestess, but you are not a goddess."

I got a grip on my panic and sorted through events. Carson had turned my psychic defenses into a shield against the magical attack—and as crazy as my life was by normal people's standards, that was even *crazier*. The whole thing must have lasted just seconds, but I was totally spent.

Why was McSlackerson still on his feet?

Other pieces started to come together, too: Mrs. Hardwicke's weird and sudden disappearance. The muting of every trace of death echo in the Pompeii exhibit. A translation of the Book of the Dead that spoke of—or instructed how to use—the power of the afterlife. My subconscious had figured it out already, because I'd warned Cleo away from my abductor. Somehow this Brotherhood was using remnants to do real magic. *Big* magic.

The idea violated my entire purpose in life and in other people's deaths. But I couldn't do anything about it with my current problem.

"Why can I still See you?" I asked the Egyptian girl.

She shrugged. "Your senses are dulled, not gone. And I will that you should See me."

Some remnants can and do appear to the average Joe, but the clarity of our current interaction was impressive for someone who looked like an Egyptian teen princess. "You can do that?"

194

"I am the daughter of Isis." Another shrug. "I can do whatever I wish."

She had the supremely casual tone of the truly arrogant, and I had a bad feeling I sounded like that sometimes. Maybe a lot of the time.

But not just then. Despair took my heart in its fist. "What if it doesn't come back?" I didn't know *how* to be normal. My Sight... it wasn't just what I did, it was what I *was*.

"This I do not know," said Cleo, impatiently. "But what I *do* know is that when you fell, your magician looked like someone had put a sword through his heart, and you've been so long feeling sorry for yourself that he probably thinks you are dead and is killing the knave now in vengeance and *you are missing it!*"

She was right. Bloodthirsty, but right. I was feeling sorry for myself, and I had important things to do, like stop Carson from doing something rash.

Not that he ever seemed to be without a plan, even when taken by surprise. *Especially* when taken by surprise. I really hoped he had a plan for stopping the attempted murderer from getting away, and for us not getting caught by the cops ourselves.

I used the statue's pedestal to haul myself up. Cleo had popped up across the hall and was gesturing for me to hurry, which I did. The wing with the old masters had bigger rooms and higher ceilings, almost like ballrooms. In the first gallery hung life-sized portraits. A huge Gainsborough and two sober Dutch masters gazed in painted disapproval as I ran past.

My steps slowed as I neared the door to the next gallery, partly because I wasn't sure what waited inside—like police or more magic or just an armed and smirking sociopath—and partly because I heard voices in taunting tones that raised more questions than they answered.

"Have you figured it out yet, Maguire?"

The voice was McSlackerson's. He was breathing hard, like he'd paused in running, but it was the name that made me stop outside the door and press against the wall to listen.

"Don't call me that," Carson snapped, as discomposed as I'd ever heard him. There was something very *personal* about his anger that made it sound like they'd argued before. "I just work for him."

"Does he know you've gone rogue, you and little Miss Ghost Whisperer?"

Had we gone rogue? This was news to me. Or maybe not. There was Carson turning off his phone, using cash at the Walmart, refusing to call Maguire for a car. Another one of those things more clear in retrospect.

"If anything happens to Daisy," Carson said, so low I strained to hear, "if she's not all right when she wakes up, I am going to stake you like you did that guard."

I believed him. There was an unshakable vow in his voice. Hearing a guy threaten to kill someone—or at least maim him—for my sake shouldn't make me feel a rush of warmth around my heart. But it did, just a little.

"Hey," said the thief, in a tone that made me loathe him even more, "if she's not all right when she wakes up, it's your fault. And you know it, or you wouldn't be so—"

Wait. Did Carson *care* or did he just feel guilty? I leaned forward to hear, but a crack of fist hitting bone cut him off. I really *was* missing the exciting stuff.

I burst into the room in time to see McSlackerson reeling back, his hand clamped to his jaw, Carson going for the follow-through punch to the gut. His fist landed with an awful, dull thud, and it looked terribly effective and efficient.

Cleo had appeared beside me, delighted by Carson's show of force. "Oh, look. He's going to kill him with his hands. Very satisfactory."

I echoed with a bloodthirsty "Very."

20

THEY BOTH TURNED at the sound of my voice, McSlackerson with shock and dismay, and Carson—his gaze lit with undiluted relief that brought a totally inappropriate flush to my face.

McSlackerson was easy to read. He must have realized the attempt to grab me had gone wrong and stalling Carson—why else would the thief still be there?—was no longer necessary. His hand tightened on his messenger bag and he raised it up high. "If you come any closer, I'll drop this, and the jackal will break."

Would it? Would *he*, after all this trouble to get it?

"What would the Brotherhood say?" I asked, drawing his attention.

His brows shot up. "Oh, you know about that?" He glanced from me to Carson. "You two *do* work fast."

"Shut up," growled Carson.

Cleo was studying the situation, walking freely around us, invisible to the guys. "I don't think the statue will break. He wrapped it most carefully."

"He wrapped the artifact up," I relayed, relishing the flare of alarm in McSlackerson's eyes and the complete lack of smirk on his face. "It might take a bump or two."

Anticipation made Carson almost smile. Yeah, that looked personal, all right. We *would* be quite a team if one of us stopped keeping secrets from the other.

He launched himself after McSlackerson, who had started running. Carson caught up with him in a few long strides and took him down in a flying tackle. The bag fell out of the thief's hand just a few inches off the floor.

The two guys, however, hit the ground with a bone-jarring crack and slid across the tile to crash against a pillar holding a Meissen vase. The pillar rocked, and I held my breath. This could be a bad day for vases.

"This is the most exciting thing that's happened since I woke up in this place," said Cleo.

McSlackerson heaved Carson off him, flipping him with an abruptness that smacked Carson's head against the floor. It stunned him and gave the thief time to struggle to his feet.

He was going for the messenger bag, and I moved to head him off. But Carson was on it. He grabbed the wires leading to the alarm on the pedestal where they'd crashed, then, with a huge stretch, he just barely got a finger on the thief. But it was enough. McSlackerson stiffened and dropped to the floor.

"What did you do?" I gasped, staring at the guy as he lay twitching like a dog chasing rabbits in its dreams. "Did you just magically Taser him?"

"Something like that," wheezed Carson, still on the ground. "You wanted to know if I could whammy someone."

"But he still lives," said Cleo, petulant with disappointment.

"Yeah," I murmured. "But he probably wishes he didn't right now."

"Is the magician going to cut out the knave's heart?" she asked hopefully.

"No!" I snapped, because I was a little unnerved by the way Carson had just dropped the guy in his tracks. "There will be no removing of hearts or any other body parts."

"Tempting," said Carson, standing up with a groan, "but there's no time for that. I don't know how quickly the zap will wear off. Grab his bag and let's get out of here."

"He stabbed a guy!" I protested. "We can't let him get away."

Carson looked at me, raising his brows. "You want to stick around and answer questions? More police will be here any minute. I don't think they're just going to shake our hands and let us go."

He was right. We'd been lucky, or the Brotherhood had been

effective in delaying law enforcement, but either way, we were out of time. There was heavy-duty mojo at work here, something the police weren't going to be able to handle. And neither was I, if I ended up in jail.

"Drag him over here," I said, pointing to a bronze Degas ballerina. Carson set his jaw, like he might argue, but then he grabbed McSlackerson by the collar and hauled his limp carcass across the room. Cleo moved primly out of the way, which was sort of funny considering she didn't have an actual body.

"Are you going to sacrifice him to your goddess?" she asked. "Normally I'd suggest a bull or a goat, but it seems a shame to waste the blood of your enemy if it might get your power back."

"What *is* it with you and the bloodshed?" I asked. "Are all Egyptian women this way?"

"I would not know," she said, with that casual arrogance of hers. "I am the daughter of—"

I rolled my eyes and unbuckled my belt. "The daughter of Isis. I remem—"

And then I *did* remember. It would have dawned on me sooner, except that I'd been in the middle of freaking out about losing my superpower.

"You mean you really *are* Cleopatra?"

"Of course." She looked down her aquiline nose—I'd never have a better chance to use that word—as if she weren't a foot shorter than me. "Who else would I be?"

In spite of everything, I gave a giddy laugh. I was talking to a remnant of Cleo-freaking-patra. No wonder she was such a vivid

201

shade. Even this tiny piece of her, tied to some artifact, was fed by the epic legend of memory.

"Well, that explains a lot," I said, trying to keep my cool. "The arrogance, for one thing."

Carson, with McSlackerson still hanging from his grip on his collar, looked between me and the space that Cleo occupied. "Do you think you can cut short the confab with your invisible friend so we can get on with this?"

Cleo's painted brows arched to the braided black bangs of her wig, then lowered into a scowl. "He is very impertinent, your magician."

"Yes, he is," I said, but I got busy binding the thief's arms around the base of the statue with my thin studded belt. I was momentarily grateful my remnant sense was wacked out, because I didn't want to know what Degas would think about knave drool on his little ballerina's slippers.

Carson sighed loudly and started going through McSlackerson's pockets. "I don't even want to know."

"Her Highness says you are impertinent." I cinched the belt around the thief's wrists tight enough to make him groan. It wouldn't have to hold long, and I didn't really care about cutting off blood circulation.

"Still," said Cleo, studying Carson from behind. "I can see why you keep him around. He is very manly, as well as adept. Power is very attractive."

"She also says you're a dish," I relayed. And I didn't bother to deny it.

"That's nice," said Carson. His rifling had turned up a wallet and cell phone, and he started flipping through the log of recent calls.

Something under McSlackerson's cuff caught my eye, and I pushed up his sleeve. On his forearm was a tattoo of a jackal, lean and pointy. I'd seen it in Egyptian art and hieroglyphs too often to mistake it for anything else. "Look at this."

"Appropriate," Cleopatra said with a sniff. "Jackals are scavengers and thieves."

I brushed the inked skin with my thumb and got a shock of remnant energy so strong my whole arm tingled. It hurt like a smack to the funny bone, even through the numbness of my psychic senses. I gasped, half in pain and half in relief to feel *anything* spirit related.

"Check this out, Carson. I wonder if this is some kind of membership badge for their brotherhood. There's something weird about it, some kind of psychic punch...." I turned to see why he wasn't answering. "Are you even *listening* to me?"

Carson was staring at McSlackerson's phone, and whatever he saw there put an unhappy knot between his brows.

"What?" I asked.

"Nothing," he answered. Except it was obviously *something*, and he wasn't telling me.

"He's lying," said Cleopatra, in a darker tone, the girlish veneer slipping away to show the formidable young woman she'd been. She turned her gaze toward me, and I understood how she'd swayed such powerful men, reclaimed and ruled the kingdom of Egypt. "Be careful, priestess. I think he cares for you, but he may care for something else more."

The way she said that made me wonder how much she recalled of her own life. Despite the time pressure, I had to ask, "Do you remember them? Caesar and Antony?"

"No. They came later." I understood what she meant—any memories of those men belonged to some other remnant. Still, there was a heaviness to her sigh. "But men are the same always. Do not doubt they love, and do not doubt their love won't matter."

There was a bang from the front of the museum, the crash of one of the doors slamming open, and the sound of running footsteps. The open chambers of the museum carried the warning clearly. Carson put the phone in his pocket and grabbed the thief's bag. "We have to go. Now."

McSlackerson, maybe warned by the same noises, flexed his bound fingers. He must have been faking unconsciousness for who knows how long. But he was tied up, and there wasn't a reason for my heart to pound against my ribs.

No reason except the daughter of Isis.

"Cleo—" I warned.

Too late. The thief's fingers closed on an intangible fold of her linen shift. Cleopatra gave a start of surprise, then shock, then fear. And then she vanished.

I watched Cleopatra disappear, grabbed at her with my psyche and felt the worst sort of nothing—the freaky Novocaine numbness where your brain knows something awful just happened and your senses try to deny there's a hole where your wisdom tooth used to be.

The last pharaoh of Egypt. It didn't matter that I knew it wasn't all of her, or that there were who knew how many other remnant versions all over the world. This one—this unique moment in this amazing woman's life—had just been used up like a Kleenex for this guard-stabbing, priceless-artifact-stealing, mafia-princess-kidnapping asshole to spit out his gum.

McSlackerson snapped the belt around his wrists and it crumbled to ash, the metal buckle tinkling to the floor. He looked from me, staring at him in shock and outrage, to Carson, holding the bag—literally—to the door, where police would be pouring through any second. Then he jumped to his feet and ran like the jackal he was.

Fury burned off the numbness. I started after him, but Carson grabbed me. "Leave him. Let's go."

He yanked me with him through a different doorway, to a dead end full of modern art. "Brilliant!" I said, strangling my voice down to a whisper. "We're trapped."

A whisper wasn't good enough. Carson clapped a hand over my mouth and pushed me against the wall next to the connecting archway, flattening us there, out of sight.

"Calm down." He breathed the words into my ear, hardly stirring any air, probably because there wasn't any air between us—pressed together from chest to hip, our legs tangled up, his cheek against mine, his lips against my hair. Pressed any tighter and we would melt into the plaster.

Even though I knew it was simple expediency—maybe *because* it was expedient and efficient and all the things Carson was when something needed doing—my heart fluttered at the feel of his arms around me and his body against mine and his broad shoulders between me and the whole world.

The police charged into the next room, yelling things like "Clear!" and "He's not here!"

"Think invisible thoughts," Carson whispered, and I gave an infinitesimal nod. Which was all I could do, because he hadn't taken his fingers from over my mouth. Maybe he didn't trust me not to give us away.

Rubber soles squeaked in the doorway. If I could have drawn a breath, I would have held it.

Then someone said, "This is a dead end. He didn't go this way."

"He's going for the back exit," said another officer, and the footsteps retreated.

Carson waited a long moment before moving, and then only to put his hand on the wall beside my head. His breath—when he finally let himself breathe—skimmed my neck and raised goose-flesh. Even without magic, without my extra senses, there was an electric zing everywhere we touched. Which was just about everywhere.

"What about the security cameras?" I whispered.

"I shorted them out when I grabbed the wire to zap our friend back there."

"Oh." I shivered, for reasons I couldn't quite untangle.

Be careful, priestess. Cleopatra's observation became a warning. *Power is attractive.*

"Okay," he said, as if shoring up his strength. He'd used as much magic as I had psychic energy *and* been in a fistfight. Still, his arms were steady as he pushed off the wall just enough to look down at me. If I hadn't been propped up, the anguished relief in his eyes, from that intimate an angle, would have leveled me.

"When you passed out," he murmured, searching my face, "I thought I'd hurt you."

I couldn't bring myself to tell him that he had. I wasn't sure I could voice it at all and keep going. I felt stretched to a fragile filament. Admitting weakness might break me.

So I didn't. "It takes more than some guy channeling a volcano to keep me down."

His rueful laugh stirred my hair. "I know that's right."

He knew so much about me, and I knew so little about him. Who was he thinking of when he asked me about remnants and ghosts? Why did he pick his truths so carefully? Could I trust him a little, or not at all?

Carson stepped back, letting his hands fall to my shoulders and giving me an encouraging squeeze. "Ready for more running?"

"God, no." But I got my legs under me anyway. Whether the cops managed to catch McSlackerson or not, we had to get out of there before they came back to secure the scene. "You owe me a helluva lot more than a milk shake and french fries."

By some undeserved miracle, we were able to slink unseen through a fire door where the alarm was already shorted out. I figured we had just minutes, maybe less, to get out before officers were stationed at all the exits; it was dumb luck—and the distraction of chasing McSlackerson—that they weren't guarded already.

We slid out the side of the building, then slipped around to the front, to get lost in the crowd that had gathered there. Four police cars blocked the drive in front of the museum, and uniformed officers stood sentry on the stairs. An ambulance waited, too, its doors ominously open, like a pharaoh's empty tomb.

"Why is it taking so long to bring out the guard?" I fretted.

"They probably want to make sure his vital signs are steady," said Carson. Maybe he was as certain as he sounded, or maybe he sensed how thin I was stretched and was trying to hold me together with hope. My ESP was blown like a fuse, Cleopatra had been erased, and the perpetrator had gotten away. But if the guard died, if we hadn't been able to save him, then what was any of this for? I might as well go home and sell magic tea and candles like the rest of the Goodnight clan.

"Come on." He touched my arm, trying to draw my attention away from the ambulance. "We're out. We've got the next clue to the Jackal. Let's not waste this lucky break."

"Okay," I said, but didn't move. I was watching the new car that had arrived. A black one. Government plates.

It was definitely the feds, no mistaking the black sedan or the standard-issue square-jawed Johnny G-man who drove it. But what were the chances that the back door would open and Agent Taylor would climb out?

The way my day had been going? Pretty damned good.

21

I RECOGNIZED AGENT Taylor's profile with less than a glance. The way he moved, how he held his shoulders. It jabbed like an adrenaline needle into my heart, but with the reverse effect. I couldn't move.

Binding promise or not, I'd had zero temptation to give myself up to St. Louis's finest. But this was *my* Agent Taylor. He would believe me. *Trust me,* I'd said in my email.

The email I'd sent told him to track down Michael Johnson. And now Taylor was in St. Louis, where McSlackerson had just stabbed a guy and one of his Brotherhood had tried to abduct me through Ancient Greece. Did that mean one of them was Johnson?

The other car door opened, and Agent Gerard climbed out. Nuts. Agent Gerard would *not* trust me. If anyone could possibly want to lock me up more than he did, I didn't know about it.

Beside me, Carson cursed, and I knew he'd recognized them. "Come on," he growled. This time it was an unmistakable order.

I hesitated too long. Maybe Taylor caught a glimpse of the setting sun on my red hair. Maybe he felt me staring at him. Maybe my psychicness had rubbed off on him. But he paused on the steps to the museum and turned back to scan the crowd.

Then he saw me and blinked, poleaxed by surprise. He must have said something because Gerard turned, too. What *he* said was easily readable on his lips, and *he* didn't blink, just charged like a bull down the museum steps.

Even if Carson hadn't grabbed my wrist and urged me into a run, the sight of Gerard barreling toward us would have spurred me on.

The crowd slowed the two agents down. I heard them shouting for people to get out of the way, and I was tempted to look back but didn't dare with Carson pulling me along. We plunged down the steep slope of the lawn, and I could barely keep my feet under me.

"Daisy Temperance Goodnight! Hold it right there!"

Crap! The full-name whammy. Oldest magic in the book. I'd *taught* Taylor that trick, the asshole.

I obeyed, only for a fraction of a second before willpower

kicked in. On the flat land it wouldn't have made a difference. On the grassy hill, though, I tripped over my feet and went down.

My fall jerked Carson to a stop, but he didn't let go of my wrist. *That* was going to bruise. He wrapped an arm around my waist and hauled me to my feet. It wasn't a long delay, but enough for Taylor to gain ground. Gerard lagged behind, probably because he was fifteen years older or maybe because he was on the phone calling for backup.

Carson dragged me after him until my legs started cooperating again. We made it through the gap in a row of hedges that walled off a sculpture garden, and I hoped he knew where we were going, because I had no idea.

"Maguire!"

The name startled me, and so did the fact that Carson glanced up at it. I whirled and found Taylor, slowing his steps at a safe distance, his gun drawn but pointed down at his side.

His gun drawn.

"Seriously?" I said, outraged. "You need your firearm for this?"

He looked not at me, but at Carson, who hadn't moved. "Step away from Daisy, Maguire. We can sort this out, but only if you let her go."

That was the second time Taylor had used that name. And inside, McSlackerson had called Carson by it, too, but I'd thought he was just being snide. *Maguire?*

"I'm sorry, Agent Taylor," Carson said, still holding me beside him. "If I don't get out of here with this girl, another one is going to die."

"We can find Alexis." Taylor spoke in an authoritative, hostage-negotiating tone. "This is what we do."

"No offense," said Carson, with a hint of cool irony that showed none of the tension I could feel in the arm wrapped around my waist. "But this is way beyond the FBI. That's why I need to borrow your girl Daisy."

"Hang on," I said. Carson gave me a "not now" squeeze, but this was important, and not just because I didn't want him to get shot. "I'm my own girl."

Taylor's gaze flicked to me, to Carson, and back again. He was smart, and intuitive, and he *knew* me. He must realize what "beyond the FBI" meant—beyond *normal*. I could see him working it out, but I could also hear Agent Gerard almost on us.

Taylor heard him, too, and came to a decision. "What do you hear, Daisy?"

I let out my held breath and gave him the *I'm okay* response. "Nothing but the rain, Taylor." *Trust me.*

His eyes narrowed on Carson, who gazed steadily back, some kind of testosterone telepathic exchange going on. Taylor confirmed when he warned, "If anything happens to her—"

That was as far as he got before Gerard charged through the gap in the shrubs. Taylor whirled, expecting an attack, and Carson dropped his arm from my waist and grabbed my hand. "Let's go."

I didn't hesitate, but I did look back, long enough to see Gerard point his weapon at us and shout something that I couldn't hear over the roar in my ears. I made out "stop" and "arrest," and I smelled the burning of bridges. Taylor knocked his partner's arm away, yelling, "Are you crazy? You could hit Daisy!"

I was pretty sure Gerard wouldn't mind.

I kept running, convincing myself that the ache in my chest was exhaustion and not my heart breaking because I was leaving behind everything that had been so important to me twenty-four hours ago.

We reached the parking lot with no more sign of close pursuit. Carson ran for a motorcycle that someone had parked illegally near a fire hydrant. He touched something—the battery, maybe?—with one hand and the ignition with the other and the engine roared to life.

He swung his leg over and ordered, "Get on."

I wanted to make him work for it—with an explanation or a plea or even, you know, a *request*. I was tired of being ordered, hauled, squeezed, and run over.

"Get on the bike, Daisy." His gaze caught and held mine, his fatigue and desperation binding me closer than any spell or bond. "I can't do this without you."

I got on the bike, like I'd known I would. A girl's life and the power to throw volcanoes at people were more important than a "please" or a promise to answer all my questions. But so, I had to admit, was "I can't do this without you."

22

I CLUNG TO Carson's waist as we zipped out of Forest Park, quickly getting the hang of shifting my weight with his. Mostly he did all the work and I just held on as he doubled back twice to make sure we didn't have a tail before heading against rush-hour traffic toward downtown.

"Are you crazy?" I shouted, hoping some of the question would make it to his ear before being whisked away by the wind that was turning my hair into a banner behind us. "Every cop in town will be looking for a guy and a redhead on a motorcycle."

"Trust me." He made two more turns and then pulled into a parking garage near a retail mecca in an old train station, stopping at the gate and hitting the button for a ticket like we were out for a day of shopping. There were plenty of empty spots, but we wound all the way to the top before he pulled into one and cut the engine.

I was off the bike before the engine died. "Trust you? *Who* should I trust? Maguire? *That's* your last name?"

He didn't go so far as to wince, but there was definitely a flinch behind his cool control. "I can explain."

"Yeah? You don't think that would have been better at the *beginning* of our association?"

"Possibly. But this isn't the best time for a freak-out."

"Really? Because twenty-four hours ago, I was a law-abiding kick-ass psychic, the go-to girl when the *freaking FBI* needed someone to interrogate the dead. And now I'm on the run, complicit in grand theft auto, *and* grand theft motorcycle, *and* art theft, *and* riding a motorcycle without a helmet. I've been kidnapped, almost twice, and nearly smothered by the ghost of the most famous volcanic eruption in history. When *would* be the best time to freak out?"

Carson watched me all the way through, without expression. "Are you done?"

"Not quite."

I reached out, grabbed the edge of his jacket, yanked him close, and kissed him.

It was an impulsive decision. But not the obvious kind. At least, not when I'd decided it. All I wanted was to seize one small moment of control. For the gazelle to get the better of the lion.

He froze when I planted my lips on his, except I'd knocked

him literally off balance, and the natural reaction was to grab on to the nearest thing, which was me. And then he realized what he was grabbing and let go like I was hot—and not the good kind.

For an age we stood there like that, me holding him by the collar of his jacket and kissing him for all I was worth, him standing there, hands up like I was frisking him, with no idea what to do about it.

It. Was. Awesome.

Because all the time he didn't know what to do with his hands, he knew exactly what to do with his lips. In fact, Carson Maguire—oh my God, *Maguire*—was twice as good at being kissed as other guys were at kissing.

The balance shifted, and he stopped resisting. I was able to slide my arms around him, skimming my hands over his back, which got an approving sound, to his waist, which got a small, warning growl, to the pocket of his jeans, which got no sound at all because he was too busy taking over the kiss, and it was all I could do to remember to grab the cell phone from his pocket.

Just as his arms started to close around me, I collected my brain from the puddle of mush it had become and stepped back. Carson nearly fell on his face, which would have been much more satisfying if I weren't swaying on knees as weak as my resistance.

"Okay," I said, pretending my voice wasn't breathless. "Now I'm done."

He just *looked* at me, and I couldn't tell if I'd just rocked his world or pissed him off. Maybe a little of both.

Whichever it was, he had to clear his throat before he could speak. "Good. Now that you've got that off your chest." He jerked his head toward the stairwell. "Let's go see what time the train leaves for Chicago."

"Why Chicago?" I asked, like that was the most important question of the moment.

"Because Michael Johnson had a return ticket there in his wallet. And if he was bringing this artifact back to Chicago, then that's what we're going to do."

He'd already turned for the stairs before I connected the fact that McSlackerson was Johnson with my feeling that Carson had some personal beef with the guy. Which meant that my partner in crime was a lying liar at *least* twice over.

Carson Maguire had some explaining to do.

The train station was just a block away, and we reached the ticket window right before it closed. Carson paid for two business-class seats with cash and nudged me to show my fake ID, which worked just fine, though I didn't think I looked like an Adelaide Schmidt.

The railway attendant pulled up the steps after us, and we found seats as the train chugged into motion. I dropped into the seat next to Carson and tried not to moan. Now that we'd stopped running, I had time to actually *hurt*.

As the train rolled past the Gateway Arch, the setting sun painted the landmark a vibrant orange, a picture-postcard vision in the middle of a craptastic day. "So how did you manage *this*?" I asked.

"The sunset? I'm good, but I'm not that good."

217

I'd meant the timing with the train, but he was facing away from me and I was worried I'd give myself away by thinking about the stolen phone in my back pocket, so I didn't say so. The sunset washed Carson in warmth, too. He'd have a Technicolor bruise on his cheek tomorrow. As he flexed the fingers of his right hand, I could see the knuckles were swelling. I was still mad enough to hope he ached in at least half as many places as I did.

The conductor came by and checked our tickets and our IDs. I watched her carefully to see if she gave us any particular attention, but she merely handed back our stubs and told us the snack car was open.

"I have to powder my nose," I said when she'd moved on. Carson gestured for me to go, then leaned back and closed his eyes. He looked tired and vulnerable and I almost felt guilty for kissing him for the phone. Almost. I'd put off calling him a liar. But I hadn't forgotten.

The restroom at the end of the train car was slightly bigger than an airplane lavatory, but not by much. I closed the door and latched it, pulled out McSlackerson's phone—the one I had liberated from Carson's pocket under amorous pretenses—and dialed a number from memory, not sure if I'd get an answer or not.

My cousin Phin picked up on the second ring and started talking without so much as a hello. "You would think a psychic would see trouble coming and know how to avoid it," she said.

This was comforting, in its own infuriating way. If Phin didn't rib me, I would know I was doomed. "Hey, Igor. I have zero time for pleasantries. I need to know if it would be possible to work magic with trace psychic energy. Like from spirits or remnants."

"Oh, *totally.*" She jumped on the idea with enthusiasm. "But you'd have to deal with the transduction inefficiencies in the energy conversion ratio from the noncorporeal to the physical mass differential."

Or something like that. I was ninety percent sure she was just pulling those words out of a hat. "In English, please?"

She translated carelessly. "You wouldn't get much bang for your buck. It takes way too much energy to do the simplest spells."

"What would you need to make that kind of arrangement practical?"

"Hmm. Some kind of potentiating transducer, maybe. Or find an unlimited power source." She laughed at this second suggestion. When I didn't, she explained, "That's funny because there is no such thing."

Nerd humor. "I get it," I said.

"We live in a finite universe, even if it is so large that it *seems*—"

"I *get* it, Phin." I was sure this was what the Brotherhood was doing, and they already seemed pretty good at it. One had used up a very strong remnant just to blow out the Taurus window, and McSlackerson had spent all of young Cleopatra to dissolve the belt tying him up. That was too inefficient to stop an army.

But it gave me an idea what the Jackal might be. "What if there were some sort of object that could either amplify energy or make it work more economically or something . . . ?"

"That would do it. But there is no such thing," said Phin. "It would be like . . . like the philosopher's stone. Legendary and utterly improbable."

"But worth killing for if it *did* exist?"

"Oh yes," she said, with maybe just a little bit of greed. "*Absolutely* worth killing over."

There was a scuffle for the phone and my cousin Amy came on the line. "Daisy! What does Phin mean 'worth killing over'? Where are you? Are you okay? What's going on?"

"Would you believe I don't know the answer to any of those questions?"

"You? Yes." Amy was not a go-with-the-flow type. "What can we do?"

Come here and help me. Risk life and psyche and indentured servitude to a magical crime boss. I wanted to keep them safe from Maguire and the Brotherhood, but I knew they would risk everything for one girl's life, if I just asked them to.

But all I said was, "Keep the aunts from worrying." I caught a glimpse of myself in the mirror and realized that would be a trick, if they could see me. Dark circles under my eyes, my freckles standing out against my pallor...

Lips like they'd been kissing someone's socks off. *I* was worried for me.

"Gotta go." I hung up before I could give in to the strange temptation to unburden my worries on my cousins. They thought I was either (a) annoying or (b) indomitable. Mostly (a). I wouldn't want to burst their bubbles in a moment of weakness.

I dialed the next number while I was still feeling strong. Agent Taylor answered on the second ring.

"Taylor," he answered, sounding wary, since I was calling his direct line.

"I have an anonymous tip," I said, knowing he'd recognize my voice.

There was a nanosecond sigh of relief, and I heard footsteps like he was in the museum. "Go ahead, caller. Any information you have would be welcome."

"There's a stolen motorcycle on the top level of the garage by the Union Square shopping center." I dropped the pretense, at least on my end. "And a Corvette in the parking lot near the art museum. Sorry about that."

"Got it."

"I'm calling from the phone of the guy who stabbed the guard in the museum. Is that how you ended up in St. Louis? You trailed Michael Johnson?"

"Yes. I got your *other* tip." There was the sound of a door closing, then he dropped the pretense on his end, too. "Daisy, are you—"

I cut him off, focused tightly so I wouldn't sway from my course. "Is the guard going to live?"

"Yes. He's critical but stable."

I let out a breath I didn't know I'd been holding. "And the officers who got hit in the Roman statuary?"

"They're fine, but scheduled for psych evaluations."

Of course they were. Pyroclastic blasts didn't just come out of thin air in Sane Person Land. "There was another guy," I said, "in the room with all the Grecian urns."

"We didn't find anyone there. Just a broken pot that the management was pretty upset about."

I leaned against the door as the train swayed on the tracks.

So, no one captured at all. No one to interrogate about Alexis's whereabouts. It was all up to me and Carson, then.

"Can you get away?" Taylor asked. "If you come in on your own, I'll help you, you know that, right?"

He didn't mean with the investigation. He meant with the criminal charges. But I chose to misunderstand him. "Agent Taylor, if you tried to help me with this one, they'd schedule *you* for a psych eval."

He paused to process what I was saying. "That weird, huh?"

"That weird. Tell Agent Gerard I'm turning off this phone, so don't bother to trace it. Also, don't call my aunts. They're freaked out enough as it is."

"Anything else?" There was a hint of humor there, in spite of everything.

"Yeah," I said, holding on to the hope of holding on to his good opinion. "Trust me."

Then I hung up and turned off the phone before heading back to my seat, body aching, brain full, and heart torn.

When I returned, Carson had the netbook open on the seat-back table and the flash drive from the mausoleum plugged in. He didn't glance at me as I sat beside him, or even pretend to believe I'd been powdering my nose that whole time. "Did you turn off the phone when you were done so they can't track the GPS?"

Jeez, how did people in *real* relationships cheat on their boyfriends? I couldn't even manage it with Carson and Taylor, and neither of them even came close to that description.

Pocket-picking lip-locks excluded.

"I'm not an idiot," I said.

"I don't think you're an idiot," Carson said. "I think you're a nice girl who hasn't ever had to think about the FBI tracing her calls."

"I'm not a nice girl." Not in the way he meant, which sounded too much like *naive*. "Any luck unlocking the flash drive?" I asked. Not that I was changing the subject or anything.

The password field dominated the screen. Carson typed, the field said *Denied*. "I've tried all her usual passwords, her favorite bands, pets, colors, birth dates, mother's maiden name...."

He must have been trying things the whole time I was gone. Maybe he was more nervous about my talking to Taylor than he let on.

"Did you try Oosterhouse's name?" I asked, and from his look, he'd thought of that. "Black jackal? *The* Black Jackal?"

He did try that last suggestion but was denied again.

"What about Latin or Greek?" I suggested. "She knows both, right?"

"Yeah," he said. "But I don't." He sat back, narrowing his eyes at the screen as if trying to stare it into submission. "It's a good idea, though."

Nice try flattering me. "Have you looked at the jackal from the museum yet?"

"I was waiting for you." He reached under the seat and pulled out McSlackerson's messenger bag, putting it safely between us. "You're the one who can tell if it has any psychic kick to it or if it's some kind of red herring."

I took out a bundle about the size of a cantaloupe, but oval. The high seat backs and the rail noise gave some privacy as I unwrapped the cloth, leaving it protectively around the fragile figurine. It definitely looked like the illustration in Oosterhouse's excavation report. The jackal-headed man was tiny, only a handspan tall. One ear was slightly chipped, but it looked like an old injury. The gold leaf from the wide collar looked good, as did the painted skirt and tiny jewels.

But as far as spirit energy, I didn't feel a thing. Maybe there was nothing to feel, but more likely I was still zapped. Though I had gotten a very powerful jolt from McSlackerson's jackal tattoo, so if this was *the* Jackal, I was pretty sure I would know it.

"This isn't the Black Jackal," I said.

"That's what Johnson said, back at the museum."

"I noticed you used McSlackerson's real name." With the password and the mini jackal dead ends for the moment, there was no sense putting off the pants-on-fire discussion. "And while we're on the subject of real names..."

He went still and then relaxed, as if he'd been bracing for the question and was relieved to have it over with. "Yeah. About that."

I gently bundled the little statue back up and slipped it into the bag. "You're going to want me in a good mood for this discussion, Liar Maguire. And I will be in a much better mood in the snack car."

23

I STARED AT the cardboard-flavored microwave pizza in front of me and added it to the debt of Carson's offenses.

"It was that or a cold turkey sandwich," he said, sliding into the booth across from me. "I guessed that you wouldn't want another of those."

He guessed right. Insult to injury, there was no Coke. Only Pepsi.

I choked it down like medicine, strictly for the sugar and caffeine, then tried to figure out where to start. The sun had gone down completely and the snack car was brightly lit, superimposing our reflections on the Illinois farmland in the window.

"So Alexis isn't just *like* a sister to you," I began. Funny that I'd never considered he could be a cousin or a nephew.

"She's my half sister," Carson said a little warily, as if bracing for another freak-out.

The clues had all been there: his status with the staff, how well he knew Alexis ... and most of all, now that I thought about it, the strange, bright remnant that seemed to connect father and son in Maguire's office.

McSlackerson had called him by his last name at the museum. When Carson had objected, I'd just thought he'd been rejecting the association. Which I guess he was, on a deeper, more messed-up level. I might have to give him a pass for now.

"And speaking of lies ..." I paused to give Carson the eye, but he didn't look like he was about to protest his innocence. He just sipped his Pepsi, waiting for me to continue. "When Elbow Patches mentioned Michael Johnson at the Institute library, you said you didn't know him."

"No," Carson said calmly, "I said I didn't know Alexis was thinking about graduate school."

I sat back, folding my arms, and prompted him to come clean. "So, speaking of *lies by omission* ... tell me about your history with McSlackerson. And don't try to tell me you have none."

The nickname almost made him smile, but he thought better of it. "It's not that much history. He and Alexis dated a while. I didn't like him then, but I thought they were done. I thought Alexis dumped him."

For a long moment there was only the sound of the train on

the tracks while I glared at him, trying to see into his skull. "We really need to discuss your definition of 'need-to-know basis.'"

He met my gaze evenly. "Mrs. Hardwicke told you that Alexis knew one or more of these Brotherhood guys. And the guy at the Institute had just told you that Johnson and Alexis dated. So you knew what I did. We had other things to talk about, like the jackal and Oosterhouse and getting to St. Louis."

True. I wasn't sure that excused him, but it was true.

"Okay," I said. I hadn't told him I'd emailed Taylor to give him Johnson's name, so maybe we should just move forward. "Let's debrief. And we'll both promise not to skip anything."

Carson scrubbed his hands over his face. "Daisy, I haven't slept in almost forty-eight hours and we've been through the wringer. The whole museum thing really deserves my best brain-power, and this isn't it. I'm baffled as to why Johnson and his brothers would stab someone to get an artifact that you say has no power."

"That's not what I said. I said it isn't the Black Jackal."

"Is that what we're calling the Oosterhouse Jackal now?" Carson asked. "Don't you think it's a little melodramatic?"

"And 'Brotherhood of the Black Jackal' isn't? I didn't make up these names." When Aunt Ivy had told me about it, I'd thought the name was a reference to Anubis. And maybe it was, but ...

"At the museum," I said, trying to remember exactly, "Johnson said, 'This isn't the Black Jackal,' and, 'We're still assembling the pieces.' Or something like that."

"Do you know what he meant?"

"Maybe. Well, no, but a little." Boy, did we have a lot to catch up on. Pointing to his pizza, I said, "You eat. I'll talk."

I told him everything that happened after I woke up over the shoulder of Johnson's comrade: the kidnap attempt, my drained psychic battery, the fact that I'd spoken with the real Cleopatra, and the way Johnson had used her remnant force to escape his bonds. I also explained that I thought he had stabbed the guard to somehow use his—I guessed *psychic energy* was the only term for it—to keep the alarm from going off.

"That's why I'm so worried for Alexis," I said. My pizza had gone cold as I'd been talking. For the first time in my life I didn't feel like eating. "And that's why these Brotherhood guys have to be stopped. They're willing to kill someone, but worse, they're willing to steal their . . . the essential spirit of them. These are remnants of people's *souls*."

Carson had listened calmly as I caught him up, but he'd pushed aside his food. By the time I'd finished, his folded hands rested on the table, knuckles white.

"I'm not like them," he said tightly. "I wouldn't use up . . . I didn't know. . . ." He broke off, to stare out the window, his jaw muscle working as he struggled with his thoughts and some emotion I didn't understand.

Finally he turned back and met my gaze. "Daisy, I'm so sorry for hurting you back there."

I was stunned. It was the most genuine apology he'd given me, for something I would never hold against him. "Carson— I'm fine. I think my mojo will come back, but even if it doesn't—" My voice broke, and he flinched. Not much, but visibly. I pulled on my brave-girl armor for both our sakes. "Even if it doesn't, I'm still here. You did it to save both of us, not just yourself. You're nothing like the Brotherhood."

He let my assurance stand for a few seconds, maybe letting it sink in. When he did speak, it was like we were going to pretend that moment of weakness hadn't happened. "I don't think they were trying to kill us. I think they were trying to do exactly what happened—drain you to exhaustion and distract me while they made off with you and the artifact."

"How would they know you could make with the deflector shield?" I asked. "*You* didn't know until you felt—whatever it was that happened when Pompeii hit me on the first time through. Did you?"

He got a little bit of a dodgy look, like he was about to tell me something else he'd been holding back. "Not on that scale. I did something like it at the cemetery. Remember, I told you to think invisible thoughts? But that was just…" He waved a hand.

"Jedi mind tricks," I finished. I thought about what Johnson had said about collecting the pieces needed for the fiendish plan. "You did have a theory that a psychic who could talk to the dead was one of the resources the Brotherhood couldn't get on their own. Why they need the Maguire organization."

"Yeah, I did suggest that." He didn't look happy about being right. "But why?"

"Maybe to read this." I put my hand on McSlackerson's messenger bag on the seat beside me. Did I feel a tingle of spirit from the artifact inside, or was that wishful thinking? "Maybe this holds a remnant with a clue to the Black Jackal."

"Which still leaves the question … What *is* the Black Jackal?"

I explained what I had put together, leaving out the part about Phin's help. "I think Oosterhouse discovered how to draw on remnants and shades for magic and somehow left that information for his disciples. The Brotherhood has been doing it all along, just on a relatively small scale. But the Oosterhouse Jackal, or Black Jackal, will let them use that spirit power more efficiently."

"Like a transistor that amplifies an electronic signal," said Carson, following the thread.

He was as bad as Phin. "It's a thingy. It makes it work. I don't need to know how." I drummed my fingers on the table. Magical theory really was not my thing, but I didn't want to risk calling my cousins again and drawing them further into the situation. "I would like to know how they do magic now, without the Jackal. It's not something everyone can do."

Carson leaned back in his seat. "Secret societies have secret rituals. Initiations."

"Symbols!" I pointed to my arm. "Johnson had a tattoo of a jackal. And when I touched it, I got a powerful jolt of remnant energy. Maybe the tattoo links the members of the Brotherhood somehow."

"Everyone has tattoos these days," said Carson, and pointed to a family sitting across the aisle from us, enjoying their snack and their train ride. The mom's pants leg had ridden up to show a butterfly inked on her ankle. "Even nice, normal Midwesterners. Even me."

"Really?" Curse my vivid imagination. "Where?"

He sipped his soda. "That's not important." But he looked pleased that I was curious.

That flustered me. Because I *was* curious, and we had known each other all of twenty-four hours, and twenty-three and one half of them had been spent on the run.

"Okay, then," I said. "If you won't tell me that, tell me about your mother."

He reacted with a very careful nonreaction. Most people would be at least a little surprised by the non sequitur. "How Freudian of you, Miss Goodnight."

"Well, I know about your father." I left an accusing beat. "*Now* I do."

He sighed like I had guilted him into talking, which was fine, since that had been my intention. "My mother was an artist who had an affair with Devlin Maguire just long enough to find out he was married and to get pregnant with me. Not in that order. She raised me on her own until she was killed during a home invasion when I was sixteen, and Maguire adopted me so I'd have his name. I'm his only son."

The way he stripped all emotion off those facts somehow made them more appalling. "Maguire simply showed up, all 'Luke, I am your father,' and adopted you? Just like that? The family court judge didn't give you a choice?"

"Maguire speaks softly and carries a big wallet." Carson shrugged. "My mother had never accepted any child support from him, but apparently he could prove he'd tried or something. Anyway, except for the name change, I didn't mind. Mom never said a bad word about my father—she never said anything at all, really. And then he shows up, filthy rich, larger than life, and paying for college, promising me a job in the family business. And there were the cars ... They're not all Ford Tauruses."

I studied him over the rim of my Pepsi can, not believing for an instant it was that simple. "So it's all about the money and the cars? That's why you're sticking around?"

"Of course." He kept a straight face except for one raised eyebrow. "What would Freud say about that?"

"I don't know," I said. "But I'm sure it would have something to do with tailpipes."

He choked on his soda and grabbed for his napkin as Pepsi came out his nose.

Score.

He mopped at the drink, but he was a lost cause, really. Before we got to the train station, he'd turned his shirt inside out to hide the bloodstains. (I'd ditched my top layer and borrowed his jacket and hoped my jeans just looked tie-dyed.) There were dark circles under his eyes and an unshaven shadow on his jaw, in addition to all the cuts and bruises.

Why was there no remnant of his mother nearby to fuss over him, especially while he was wounded? That was exactly when mothers like to check in on their kids. I remembered him asking me, on the dark road the night before, about remnants, if I saw anything around him. Had he known somehow that she wasn't around?

I wanted to reach across the table, to take his hand and lace our fingers together the way our lives seemed to have become laced. I didn't, but I gave in to the impulse to share something else that linked us.

"My parents were killed, too. By Dad's business partner. Nothing like your dad's business. Computer parts. But it was over greed and a bigger market share. Would you believe he cut the lines to the brakes on their car? One steep Hill Country embankment and—" I made a fatal arc with my hand. Very dramatic.

My emotions weren't in the words. They colored outside the lines of the story, and he watched me as I told it, reading my feelings like I read spirits.

"How do you grow up with that," he asked, "and not be all..."

I raised a brow, mirroring one of his favorite expressions. "Jaded and bitter?"

He acknowledged my point with a tip of his head, then turned the mirror back on me. "You pretend to be jaded. But you have this glow of ... *decency* about you—"

"Now you're just being insulting."

"—and a belief in the basic decency of others. How do you keep that, seeing what you see?"

"My aunts, of course. It's their fault. I wanted to start an indie girl band, but I couldn't get up the proper angst." I sighed hugely. "Now you know my secret shame."

He just gave me a *look*. "I've pretty much known you were an idealist from the beginning, Sunshine."

Well, that explained the nickname, I guess.

Across the aisle, the kids were experimenting with the ripples the motion of the train made in their cups of soda. I watched them for a moment, then said, "I don't think it's idealism to believe the universe is a decent place, or that people are more good

233

than bad. It doesn't make me *unaware* of the bad in the world, just more determined to add to the good."

I glanced back to find him watching me with an enigmatic expression. I'd gotten better at catching the glints of truth beneath his surface calm, but this time I couldn't make out his feelings. Amusement, warmth, regret. Those were enough to make me blush.

"Besides," I said, flustered and determined to break the tension, "my idealism isn't *that* secret. I drive a Prius."

He shuddered. "I can't believe I let a girl who drives a Prius kiss me."

Awkward. Pause.

"I just did it to steal your phone."

"I know."

Damn. I mean, I knew he knew I had it, but damn. "I'm a lousy pickpocket."

He laughed, looking sheepish. "Actually, this time I didn't notice until you went to the restroom."

Kiss distraction achieved. That was progress, I guess. And nice of him to admit it. That was progress, too, though I wasn't sure what kind.

"Do we have a plan for Chicago?" I asked, changing the subject. Again.

"Find a place to crash." He rubbed a hand over his face, wincing when he hit a cut on his cheek. "But now that I don't have to protect my secret identity, I've got an idea."

"Is it stately Wayne Manor?" I asked. "I always figured you for more of a Batman guy than a Superman one."

"More like a penthouse," he said as he gathered the greasy

remains of our microwave pizza. "But there is a butler, and he's a very good cook."

"Carson, *darling boy,* come and give your aunt Gwenda a hug."

He did, and his aunt air-kissed both his cheeks, the sleeves of her hostess gown fluttering but the cocktail in her hand absolutely steady.

I wasn't sure what to expect when the taxi from Union Station had dropped us off at a skyscraper of condos near Chicago's Magnificent Mile. The doorman had eyed us askance, since it was after eleven and we were looking rough, to say the least. But Carson had a quick word with him, showed him his ID—maybe even his real one—and after a phone call, the doorman sent us up to the twenty-third floor.

"Isn't your dad going to know we're here?" I'd asked in the elevator. He'd told me Maguire owned the penthouse, keeping his sister there and out of his hair. Also, I would bet the feds kept tabs on all Maguire's properties, even on a day when his son *wasn't* on the run from the law.

"Maybe," said Carson. "But by now, if he really wants to know where we are, he does. I've been careful but not that careful." He'd shrugged as the elevator pinged for our floor. "Besides, Gwenda won't tell him. She's sort of like Switzerland that way."

Aunt Gwenda was older than her brother, midsixties or a well-preserved seventy. Maybe she'd had work done, or maybe she had really great bone structure. Her zygomatic arches were sculpted just like Carson's.

"You look wonderful, Gwenda," he said. "Are we interrupting a party?"

"This old thing?" She gestured to her hostess ensemble. The butler—yes, a real butler—had shown us to the kitchen, but a murmur of conversation came from deeper in the apartment.

"It's just a few friends, darling," she added, with a sip of her cocktail. "You must think this is awful with Alexis missing, but it's been scheduled forever and Devlin said to behave as normally as possible."

"I understand," said Carson, all smoothly sociable, not a bit stony. "Speaking of all that..."

Gwenda held up a hand like he hadn't already trailed off. "I don't want to know. And don't worry, I won't tell anyone you're here. *Including* my brother."

"Thanks." He flashed her a handsome-devil grin and got an indulgent-aunt smile in return. The guy was scary adaptable. With perfect manners, he stepped back to introduce us. "Aunt Gwenda, this is Daisy. We need a place to stay for the night."

"You poor darling!" she exclaimed, as though she hadn't taken my measure as soon as she'd come into the kitchen. "We must get you into a hot bath as soon as possible."

I put on my company manners, too. I do have them. "That sounds wonderful, Miss Maguire."

She hooked her free arm through mine. "You must call me Aunt Gwenda. We shall get you all fixed up, my dear. Are you hungry? Will canapés do, or shall Matthew whip up an omelet?"

"Yes, please," I said, in a daze of yes-yes-please-feed-me.

When I glanced at Carson he was looking very smug. Not that this made us even.

Well, maybe it made up for the pizza.

Matthew was the butler. He was young and handsome and, as promised, a great cook. He fed us while the party wrapped up down the hall, then Carson called first dibs on the shower, which suited me because I called seconds on canapés.

When Aunt Gwenda swept back into the kitchen, she laid a pile of silky fabric on one barstool, then took the other beside me. "I brought you something to sleep in, darling. I can have those clothes washed for you, or we can just toss them out and start over. I'm sure I have something you can borrow."

"Oh, I couldn't possibly—"

"Of course you could." She patted my hand. "I wish you weren't here on *business,* so we could talk about you. Carson has never brought a girl anywhere near the family before."

Matthew the butler and I exchanged glances as he refilled my orange juice. "No offense, Miss Maguire, but I can sort of see why. *You* seem very nice, but..."

"But my brother is a dreadful man." She gave a what-are-you-going-to-do shrug. "At least I have a lovely home and a delightful niece and nephew."

I was not going to get an opportunity better than this. "Did you know Carson's mother?"

"Sadly, no. I understand she was a very talented artist. But I didn't even know I *had* a nephew until he came to live with Devlin."

"What about Alexis?" I asked. "Where is her mother?"

"She moved away ages ago. Remarried now. To some foreign count, can you believe it?"

That was one of the more believable things I'd heard in the past two days. "What's Alexis like?" I asked. Carson spoke fondly of her, but I still had little read on her personality.

"Very smart. *Book* smart, just brilliant. She doesn't get that from our side of the family." Gwenda poured some orange juice into the remains of what I assumed was her vodka. "But she's clever, too, like a Maguire. Well, she'd have to be. Devlin is a manipulative bastard, and she had to learn to get around that, learn to work his system so she could have some independence and happiness."

I couldn't find fault with that. No wonder Carson was so cautious with his truths, and he'd only been in that environment since he was sixteen. What would he be like if he'd been raised as Maguire's only son? Probably less conflicted, and not in a good way.

Gwenda patted my hand once more. "You toddle off and have your bath, or a nice hot shower. Second door on the right, down that hall."

I thanked the butler again for the midnight snack, then took the bundle of pj's Aunt Gwenda pushed at me and followed her directions. It was weird not feeling a shred of spirit energy anywhere. Full-on apparitions like Cleopatra or Mrs. Hardwicke were rare, but snatches of color, voices, or emotion were the background music of my life. It was sort of lonely without them.

Down the hall, I opened the second door on the right and found my temporary bedroom. I also found Carson coming into the same room through a different door, wrapped in a towel and nothing else.

24

IT WAS A big towel, but there was a lot of Carson.

I mean, he was really tall. And *really* well built. No wonder he'd been able to toss me over the cemetery fence, then vault it like a bump in the road.

I stood there with my mouth hanging open and, I don't know, some sound coming out, because he made a shushing motion with the hand not holding the towel and then hurried to pull me into the room and close the door.

"Aunt Gwenda has made an assumption," he said. "And I sort of let it stand because it's simpler this way. I swear this was not my idea."

He was very apologetic and earnest. In fact, he seemed rather panicked that I was going to get the wrong impression. From him wearing a towel. And nothing else. Because no one would get the wrong impression from that.

"Let me put on some clothes," he said, when I continued to say nothing.

I decided to study the decor while he grabbed a stack of something from a chair and returned to the adjoining bathroom. That was when I noticed there was only one bed. It was a big bed, but there were two of us.

He came back quickly, wearing a pair of sleep pants and a long-sleeved T-shirt. "Look, I can grab the comforter and a couple of pillows and sleep on the floor. It's not a big deal."

"That's stupid." My brain had finally started working again. "I saw your bruises." Boy, had I. "You don't need to sleep on the floor. We'll put a pillow wall down the middle or something."

"Are you sure?"

I clutched my bundle of pj's to my chest and walked past him to the bathroom. "Carson, after the day we've had, if you can do anything other than sleep, you're not just a magician, you really are Superman."

The shower had five types of massages, and I tried them all. And not just because I was delaying going out there and facing Carson. I was *thinking*.

There were still holes in some of my theories, simply because I didn't have the pieces to fit. But nothing was totally unraveling. If Alexis and Johnson were close, it made sense that they would have shared information about Oosterhouse and his secret society. Maybe they split when she realized how the magic drew its power, or how far the Brotherhood was willing to go to get the Jackal. But they still needed her knowledge, or Maguire's resources, or whatever was on the flash drive, so they took her.

If the Brotherhood took her. I'd argued all along that they must have, but there was something weird about the way Johnson had reacted when I demanded he let her go. He'd seemed surprised. Was it simply because I'd thought the small jackal figurine he'd stolen was *the* Jackal?

Too many missing pieces. The password to the flash drive, the information on it, the reason the Brotherhood wanted the artifact from the St.Louis museum...

I admitted that I was going to run out of hot water before I ran out of questions. I also admitted I was stalling, and forced myself out of the shower.

Putting on the loaner pajamas, I brushed my teeth with the guest amenities, then checked my reflection in the steamy mirror. The pj's were green silk that brought out the color of my eyes and the purple of my bruises. Fortunately, most of those were covered.

No more stalling. So the silk was clingy when I moved and it was kind of obvious I wasn't wearing a bra. I was just going to walk out and get under the covers like it was no big deal.

I walked out to the sound of snoring. Carson sprawled facedown on half of the bed.

The middle half.

Ass.

"Move. Over." I pushed him until he rolled to one side, then I started putting pillows down the middle of the bed. Before I got to the one at the top, I stopped and looked at him.

I was not the type to get soft, squishy feelings for a boy. I liked guys who made my heart race, not ones who made it melt. But Carson asleep and ragged and vulnerable? He did both.

Odds were, not many people got to see this. Why did he walk such a tightrope, hating Maguire, but working for him, playing his game. Adapting. *Here* was a guy who was clever.

Clever and powerful. Cleopatra had the right of it. Dangerous and irresistible.

"Carson," I whispered. He made a sleepy, not-really-awake sound. Perfect. I didn't have any scruples about questioning his subconscious. "Carson, what hold does Maguire have over you? Why do you stay with him?"

He gave a drowsy hum and muttered something. I leaned closer to hear and he whispered, "Nice try, Sunshine."

I hit him with the pillow, but not very hard. "Ass."

Cracking open an eyelid, he looked at me, then the pillow, then me again. "If you're going to put that brick in the wall, you'd better do it. I can see down your top."

I whacked him again, plenty hard, then thumped the pillow into place, completing the feather fortress. When I collapsed on the bed, I couldn't see him at all.

Carson rolled over and turned off the bedside lamp. I stared at the dark ceiling, exhausted, but my mind was racing too fast for sleep to catch up, still trying to find the pieces to fill all the holes.

The Oosterhouse Jackal, the Black Jackal . . . *Were* they the same thing? If not, then what *was* the Black Jackal?

Twice through the Veil I had seen something, a lean, hound-like shadow. Was this the power of suggestion, or something real? And if so, what? And what did it want? The threshold to eternity—whatever lay beyond this world—was a one-way deal.

At least, I thought so.

On the other side of the pillow wall, Carson stirred, like he was restless, too. I had one more thing on my mind, and it wasn't any kind of transcendental question.

"Hey," I whispered, in case he was sleeping.

"What now?"

"Back in the garage, when I stole the cell phone . . . Why did you wait so long to kiss me back?"

"Because I have this weird policy against kissing girls under a magical compulsion to obey my father." There was a loaded pause and then, "After we find Alexis, it will be a different story. Just so you know."

Great. Now my heart was racing as fast as my brain. What would he say if I told him that I hadn't felt coerced much at all since we hit the road?

I wasn't going to find out what he'd say to that, because the next thing I heard from his side of the wall were his snores.

• • •

I finally slept, dreamless as the dead. But when the washed-out light of dawn edged the curtains in the unfamiliar room, I heard a voice calling me, so faint that I wasn't sure I wasn't still asleep.

"Wake, Daughter of the Jackal. You've slept too long."

Awake or dreaming, I opened my eyes to find a spirit beside the bed.

For a second, my sleep-fogged brain Saw a canine-headed figure, but it faded, leaving a gray-haired man dressed in sweat-stained khaki, looking down at me with a benevolent smile.

"At last! Wake up, young lady. I've been waiting for you for a very long time."

25

WAKING UP WITH a dead guy standing over me was a helluva way to discover that my systems were back online.

I shot to the head of the bed in a crab-walk that knocked over all the pillows and woke Carson. He pushed off the avalanche of bedding and searched for the threat.

"What's going on?" he demanded when he didn't see anything.

I grabbed his shoulder and pointed, not sure what I expected to happen. Or maybe I had some idea, because I wasn't totally surprised when Carson Saw the khaki-clad shade across from him and vaulted out of the bed.

"What the—?" He looked from the apparition to me and back again. "How am I seeing this?"

When he'd moved, I'd pictured my psyche stretching to keep contact. It was only a few feet, and we couldn't hold hands *all* the time. "I've got my groove back," I told him. "And I'm sharing. Like in the museum, but with less life-and-death peril."

"Are you sure about that last part?" He eyed the shade warily. A full apparition was an unnerving thing to wake up to, even if you're used to them.

The ghost raised his hands in apology. "I beg your pardon. I am intruding on your tryst."

The old-fashioned word made everything—the mild-mannered shade, my pajamas, Carson's wicked case of bedhead, the fact that I was crouched like a ninja on the mattress—feel kind of farcical. I edged over and stepped down to the floor. That was a little better.

"It's not a tryst," I said.

Carson, still wary, or maybe just grumpy, said, "That's not his business. Who is he?"

I already had a good idea. The shade had gray hair and a close-cropped beard, and a tanned face, lined from years of squinting in the sun. But he looked hearty and ready for an expedition, dressed in a field jacket and cargo pants.

He gave a small, good-natured bow. "Professor Carl Ooster-house, at your service."

Yes! I tried to be cautious about my excitement, but maybe, *finally*, we were getting answers.

I glimpsed a writing desk against the wall, where two messenger bags—Carson's and Johnson's—hung from the back of the chair. On the blotter were the netbook, the flash drive, and the jackal-headed figure from the museum, unwrapped and lying carefully on top of its padding.

"This must be why the Brotherhood wanted to steal the artifact yesterday," I said to Carson, not hiding my hope very well. The shade was attached to the figurine, and when my mojo kicked back in, it must have pulled the remnant out of hibernation.

"Do you know where you are?" I asked Oosterhouse carefully. He seemed very coherent for a recently dormant spirit. But you can't just spring on someone the fact that they're dead.

"Beyond intruding on your privacy?" asked the professor, the glow of his good mood undiminished. "I am uncertain. But when I felt myself pulled from my own slumber, I couldn't quite contain my excitement."

"I don't understand," I said, assuming I hadn't dreamed the words that had woken me. "How could you have been waiting for me?"

"An overdramatization." He gave a rueful grimace. "It's a failing of mine. I should have said, I've been waiting for someone who can do what you do. You're the answer to a lonely soul's prayer."

Ah. Unfinished business. That would explain how cogent the remnant was. Clear goals gave spirits strength and focus, the same as the living.

Oosterhouse, hands linked behind his back, strolled to the

desk. Carson stepped forward like he could stop him, but it took him out of my reach, even psychically. Numskull. Not only could he not touch Oosterhouse, now he couldn't see him.

The shade bent to look at the figurine. "Ah yes," he said, with a note of pride and nostalgia. "I found this on an expedition on the west bank of the Nile, across from Thebes. Now they call it the Valley of the Kings. What exciting days those were. Hot, tedious, dangerous. Half killing ourselves to find a tomb, only to discover it already plundered in antiquity. I may not have found much gold, but ah, the riches of knowledge..."

He seemed prepared to go on about the riches of knowledge for some time. Interrupting him was difficult, because as a spirit, he didn't have to stop for breath.

"Ask him about the Oosterhouse Jackal," said Carson.

Oosterhouse stilled, then turned. "Ask me yourself, young man." He sounded very professorial just then, as if Carson had interrupted a class lecture. "I can hear you. But I'm not sure what it is you speak of. Perhaps a better-constructed question is in order."

I didn't want to relay that, so I moved closer to Carson to loop him back in, letting him see and hear Oosterhouse again. "What about the Brotherhood of the Black Jackal?" I asked, watching him closely for flickers in his emotions. His start of recognition at the name was small but obvious. "What can you tell us about them?"

He paused, as if to collect his thoughts. "I have not heard that name in quite some time. I believe we are in the twenty-first century now?" He shook his head and chuckled. "A new millennium. It seems incredible, yet also incredibly short, when one considers that our excavations uncovered tombs buried beneath the sands of *multiple* millennia—"

"About the Brotherhood?" Carson prompted.

Oosterhouse flared with disapproval. He changed subjects, but without acknowledging Carson. "My areas of inquiry concerned the occult aspects of ancient burial rituals. I tutored a number of students who gave themselves that name as a novelty. I believe they disbanded when I, ahem, left my teaching position to return to the field." He scratched his beard thoughtfully. "Possibly someone has revived the name as a schoolboy prank."

"It's no prank," Carson said. "They're willing to kill and kidnap people to get your artifact. Clearly they want something more than novelty."

Oosterhouse grew sober. "That is regrettable. But now I understand. I've slept for some time, unremembered. But recently something has called me awake. I thought it might be you, dear girl, and your gift." He gave me an oddly fond smile, as if my ability to hear and see him tied us together somehow. "But if someone is searching for the Jackal, that would also explain my waking."

"Can you help us?" I asked the professor. "I don't even know *what* the Jackal is."

"Ah. Well." He clasped his hands behind his back again and rocked on his heels. "This is the pinnacle of my research into the alternative funerary practices of a splinter cult of the late Middle Kingdom near Thebes. The Jackal is a very powerful thing. It is capable of channeling *unlimited* energy—"

"Unlimited?" I asked. "I thought there was no such thing."

It was my turn to get the professorial frown. Oosterhouse did not like to be interrupted when he was lecturing.

"I think I am in a better position to understand the minuscule difference between infinity and *almost* infinity, my dear girl." Then he gave a wistful sigh. "I had such plans. What great things I could have accomplished with such power."

He seemed to fade with the sigh, and I thought at first that emotion dimmed his image. But his shade was weakening, the details hazing together in the pale dawn light. He might be well defined, but he was nowhere close to unlimited.

"Dr. Oosterhouse." I rushed to pull him back from his memories. "Do you know where the Jackal is? It's vital we get to it before the Brotherhood does. A girl's life is at stake." When he seemed to dither, I appealed to his pride. "You wanted to use it to do good. You're the only person who understands how dangerous this thing could be in the wrong hands."

"You mistake my hesitation, my dear." His fading shade gave me a Santa Claus smile. "I will tell you where the Jackal is. But I ask for your help in return."

"Of course," I said. "Whatever you—"

"Hold it." Carson had been quiet, letting me handle the professor. Now he objected like my legal counsel. "What is it you want?"

Oosterhouse's eyes narrowed. "You are an impertinent young man. But, being a gentleman myself, I appreciate your protective gesture." He smoothed his ruffled feathers and went on with his request. "I am tired of sleeping and awaking here. Tired of being this"—he gestured to his form—"shadow of myself. I wish you to open the door to the afterlife so I can be complete, my soul whole once more. If you do this for me, I will show you the Jackal."

I had agreement on the tip of my tongue when Carson stopped me again. "This is how it's going to be," he said, in a voice to be reckoned with. "You show us where to find the Jackal and tell us its secrets, and only *then* Daisy will do her thing."

"Does Daisy get a say in this?" I snapped.

Oosterhouse kept his gaze on Carson. "Yes, why not let Miss Goodnight make her own decision?"

My surprise shook me out of my snit. "How did you know my name?"

The professor gave me an avuncular smile. "My path crossed with a Goodnight before. Quite an interesting young lady, and you have the look of her. Add in your, shall we say 'spirit'— if you will forgive a pun—and it is not much of a guess who you are."

Oosterhouse was fading quickly now, the air chilling as he pulled heat energy to stay visible. I didn't have the strength to hold him there. "I need to rest before I can open the Veil," I said. "Tell us where to look for the Jackal, and when we find it, I promise I'll send you on."

The shade sighed, the ghost of a gesture of resignation. "You truly do not understand how powerful you are, young lady. What a shame the Brotherhood of the Black Jackal has re-formed only to become petty criminals. With the knowledge I passed down to them, and your gift . . . oh, the wonders you could—"

"I agree, she's amazing," Carson said. "Which won't do any-one any good if she keels over from the effort of keeping you here. Tell us how to find what we're looking for."

Oosterhouse gave him a glare colder than the plummeting room temperature. "Very well. As it happens, I will still need to guide you once you find my grave. Find the artifacts that lie with my bones, and I will show you the Jackal."

And with that, he faded completely, leaving nothing but an icy fog that vanished in a swirl of heat from the radiator.

26

"YOU HAVE GOT to be kidding me," said Carson, staring at the spot where the ghost had been. "Find the artifacts that lie with his bones? How do we do that?"

"Find his grave," I said, going to grab the robe Gwenda had given me with the pajamas. "And a shovel."

"That's not funny."

"That's because I'm not joking." Belting the robe, which wasn't much heavier than the pj's, but adequate now that the ghost was gone, I headed for the door. "I never joke about disinterment."

Carson followed me, unappeased by my calm. "Where are you going?"

"To get some breakfast. I'm not planning any tomb raiding on an empty stomach."

He must have seen the sense of that, because he followed without argument.

Aunt Gwenda was, no surprise, a late sleeper, but there was a note from her on the kitchen counter telling us to make ourselves at home since Matthew had the morning off.

The apartment was sort of urban vintage—exposed brick walls and beams, wood on the floors, copper or brass on the fixtures. The kitchen was huge and the appliances were commercial grade and intimidating.

Carson headed for the coffeemaker—an apparatus that looked like it could pilot the space shuttle. Maybe someone had gotten a bargain when NASA shut down that program. "The note says there's a bag of bagels by the toaster. You can work a toaster, right?"

"Of course," I answered. Neither of us said anything while Carson ran the coffee grinder, but once he'd measured out the grounds and, I don't know, programmed a geosynchronous orbit, he turned to me.

"Where's the ghost now?" he asked.

I did a quick poke around with my psychic senses. "There's just a faint trace of him in the bedroom, where the artifact is. Manifesting that long wore him out."

He leaned against the counter and folded his arms. Not a receptive sort of posture. "Are you sure he can't hear us? The Egyptian girl at the museum, she could leave her object."

"You mean Cleopatra?" The reminder brought a fresh pang of failure, that I hadn't protected her. "She was an extremely strong shade, thanks to her place in history. *This* poor guy—"

"Poor guy?" Carson echoed.

"Well, his institution booted him out. They were willing to keep the artifacts he collected, though."

"I'm worried there was a reason for the Institute to distance themselves. Something more than just eccentric theories. I think you're identifying a little closely with this one, Daisy. He's not one of your lost lambs."

"It's not that," I protested, maybe a little too much. "People like to be remembered. You heard the guy at the Institute—no one outside the archives has ever heard of him, in Egyptology, where *everything* is about being remembered."

"No one outside the archives and the Brotherhood," Carson said.

"You just don't trust anyone, do you?"

"No. And your bagel is burning."

Nuts! I popped it out of the toaster, but the damage was done. Tossing the blackened bread into the trash, I turned on Carson as if that were his fault. I found him standing much closer than I expected.

He spoke low, as if he really thought Oosterhouse's remnant could be listening from the other room. "I think he knows more than he's saying. Which is a lot of words and not a lot of information."

I pitched my voice the same way. "He's a *professor.* Of course he uses big words." I grabbed the bag to take out another bagel.

"Here's a big word for you, Sunshine." He didn't move out of my way, so I had to reach around him. "*Obfuscate*. It means 'to blow smoke up someone's ass.'"

I scowled. "You're cranky before caffeine. Isn't the space shuttle done making it yet?"

"I'm *cranky*," he said, finally moving to get two mugs from a glass-front cabinet, "because—call me squeamish—I'm not exactly thrilled about desecrating a grave. We dodged that bullet with Mrs. Hardwicke, and now it's coming back."

"You'll steal cars and museum artifacts and snatch reasonably innocent psychics off the street, but you draw the line at digging up bones?"

He finished pouring before he answered. "One, cars are just *things*. Two, my plan was to take good care of the psychic and return her undamaged. A grave, though . . . that's like spitting on someone."

The coffee he held out to me was extra light and extra sweet, exactly the way I'd fixed mine at the diner forever ago. When I reached for it, he didn't let go until I met his eye.

"Three," he said, with the ring of an oath, "I'm not drawing the line. I'd do whatever it takes to rescue Alexis. And if this Jackal *is* an unlimited power supply, it's almost as important."

"Okay," I said, solemnly accepting his promise and noting his priorities. "Let's say we manage to find the Jackal. I think maybe it's time to talk about what we're going to do with it."

We *had* to rescue Alexis. But I didn't want to hand over that kind of power, infinite or not, to the Brotherhood. Or, for that matter, to Maguire.

"We use it to get her back," said Carson, without hesitation. "To find her and rescue her."

"And not hand it over?" I asked, making sure we were clear on that.

"And not hand it over."

There were so many problems with that idea, but I wanted to believe we could do it. That *I* could do it. Rescue Alexis ... and Carson, too, from the hold Maguire had on his loyalty.

"I'm in," I said, offering my own promise. "And it has nothing to do with the triple swear or any threat from Maguire. This has been voluntary ever since I realized they were messing with my remnants. And whatever is between you and your father—"

He gave me no warning before he kissed me. Didn't move closer, didn't take me in his arms, just swooped in and stopped my words with his mouth. Thoroughly. He drank down whatever I was going to say, and when I was speechless, only then did he lift the coffee cup from my hand and put it on the counter behind me. I almost didn't notice because he did it without taking his lips from mine.

It was a perfectly choreographed move, a short step to wrap his arm around me and press me up against the cabinet. Not that I offered any resistance. I kissed him back, savoring the play of his lips on mine and the taste of black coffee on his tongue. I was revising my preference for cream and sugar, and revising my stance on guys who made me feel melty inside. Because I was melting like ice cream on a hot San Antonio sidewalk.

His free hand came up to my neck, lacing his fingers in my tangled hair as he kissed along my jaw, his chin deliciously scratchy on the ticklish skin under my ear.

"Maguire owns this apartment," he whispered. "It might be bugged."

It took me a moment—or two, or three—to figure out what that had to do with our current entanglement. I couldn't remember if I'd been saying something we wouldn't want Maguire to know. Jeez, I couldn't remember how to *talk*.

Oh, wait, yes I did. I jabbed a finger into his shoulder and pushed him back so I could see his face. "You kissed me to shut me up?"

Carson met my narrow-eyed glare with humor and zero apology. "No. But it makes a good excuse. And paybacks are hell."

So I gave him a punch in the ribs, but not very hard at all. "You're a pretty good kisser for a jackass."

His brow lifted. "Have you kissed a lot of jackasses?"

I pretended I wasn't leaning on the counter because I was weak in the knees. "At least one too many."

"Ouch." His hands slid off the silk of my pajamas with only one side trip over my hips, almost brief enough to be accidental. Then he pointed to a computer tucked away on a small built-in desk. "I'll take care of breakfast. You find us a grave to rob."

Okay. So I guessed we were moving on now. But something had changed, not because he'd kissed me. Because I'd confessed what I'd known since last night—that I was here voluntarily. I guess that made us partners.

I went to the desk, woke the computer, and pulled up a browser. Researching obituaries was nothing new to me, and I remembered the year of the professor's death, which was an advantage. So I felt strangely optimistic as I went to one of my favorite online obit archives and started a search for Carl Ooster-house, date of death, 1941. Maybe it was the familiar territory. Maybe it was the concrete goal.

It didn't take me long to find the obituary, and I started reading the important parts aloud to Carson. "Noted German-American archaeologist Carl Oosterhouse ... emigrated before World War I ... numerous expeditions ... University of Chicago ... blah blah blah stuff we know ..." Then my heart took a dive, along with every hope of solving this problem with a shovel and a bit of nerve.

I must have made a sound or cursed or something, because Carson came to see what I was reading. I pointed to the screen. "... was returning from an expedition to Northern Africa for the purpose of saving as many artifacts as possible from the destruction of war, when the British transport ship was sunk by a German U-boat. All hands and all cargo were lost."

Blessed Saint Brendan. Those poor sailors. I had a short list of ways I would prefer to go—my gift gave me a bit of insight on the subject—and drowning was not on it.

The shipwreck was a dead end for Carson and me, too. "That means no grave to dig up," I said. "Not unless Maguire has a sideline in deepwater salvage."

Carson turned away from me, paced to the toaster, and stared into it, hard enough to brown the bread himself. His arms were braced on the counter, his shoulders tight with frustration.

"Dammit," he said.

"Yeah," I answered. My heart was on the floor and I was tempted to crawl down there and join it.

He turned back abruptly, still vibrating with tension. "Google *deepwater salvage* and *Egyptian artifacts.*"

I supposed a shot in the dark was better than giving up. Pulling myself out of my dejected slump, I typed the terms into the search field.

"There's a lot of hits, but they're really scattershot."

"Add *Chicago.*" I did, and he came back to read over my shoulder, pointing at a news article from the *Chicago Tribune*. The headline: EGYPTIAN MINISTER OF ANTIQUITIES SEEKS RETURN OF SALVAGED ARTIFACTS.

I glanced at him, too close to really focus. "Are you the psychic now?"

He shrugged and continued to read the article. "A hunch. Something lodged in my subconscious."

"What?" I asked, trying not to suspect he was holding back information.

"Something I read a while back." Before I could push for more than that, he gave me the recap of the article. "A deepwater salvage company, funded by a private collector, recovered some artifacts from a shipwreck, one that sounds a lot like what you just described."

"Who's the private collector?" I asked.

He pointed to a name. "It says the Beaumont Corporation. So whoever owns that." I'd rolled the chair to the side to give him a better view of the screen, and me a better view of his face as he read. "But there's no written provenance to say whether the stuff was removed from Egypt before or after it was illegal to do so, and the British have their noses out of joint since the wreck may fall under the underwater war grave protection act..."

"I get it," I said. "Big legal battle. Where are the artifacts now?"

He smiled as if he'd conjured them himself. "On display here in Chicago."

Holy cats, what a lucky break. Maybe too lucky. Maybe too convenient. Maybe I didn't care, if it led to the Jackal, the Brotherhood, and Alexis.

"Are there pictures?" I asked, reclaiming the computer mouse. I clicked on a link (helpfully labeled PHOTOS). The first was of a team working to restore and preserve the items. The next, a picture of the collection in an exhibit. The caption said ON LOAN FROM THE BEAUMONT CORPORATION, and prominently featured, was a large basalt statue of the god Anubis in his animal form.

A black jackal.

So close. Light-at-the-end-of-the tunnel close.

What had the shade said? *Find the artifacts that lie with my bones.* "If that statue sank with Oosterhouse, it *did* lie in his grave—his watery, unmarked one. If it's the one, I'll know as soon as I see it."

"Seeing it is going to be the easy part."

He tapped the banner of the Web page and I understood what he meant. Stealing from the Field Museum was going to be a helluva lot harder than jumping another cemetery wall and digging up a grave.

27

FIRST, WE HAD to case the joint.

"We have to what?" asked Carson, when I'd put it in those words. "Are we in a gangster movie?"

I shrugged. "Outdated slang is sort of an occupational hazard."

We were walking through the park that housed the museum and it was raining—a cold, miserable, umbrella-defeating drizzle that hung in the air and seeped through my clothes. Aunt Gwenda had had too much fun dressing me. I looked like a refugee from an Anthropologie catalog.

To top it off, we'd parked in the farthest possible parking lot.

"Dude," I said, shivering in my raincoat. "What if we need to make a quick getaway?"

Carson gave me the side-eye, one brow raised. "Have I yet failed to provide timely transportation?"

He had a point.

A tunnel under Lake Shore Drive gave a break from the rain, but when we came out the other side, my feet failed me. I could only gaze in awe at the huge—sweet Saint Gertrude, *really* huge—neoclassic home of the Field Museum of Natural History. City-block huge, so large that the far edges of the building's wings disappeared in the misty drizzle.

"Three stories of exhibits," said Carson, stopped beside me as I stared. "More levels of storage below. Over twenty million artifacts, only a fraction on display."

"Stop," I said. "You're making me dizzy." I hoped it was simple intimidation and panic. But that was a lot of artifacts. That was a *lot* of people's history. If only a little bit of it was haunted, I might be in trouble.

"You'll be fine." Ducking under the edge of my umbrella, he put his arm around me and started walking again. "You had a hearty breakfast, a second breakfast, and elevenses. You should be ready for anything."

I decided to accept the encouragement and ignore the teasing as we climbed the stairs—there were a lot of them—and went in. While Carson bought our tickets, I scoped out the steel gates and doors that would seal the museum shut after closing time, not to mention the security cameras with their eagle eyes.

Another day, another museum. I only wished I felt as confident as I had the day before.

This place wasn't just bigger in size. It hummed with a hundred years of visitors and curators and researchers, the living, breathing stuff that was only background noise to my particular psychic channel.

But as for that—I'd *never* felt such an orchestra of remnant sensation. It sang to me, pulled me like gravity, but in all directions. Up, down, sideways. It was so finely tuned, so well balanced, no one part stood out. The harmonic vibration of it made me feel a little drunk.

"Hey," said Carson. "Come back to earth and have a map."

"Thanks." I unfolded it, reading as I trailed behind him. He gave our tickets to a guard and our raincoats and my umbrella to the coat check attendant, all while I got my bearings from the exhibit descriptions on the diagram.

"*The man-eating lions of Tsavo*," I read. "That would be one of the things ringing my bell. The *Grainger Hall of Gems*. Haunted jewelry would do it." Once I identified the things tripping my radar, I felt more secure, knowing what to avoid. "Oh, super. The *Inside Ancient Egypt* exhibit features twenty-three human mummies. That would *definitely* do it."

Carson plucked the map from my hands, forcing me to look around. We stood in a vaulted marble hall that made the twenty-foot totem poles beside me seem like a pair of toothpicks. It looked as long as a football field. Columns lined the first floor, leading to the wings on either side, and above that was a gallery that wrapped around the central space. In the middle were two full-grown elephants—taxidermic specimens, that is—and far, *far* on the other end was a dinosaur.

I may have squealed with excitement.

"Throttle back, Sunshine," Carson said with a laugh.

"I can't help it." I bounced on the balls of my feet in spite of myself. "I *love* the T. rex."

"Of course you do."

The Tyrannosaurus rex skeleton—the most complete ever found, according to the brochure—had been posed as if frozen midrun, her body stretched out, her tail horizontal to balance her gigantic skull and rudder her massive body through the Cretaceous swamp. Her bones had a beautiful fluidity that simulated motion so well, I almost thought I was Seeing her with my psychic senses.

Of course, remnants required a human involved somewhere, and there were no people around when dinosaurs ruled the earth. On the other hand, humans had dug up these fossils and cleaned them and mounted them with dedication and care. She was viewed by millions of people, and even had a name. Sue. Maybe she *did* have some kind of remnant.

But dinosaur bones weren't why we were there. Though just for a moment, I wished they were. I wished Alexis were safe and Maguire were arrested and Carson were happy. I wanted to hold his hand with no ulterior motive, and see if we had anything to talk about if we weren't chasing jackals and running from everything else.

"We should get on with it," I said, squaring my shoulders, at least figuratively.

The museum would have been crowded if it were smaller. It was Friday afternoon, and the place was full of schoolkids on field trips. It was hard to maintain the proper tension levels about the twenty-three mummies while fourth graders raced to the ancient Egypt exhibit, daring each other to descend into the replica tomb.

Mastaba. The proper name for the tomb entrance slid into my mind as if someone had whispered it.

Carson and I let the fourth graders get ahead of us and entered the antechamber of the tomb, hung with slabs of real hieroglyphs that made my vision go double between the then-and-there and the here-and-now.

"You okay?" Carson asked. "Give me a heads-up if you're about to go under."

"I won't go under." At least, I hoped not. Twenty-three mummies in here and, somewhere, an artifact that might transform their remnants into unlimited power. There were only about a hundred or so *other* ways this could go wrong.

The stairs to the exhibit-tomb were authentically dim, but they had inauthentic handrails. Below, the light was faint and I sensed the rustle and flicker of spirit traces, not decently sleeping, as the dead should be, but waiting and watching. Curious about what I was doing there.

That made twenty-four of us.

There was a mummy case at the bottom of the stairs. Wisps of human memory clung to it like cobwebs, brushing pinpricks over my psyche as I passed. *I'm just visiting,* I told anything that remained. *You're safe from me.*

In the next chamber, kids jostled each other, pressing their faces close to see the mummies, dark as old wood, behind the glass. Some were at rest in their cases, some still cocooned in their wrapping. Some were not. One had been unwrapped from the neck up—layers and layers of linen pulled back like swaddling around the man's head, dried skin over hawkish nose and sunken features.

Their remnants endured as a whole, time eroding personality. Their bodies remained, scraps of leather over brown bone, but the individual spirits had melded into one collective consciousness.

Just as well. I gazed at the unwrapped mummy, pretty certain that gawping ten-year-olds weren't what he had in mind when planning for eternity.

Carson tapped my shoulder from behind and I jumped, because I might be all enlightened and respectful of mortal remains, but dude . . . *mummies.* They were always tapping people on the shoulder right before they strangled them.

"Over here," he said. "I think I found it."

Around the corner, the exhibit was set up to look like a preparation room. Murals showed priests readying a body for the afterlife, presided over by the canine-headed Anubis. And in the center, guarding the entrance to the tomb, was the god in his animal form.

A black stone jackal. The basalt statue had a polished gleam and an ageless stare. But was it *our* Black Jackal?

It was on a pedestal with no glass and very dramatic overhead lighting. I glanced around for spectators—a guard and a museum guide were both busy with fourth graders—then flexed my fingers to get my blood flowing. Careful of alarms, I held my hands toward the statue and let my psyche scan its points and curves, reaching toward its stone heart for anything that remained inside.

"Is this it?" Carson asked.

There was certainly power and potential, but it was locked down deep somehow. I answered him slowly. "I expected more of a kick, maybe something from the sailors that died on the same ship only eighty years ago. There's just a faint trace of them."

"But it is the artifact from the news article?" he asked.

"I'm sure." We stood shoulder to shoulder, gazing at the statue like it was the Mona Lisa and we were trying to solve the Da Vinci Code. "What do we do now?" I asked.

Carson ran his eyes over the lean canine shape. "Now we make a plan for how to get it out of here."

"I'm open to suggestions." That was going to take a lot more than a Jedi mind trick. The statue was actually dog-sized. Not Chihuahua tiny, either. Even if we could get it off the pedestal without triggering an alarm, we weren't going to be able to walk out with it in my purse.

"Can we use magic?" he asked, under cover of the kids squealing over the mummies. "The Brotherhood used it to break into that case in St. Louis."

"Yeah, but they had to stab a guard to get the energy for it. That's sort of a deal breaker for the good guys."

Circling the statue, he asked, "Can we use the Jackal itself? Is there an on switch?"

"I don't know," I said. "Let me just look that up in the instruction manual."

Carson glanced at me over the statue's back, calmly intent, reflecting none of my frustration. "Hey. I'm just pitching ideas here. Don't bite my head off."

He was right, and I gave a guilty squirm. "Sorry. I just hate not having the answers." It was painful to be *so close* but still lack the one variable to let me solve for *x*. "Plus, all this"—I waved a hand to encompass the mummies, the museum, all of it—"isn't helping. It's like standing in an electrical field."

"It's okay. Let's just focus on the Jackal." He was right about that, too. "Is any of that electricity coming from the statue?"

I focused my other Sight to look again. "Barely. Which is weird. I wouldn't expect ancient pharaoh, but I should be getting more from the deaths of the crew of the transport ship. Not to mention Oosterhouse."

"No," said Carson, hiding none of his dislike for the professor. "Let's not mention Oosterhouse."

Behind him, one of the field trip teachers wrapped her sweater tighter, glancing around for a draft. The room *had* chilled, so slowly I'd only just noticed it. I didn't fool myself that it was the air-conditioning. Some very real spirit had slipped into the replica tomb.

It didn't come from the crumbling mummies or the artifacts of embalming. This was something familiar.

The shade of Oosterhouse appeared, fading in like breath fogging on glass. He looked exactly like the remnant on the artifact we'd left at the apartment, but he shouldn't have been able to travel so far from it. Yet he looked at me with recognition.

"How are you *here*?" I whispered. "Do you haunt this jackal, too?" No one else—including Carson—reacted to anything but the chill. The shade must be drawing a huge amount of energy to manifest, even to just me.

"You've done it," he said, as jovial as Santa at Christmas, ruddy cheeks flushed above his white beard. His excitement seemed to draw an answering pulse from the jackal. "You've found the part of me that was missing," said Oosterhouse. "I felt it waken, and it pulled me here."

I felt the stirring spirit, then, a remnant of Oosterhouse in the basalt jackal, so faint that I'd only felt the potential of it. How could such a small or dormant trace have the power to bring the other shade to it?

"What's going on?" murmured Carson, close at my shoulder. "You've got a funny look on your face, and I don't like it."

Him and me both.

The teacher rubbed the back of her neck, as if soothing a prickle of unease. She hurried her students along, leaving Carson and me alone with one specter and a collective of ancient shades.

"Oosterhouse is here," I told him, turning to watch the professor move around the room, taking in the dioramas and displays of the mummification chamber with avid curiosity.

Carson looked startled. "I thought you said he couldn't leave the artifact."

"I didn't think he could."

The room kept getting colder and the shade kept getting

stronger, as if the place was feeding him somehow. That was not good. I glanced at Carson and realized with my own shock that he was watching the spirit, too, without any help from me.

"Can you See him?" I asked.

"Yeah." He didn't sound happy about it. "I don't know how."

Oosterhouse finished his perusal on the far side of the stone jackal, standing with his back to us, hands linked behind him as his ghostly gaze roved over the murals and hieroglyphs decorating the replica tomb. "How fortuitous that we should end up here. This shall do nicely."

"Do for what?" I asked, the bad feeling turning into more of a stab of dread.

He seemed buoyant, happy I'd asked. "A sense of ceremony, dear girl."

"What does that mean?" asked Carson. Apparently he could hear as well as see him.

Oosterhouse turned with a condescending smile. "I'll explain slowly, my boy. Try to keep up. You have found the piece of my spirit which lay with my bones. My *ka*. Now only the *akh*, the part waiting in the afterlife, remains."

"You're speaking in riddles," snapped Carson. "Is this the Oosterhouse Jackal or not?"

"What you seek is here." He laid his hand on the jackal's head, fingers spread between the pointed ears. When he shifted his gaze to me, his eyes were dark with feverish intensity. "Keep your promise, *Kebechet*, and I will show you the secrets of the Black Jackal."

"What did you call me?" My breath misted in the air and

frost crept up the glass of the display cases, but it was nothing compared with the cold premonition uncurling in my chest.

"Daughter of Anubis," said the professor, shadowed eyes holding mine. "Protector of the dead. Only you can help me. No one else can do what you do."

"He's playing you, Sunshine." Carson's voice was all gravel and warning. "Don't let your ego make you do something foolish."

Annoyance broke the specter's hold on me, and I turned a scathing glance on Carson. "I'm not an idiot."

Even if what the professor said about me happened to be true. I didn't know anyone who could do what I do.

I gave Oosterhouse my attention once more, but I was back in control. "Tell us how the Jackal works," I said. "Then I'll open the Veil for you to move on."

"You have the book, don't you?" His earnestness rang false. But remnants couldn't lie. "It will tell you all you need to know."

"What book?" I asked, then realized I *was* an idiot. "The Book of the Dead?"

"I know you have it. I can sense it." All sincerity vanished, leaving only the glitter of avarice in the specter's gaze as he pointed to Carson. "He is carrying it now."

I shot a look at Carson, who was coming to the same realization that I had. Alexis hadn't hidden a *clue* to the book or the Jackal. We'd been carrying Oosterhouse's translation of the Book of the Dead all this time.

Carson reached into his pocket, pulling out the mummy-shaped flash drive. "You mean this?" Oosterhouse's gaze seized on it hungrily. "First, the secret of the Jackal."

Something moved behind me in the dark. I whirled, and kept turning as three, then four, then five young men stepped into the replica tomb, blocking all the exits. I recognized two of them, even without the jackal tattoos on their arms.

"Hey, Maguire," said McSlackerson. "Thanks for bringing that flash drive along. I'll just take it off your hands."

"Hey, Johnson," said Carson. "Not arrested yet, huh?"

I ignored the banter, busy trying to figure out what I was Seeing. Cupped in Johnson's fingers was a basketball-sized incandescent glow of raw power. With dawning horror, I realized why there was nothing but a trace of the drowned sailors on the statue. Johnson held them *all*. He had stolen the fire of dozens of deaths—dozens of remnant souls—and he held them between his palms like a balled-up snarl of yarn.

"Carson—" I warned, too late to do him any good.

Johnson pulled free a strand from the tangle and snapped it like a whip. Power made a wave of the air and washed over Carson before he could dodge. His next breath was nothing but a drowning gurgle. He struggled against it, doubled over, and heaved up a spew of dark water that stank of brine and diesel fuel.

"Stop it!" I called up my defenses and lunged toward Carson, trying to get close enough that he could use my shields to push the magic away, out of his lungs. But two of the brethren snatched me by the arms, pulling us apart.

"Give me the flash drive," said Johnson, letting Carson grab half a breath before throwing another thread of drowned spirit at him. Carson dropped to all fours, sputtering salt water from his mouth and nose. But he managed to lift one hand—and one finger—to McSlackerson.

"Carson, you idiot!" I cried, wondering why no guards were coming, wondering why some sort of alarm wasn't going off. "Give it to him!"

The file was encrypted. That would give us time to think of *something*, some world-saving plan. But we couldn't do anything if he was dead.

On his hands and knees, Carson wheezed and spewed. "Alexis first. Where is she?"

Johnson unraveled another thread and spun a darker threat. "You're not in a position to bargain, Maguire. There are a lot of cute little kids in the museum today. They're all eating lunch right now, just on the other side of that wall. Maybe we should see how far this magic will reach."

The next shred of spirit left Carson heaving helplessly on the ground. I wrestled against the guys who held me until I thought my shoulders would pop out of joint.

Oosterhouse whirled to me, so quick, so intense that his form blurred. "Hurry, my girl, and we can save him. If you open the Veil, I can help you."

I didn't question *how* he could do what he said. I couldn't afford to doubt him and be wrong. With herculean effort I pushed back my panic and my tears and found the song inside me that called the curtain between us and eternity. I let my whole soul ring with it.

The Veil was sluggish to answer, and I pushed it, poured my desperation into the ethereal serenade until slowly the air began to shimmer behind the shade of Oosterhouse.

"You must cut my *ka* free from the statue," he said, shouting over the bell-tower racket of my psychic call.

He'd used the word before, and I knew what he meant. I pictured my shadow self unknotting the threads of his silent, weak remnant in the heart of the statue. As they loosed, they blew toward the Veil but met Oosterhouse standing between. There was only one phantom strand remaining tied to the statue as they tangled around his grandfatherly form, sinking in, reuniting....

Reclaiming.

The Veil changed, brightened along the edges with warm yellow light. In the next moment it opened, like a daylit doorway to a tomb. A figure stood silhouetted by the blinding glow, the same shape depicted on the walls around us.

It towered over Oosterhouse's shade. The two figures superimposed and merged as the glare became blinding. The guys holding me let go, and I shielded my eyes as every display case in the room shattered.

Glass rained down and the awful brilliance became red-tinged darkness and ringing silence. When I could see again, the Veil had disappeared, and so had the fusty-looking professor with his neat white beard and khaki kangaroo pockets.

In his place was a jackal-headed god.

"*This* is the thing you seek," he said, in a voice that flooded the room like the Nile. "I *am* the Black Jackal, and now is the end of all things."

28

W HAT. T HE. H ELL.

No one moved. There was only the plink of glass shards falling and the sound of Carson pulling in air like he'd just swum up from the depths of the ocean. The brethren stood slack-jawed, staring at the jackal-headed apparition that loomed larger than life at the head of the preparation chamber.

Then Johnson dropped to one knee. The rest did the same, bowing before the figure of the canine-headed man who used to be Professor Oosterhouse.

This? Was not an improvement in our situation.

"Thank you, my brothers, for remaining true. Your loyalty

will be rewarded." The voice that rolled from the Jackal was the professor's, but shaded with darkness and the resonance of eternity. "What I have, I share with you, and together we will start a new dynasty that will endure age upon endless age."

"Thank you, my lord," said Johnson, lifting his head. The other guys took their cue from him. Their shock had faded to wary awe, and what looked like anticipation and greed.

Carson hauled himself to his feet, staring at the Jackal in disbelief, then turning to me over the heads of the kneeling minions. "Daisy, what did you *do*?"

"Nothing!" I managed a horrified protest. Except I'd obviously done *something*.

"You opened the door to the afterlife and freed me," said the towering figure. "I died a man, with a weak body and powerful knowledge. And I have come back a god."

Wow. Forget the sacrilege. That was some supreme arrogance right there.

Was there really a jackal-headed god standing before us? That was what it looked like to my eyes. But to my Sight, it was Oosterhouse. Not the gray-bearded professor who had talked me into opening the Veil for him, but a younger man. Tanned, blond, and fit—he was bare-chested, wearing the draped linen skirt and heavy gold ornamental accessories of an ancient Egyptian priest or royal.

He pulsed with vitality, and I realized I wasn't looking at a remnant of Carl Oosterhouse. He was too substantial, too *present*. I was looking at the real thing. His spirit. His soul come back from beyond.

That wasn't supposed to happen.

But it had. This was real, and this was really bad.

Johnson rose to his feet and gestured to the others to get up as well. "What should we do with these two?" he asked, meaning Carson and me.

The Jackal Oosterhouse turned to me. "Will you join us, Daisy Goodnight? Think what wonders you could do with your power and ours. I've heard you speaking with young Maguire, and I know you have great ambition for remaking the world."

But I didn't. The world wasn't perfect, but remaking it to my own design wasn't the answer. I wanted to fight the problems, not *be* the problem.

"Bugger off, Professor," I said. His try at temptation had pissed me off, because he'd been playing me all along. And there's nothing this idealist hates more than abuse of her good nature. "If you were a god, you could have opened the door yourself."

He rippled with fury; as solid as he looked, he still had no body. Over the roar of adrenaline in my ears, I heard people coming to investigate the crash. Oosterhouse did, too, and the wave of anger passed, becoming a gloating smile, which was much worse.

"You need proof, my girl?" he said. "I will give it to you, as thanks for your role in reuniting my spirit."

He drew himself up, breathing in the dust of antiquity that swirled out of the broken cases. His figure swelled, his barrel chest expanding. I felt a pull across my psyche, all over, like silk dragged over my skin, and I realized he was drinking in not air but the remnant spirits of twenty-three human souls.

The dust circled him like a vortex, and he gulped it all down, growing larger, brighter. Then he breathed it out again, an impossibly long exhale, blowing life into the desiccated corpses around the room.

They stirred like sticks in a thunderstorm, rattling and trembling, then rising from their sterile museum tombs.

With jerking motions they came, fragile wrappings ripping, trailing like scarves. They peeled off their cocoons of rotting linen and they climbed out of their cases and they pushed open their sarcophagi. The Brotherhood minions scrambled, wide-eyed, out of the way of the animate dead as they shambled out of the chamber to the halls beyond. Children, guards, patrons—their terrified screams rang through the exhibit.

Three of the undead grabbed Carson. They were indomitable—held together not by brittle tendons or dried muscles but by magic. They bloodied his nose and twisted his limbs, and then I lost track, because they came at me.

I stumbled away, horror wrenching a sandpaper shriek from my throat. It wasn't their grasping arms or leathery flesh that terrified me. I didn't dread the touch of dust and ancient bodies but the touch of the spirits trapped inside these abominations that warped everything I believed in.

The undead circled me, and I could feel the shredded souls trapped in the magic that animated them. They'd been rent apart, chewed up, and spit out. Snatched from any hope of the eternity they'd awaited for thousands of years. Transformed by Oosterhouse into a consumable power source.

No—not Oosterhouse. The Black Jackal.

He had Oosterhouse's face, but the eyes burning with power were alien and frightening. He wasn't a god, but he wasn't any remnant of human anymore, either.

"I will give you one more chance," he said as the undead held me bound with bones as strong as oak. "Bow, Daisy Goodnight, and become one of my brethren. I would rather have you freely than enslave your spirit."

Carson fought against the undead that held him immobile with a bony arm across his throat. "Don't you dare, you son of a bitch. Let her go. I'll do whatever—"

He broke off with a wheeze, and for a horrible moment I thought *he* was broken—his neck, his windpipe, or some other vital, fragile thing. But Johnson, stepping forward, had cut off Carson's words with nothing but a gesture.

"Quiet," he said. "You've done your part, Maguire. We don't need anything else from you."

Carson was turning purple from the relentless bony hold on his throat. He tore at the dried flesh and it crumbled under his clawing nails, but the ancient undead wouldn't let go.

How do you fight something that just won't stop?

Use us, Daisy.

I shuddered at the hum that ran through me—the perfectly tuned collective spirit of the place. A century of scientists, academics, archivists, their psychic traces permeating stone and steel and glass until the building itself sang its offer to me. The unified remnant was as fresh as a wellspring amid the muddy magic in the room. I reached for it and it infused me, not with a swelling rush but with a slow seep of support and bracing, ghostly cold that reminded me who I was.

I was Daisy Goodnight. And no lame-ass mummy-raising Boris Karloff knockoff was going to get the better of me.

My Sight found the lines of power that connected the Jackal to the undead that held me. With my new strength, I broke the ties like fragile thread and the mummies collapsed into piles of chunky ash. Magic cut off, the fragile remains could not stand the physical strain.

Johnson turned as if to stop me, but he was startled and I was quicker and shoved him into the wall with only a gesture. A push at the undead that held Carson and they flew apart like piles of leaves in a gust of frigid wind.

Carson sagged, gasping for breath—only for a nanosecond, though, before he charged Johnson, picked him up, and slammed him again into the exhibit wall in a hail of grunts and plaster.

"Where is Alexis?" he demanded, giving him a shake. Johnson fought back, but it was kind of an unfair match.

The Brotherhood goons seemed uncertain whether to rescue Johnson from Carson. As for the rest of the mummies, the only signs of them were the screams from beyond the exhibit.

The Black Jackal just laughed at our struggles. He glowed with power, stolen from the spirits, from the upheaval of terror. "Grab the girl," he told the dithering minions. "And meet me in the place you've prepared."

I couldn't let him vanish. He was still just a spirit, an über-ghost created by the re-joining of remnants and soul. I was responsible for that, and worse, I'd untethered the piece from the stone jackal. I could not let him escape to wreak havoc on all of Chicago or beyond.

With all my strength I grabbed the fabric of Oosterhouse's soul, clutched the shreds of the human being that had made the Black Jackal. I didn't know how to fight a self-proclaimed god, but I knew how to handle pieces of a spirit. By binding the remnants of Oosterhouse to this place, I could leash the creature he'd become.

He seemed to realize what I was about to do. "Stop her," he told his minions. They didn't move, maybe because I didn't *look* like I was doing anything, and the Jackal snapped, "Idiots! Grab her! Knock her out!"

They rushed me, but Carson shoved Johnson into their path, flattening two like bowling pins and linebackering another into an empty mummy case. There were five of them and one of him, and I don't know how he did it, but he kept them off me.

"Whatever you're going to do, Sunshine," he said, slamming the lid of the case and trapping a minion inside, "do it now."

I used every bit of my strength to tie Oosterhouse, and the Black Jackal with him, to the foundation of the gigantic museum itself. I went down to the sublevels, where nerdy scientists spent their days, nights, and happy afterlife. Their remnants were faint but mighty, and they grabbed on and knit the Jackal's essence to the bedrock.

He flailed at the binding, the power of his fury sending his minions staggering. It bought Carson and me a few seconds to get our feet under us. I couldn't remember falling, but as I staggered upright I had cuts on my hands and knees from the shrapnel of the museum display cases littering the floor.

"Come on," said Carson. "Let's get out of here."

I pressed a bloody hand to my aching head. "We have to clear out the museum. I don't know what the Jackal will do to try to get loose. I bound him, but he can still work his magic. And there is a freaking *arsenal* of remnant energy here."

"I don't think clearing the museum will be a problem," said Carson as shrieks continued to echo through the building.

The Jackal realized we were escaping. He spread his arms and the Brotherhood got up, riding a wave of renewed energy. Johnson, whose nose was obviously broken, looked at Carson with murder in his blackening eyes.

"Brethren who bear my mark," said the Jackal, like a priest at an altar, "I am the guardian of the well of souls. What I have is yours. Take it and use it well."

Then he blew another infinite breath, like he had with the mummies, breathing power into the henchmen. Raw power, raw energy ten times more potent than any I had ever felt.

It just kept coming. There didn't seem to be any end to it. Where was it coming from? Not anything in the room, from some bottomless well . . .

I am the guardian of the well of souls.

I shuddered at the idea. Surely that was another over-dramatization.

"Get them," said the Jackal, abruptly pragmatic. "And if you can't bring them back alive, just bring back the book."

The brethren turned toward us. The shared power that the

Jackal had given them crackled like a static field that prickled my skin and raised my hair.

Johnson smirked through his split lip and wiped the blood from his mouth. "With pleasure," he said.

Carson grabbed my arm and started pulling. "Now. We're going *now.*"

I was already moving.

Carson and I ran through exhibit halls, following the trail of undead looters—shreds of ancient linen wrappings caught on toppled signs, a spatter of blood on a torn display. Ahead of us were the screams of terrified children and behind us was the sound of pursuit.

"Come on," said Carson, like I needed to be told twice.

We burst out of the exhibit into a hallway, with Johnson on our heels. I glanced back in time to see him push out his hands, just like he'd pushed the ghost volcano at us before. I flashed on the drowning magic he'd used against Carson, just as a wall of water gushed from nowhere and washed my feet out from under me.

I crashed into Carson and we went tumbling over each other, swept down the hall until we smacked up against a glass case, arms and legs in a sodden tangle.

"We've got to stop meeting this way," I wheezed, after I spit a mouthful of salt water over his shoulder.

"No promises," he said, climbing off me as the wave receded. "Not if we make it out of here."

There was an incentive, if I needed one other than staying alive.

Carson rolled to his feet and helped me up as Johnson stalked toward us, shoes squishing on the wet floor, murder in his eye. The one that wasn't swollen shut.

"How do you like taking orders from a dead man?" I asked him.

"No problem when it's something I want to do anyway." He pushed the air again, and I caught my breath, ready for another flood. But nothing happened. The last deluge had used the remains of *that* ghost magic. Something else was coming.

I waited, braced, until a predatory growl behind me sent a primal jolt of fear through my veins. Carson tensed beside me, and Johnson said, with a sneer marred by his fat lip, "I'll let you run. Just for grins."

A feline roar, close enough to rattle my teeth, put the spurs to my heart and my feet. Carson's, too. But I took enough time to read the sign on the case behind us: MAN-EATING LION OF MFUWE.

Something like a shade pulled free from the sad stuffed and mounted specimen. It shook itself as if waking from a nap, then leapt, passing through the glass and landing on the tile with prowling grace.

I didn't realize I'd gone still until Carson grabbed my arm and pulled me out of shock and into motion. We ran, sliding on salt-water-slick floors, and made it to the stairs. The click of claws on marble pursued us, and I glanced back to see golden-green eyes glowing with stolen power. The outline was hazy, but teeth and talons gleamed. It was a construct of magic and the ghosts of its victims, and it was made for killing.

Taking the stairs two at a time, I kept pace with Carson. "Those claws," he asked as we rounded the landing, "are they as real as they look?"

"I don't want to find out the hard way," I panted. "The volcanic ash was real enough. And the water—"

I broke off. We'd reached the main hall on the first floor, and chaos. I hadn't had time to wonder if the mummies could climb stairs, but now I knew. With no definite instructions, the undead ran amok, chasing sightseers, terrorizing children. Just... grabbing people. And anyone they grabbed, they would Not. Let. Go.

Teachers held off mummies with umbrellas and satchels, trying to get their students to the doors. Security guards shouted over the noise, "Keep calm! Move in an orderly fashion to the exit!" But trying to maintain order was a losing battle.

The lion's claws scrabbled on the stairs. Carson and I split, diving out of the way as the beast leapt into the hall with a roar that shook my bones. It sprang on the nearest thing that moved—a man grappling with one of the undead—and took them both down with one swipe, slashing the man's leg and shredding the ancient corpse like confetti streamers.

The crowd screamed, making a deafening echo in the enormous hall. The panicked rush for the doors accelerated to ramming speed.

"Hey!" yelled Carson, getting the lion's attention. It turned, snarling, away from the easy pickings of the herd in the hall and focused on him with specific intent. "Handle the mummies," he told me, already backing away. "I'll take care of the lion."

He was gone, running full-out for one of the side galleries, before I could ask what he planned to do. I ran for the lion's victim; his blood made a garish arc across the white marble floor, and I pulled off the scarf I wore and tied it around the man's thigh, stanching the dribbles.

"That was a lion." His voice was flat with shock. "And a...a..."

"Yeah," I said. I couldn't see the brethren, but I knew they must be around, keeping the power flowing to the mummies. How else were they still so strong this far from the Jackal?

"Police!" came a shout. "Everyone stay calm and—"

The officer broke off as he got a look at the carnage in the hall. "What the—"

The rest was drowned out by the skull-ringing clang of the security doors on the far side of the hall slamming shut. A moment later the heavy gate of the remaining exit started rumbling down.

A policeman on a radio yelled for someone on the other end to raise the gates. The rest were shouting, "Go, go, go!" and hurrying the wounded through the closing gap to freedom.

"This guy needs help!" I called. An officer and a tourist hoisted the man up and half carried him toward the door. One of the undead marauders lunged after them; the reins of power that tied them to the Jackal and the Brotherhood glowed to my Sight. I was so close I could grab them with my psychic hands and rip them free.

The mummy collapsed, kicked apart an instant later by fleeing feet.

There was a shudder in the web of magic that animated the remains. Slowly, they turned their empty-eyed faces toward me. I'd been spotted. One of the brethren must have given them new orders.

At least they abandoned the innocent bystanders. Some part of me registered guards and police helping the shocked patrons to the exit, but most of me only had eyes for the undead that were backing me toward the towering skeleton of the tyrannosaur.

There were so *many* of them. My psyche couldn't reach all of them—

Unless I let them get really, really close.

"Daisy!"

I thought I heard my name, shouted from amid the melee of escapees near the doors, but between the screaming and the yelling and the grinding of the gears on the security doors, I couldn't be sure, and I couldn't take my attention from the advancing undead to look.

There'd been a shift in the magic around the walking dead, the ropes of power thinning to mere puppet strings. I wouldn't have a better chance to shut them down. I hauled up the strength to slam closed a psychic door between the Jackal and the mummies, cutting them off from his control, freeing their abused bodies.

Without magic to knit them together, they crumbled and cracked. Dry, brittle bone and parched flesh turned to rubble and dust around me.

"Those were priceless! Priceless artifacts!" A hysterical woman in a business suit came out of hiding, fueled by outrage.

"They were more than that," I said, too shaky from the effort to be angry. "They were people."

The woman was accompanied by a guy in a lab coat and a woman in glasses. Nerd types, straight from central casting. "Forget that, Margo," said Lab Coat. "Let's get out of here."

With an almighty clang, the security doors slammed closed. Margo screamed, then shrieked again when another handful of stragglers, led by a security guard, emerged from one of the exhibit wings.

"You didn't make it out, either?" asked the guard.

I let the others answer him, and started worrying about Carson. He'd seemed like he knew what he was doing when he ran off, but he'd been gone so long—

A lion's furious growl rolled out of the wing to my right. I spun toward it—and then whirled again as another roar answered the first. The sounds echoed through the huge hall, but it was unmistakably a second animal.

"That came from the African hall," said a woman with glasses.

"How many man-eating lions are *in* this place?" I asked.

"Three," she said as our band of stragglers clustered together. "One from Mfuwe and two from Tsavo."

Margo screamed again as the first lion, looking bigger and toothier than ever, burst from the hall of Ancient Americas. Behind him came the glowing shades of a half-dozen ancient Americans, each carrying a spear capable of taking down a woolly mammoth.

Limping behind them, holding a spear of his own, was Carson. As the clan of the cave bear drove the snarling beast toward one end of the Great Hall, he backed toward us, keeping the tribesmen in his eye line.

"Good to see you," I said—a massive understatement, but I didn't want to break his concentration. "You found some friends."

He nodded without taking his gaze from the anthropological apparitions. "So did you. What's the situation?"

I glanced at the tight knot of stragglers. "Trapped like rats, I think."

"No service?" Margo tapped her cell phone with rising hysteria. "How can there be no service?"

Lab Coat just looked at her. "How can there be *mummies?*"

"They know people are trapped inside," said the security guard. He meant to be reassuring. But my "they" was different from his. The world outside knew we were here, but so did the Brotherhood.

A prowling growl from the shadows raised the hair on the back of my neck. No one screamed this time; they all froze with a collective held breath.

"I don't think we can hold them all off like this," said Carson, meaning him and me. "We need a place that we can fortify and make a plan."

"But where?" I whispered. "This place is full of things that are full of spirits."

"What about the library?" asked Glasses Lady. She wore a staff ID badge, but I couldn't see her name. "There's a landline, and the reading room locks. And if things get really bad, the rare book vault is hermetically sealed and impenetrable."

"Sounds good," said Carson. "Daisy, take the lead to feel out anything in the way. I'll follow—I can at least keep the big lion at bay for a minute or two."

"Who put the kids in charge?" demanded an old guy with "retired tourist" written all over him. He and the woman with him were the only ones of the seven not wearing museum badges.

"Do you have a better idea?" asked a quiet man with a Morgan Freeman soul patch. "I, for one, refuse to be done in by a scientific impossibility."

"Then let's go," said the security guard, and we started for the stairs, the snarls of the lions snaking after us.

I prayed I wasn't leading everyone from the frying pan to the fire. Remnants respected certain barriers . . . but these weren't ordinary shades. These were weapons made of spirit, memory, and magic.

Please, God, don't let me be the scientific impossibility that does us all in.

29

AS WE MADE our breathless way to the third floor, Glasses Lady introduced herself as Marian. Marian the Librarian. Once the nine of us—the security guard and Carson bringing up the rear—had filed into the large reading room, Marian pulled her key card from under her sweater, ran it through a reader next to the door, then entered a code, locking us in.

It seemed like an electronic lock would be particularly easy to undo with magic. But I was just guessing. Until two days ago, I hadn't thought magic could materialize stuff out of thin air. Maybe a physical lock wouldn't make any difference.

The security guard—his name tag said SMITH—went directly to a phone on the desk and punched in a number. Besides him and Marian, there were Lab Coat, Soul Patch, Margo the administrator, and the retired couple, all anxiously watching Smith, waiting for word of rescue from outside the museum.

"Bad news," he said as he hung up. "There's some sort of problem with the computer that controls the locks. We're stuck here for a little while."

Carson pointed to the door. "Is this lock controlled by the same computer?"

"Hey," said Lab Coat, "if they hacked the computer to bring down the security gates, they could open this one."

"Who are *they*?" asked Margo.

"Whoever's behind the mummies rising and stuff," said Lab Coat, almost laid-back in comparison with the administrator's tightly wound hysteria. "Someone's got to be, right?"

The question was half rhetorical, half aimed at Carson and me. Instead of answering, Carson propped the spear he was carrying against the wall and gestured to one of the massive library tables. "Let's move this in front of the door."

It took four of us to get the barricade in place, which seemed to make everyone feel better. Everyone but me. Walls seemed so flimsy next to the power I'd felt from the Jackal and his minions.

Going on instinct, I climbed onto the table so I could put my hands on the wall near the electronic lock. I'd kept a thin trickle of contact with the museum's ghosts, but the connection swelled in a rush of approval when I focused my intent on protection. The collective remnant pulsed through the walls like the building's own psyche; it took only a little direction from me to shield this room from spirit animal attack. I felt the defenses take hold, almost like a change in the air pressure in the room, and I let myself take one long breath of relief.

"Okay," I said to Carson, who I sensed standing protectively close as I worked. "I'm not sure it will hold against the Jackal if he goes thermonuclear, but it should keep the minions and their magic out."

Carson cleared his throat and I turned to find our whole band of refugees staring at me, eyes full of questions. "Maybe it's time for you two to tell us what's going on here," said Smith.

The Goodnight ability to make fantastic things sound reasonable saved a lot of hassle, but took some faith, because you just had to jump in with the truth. So I did, keeping it simple: "Evil secret brotherhood. Raising the dead. Taking over the world."

They stared at me for such a long moment that I wondered if the Goodnight charm had failed me. Then Soul Patch said, "Is that all? Secret brotherhoods have been trying that since the beginning of time."

"If we're going to be here a while," said Marian the Librarian, "I have an electric kettle and instant coffee in my desk."

The group dispersed. Except for Carson, who offered a hand to help me down from my perch on the table. He kept his voice a low rumble, and a bemused smile hinted at one devilish dimple. "You are impressive, Daisy Goodnight."

"Yes, I am," I said through my blush.

He grinned. "I wish I'd met you in a normal week."

I snorted to cover another flustered rush of heat. "In a normal week, we never would have met."

The others had clustered around one of the library computers. "Come look at this," said Lab Coat. There was a breaking-news Web page with the headline HOSTAGE CRISIS AT NATURAL HISTORY MUSEUM. HALLUCINOGENS USED TO CAUSE PANIC.

"Hallucinogens," Carson said, reading over Lab Coat's shoulder. "That's the story they're going with?"

"Just wait." Lab Coat switched to a grainy video of the patrons running from blurry, dark figures, and one really good shot of my face as the mummies converged on me. "You're a YouTube sensation!"

"Awesome," I said, not feeling awesome about it at all. "Famous on the Internet." Then a detail from the news site's splash registered in my brain. "Go back to the main story for a sec."

When he did, I scanned quickly, finding the line right away. *FBI agents already on the scene.* So it was more than possible I hadn't imagined someone calling my name in the chaos. Since Taylor had Johnson's name, he could have tracked him back to Chicago.

First things first. I turned to Carson and held out my hand. "Flash drive." FBI or police, sooner or later, someone was going to send in a SWAT team to rescue the hostages, and that would be the end of my chance to put an end to the Black Jackal. I *had* to figure out how to do that before he worked loose of my binding or I got arrested.

Carson dropped the drive into my palm. It seemed to have

faired well even after we'd gotten drenched. The plastic case was damp, but under that it was totally dry.

Marian had straightened from the YouTube watching and stepped over to watch us instead. "What do you need?" she asked.

"Answers," I said.

"Well," she said, with a hint of a smile. "This *is* a library. So we came to the right place."

Finally a glimmer of hope.

Right before the lights went out.

30

THE GOOD NEWS? There was still emergency lighting. It cast the room in a garish red glow, and Smith explained that the security system was on a different power grid. Or something. All I knew was it wasn't completely dark and the doors were still locked. The psychic defenses were still in place, too.

The bad news was we were cut off, trapped without phone, Internet, or Coca-Cola. Every once in a while we could hear a far-off bang, and Margo would fret over something else being broken. Stranger still, I could feel subtle, earthquakelike shifts in the psychic atmosphere, deep in the infrastructure of the building, as the Jackal tried to get free.

A rumble echoed from below, and Margo groaned in harmony. "Please don't let it be Sue," she whispered like a mantra. "Don't let it be Sue...."

"She is seriously worried about that dinosaur," I whispered to Marian.

The librarian glanced at Margo with sympathy. "Sue may be one of the most valuable things in the museum. She's truly one of a kind."

"Let's focus," said Carson, drawing me back to the current task. I sat in front of the librarian's laptop, where we'd plugged in the flash drive and were trying every password we could think of. Fortunately the computer had a full charge.

Not only were we trying words in English, but we tried them all in Spanish, French, Italian, Latin, Arabic, and Greek (ancient and modern), thanks to Marian and Soul Patch, whose name was Fred.

"How do you say 'Black Jackal' in Egyptian?" I asked, feeling like we were missing something obvious.

Fred considered the translation. "Try 'Kemet Sab.'"

I did. Nothing.

Carson had been standing behind me, leaning over to see the screen. He straightened, rubbing his shoulder. I was sure it was one of many bruises. "This is crazy. For all we know, it could be some random string of numbers or letters. And time is running out."

Lab Coat started whistling the theme to *Jeopardy!* Carson shut him up with a knife-edged glare. "That's not helping."

"Chill," I said, trying to hide my own nerves. "I know you're worried about Alexis. I'm worried about the city of Chicago. These people are worried about getting out of here. We're *all* worried."

He didn't apologize, but he did compose himself. Not that I'd go so far as to say *chill*. "Okay. What languages haven't we tried?"

Fred suggested, "German. A lot of Egyptology papers are written in German."

So we started trying things in German, except now *I* had the theme from *Jeopardy!* stuck in my head. I'd never even asked how Alexis had done on the contest—

My fingers stilled on the keyboard as one half of my brain slapped the other half for being an idiot.

"What's wrong?" Carson asked.

"*Jeopardy!*" I said. "Your answers must be given in the form of a question."

I typed into the password field: *What is the Black Jackal?*

A new window telescoped open, filling the screen. I crowed in triumph, and Marian and Fred jumped from their seats and crowded in to see.

My bubble of victory popped. "It's in hieroglyphs."

Fred turned the laptop to get a better look. "Not hieroglyphs. It's hieratic. A sort of transitional stage between picture writing and cursive-type writing called demotic. Hieratic was the language of the priests." He followed the first line of text with his finger. "Ah yes. This is a Book of the Dead."

"So you can read this?" Carson asked, sounding hopeful.

Fred shook his head as he scrolled down. "I recognize the opening passages. A proper translation of the details and specific semantics would take months. At least."

A groan rumbled through the room, and it wasn't from me. Though it could have been. The sound came from far below us, like the protest of a gigantic radiator.

What were the Jackal and his minions doing down there? The more time we spent here, the more time they had to fortify and prepare for whatever they were planning.

While Fred studied the document on-screen, I turned to Carson. His expression was stoic, but I could feel the tension in him. "When you asked Johnson about Alexis," I asked softly, "what did he say?"

"Nothing." He scrubbed a hand over his tired face. "But I get the feeling she's close. I can't explain how."

"You don't have to explain it to me." I wished I were the type who could take his hand and comfort him, or that he were the type to invite sympathy. But all his walls were up, so I went back to the matter of the book.

This was one of those times when some Harry Potter—esque magic would be helpful, if I could just wave a wand and say some faux Latin and the words would realign themselves on the page. But I doubted even mad scientist Phin could pull that out of her bag of tricks.

A lightning bolt of an idea goosed me out of my slump, so abruptly that I startled a shriek out of Margo. No, not Phin. That was the wrong Goodnight to ask.

Turning to Marian, I said, "I need a book."

"Well, I *am* a librarian." She pointed to her glasses and bun.

Casting back through the week that I'd lived in the past twenty-four hours, I recalled the title I wanted. "*Female Pioneers in Archaeology.* Or something like it. I need pictures of women archaeologists of the nineteen thirties."

"Ancient Egypt is nine-three-two," she said, giving the reference number. "I can't be more specific because the catalog is all on our mainframe, and that's down with the power."

See? Sometimes you *needed* drawers full of manila cards.

Marian found a flashlight in her desk, and Carson insisted on going back into the stacks with me. As if I had the least interest in going there by myself. In the reading room with the others, there was an illusion of security. The looming shelves of books were dark and cold, and the emergency lights didn't reach into the corners. I stuck so close to Carson that I could feel his body heat.

"You really think you can call up your aunt Ivy from a picture in a book?" he asked. I hadn't told him what I'd planned, but I didn't suppose it had been hard for him to guess.

"I'm going to try." For a moment there was just the sound of our steps on the tile floor. With the others around, we hadn't had time to debrief or compare notes. "How did you manage to raise the shades of those Neanderthal warriors?"

"Desperation." He shone the flashlight at the end of each row of shelves, looking for the 900s.

"I suppose the fact that the Brotherhood was here and waiting for us supports your theory that they knew all along where the Jackal was. Or rather, the artifacts they needed to raise him."

"And now we know why they needed you," Carson said, with no hint of *I told you so*.

"To open the Veil." A knot of emotions twisted in my chest, all having to do with how stupid I'd been. "I can't believe Oosterhouse played me that way."

"I did say I didn't trust him."

There it was. The *I told you so*. I stopped in the aisle, in spite of the dark. "But remnants cannot lie! They *can't*."

Carson stopped, too, and though I couldn't see him well, I thought he softened a bit. "Well, he didn't lie, did he? You opened the door to the afterlife, and he sure as hell showed us the Jackal."

I clenched my fists in front of me, like Oosterhouse was standing there. "I'd like to wring his ghostly neck. He had a lot of nerve abusing my secret idealism that way." A thought occurred to me. "Do you think he heard the whole conversation on the train, and only pretended he'd been awakened just before morning?"

"You're the spirit expert." He studied me for a long moment. "When the Jackal pointed out how much good you could do if you joined them, were you tempted at all?"

"I'm *already* doing good." I believed that with conviction. At least, on the whole, even if I had screwed the pooch by opening the Veil for Oosterhouse. "And what he actually said was 'remake the world.' Not even I am arrogant enough to think I have any business doing that."

"But we have the book," said Carson. "And it must be important or they wouldn't still want it. It has to be the key to their power." He caught my hand, and I felt a tingle, like when our abilities meshed. "If we could use the secrets in the book, think of how much *more* good you could do. You wouldn't just solve murders after the fact. You could stop them from happening. Keep more people from being hurt or killed."

Back in his aunt's kitchen, we'd talked about finding the Jackal and using it—if it had turned out to be a powerful artifact and not a megalomaniac überghost—to rescue Alexis. But Carson seemed to be talking about something different.

"This power uses up spirits, Carson. There's nothing good about that."

"Until we translate the book, we won't know if it *has* to. Your affinity for spirit energy and my ability to channel power into magic might get around that."

"Yeah," I said slowly. His reasoning was more tempting than anything the Black Jackal had put before me, but that didn't make it right. "I could also sprout wings and fly. But I'm not holding my breath."

"Even with what happened to your parents?" he demanded. "What if you could stop that happening to someone else? What if you could take that guy who killed them and boot him into an early hell?"

"*What if?*" I echoed. I wanted to be shocked or offended by the idea, except that I didn't have room to throw stones in my glass house. "You think I haven't worked out exactly how I could shove Mom and Dad's murderer through the Veil? But that's not my job."

"Right. St. Gertrude. I forgot." He turned away, taking the flashlight and turning to search for the female archaeologist book. "But I'm just the son of a crime lord."

The gravel in his voice knocked the wind out of me. How could I not have heard it before? That when he said "your parents" he really meant "my mother"? I *was* an idiot.

"Carson..."

"Forget it." He ran the flashlight beam over the spines, reading titles. "Let's just find your aunt."

Deal with ghosts long enough and you know when to push the stubborn ones. "Do you know who murdered your mother?"

"Of course I do," he said, like we were talking about who fumbled the ball in last night's baseball game. "Devlin Maguire ordered her killed so he could raise his son in his own image. Especially since the kid had some pretty useful talents. And just to make sure the kid follows orders, he finds a witch to put his mother's soul in a jar that he can keep in his desk."

Horror washed cold over me. A helpless, trapped soul was more wretched than I could imagine. But it was the flat ribbon of Carson's voice, the grief and anger ironed out of it by time and helplessness, that cinched the strings of my heart so tight it was hard to breathe. "Why didn't you *tell* me?"

His gaze swept over my face, his own expression closed, all business. "Because you would look at me like that. Like one of your lost souls. I'm not. I don't need your pity."

"No." Except *yes*, more than ever. "But you do need my help."

"Yeah." He dropped a book into my hands; I only caught it by instinct. "I need you to translate that computer file so we can use it to rescue Alexis and vanquish this son of a bitch."

I clutched the book to my chest. "You're choosing *now* to push me away? We need to stay a team, Carson."

He folded his arms and gave me nothing. "We are. We're a great team, Daisy. I would never have gotten this far without you."

"Trapped in a library by man-eating lions and a self-appointed demigod in the basement?"

He laughed, then tried to pretend he hadn't. "Well, maybe not."

"So... all the rest of... everything?" I hated myself for blushing, for not being able to say *kissing* out loud. "That was just to win me over?"

His shrug might have been convincing two days ago. "I told you at the beginning. I am not a nice guy."

"Keep telling yourself that," I said, already mad and boiling up to furious. How dare he let me glimpse into his soul and then slam the door. "Because I told *you* at the beginning, I think you lie to yourself more than anyone."

"That's what criminals do."

"Do you think I would be working with you if I thought that was all you were?"

"Yes. Because you're sworn to find Alexis, and you're determined to stop the Brotherhood and the Black Jackal."

"I would have figured out some other way."

"Right. With your darling Agent Taylor."

"Exactly." It was a jab at him, and I knew it. There was no

comparison between the two—talk about apples and oranges—but Carson seemed sensitive on the subject, so I used it, because I could be a jackass, too.

If he flinched he didn't show it. He just put a finger on the book I held clutched to my heart. "Translate the computer file, Sunshine. And when this is over, you can go back to solving mysteries with your rookie G-man and putting ghosts to rest with your wacky family and forget all about me."

I hadn't gotten as far as thinking about when this was over. But at least he was confident we would succeed. A lot more confident than I was, about that or anything else. Especially that bit about forgetting him.

But what I said aloud was "Fine."

And he said, "Fine."

"I'll go get started," I warned, giving him the chance to call me back and fix this, to make me stay so he could explain why he was working so hard to be a jackass.

He did none of those things. He just said, "So go."

So I did.

31

BACK IN THE reading room, I put the book on the table next to Marian's laptop, determined not to let emotional distractions interfere with what needed to be done. But it wasn't that easy.

Carson, usually steady as a rock in his own rebel-with-a-cause way, was all over the place. The psychic tenor that ran through the building kept shifting, like tectonic plates, which did not make me feel better about whatever was going on outside the room. And without the power on, it had gotten really cold.

The rest of the group was in the librarian's office, where it was warmer, and Lab Coat was trying to see if he could connect

307

a laptop to the security camera feed, even with the main power off. Marian had wanted to stay, but I warned her she wouldn't see much.

So it was just me and Carson. Nothing awkward about that.

Once I'd found Aunt Ivy's picture, I propped the book open on the table and rubbed my hands together to get the blood back into my chilly fingers. "Ready?" I asked, and looped Carson in with my psyche, the way I had with Oosterhouse in the apartment.

"Ready," he said, and got out of the way to let me work.

The picture was black-and-white, showing Ivy with her hair pulled into a braid, her foot braced on a rock, an artifact in one hand and a trowel in the other. But I pictured her in color, as I'd seen her at the Institute museum.

I focused on our similarities, on the links we shared in the chain of our DNA. I called to any remnant I could reach by any stretch of imagination. I pulled as if I could bring her all the way from 1932, and despite the cold, a sweat of effort stung my cuts and scrapes.

After all that, my aunt appeared with staggering abruptness, like I'd yanked with all my might on a door that hadn't been locked. I caught myself on the table as Ivy, looking exactly as she had before, glanced around, getting her bearings. I was ready to introduce myself all over again to this new shade, but when she saw me, recognition lit her face.

"Daisy! Good grief. You look awful."

"It's been a rough couple of days," I said, wondering how to even start to explain.

"Did you find it?" she asked urgently. "The Jackal? Did you get to it before the Brotherhood?"

"How did you know—" The question confused me, and not just about how to answer it. "Are you the same shade from the Institute?"

"Of course," she answered impatiently. "Don't sound so surprised. Goodnights go where they're needed. I told you: you're never alone."

I didn't know how to wrap my head around that. And she was waiting on my answer to her question. "It's really complicated. The Jackal isn't a thing . . . Well, I'm not sure what it is, exactly, I just know that everything is a huge mess and it's my fault and I have to make it better."

The words came out in a guilty rush. I hadn't just been naive. I'd been overconfident, so sure I knew everything, could handle any spirit. I'd created this situation by playing into Oosterhouse's hands, and all I'd been able to do since was plug holes on a sinking ship.

Ivy's shade walked through the table and laid her hands on mine. Sensation raced up my skin and sank into the heart of me. Reassurance. Willpower. Permanence. A steady foundation in a rocky world. "Anything you need is yours. You have generations of Goodnights at your back, Daisy. More than you know."

While I still reeled from that, she stepped back and dusted off her hands in a down-to-business way. "Now. What do we have to work with?"

Feeling more confident—except for the part where I realized Carson had heard all of that—I told her, "We have the Book of the Dead. Oosterhouse's book. At least, I'm pretty sure." I gestured to the laptop, where hieratic writing filled the screen. "Can you read it?"

She leaned in, fascinated by the computer. "What wonder is this! Is it some sort of electronic tablet?"

"Not exactly, but we have those, too. It *is* electronic, though. The writing is stored inside."

"Hmm." She tapped a finger against her cheek. "Ordinarily, it might take a few days. But let me see...."

Before I could stop her—remnants and electronics don't always mix well—she placed her hand *inside* the laptop. The screen flickered and flashed, and the picture writing scrolled upward, faster and faster until it was nothing but a blur of pixels.

The blur became swirls and fractals and finally resolved into letters. English letters. Ivy staggered back, her image wavering. I reached to steady her, and the air she occupied was frigid.

Carson had sat back to let me work, but at that he straightened, as if he would help. "What's wrong?" he asked.

"Everything," Ivy answered him, her voice still weak. "With the secrets in this book, one could achieve what the pharaohs only dreamed of—innumerable worshippers, eternal power, and eternal life."

"How?" I asked, giving her as much of my strength as I could. "I've guessed at some of it, but until I know exactly what's happened, I can't undo it."

She sat in one of the chairs, as if she had substance. "The soul, according to ancient Egyptian afterlife beliefs, has three parts: the *akh*, which journeys to the afterlife; the *ka*, which remains in the burial tomb; and the *ba*, which can fly about and pay calls and such."

"Okay." That sounded at least a little like my understanding of remnants, except the flying-around part.

Ivy nodded to the computer. "This Book of the Dead contains a ritual that allows one's *akh* to come back from the afterlife, and by rejoining with the other parts, become a creature of both worlds, able to call on the power of the dead to work magic."

"What about the Brotherhood?" Carson asked. "Where do they fit in?"

Ivy tilted her head to study him before she answered. "The deceased needs a priest and acolytes to help him reunite his spirit. Since he is, after all, deceased. Whoever bears the mark of the pharaoh—though really it could be anyone with enough riches and power to rate acolytes—holds a share of this power."

"Ha!" I slapped my hand on the table. "It *is* magic tattoos."

Carson didn't quite roll his eyes. "But the Brotherhood have been doing magic since we met them in the cemetery."

Ivy might not know what he meant exactly, but she seemed to follow well enough. "The mark gives some small power, but the more pieces of the pharaoh's spirit the priest possesses, the more easily he and the acolytes can work magic. Which I'm sure comes in handy when doing the master's bidding."

Then she looked at me and asked the question I'd been dreading. "How many pieces of the Jackal do the Brotherhood have?"

"All of them." There was no sense in hiding it. "The shade of Oosterhouse—his *ba*, I guess—tricked me into opening the Veil for him."

Carson spoke up, surprising me. "It wasn't her fault. She was trying to save me."

Ivy's image wavered with alarm. "It doesn't matter why. It matters what he and his acolytes can do now. Where is he?"

"On the first floor, in the Egypt exhibit," I said. "I managed to bind him, but the Brotherhood have us trapped in here."

"You must keep them from getting the book. If the Jackal gets loose, he can draw on all the ghosts in Chicago for power. And if he completes the ritual, he can go anywhere, have access to all the souls in history."

I fell into a chair, vividly recalling Phin telling me we live in a finite world. But all the souls in history? Maybe not infinite, but that would make little difference to the people he would rule.

"How can we stop that from happening?" I asked.

She considered the question grimly. "You have him bound. You could entomb him and leave him for later generations to deal with."

I rubbed my pounding head. "I don't think the city of Chicago would be thrilled with my collapsing their nice museum on him. So entombing isn't really doable."

"Then we have to think of something else," she said. "The book has instructions for unbinding the Jackal's *ka* from his grave. That can only be done once the spirit is rejoined. You didn't do that, did you?" When I shook my head—I'd only had the grave remnant half untied from the Anubis statue—she looked relieved. "Then I'll wager his acolytes are preparing for that ceremony, hoping it will work on your new binding as well."

"And once it's unbound?" asked Carson. "What then?"

"The reborn pharaoh is still just spirit," she explained. "He needs a body. The last step of the ritual will transfer the binding from the tomb to a living person. A host."

"Like possession?" Carson asked, more calmly than I would have managed.

Ivy paused, as if reviewing the text in her mind. "Even with a perfect translation, this subject matter is esoteric. But there's more a connotation of a symbiotic partnership."

Whatever Carson was thinking, it etched a deep V between his brows. "So the host would have the Jackal's power?"

I didn't want to let it get that far. "What if I sent his spirit back beyond the Veil?" It seemed an awfully simple solution.

"That might work." She seized the idea with growing enthusiasm. "The book warns that the gods would be jealous of a new brother and might try and cast him back to the afterlife. Rending and sundering of spirit flesh was mentioned."

"That sounds promising," I said.

"But you'd have to do it before he's bound to a host, or more than spirit might be torn asunder." Her frown deepened even more. "If the Jackal knows you can open the Veil, you're in terrible danger, Daisy. You are the biggest threat to him. And the biggest prize. If he kills you, he might be able to take your power over the gate to the afterlife. And then…"

And then the Jackal would not be confined to the spirits on this side of the Veil. Not just all the remnants in history, but all the souls in eternity. What was more infinite than that?

"That's not going to happen," said Carson. I didn't know if he meant the raiding of the afterlife or the possibility of the

Jackal sending me there. When he used that steely voice, I really didn't care. We stood apart, but his conviction warmed me.

Ivy measured him with a long look, but didn't say anything. She didn't have a chance before Lab Coat popped his head out of the office door.

"Hey, guys," he said. "You might want to come look at this. Either we're about to get rescued, or things are about to get weird."

Carson and I exchanged glances and headed for the librarian's office. Halfway there, I realized Ivy was following, and turned back.

"Aunt Ivy," I began, aware that Carson had paused as well, watching the exchange. I thought about dropping the psychic connection that let him hear Ivy, but worried that would put another pebble in the shoe of our limping partnership. "You know it's really dangerous for you here, right? These guys can zap you like that." I snapped my fingers.

She grinned. "I'm just a scrap of spirit, Daisy. My soul is safe in the beyond and I have no body to damage. But even if I did, my place would be with you."

My hero worship was in danger of turning into real affection.

In Marian's office, the band of nerds was clustered around the other working laptop, but they moved back as Carson and I came in. Margo was already wrapped in the afghan from the office couch, but she shivered when Aunt Ivy slipped through the wall.

When I was dead, I wanted to be like Ivy, the type of remnant who made my own doors.

We huddled around the screen for information the way castaways huddle around a campfire for warmth. Lab Coat had managed to hack into the security camera feed using his own brand of techie magic. The picture was sepia with night and blurry with rain, but I could see a helluva lot of cars, vans, and flashing lights.

"What are we looking at?" asked Carson.

"This is the drive outside the north entrance of the museum," said Smith, pointing to the screen. "This is the police, the armed response team, news crews, and—"

"And the FBI," I finished. I recognized Taylor's profile and Gerard's bulldog tenacity. They were standing side by side, watching a big, black car pull into the drive behind the police barricade. It parked, and about fifty cops and detectives went over to it.

Devlin Maguire climbed out of the limo. Proof that my psychic powers don't include premonition.

"What is *he* doing here?" I couldn't fit him into my mental jigsaw puzzle. But there he was, big as life, unmistakable from the cut of his perfectly tailored raincoat to the size of his charisma. I even caught a glimpse of platinum blond near his shoulder before the reporters engulfed him. It appeared that he'd brought his pet witch, Lauren.

The news camera lights made him stand out even in the security video feed. Maguire looked like a president taking a press conference. There was no sound, but he made confident, reassuring gestures to the reporters, while Taylor, Gerard, and half the police force waited on him to finish.

I glanced at Carson to see if he was as surprised as I was. I couldn't tell, because he'd gone to that cool, impassive facade he wore around his father.

The man who'd had his mother murdered.

"Maybe this is good news," I said, then felt stupid when he cut his gaze to me, his subtext clear: How could this possibly be good news? "Alexis must be here, in the museum somewhere. The FBI could have come with Taylor, but Maguire wouldn't be here unless the kidnappers called him."

At Carson's continued stare, I realized my error. "Or he could be worried about you," I said, just babbling now. But how *did* you tactfully navigate such a screwed-up family dynamic?

"He's not here because of me," Carson said grimly, but he didn't explain more than that.

"So who *is* that?" Marian asked. "It's not the mayor, though you'd think so from the press."

"Why . . . that's Devlin Maguire!" exclaimed Margo, leaning into the screen. "He is a *major* contributor to the museum, and has come to a number of our gala events with his sister, Gwenda, who is on the fund-raising board." She glanced at me, and showed she had been paying attention to more than the moans and groans from the floor below. "I believe Mr. Maguire is a shareholder in the Beaumont Corporation, who loaned us the basalt Anubis statue—the black jackal that you've been so interested in."

Hold. The. Phone.

I reeled at the implications of that and turned to Carson,

more baffled than accusing. "Did you *know* that? Is that why you remembered that article about the deep-sea recovery?"

"That's how I came across the article," he admitted. "Doing paperwork."

His tone was too careful. There was more, and when it connected, I thought my brain would short-circuit. "Does that mean that Maguire knew what the Oosterhouse Jackal was all along?"

Carson gazed back at me levelly. "The problem with you, Sunshine, is that you are so honest, you never expect anyone to tell you a lie."

"Did *you* know what the Jackal was?" I asked, my voice cracking. I knew there were other people in the room, was aware of them pretending not to listen, but they seemed very far away.

"No. I had no idea." A chink opened in his armor, and a little bit of last night's Carson came out. "You don't have any reason to believe me, of course."

True. But he also didn't have any reason to lie at this point. And I had more important things to do than burst into tears or kick his ass. Or kick his ass and *then* burst into tears.

The phone on the librarian's desk rang. Everyone stared at it like a piece of alien technology. "When did the phone start working again?" asked Marian.

"I don't know," said Smith, picking up the receiver. He listened for a moment, then held it out to me. "For you."

I was, I suppose, expecting it to be Taylor. I managed not to fall over when I heard Devlin Maguire's voice rumbling through the line.

"Miss Goodnight," he said, "I am reliably informed that my daughter is inside that building. You have discharged your duty by leading us here—though perhaps with more drama than I would have liked."

At his words, the rope of obligation fell loose from my psyche. I'd become so accustomed to the constant tension, I swayed a little before regaining my footing. "Reliably informed by whom?" I cared less about the geas and more about seeing Alexis safe. "Did they say where?"

"That is no longer your concern."

His dismissal made me angry and distance made me brave. I turned my back on the room and hissed into the phone. "I know you knew about the Oosterhouse Jackal the whole time that Alexis has been in danger. Now she's in here with a bunch of madmen. You should value your family a little more, Mr. Maguire."

I was looking at him on the computer when I said it. I don't know how he knew—how did he know we were in the library in the first place?—but he raised his gaze to the security camera and looked right back. "Our business is done for now, Miss Goodnight. Please, if you would be so kind, put my son on the line."

At that casual "for now," I bridled my anger and handed the phone to Carson without further comment. It was a short conversation, consisting of only single syllables on Carson's end before he hung up the phone and addressed the library refugees.

"The, er, terrorists occupying this building have agreed to let you go. The police are going to send the armed response team up the fire stairs to come get you. Stay put until they get here."

"Terrorists?" Lab Coat echoed. "Mummy-raising terrorists?"

"What about you?" asked Marian. "You said *we* should stay here. What are you going to do?"

He caught himself rubbing his bruised shoulder again, and dropped his hand. "I'm delivering part of the ransom so they'll let my sister go."

The others reacted with worried acceptance as Carson walked out of the office. I stormed after him, much more vocal about my opinion of this idea.

"What part of the ransom?" I asked, following him to the laptop, where he pulled out the flash drive. "The book? That wasn't part of the deal."

He capped the flash drive and put it in his pocket. "You really think that matters? It's part of making the Black Jackal, if you want to split hairs."

"We can't give them the real flash drive," I argued. "We have to give them a decoy."

"*We* are not doing anything." He retrieved the spear he'd brought from the ancient America wing, then picked up one end of the table with his free hand and swung it out of the way. I wasn't sure what that was supposed to prove. That he could channel Neanderthal strength? How much would that help against lions and Jackals and backstabbing brethren?

"You need me to watch your back," I said, sliding between him and the door.

"*You* need to stay away from the Jackal," he said. "I heard your aunt's warning, too."

He didn't retreat from the door, which meant he didn't retreat

319

from me. I wasn't used to having to plead my case. People either listened to what I had to tell them, or they didn't and I didn't care.

I cared a whole lot now. About stopping the Black Jackal and the Brotherhood, about protecting Alexis, and about Carson.

"You *know* there's got to be a double cross in the works. You need one person there you can trust. If not for your sake, then for your sister—"

He took me by the shoulders, gazing down at me with surface calm and fathoms of emotion below.

"Stop. Talking."

"But—"

"I need you to promise something. If anything happens to me, get into Maguire's house. Tell Agent Taylor that if he needs probable cause, look into the Beaumont Corporation. There's a safe in Maguire's office, behind the bookshelf. That's where he keeps my mom's soul. Let her go for me, okay?"

His measured composure frightened me more than an impassioned plea. "You know I will. But why does this sound less like making a plan and more like saying goodbye?"

My worry made him relent with a soft laugh. "I'm not planning to jump into Mount Doom with the One Ring or anything. But I might be in jail. And you probably won't want to see me again. So I'm making a contingency plan."

"Don't be an idiot." He still held my shoulders and I started to push him away but somehow ended up holding on instead, grabbing a fistful of his shirt.

"Ow." He covered my hand with his. "Johnson left some bruises there. Be careful."

"Be careful?" I socked him, in case *that* got through his stubborn head. "You're talking about facing an überghost who can raise the freaking dead. Why would you not take along someone who can *vanquish* ghosts, you jackass?"

"I'm going to miss these pet names of yours, Sunshine."

"No you're not, because I'm going with you."

I yanked my hands from his and tried again to push him back a step. But as my fingers touched his shoulder, a shock raced along my nerves, raising gooseflesh and shivers all over me. Not good shivers, either.

Remnant shivers.

"What is that?" I demanded, with a rising note of... of *everything.* Panic, betrayal, hysteria. Because I'd felt a shock like that from living skin only once before—when I'd touched McSlackerson's tattoo in the St. Louis museum.

The Black Jackal's mark.

Carson closed his eyes and sighed, an exhale of regret and inevitability. "That was a mistake I made. And it's why you can't come with me. You want to send the Jackal back to the afterlife, and I can't let you do that. Not yet."

I couldn't make those words make sense, and I couldn't make myself move away as he brushed back my hair—and I couldn't resist as sudden darkness dropped the floor out from under me.

The jackass had whammied me. There were strong arms holding me and a warm kiss on my neck and a whisper in my ear, "Don't hate me too much, Daisy. And don't forget about my mom."

And then nothing.

32

"DAISY GOODNIGHT, YOU are under arrest for the obstruction of a federal investigation, evading custody, conspiring to commit motor vehicle theft..."

There might have been more, but Agent Gerard's voice merged with the buzzing whine in my head. The armed response team had arrived. I was stretched out on the couch in Marian's office, and Gerard looked like the devil himself in the red emergency lights.

"You can't arrest her while she's semiconscious," said Agent Taylor. I hadn't awakened at the armed forces busting through the door, but at Taylor's hand on my shoulder. I'd nearly cried at the sight of his familiar, loyal face.

I nearly cried for a lot of reasons. The headache beating at the inside of my skull was the least of them.

I was angry and hurt and mad at myself for *being* hurt, but most of all, eating up all those emotions like a lion in the pit of my stomach, was worry for Carson. Almost as much worry as there was fury.

How far back had he betrayed me? If he'd been in on the Brotherhood's plan, he was an *impossibly* good actor. And there was no faking the animosity between him and Johnson. But all the same, he'd been keeping secrets from the start.

Don't you ever want to take that guy and boot him into an early hell?

Carson wasn't after power. He was after vengeance.

"We need to go, sir," said one of the guys in black fatigues. Taylor and Gerard had them on, too.

"Just give me a sec," I said, sitting up slowly. More slowly, maybe, than necessary. I needed time to think.

Taylor crouched beside me, watching me like I was going to break. Behind him I could see my museum comrades closing ranks on Gerard.

"You can't arrest her," said Lab Coat. "She saved us from those mummies. And a big-ass lion."

"Sir," said Captain Fatigues, intervening between the nerd and the agent, "you've been exposed to a hallucinogenic substance, and we need to get all of you out of here and to medical attention."

Gerard had already turned back to me. "Where is your buddy, Peanut? Reenacting *Die Hard* downstairs?"

I tried to glare up at him, but it hurt my head. "Don't. Even. Start."

"Sir," said Taylor, standing to face the senior agent, "may I remind you that Miss Goodnight has been a hostage for forty-eight hours. And that we found her unconscious in a building under siege by terrorists"—Gerard gave a snort, and Taylor ignored him—"so we might cut her some slack."

Gerard looked apoplectic, and I really didn't want to be arrested, or to get Taylor in trouble. So I played my ace. "Be nice to me, Special Agent Gerard," I said. "I can get you probable cause on Devlin Maguire."

Captain Fatigues stood in the door. "We really can't waste any more time, sir."

Gerard gave me a long glare, as if he resented me for giving him what he wanted. Finally he stalked off to join the others in the reading room. Taylor took my hand and pulled me to my feet. I overbalanced and caught myself on his chest. It wasn't on purpose, but it was convenient.

"I can't leave," I whispered.

"Daisy," he said, steadying me by the shoulders, "you have to. Once you're all safe, the armed response team is going to go in after the hostiles downstairs."

"They can't." I stepped back out of his hold. "Forget that Carson and Alexis are down there somewhere. So is a monster—a madman who can do things you can't even imagine."

"That's why the professionals are going to handle it." He was using his calm-the-overwrought-witness voice and I didn't like it. "They'll do everything they can to keep the civilians safe. We're not letting Maguire into the building to negotiate, and I'm not letting you—"

"Maguire!" I wrestled my voice down, because I did sound overwrought and I didn't like that, either. "He can't come in here!"

"That's what I just said."

"He's been involved since the beginning! He knew about the Black Jackal, and he must have known about the Brotherhood...."

"You mean the kidnappers?" asked Taylor, looking at me like I'd really gone off the rails. "You're not seriously suggesting he kidnapped his own daughter, are you?"

"Maybe." It did sound crazy, but it had gotten Carson and me on the hunt for the remnants of Oosterhouse. More than that, it had gotten me *here*, to open the Veil for the Black Jackal.

"But why?"

"Power. I don't know—I haven't got that all worked out yet. Something about the symbiotic relationship..."

Now I was just babbling thoughts as they came to me, thinking out loud. Captain Fatigues appeared again in the doorway, like a dad calling curfew. "Agent Taylor," he said, in a don't-screw-with-me tone, "everyone else is gone. You're the last out."

Taylor took my arm to steer me toward the exit, but he didn't rush me. As soon as Fatigues's back was turned, I whispered, "I swear I'm not going bughouse. Bullets won't do any good here. In fact, dead people will make this about a million times worse. This is World Series weird, Jack. You have to trust me."

We had a bargain that I couldn't call him Jack until I was eighteen. This situation called for jumping the gun.

And it worked. He stopped in the doorway and faced me, grave and conflicted. "Daisy, if you don't toe the line, I'm not sure I can keep Gerard from arresting you."

"*Jack.*" I used it again. "If I don't stop this guy, Chicago will be a ghost town. *Literally.*"

He studied me closely, his face hard angles in the red emergency lights. "You're serious."

"I never joke about ghosts running rampant through the streets. Ghosts of mobsters, ghosts of the great fire, ghosts of Mrs. O'Leary's freaking cow. The sleeping dead pulled from their graves and every shred of their spirit erased from existence. All to fuel magic. Big, real, take-over-the-world *magic.*"

Another too-long inventory of my face. If we weren't such good friends, if the world weren't in such trouble, I might blush.

"And this isn't just about one guy in trouble?" he asked, stabbing me in the heart.

"No! What am I?" Outraged. That was what I was. "I'm not some lovelorn twit. It's about saving the city and every remnant soul in it from a megalomaniac with delusions of godhood."

And also a guy too stubborn to admit he needed saving.

"I didn't mean lovelorn," said Taylor, proving he did know me after all. "I know that you would risk anything for just one soul in danger. But for a whole city, I'll go with you."

I threw my arms around him in a relieved and rule-breaking but completely justified bear hug. After a second, his arms wrapped around me so tightly my bruises squealed. Or maybe I'd made that sound, because he eased off, but didn't let go. "You need to stop scaring the crap out of me, Jailbait."

Yeah, I probably needed to stop hugging him, especially if he was going to call me that. But the uncomplicated security felt so good that I let myself indulge a moment longer. It was a good thing no one else was there, or my badass image would be wrecked forever.

Wait. Why *were* we alone?

I straightened so fast that I almost knocked Taylor in the jaw. "Where's Captain Fatigues?"

He didn't ask who I meant. In a practiced motion he pushed me behind him with one hand, and pulled his firearm with the other. "Stay back."

Like hell I would. I knew how many man-eaters there were out there. And that was just the lions.

The reading room was all red and black shadows, as macabre as a horror movie set. It took me a moment to realize the puddle of darkness beside the first table was a sprawled body. Ignoring Taylor's warning, I hurried toward it and found Captain Fatigues down but not dead. He was deeply unconscious, maybe even whammied.

"Don't shoot!"

The words came from the inky rectangle of the open hall door. A female voice. A petite figure stepped into the room, spiky platinum hair dyed crimson by the light.

Taylor kept his weapon trained on the punk-rock witch, even after he recognized her. "You were at Maguire's house."

"Of course I was." She took another step into the room, and as she did, she seemed to leave her skin behind. The illusion burst gently, like a dandelion puff in the wind. All that remained was the real girl, one I'd only seen in photographs.

Alexis Maguire.

"He's my dear old dad, after all."

33

"WHAT'S GOING ON?" asked Taylor, obviously unsure if he should keep his gun aimed at her or not. "That looks like Alexis Maguire."

"I think it is." After all the shocks of the night, I felt numb, hollowed out, and spent. Maybe that was why the pieces fit together so easily. The dandelion-puff bits of illusion hung in the air, smelling of lakeside mud and blood spatter. "Did you kill your bodyguard for the power to make that disguise?"

She shrugged. "It had to be good enough to fool Carson. He can be reluctant about the messy stuff. And I figured you'd get along better if you sensed his sincere worry about me."

I allowed myself to feel a moment of relief that Carson didn't know everything, that he'd been played, too. "Was there ever a real Lauren?" I asked.

"Of course," said Alexis, with a chilling lack of concern. "But she had to go, too. She was a little too insightful."

Taylor put it together more quickly than I'd have thought. But then, I'd warned him it was world-class weird. "So . . . you faked your own kidnapping?"

"Obviously." She caught the confusion that flashed over my face. "Questions, Miss Goodnight? I'll let you ask a few."

I voiced the one foremost in my mind. "How did someone as smart as you end up taking orders from someone like Michael Johnson? He's the leader of the Brotherhood, right?"

Annoyance twisted her features. "I let him think he was. But once we'd identified all the pieces of Oosterhouse, I had my own plan. I knew that moron Johnson would make an unholy mess of things, which he has." The cool slipped back into place. "Still, it's not unsalvageable. And he has his uses. A priestess needs acolytes."

Taylor spared me the barest glance, keeping an eagle eye on Alexis. "What's she talking about?"

I fumbled for a quick explanation, but Alexis spoke first. "I'm sorry, Agent Taylor. There's really not time to bring you up to speed. Why don't you take a little nap?"

She merely nodded and Taylor collapsed, and my heart with him. I was just barely fast enough to keep his head from hitting the floor. His gun fell out of reach with a clatter.

"He'll be all right," Alexis assured me as I felt for his breath and pulse. "He's a strong one. And cute. No wonder Carson sounded so jealous."

I ignored her jabs and lowered Taylor gently, then stood, taking back the height advantage. It was the only one I had. While I was at it, I felt around for Aunt Ivy and got only the faintest resonance. I pushed back fear for her with hope that she had sense to retreat.

"How much does Carson know?" I asked. "Not, I assume, that you're a cast-iron bitch and murderer."

"I think he's figured it out by this point. He was pretty shaken when he came downstairs and saw through my illusion, though he tried to hide it." Alexis had sauntered sideways while she spoke. I didn't realize where she was headed until she picked up Taylor's pistol. "Carson said you would be gone by now, not to bother to come look for you. I think he underestimated your superhero complex."

"People do tend to underestimate me."

"Not me," said Alexis, handling the gun as easily as a fashion accessory. "I've been on the lookout for someone like you ever since I found Oosterhouse's Book of the Dead. You were just what I needed. The problem was how to convince Carson to go along with kidnapping you. He'd left the Brotherhood already. *Ethics,* he said. In his position, can you believe it? That boy is seriously messed up."

That was a mistake I made, Carson had said, when I'd discovered the Jackal's mark. *I'm not like them,* he'd told me on the train. I still believed that. I *had* to, or I'd have to start doubting everything I knew.

"Where is he now?" I asked.

331

"Downstairs, waiting on Dad. With all those conflicted principles, I wasn't expecting him to come onboard with me so easily. But his finding out that Dad played him—and worse, forced him to put you in danger—has got him rethinking alliances, which is convenient for me."

No wonder I had so much trouble putting the jigsaw puzzle together. This picture had more double crosses than string art.

"So your father," I prompted, since she seemed to enjoy my questions, "he was the mastermind behind this whole thing?"

She grinned, her straight white teeth gleaming in the dim light. "That's what *he* thinks. That's the trick with managing Dad—nothing magical about it. You just have to make him think something is his idea. Carson, too, in the opposite way. I knew putting you on the run together would bring out all his protective instincts." She paused for thought. "I *did* seriously underestimate his hate for Dad. It's kind of oedipal, don't you think?"

"Except for the part where his dad ordered his mom killed. That isn't how the play goes."

"Whatever." She sighed heavily. "If I'd known, I would have just *asked* him to help me. Subterfuge is a lot of work."

It sounded like she had a plan for Maguire—and maybe Carson, too. He must be playing along with her, but if he had a plan beyond that, I was pretty sure it didn't account for the fact that his half sister was a sociopath.

"But what do *you* get out of it?" I asked. Taylor had once told me that sometimes the best interrogation technique was to shut up and let the suspect spill his guts. It was like a compulsion, whether they felt guilty or proud of what they'd done.

Alexis? Did not feel guilty.

"Power. And dynasty, of course." She checked her phone, a very businesslike gesture. "I need Carson's help, which means I still have a use for you. He almost wrecked it, giving you the chance to escape. But here you are." She flashed another grin. "I love it when a plan comes together."

I had a bolt of inspiration. Not the good, get-out-of-this-jam-with-everyone-you-care-about-alive kind. But the bad, this-shit-is-so-much-deeper-than-I-thought kind. I should have kept my mouth shut, but I had to know if I was right.

"Did you make Maguire think it was his idea to kill Carson's mother?"

Her smile vanished, and something deadly sparked in her eyes. "Can you blame me? I had to discover by *accident* I had a brother. And when I found out he had the same weird talents I did? Of course I wanted him in the house. I'd always wanted a sibling, and Dad always wanted a son. Everyone wins."

"Except Carson's mom."

Alexis gave an *Oh well* shrug. "It's time to go downstairs. Dad found a way in, and everything is set. But since I just got Carson onboard and you're a bit of a wild card, I think you should take a little nap, too."

"Wait!" I said . . .

Just before everything went dark. Again.

I woke to the flickering of torchlight on hieroglyphs and the rhythmic chanting of men's voices. My arms ached, and when I tried to move, I found I was sitting on the floor, my wrists tied behind me and around the base of the statue of Anubis, in the reconstructed tomb in the bottom of the museum, where this had all started that afternoon.

You have got to be kidding me.

Bound and gagged like a pig at a luau.

I couldn't speak. My mouth felt like it had been stuffed with old sweat socks.

Nightmare shadows loomed on the ceiling and walls, cast by deformed heads and cloaked figures. The Brotherhood stood in a semicircle around me, wearing jackal masks and some sort of robes, and it was all too weird and too terrifying at the same time. Their chant had the ring of ritual, and it raised a sort of electricity in the air, a potential of power. As if they could call *anything* and it would answer.

The semicircle faced an altar, and that raised my hackles, too. Behind it stood Devlin Maguire. To his left, his daughter, Alexis. To his right, his son, Carson, eyes straight ahead. A dynasty in the making.

The big man raised his arms in invocation. The chanting dropped to a hum, and Maguire spoke over it. "The Brotherhood of the Jackal has formed. We call our mentor and master, the Black Jackal, and offer him a body so that he can live again and we can share his glory."

Oh, you have so got to be kidding me.

34

A *BODY*?

Ancient Egyptians didn't go for human sacrifice. But there I was, in the middle of the semicircle of brethren, tied to the statue of the jackal like some kind of offering.

I'd managed to sit up with my back to the pedestal, my arms stretched behind me, wrists bound to something yielding but inescapable on the other side. I gave a few experimental yanks and the something yanked back with a very annoyed grunt.

Oh. *That* was where Taylor was. I was relieved he wasn't lion chow but otherwise was not happy to hear from him.

And Carson... Carson still hadn't looked at me. His jaw was

set, his muscles tight. Surely he would find a way to give me *some* clue as to what he was planning.

Suddenly Ivy was there beside me. I jumped, then pulled at my bonds, and barely remembered not to talk out loud to her.

"I am so very sorry I didn't stay to watch your back," she said, guilt flavoring her apology but not prolonging it. "I thought it was important to reconnoiter for you."

Get out of here! I told her. *It's jackal central! Are you nuts?*

"I will. But it's important I tell you what I know." She glanced at the Maguire family behind the altar. Everything seemed in stasis, but it was only in comparison with the speed Ivy's shade was telling me things in psychic time. "The young man won't look at you because he doesn't want them to use you against him. He has a plan. It's a catastrophically stupid plan, but I have no way to stop him."

How do you know? I asked, still terrified for her. But I had a hunch that made me terrified for all of us.

"I spoke with him." She absorbed my reaction to that even before I could. "You mean he *doesn't* share your ability to speak with the dead?"

No. He has the ability to borrow it, though.

Until now, he'd only done it when we were touching, or close. But he had the Jackal's mark, and it was a whole new ball game now. My horrible hunch said my talent for speaking with the dead wasn't all he'd borrowed.

He's planning to push the Black Jackal back through the Veil.

"He thinks he can, yes."

That wasn't all. I knew what Maguire meant about offering

the Jackal a body. Not a sacrifice, but a host. If Maguire thought he would remain in control of all that power, he would take it. And I didn't think Carson cared if sending the Jackal back to the afterlife sent Devlin Maguire, too.

Psychic time or regular time, we were out of both. I could feel the Jackal prowling within the bonds I'd anchored to the foundations of the building. This room was the limit of his tether, but not a stretch.

Go, I told Ivy. If I could force her away, I would. *He's coming.*

She went, with a fleeting touch of her spirit to mine, spending no time on words. Then she was gone, really gone, and safe.

I looked at the altar, subjective time back to normal. A pulse beat in Maguire's neck, above the collar of his shirt. He wore his suit like a vestment. There was something else, a muted psychic hum. I'd felt it once before in his office. However he'd contained the soul of Carson's mother, he had it here. *Here,* where he was about to raise a soul-eating monster.

What an arrogant ass.

I didn't think Carson could sense it. I'd had seventeen and three-quarters years to learn how to use my gifts. What made him think he could master them instantly?

Simple. He was the son of an arrogant ass.

The air stirred with a shimmer, the Black Jackal appeared inside the semicircle of his brethren. He wore the guise of the jackal-headed god, but I could See through the illusion to the shade of Oosterhouse. Handsome, young, fit . . . and bare-chested, like a Yul Brynner Rameses.

He put his hands on his hips and studied the surroundings

337

with a sneer. The tomb had seemed very real when I'd awakened to chanting, but behind the genuine artifacts were black exhibit walls, and the torches were merely flashlights and electric lanterns. It was all just set dressing next to the self-proclaimed demigod.

Maguire spoke from the altar like it was a boardroom table. "Welcome, my lord. As you see, we are ready to proceed with the ritual."

The Jackal encompassed Maguire in his disapproval. "You managed to secure the book?"

"I never lost the book," said Maguire, cool and in charge. "I always knew where it was." He placed one paternal hand on Carson's shoulder, the other on Alexis's. "My son had it, and my daughter translated it, and together they brought you Miss Goodnight."

At last Carson's guarded gaze flicked toward me, as if to see if I believed that he'd been working with Alexis. I trusted he hadn't, but I was still pissed about everything he *had* done, including delivering the Jackal exactly what he wanted. Not me, but the power to open the Veil.

The Jackal finally gave me his attention, and the air crackled between us with opposing psychic forces. He strode to where I was bound and stood over me, his shadowed eyes glinting. It hurt to look at him, as if the twisted magic that made him burned the answering magic in *my* soul.

His gaze roved over me in a vile way. "You've brought her," he said, "but you haven't broken her. How will you convince her to play her role?"

Maguire's voice was a smooth, ringing promise. "If she does not unbind you, Agent Taylor will die in disgrace as part of the plot to kidnap my daughter."

Taylor tensed at the threat, pulling at the ropes that bound us. More than that, I could sense the horror the threat gave him—not the death, but the dishonor. Though I was guessing he didn't much want to die, either.

I managed to twist one hand until I could link a few fingers with Taylor's as Maguire continued. "However, if she complies with the ritual, her friend will merely be killed in the line of duty."

Wow. He wasn't even pretending he wasn't going to kill us. Taylor's fingers squeezed mine, but I didn't find that reassuring. My choice was doom him to disgrace or doom him and every other soul in this world to oblivion.

Maguire stood, shoulders back, supremely confident. He saw himself as the pharaoh here, and Oosterhouse as his pawn. Beside him, Alexis glowed with the same conviction of control, and in his own way, underneath his mask of compliance, Carson seemed steady in the idea that he could turn the tables.

They were all cataclysmically wrong.

"I like the way you think, Maguire," said the Jackal, indulging him. "The problem is your sense of scale. I know a man like you understands the importance of, what do they call it now? Shock and awe."

As quick as a thought, he plunged a spectral hand into my chest. Icy cold punched through my ribs, burning, cracking, seizing my heart. He twisted, tearing a scream from my vitals. It was the worst pain I'd ever felt in my life, but worse still was the moment when he grabbed the threads that connected Ivy to me and used them to pull her shade from thin air.

"Hello, Professor Goodnight," he said. She dangled from his grip on her throat, her hands grabbing at his thick, tanned forearm.

"Oosterhouse." Aunt Ivy managed to wheeze with contempt, as if they were academic rivals and not one spirit choking the afterlife out of another. "I should have known. No one who likes to hear himself talk as much as you do has altruism at heart."

"I'm so glad this turned out to be you," he snarled. "Women—and Goodnights—need to know their place."

He tightened his fist, and Ivy screamed. I did, too, straining at my bonds until my joints threatened to pop. But I was helpless to stop the Jackal as he pulled the remnant essence of my aunt into his fist like he was wadding up paper.

Her image shriveled but her scream multiplied. It reverberated in the chamber, shook the walls until they began to transform. The ancient panels of stone on display spread like spilled water, covering the walls until the tomb was no longer curtains and plaster but stone and dirt and stuffy air. The electric light warmed, turned to smoking flame and dancing torchlight.

And the scream still didn't stop. The air shimmered around the Jackal's hand, and every cell in my body shuddered in recognition and resonance. Through my link to my aunt, he used me to call the Veil. It didn't hum. It shrieked as he dragged Ivy's soul from beyond like a magician pulls a never-ending scarf from his pocket.

Her *soul.*

"Stop!" I screeched around the cloth gag between my teeth. "I'll do it! Just stop—"

Stop before there's nothing left. I sobbed the last, unable to form the words. Tears blinded me, and I blinked them away because I didn't want to be sightless in front of this monster.

The scream, the Veil, and all trace of my aunt vanished. With a cutting smile of victory, the Jackal opened his fist. He waved, and the gag in my mouth crumbled to foul-tasting dust. Leaning close he hissed in my ear, "Now do you believe I am a god? Submit, or I will destroy every dead witch in your interfering family. I don't think even you realize how close they are, thinking they can protect you. But they can't. Not from me."

He took my broken sob as an answer and stood, swollen with pride and malice. I had underestimated him. And underestimated how much I had angered him by leashing him like a dog.

And he'd treed me like a cat. Now I had to keep my balance in gale-force winds until I figured out a way down.

I got up enough spit to talk and enough backbone to brave this out. "I'll do it. But keep your paws off my family." I looked toward the altar, where Alexis and Maguire waited. Carson's facade had cracked, his face pale and his gaze tortured.

It would have been nice if I'd had more than the SparkNotes version of the Book of the Dead. I could only extrapolate from what Ivy told me and try to make it sound good. The final step, Ivy had said, was to unknot the pharaoh's *ka* from his resting place and bind him to a host. There was still a wisp of a thread binding Oosterhouse's *ka* to the statue—but that hardly seemed to matter next to the far greater binding I'd worked on him and would now have to undo.

"Choose your host," I announced to the room, hoping that drama would pass for authority. "To unbind the Jackal, I have to bind him to something else, or he will fade away."

Carson looked at his father, expecting him to step forward. But Alexis spoke first.

"I volunteer," she said. Power and dynasty, she'd told me she wanted. What had the book promised her that she thought the Jackal's power would be hers to exploit?

Her offer shocked Carson, and he stared at her as if another illusion had shattered. But he didn't have time to re-form the pieces, to realize the full scope of her deception, because Maguire dropped the next bomb.

"I volunteer my son," he said, one hand on Carson's shoulder, the other spread in a theatrical gesture of offering. "As a sign of my faith in our accord."

"*What?*" shrieked Alexis as every shred of emotion leeched from Carson's face. "I've been loyal to you this whole time!"

"Yes," said Maguire, in an implacable tone, fully believing her and fully not caring. "And I know you will be loyal to your brother—your knowledge and his innate talents will build our assets beyond what anyone could possibly imagine."

Dynasty. Maguire wanted it, too.

"What's going on?" Taylor said around his gag, while Alexis raged with escalating hysteria. The Jackal was enjoying it, drinking in the drama as if he had all night.

"Trouble," I whispered back. "And worse trouble if I can't figure out what to do about it. Carson had a plan, but Maguire just cut him off at the knees."

"Man, can you pick 'em."

"Shut it, Taylor. You don't even know." My eyes were on Carson, who'd gone still with leashed intensity. "If you get loose," I told Taylor, "make a run for it."

He laughed—actually laughed. "Do you know me at all?"

Okay. So none of us were runners.

I was watching Carson for signs he was about to act. I was watching the Jackal for the same thing. I should have been watching Alexis.

I should have remembered that she must wear the Jackal's mark, too.

Suddenly the air crackled with remnant energy, and Maguire was airborne. With a gesture, Alexis had slammed him into the stone wall, loosing a shower of pebbles and dust. Maguire's oak-tree body dropped to the floor with a bone-shattering crack and didn't move.

Neither did anyone else. We watched in shock as Alexis picked her way over the rubble she'd released and bent over her father, reaching into his jacket. When she stood, she held a small glass vial. In it I could sense the muted blaze of a woman's soul.

The Jackal began to laugh. Around us the brethren shuffled in confusion, not sure whom to back in this mutiny.

Alexis ignored them all. With chilling efficiency she grabbed one of the museum's mummification tools, then placed the fragile vial onto the altar and raised the ancient hammer over it.

"Yield to me, Carson," she said. "Or I let the Jackal have your mom."

"No, Alexis." His fury finally boiled to the surface, though he reined it in with clenched fists. "Let her go, and then I'll yield."

I tore my gaze away and looked at the Jackal, who watched the drama hungrily. If Alexis freed the soul, he would take it anyway.

"Stop it, both of you!" I shouted. In my family, you learn early how to deal with extreme sibling rivalry. "No one gets anything until I unbind the Jackal. So shut up and let me loose."

"Untie her," Alexis ordered the brethren. "But keep a tight hold on her buddy."

The minions weren't so confused they didn't follow orders. They wrenched the ropes off Taylor's and my wrists and hauled us both to our feet.

"Now," said Alexis, with the hammer still poised over the vial. "Release the Jackal from his bonds and complete the ritual."

I rubbed my wrists, shaking the blood back into my hands, and looked from her to Carson. Finally—*finally*—he met my eye. He gave an infinitesimal glance at Alexis, then the slightest hint of an *It will be all right* nod.

How, by Saint Peter's giant gold key, was this going to be all right?

"Enough stalling," said the Jackal, reclaiming the room. Didn't Alexis see that he'd *allowed* her to have her tantrum? His image glowed with power. How did she expect to control that if they were bound?

344

"Do your magic, witch," the Jackal said to me, and I didn't correct him. "Play your role and you will all live to serve me."

The limb I was on was shaking, and I dug in with my claws. "Okay," I said. "Let's do this thing. Show me your tattoo."

"Why?" demanded Alexis.

To get her to set the hammer down, away from Carson's mother, of course. But aloud I said, "For a point of focus, in a place you're already bound once to the Jackal. I don't want to get this wrong."

She exhaled in irritation but pushed up her sleeve, revealing a delicate scroll of black ink on her forearm, just below her elbow. "Don't screw this up," Alexis warned. "Or *both* your boyfriends will wish they'd never been born."

Maybe I could still make this work. I couldn't send the Jackal through the Veil until I'd unknit him from the building. But if my timing was very, very good . . .

"Stop stalling," said the Jackal. Then to the Brotherhood he said, "Give her some encouragement."

The sound Taylor made as a brethren's fist hit his kidney was all the encouragement I needed. With the Jackal to my right and the ancient altar and the Maguires to my left, I closed my eyes, braced my feet, and let the psychic hum of the building creep through its stones and into my body.

The song was so out of tune that it hurt my heart. The once–perfectly balanced orchestra of shades and remnants, of psychic echoes and resident ghosts, had skewed to a jangling garage-band cacophony.

345

The Jackal's stolen magic had tainted it, and his struggles to pull free had made it worse, snarling the threads that held him. I picked through the tangle, loosing the ties one by one, and tried not to listen to the warnings of the building's shades.

With one knot left, I instructed them, *Tell Carson to open the Veil on my signal;* then I opened my eyes a crack to see if he got the message, hoping the ability he'd borrowed from me would last. His gaze flicked to mine, and I knew we were going for it.

Now. The Veil shimmered into being, not smoothly, but there. I snapped my last knot, then formed the threads of the bindings into an arrow and sent it with all my heart, all my strength toward the portal to eternity.

The Jackal roared, and his image stretched and distorted, pulled toward the Veil but caught—snagged on the black jackal statue that had lain with his bones. I'd forgotten the only tie I hadn't made myself.

I cut it with a thought, but the damage was done, inertia destroyed. The Jackal took control of his own path hitting Carson and knocking him to his knees.

Carson grabbed his shoulder with a cry, shuddering as if he'd been hit by a real arrow, muscles heaving as he breathed through some pain or stress and finally quieted.

"Carson?" I asked, when he still didn't move.

"Yeah," he said tightly. "I'm here."

"And the Jackal?" I whispered, almost afraid to know.

He tugged his shirt over his head. On the back of his shoulder, above his shoulder blade, was the jackal tattoo. Unlike Johnson's simple outline and Alexis's girly scrollwork, this ink had character, with a sense of movement and a hint of a wolfish, trickster grin.

More than a hint. In the torchlight, the eyes gleamed with victory.

Carson finally answered, "He's in here, too."

35

"No, *no, NO!*"

Alexis grabbed up the hammer and brought it down toward the glowing glass vial on the altar. Before it could land, Carson had snatched up the tiny jar, holding it safe in his hand.

"Stop being a brat."

Who was talking? The Jackal or Carson? It *sounded* like Carson, except for the cavalier way he dismissed the half sister he'd broken all kinds of laws to save.

"A brat?" Alexis echoed, but she sounded back in control of herself. "I gave this to you. I did all the groundwork. I formed the Brotherhood and you left it. You don't *deserve* the Jackal."

"But I've got it," he said calmly. Turning to the slack-jawed brethren—they'd ditched their masks ages ago—he said to the ones holding Taylor and me, "Let them go. Now."

Whether compelled or just confused, they did. Taylor ran to Maguire, who still hadn't moved, and checked him for serious injuries. I followed, mostly to put distance between me and the henchmen. "He'll be okay until we get an ambulance," Taylor said. "We'd better not move him until the armed response team gets here."

Alexis finally did something clever, seizing the closing window of opportunity to regain the Brotherhood. She swooped over and caught Johnson by the front edge of his robe. "You don't want to wait here for the SWAT team to come in, do you?"

"Of course not," he said, looking down at her with poorly disguised adoration.

"That's what Carson would make you do," she said, sweeping them all up in a wave of charisma a lot like her father's. "All of you who don't want to go to *jail*, come with me."

No one wanted to go to jail, apparently. I didn't know how to stop them, and Carson seemed to be fighting his own battle.

"Here," he said, holding the vial out to me. I put out my hand, skin already shivering at the proximity of the imprisoned soul, and Carson dropped the tiny glass into my palm. He was leaning heavily on the altar. "Take care of that for me."

Taylor had stood, and he looked from me, to Carson, to the glow in my hand. "What is it?" he breathed, almost reverent. Maybe a soul was profound enough for even a nonpsychic to feel.

"A soul in a bottle," I said.

He was silent a moment. "You're right. This is World Series weird."

Carson laughed, but it was a shaky sound. "Get Daisy out of here before all hell breaks loose, okay?"

"Okay," said Taylor, like they'd formed their own brotherhood. A brotherhood of jackasses.

"Are we really discussing this again?" I demanded. "*Here* is exactly where I need to be when hell breaks loose."

"No," said Carson, his tone inarguable, all the shakiness gone. "You need to get out. Now."

Taylor grabbed my hand and breathed a warning. "Daisy..."

The fear in his voice stilled my attempts to shake him off, and I followed his gaze. What he could see from his angle, but I couldn't, not until he pulled me closer to him, was the tattoo on Carson's back.

The jackal silhouette now covered his entire shoulder blade. As I watched, it *moved*, flexing whippet-lean muscles, and its mouth curved in mocking laughter.

I reached out to touch it, to feel how deep the connection went, to make some wild stab of a guess at how I could pull the Jackal free from Carson without irreparably damaging him. But a charge like electric needles pushed me back, even before Taylor grabbed that hand, too.

"Go," Carson said again, his voice gruff. He'd always sounded older than he was, but now he sounded ancient. "I'll take care of the Brotherhood."

He grabbed his shirt from the floor and shook it out as he followed Alexis and her band from the tomb. As soon as he crossed the threshold, there was a rumble, and a rain of dust that grew into a hail of rubble.

"Let's go," said Taylor. "This place is going to come down."

"What about Maguire?" I didn't think the room would collapse, just revert to how it had been. But a falling slab of hieroglyphs could crush the man all the same. Even if he deserved it.

We supported his neck and dragged him out of danger, into the corridor, which was unmarked by magic or debris. We barely made it before an almighty crash shook the walls and brought the rest of the stone in the tomb behind us smashing down.

"That came from above us," I said, and ran for the stairs before Taylor could stop me.

At the top of the stairs out of the tomb, the hunting-cat screech of a lion made me stumble over my own feet. My feet and my total lack of a plan. Not that that was enough to stop me, but it slowed me down enough for Taylor to catch up.

"Daisy, stop." He grabbed me when I would have charged out into the main hall, and pulled me into the shelter of the exhibit door. "Listen. That guy—"

"Carson," I corrected. Insisted, because I couldn't let myself believe he'd become the Jackal.

"Carson," Taylor agreed. "He was barely holding on. And he's right. We need to get out of here."

"And do what?" I asked. "Let them fight to the death? Let Alexis kill Carson and take the Jackal? Or let the monster take over Carson completely?"

"How about let the armed response team come in and arrest them all?"

"Taylor!" I wrestled my voice down to a whisper. "There are three man-eating ghost lions out there! You think they can handle that?" There was another crash from the hall, making my point.

"What's the alternative?" he asked.

That was a good question. "I have to unbind the Jackal from Carson before it can totally possess him."

"You can do that?"

"Yes," I said, hoping it was true. I didn't have a plan B.

"Okay. I'll call—" He stopped, with his hand on his fatigues pocket. "My cell phone is gone."

"So's your weapon," I said, in case he hadn't noticed that already. And in case that changed his mind, I slipped through the exhibit door into the first-floor gallery.

"Daisy!" he hissed, hurrying after me from shadow to shadow. Ahead was the main hall, lit by the moonlight streaming through the skylights and amplified by the white marble. I could clearly see the two elephants, and Sue the T. rex in her eternal run. There was mummy dust everywhere, and both totem poles had fallen, like mammoth trees blocking one set of doors.

Everything else I saw with double vision, psychic and physical. Man-eating lions weren't the half of it. They prowled through ranks and ranks of hunters and soldiers from every culture represented in the museum and maybe a few that weren't. On one side of the hall were Alexis and the Brotherhood. On the other, facing

352

them and their spirit host of animals and ancient warriors, was Carson, standing alone.

Alone, but somehow equal to all that. Even from the shadows I could feel the hum of power from him.

"Last chance to give it up, Carson!" called Alexis.

"It's not that easy, Lex," he said, his voice carrying across the hall. "The Jackal chose me. You have to convince *him*."

"I can do that."

She said it with conviction, and it was clear she expected something amazing to happen. But her warriors just ... stood there.

The Brotherhood must have felt something. Johnson stared at his tattoo with disbelief, but it was Alexis who screeched, "You *bastard*!" loud enough to rattle the rafters.

Carson raised his hand as if catching a baseball, and it took me a minute to realize what I was *not* seeing. The Black Jackal had sent the Brotherhood after Carson and me armed with a share of all his power. And Carson had just called it all back.

"The Jackal giveth," he said, "and the Jackal taketh away."

He stirred the air like a huge cauldron. The shades in the hall dissolved, became a fluid swirl of mist with snatches of tooth and claw and spear. It cast a sickly light on the marble hall as it circled, catching the Brotherhood up in a whirlpool prison.

"Holy crap," whispered Taylor. "That's all ... ghosts?"

"Spirits. Yes." It was really impressive, and utterly terrifying, the effortless way he controlled it.

Not it. *Them.* Remnant shades of ancient memory.

I glanced at Taylor. Something metal glinted in his hand. "No one took my backup revolver," he explained, sounding relieved. "Those henchmen aren't exactly the brain trust."

Then he gave me a serious, this-is-real-and-shit-is-about-to-go-down look. I knew he hadn't ever shot anyone, but I also knew he'd trained for it. "Are *you* aware of the biggest threat in the room? Look."

I did. Worse, I heard. The imprisoning circle of spirit was tightening around the Brotherhood with hunting-cat snarls and the escalating beat of tribal drums. There was a cry of pain as one of the brethren got too close and drew back a slashed arm, blood dripping on the tile.

"Please don't shoot Carson," I said, more plaintively than I intended. "I'm not sure that will stop the Jackal."

I was not sure *what* would stop the Jackal. But I had to find out.

Another scream, this one from Alexis. It was harder to see her and her minions through the circling glow.

"Let's go," said Taylor. "Get Carson to stop. I'll cover the girl and make sure she doesn't get away."

"Okay." I think he expected me to wait for a count of three, but I didn't. I charged out of the shadows and stepped between Carson and the swirling remnants. "That's enough!" I shouted. "You're just torturing them!"

He didn't look surprised to see me. He looked so *normal*— way more normal than he should look with that much power inside him.

"They'd do the same to you," he said, very reasonably. "Alexis would have killed you and used your soul to fuel her magic. And you're worried about a few cuts and scrapes?"

"Not the Brotherhood," I said, though I meant them, too. "The remnants. You *know* what they are, and you're toying with them."

He waved a hand and the whirlwind ceased. The spirits dissolved again, this time into a fog lying low on the floor, spreading in abstract phosphorescent eddies. All except the Native Americans that Carson had first summoned an age ago. They stood guard around his half sister and the half-dozen brethren.

"Don't move," said Taylor, his gun drawn and aimed at Alexis. "None of you. Put any weapons you have on the ground."

Only the brethren looked worried. Alexis fumed and the shades of the warriors didn't react at all.

Carson strode through the spectral fog, bridging the distance between us. "Don't you think that's a little redundant, Agent Taylor?" he asked, nodding to the spear carriers, then the agent's gun.

"I'm too conventional to leave this to ghost guards," said Taylor. "And I don't trust you."

"You shouldn't," said Alexis, standing with her hands obediently in the air. "You should just stay out of this, junior G-man."

Johnson spoke up. I guess he hadn't completely lost his spine with Alexis around. "And how are you going to arrest all six of us by yourself?"

Carson made an annoyed sound. "I don't mind helping him with that, asshole."

The shades of all the Native American tribesmen standing

guard on the brethren simply vanished, *gone* without so much as a wisp of woodsmoke in the moonlight. In the same moment, Carson snapped his fingers and five guys dropped to the floor, whammied into unconsciousness from twenty feet away.

I was so stunned that it took me a second to realize Alexis was still standing there. Taylor swung around to include Carson in his sights, too, as best as he could. "Don't move, Maguire. World Series weird or not, I'm not messing around."

The siblings ignored him. "Did you really think I'd be dumb enough not to protect myself from that trick?" Alexis sneered.

"Are you dumb enough not to realize the Jackal would tell me everything you've been up to?" Carson fired back. "How could you kill Lauren? She was always nice to you."

"She was way too insightful," said Alexis, and I guessed that *would* be a problem when you were constantly playing everyone in your house. "But she taught me some really useful tricks of my own."

She snapped her fingers in a mockery of Carson, and there was a magic-show flash, blinding in the near dark. By the time I could see again, Alexis was gone.

"Dammit!" said Taylor, searching the hall for any trace of her.

I could see her wake in the glowing fog around our ankles, and pointed toward the Hall of African Animals. "That way."

"Don't bother," Carson growled. Two lean feline shapes rose from the mist, prowling toward us like visible shadows. "Find her," he told them, and at my inarticulate sound of horror he added, "Bring her back alive."

Then with a gesture, he sent them off like a pair of hunting dogs.

Taylor had reached his limit. "No more magic. Daisy, do something about this, or I will."

Carson looked at him, bemused. "What is it you think you're going to do, Agent Taylor? Alexis was right about one thing. You're better off staying out of this."

Then he dropped him like Sleeping Beauty.

It was just Carson and me.

No, that wasn't right. The glow of the spirit fog at our feet cast a faint but distinct shadow on columns and ceiling, towering over us both. The shadow of a jackal-headed man.

36

"OH MY GOD, Carson. Stop doing that! You're going to give someone brain damage."

My flippancy was a facade. Inside, my heart pounded like a subwoofer in a dance club, but running to Taylor's unconscious body gave me an excuse to hide my horror. Showing fear would let the Jackal know I'd seen him.

"He's fine, right?" Carson wasn't careless, but his tone was casual. *No damage done, so what's the harm?*

He walked toward me, his shoulders loose, his gait easy. He moved like a complete stranger, and I had to force myself not to back away.

"Stop worrying," he said. "The brethren are rounded up for the police, and we'll have Alexis in a few minutes. I've taken their power back. And if she does manage to get out, we'll track her down. It's all good."

"It's *all good*?" I echoed, flummoxed and frightened. Forget the fact that it was *not* all good. It was anything *but* good. This was not the Carson I'd spent the past forty-eight hours with.

"Carson, you need to let me unbind the Jackal from you. *Now*." As illogical as it was, I whispered that last part, as if the parasitic spirit couldn't hear me. "While you still have a little bit of control."

He caught my hand and, with a grin, pulled me close. "I have complete control. Let me show you."

I held him at arm's length and powered up my deflector shields. "Listen to yourself. You're trying to kiss me in a room full of shades, with six unconscious bodies on the floor. Does that seem normal to you?"

He'd kept his hands on my waist, but drew back to consider me. "And that's worth putting up the psychic force field?"

"Do you blame me?" I asked. "I've had all the whammy I can take today."

He took my hands and squeezed them in apology. "I was just trying to protect you. I had no idea what I was doing, other than that. But, Daisy, this worked out better than any plan I could have made."

"Except for the part where you're possessed by a self-proclaimed demigod!"

"But I'm not!" He squeezed my hands again and drew me

away from Taylor's sprawled body. "I can feel the Jackal in the back of my head, but he's not controlling me. Maybe it's my ability to channel and convert types of energy, I don't know." He gave a disbelieving laugh. "Hell, maybe Maguire knew that when he volunteered me, though I think that's giving him too much credit."

"Carson," I said, trying to pull him back to earth. "You are not sounding like yourself."

"How do you know? I've forgotten what 'myself' feels like. I haven't felt normal since my mom died." He laughed again, with genuine humor and joy. "I can feel her. You've got her soul in your pocket. That sounds like it should be a song title."

I didn't like buoyant Carson. It just wasn't right.

"This can be the new normal," he went on, oblivious to my tension, even when he slid his arms around my waist. He nodded to the prone brethren. "This can be what we do. Doing good. Stopping evil. The weird stuff that your FBI partner isn't equipped to handle. Now *we are.*"

He was serious, and he was earnest, and he was so *wrong.* Some deep-down part of me wondered what I would say if he was Jackal-less, if he'd never hidden any truth from me. I had a feeling it would be the same thing, it would just hurt even more. "No, Carson."

"Why not?" He pulled me tighter against him, so I had to lean back to look at him. "Come with me, Daisy. Think of all the good we can do."

Goodnights don't run.

360

Some memory whispered that in my ear. Maybe even some shade. But it was the truth. I was a face-the-music kind of girl. "Or you could stay," I said, knowing I'd have to make him somehow.

"I can't." He slipped his hand around the back of my neck, pressing his forehead to mine. "So this is where we split."

Like Humphrey Bogart and Ingrid Bergman at the airfield in *Casablanca*. Only Rick hadn't said goodbye by kissing Ilsa like there was no tomorrow.

That felt like the real Carson. Not flippant or entitled or arrogant . . . Okay, maybe just the right amount of arrogant. The kiss was deep and dark and a little bit desperate, as if he had to drink all of me in or never get another taste.

It didn't last long. Long enough for the ache of loss to blossom. Long enough for the taste to turn to smoke and sand.

I pulled away in horror. Carson looked back at me in confusion turning to alarm. "What?"

My arms had gone around his waist, and I took hold of the tail of his shirt. Twisting out of his arms, I yanked up the fabric and got a look at his tattoo.

He was too stunned to stop me. *I* was too stunned to move.

The inky jackal skulked across his skin. It covered his whole back, and blue eyes glittered like gems. They winked, telling me they'd seen me. Heard me. Tasted me.

I made a noise—disgusted, terrified. I didn't plan, just reacted. I grabbed the tattoo like I could peel it from his skin. It gave some in the middle like a blistered sunburn, then snapped back. The jackal snarled, lashed at me with gleaming teeth, and a

361

blast of magic flung me backward, where I hit the floor and kept sliding.

"Daisy!" When my eyes uncrossed, I saw that Carson looked as stunned as I was. But above him I saw the shadow of the Jackal, huge and laughing and triumphant.

I crab-walked backward from the apparition, through the swirls of spirit fog. It tingled in greeting, recognizing me from all my efforts that day. But as the Jackal's shadow condensed and fell over Carson, fell *into* him, soaking in the way ink soaks into paper, the mist began to scratch and nip and bite.

When Carson looked up, his eyes were brilliant blue.

This was the exact opposite of *all good*. What looked out of his eyes now was inhuman, alien, and merciless.

"Why couldn't you just cooperate?" said the Jackal. "I could have made the boy happy, given him what he wanted, let him keep the illusion of control. This is all your fault."

He spread his arms and the spirit mist coiled in on itself, taking a new shape. "Remember that," said the Jackal. "Though you won't have to remember it long."

I couldn't even say what the thing was, other than *huge*. It had the mane of a lion and the teeth of about fifty sharks, and it bristled with scales and spikes and bones. Every time my eyes focused, it shifted, like trying to catch the red spot on your vision after a camera flash. But it was solid enough. Talons like giant flint arrowheads threw up sparks as they scraped the floor.

It was nightmare given form.

I'd scrambled backward and hit something—the railing

around the tyrannosaur—and I used it to pull myself to my feet. Only hours ago I'd stood in almost the same spot, listening to the symphony of spirits that saturated the museum. I reached for them now, and found the psychic space where they'd been empty, like a raided tomb. What hadn't been used up by the Brotherhood or the Jackal had been pulled in and warped by the monstrosity in front of me.

Johnson and the brethren lay in a heap, not that they would help me. Taylor hadn't moved. The doors were locked. The museum was empty, and every shade in it was standing against me.

I'd never felt so alone.

Except... I was never alone.

The nightmare beast churned the air with a semblance of breathing, and it took a lot of willpower to close my eyes and Sense it with only my psyche. I shook out my hands, rushing blood through my veins and energy into my own living spirit. And I reached, harder than I'd ever reached before.

Not out. But in.

I reached into my cells, into my DNA, into the mitochondria that made me. I found that essence of myself that was Goodnight, the daughter of kitchen witches and psychic detectives and interfering busybodies. I was a guide to lost souls and the patron sinner of the recently dead.

I was part of something eternal. And the whole was present in the part.

I knit the strands into threads and the thread into a banner that called my family to aid me. The hot spirit breath of the nightmare stirred my hair and the flint-on-stone scrape of its talons made my teeth ache before I got an answer.

But it was definite when it came.

The giant bones above me rattled as ghostly lungs stretched skeleton ribs. Sue the Tyrannosaur shuddered awake.

37

DINOSAURS DO NOT have ghosts, as far as I know. I mean, maybe I'll get to the great beyond and find it's like Jurassic Park there. But Sue had been imbued with personality by everyone who worked on her bones, and everyone who visited, studied, and virtually lived in that museum. All of Chicago and visitors from all over the world loved her.

In that sense, she did have a spirit, and the collective of Goodnight remnants breathed life into her. The shade of Sue the Tyrannosaur took shape on the bones. Thick muscle and tough hide, gigantic teeth, and forty feet from her nose to the tip of her whipping tail. Then spirit shook free from fossil, and the shade pulled away from her skeleton with a bellowing roar.

She might not have a ghost, but she sure had a psyche. And she was *pissed* at the mess the Jackal had made of her museum.

Looming protectively over me, she gave another piercing roar at the Jackal's monster. My ears rang as Sue leapt over the railing and advanced on the nightmare, shaking the building's foundations as if she were muscle and bone instead of magic and memory.

The beast gave a feline roar in return and pounced, trailing shreds of spirit. Sue batted it away from me with a whack of her tail, sending it streaming across the hall like a comet.

The crash woke the unconscious brethren, and the dinosaur shade stomped toward them, sending them scrambling like cockroaches caught out by the light. Her tail whipped dangerously close to Taylor, who hadn't moved.

At the end of the great hall, the Jackal gathered his spirits and his strength and re-formed his Frankenstein nightmare. The T. rex headed for a preemptive strike on the monster, but the Jackal, with a push I could feel across the room, sent his creature in a blur past her, not toward me, but toward Taylor, who still hadn't moved.

Sue made an astonishingly tight turn and ran after the beast, flattening out in the straightaway. I ran for Taylor, too, skidding to a halt beside him and flinging up all the psychic shield I had. It wouldn't be enough, but it would be a try.

The beast was almost on us when Sue struck, her massive

jaws grabbing the back of the nightmare's neck with a *crunch* that made my psychic teeth hurt. She shook the construct like a dog shakes a rat, and it flew apart into the remnant wisps that had made it.

What was left of them.

The Jackal stalked toward me. I stood up and squared my shoulders. From far away he looked like Carson, but the closer he came, the more I saw the stranger. "We aren't done," he said, when he was very close indeed.

But we were. A gunshot rang through the hall.

I didn't know how it happened or how I even saw it. Maybe it happened in psychic time, neuron fast. But for an instant of an instant, Carson was Carson again. In the next he slammed into me, knocking me to the floor. And in the next he staggered and pressed a hand to his chest. I felt the pain as if it were my own when I saw the blood bubbling up from under his fingers.

I didn't think about the Jackal. I didn't think about the gunshot. I thought only about Carson and jumped to my feet, flinging myself to help him.

Another shot cracked and a bullet thunked into the taxidermic elephant near my head. Sue lowered her head and roared, and I spun like an idiot and just *stood* there as Alexis took aim at my heart.

A trio of gunshots. One. Two. Three. A quick, professional grouping, and then a thud. I was on the floor again, but only because the T. rex's tail had knocked me down. When I got the nerve to look, I saw Alexis on the ground, sprawled motionless. And behind me was Taylor, propped up on one hand with his backup revolver in the other.

Sue's image was fading, as if forcing me to duck had been the last of her—of the remnants'—strength. As for Alexis, Taylor rolled to his feet and hurried over to her, kicking away the weapon, then checking for ... just checking.

I turned toward Carson and got another shock. He was still on his feet. Grabbing the hem of his shirt, he pulled it off and threw it aside. The wound frothed with blood, but as I watched, out came the bullet, spit by his body like a watermelon seed.

Carson was gone again, and the Jackal looked at me with his unnatural blue eyes and foreign smile. "Lucky for your friend that you did not pull me loose when you had the chance."

His shadow on the floor began to lengthen and broaden. I was seeing double: Carson with my eyes and the Jackal in full pharaoh regalia with my Sight.

The Jackal was healing his body—Carson's body—and strengthening himself, but *how*? I was tapped out. Where was *his* new power coming from?

A shade appeared beside me in a puff of frigid air and urgent warning. "Call the Veil for the girl," she said, in a voice I knew only from my lullabies.

"Mom?"

"Call it," she said. "Before there's nothing left of her."

The girl. There was only one here besides me. My gaze flew to Taylor, still kneeling beside Alexis. He caught my eye and shook his head.

Why hadn't the Veil appeared? Where was her *soul*?

I heard it then, a tiny keen that faded as the Jackal's shadow grew more massive.

"You mustn't call it," said a gruff voice on my other side. Aunt Diantha, who knew more about shades and remnants than anyone else, even before she was one.

"But Alexis—" I couldn't let her soul be consumed, no matter what she'd done.

"That *abomination*," said Aunt Diantha, meaning the Jackal, "is keeping the Veil from opening with his hold on the girl. But you must not call it. That's what he wants you to do, so he can use the young man's power to steal yours."

I had to open the Veil without calling it. Like I hadn't had enough puzzles today.

"Daisy," said my mom, "do something! The sound . . ."

I remembered Ivy's scream, and I didn't know how the Jackal was keeping Alexis's own from me, but Mom could hear it and it had brought her shade to tears.

The Veil . . . I only called, I didn't control. It opened when it was needed.

With a bolt of inspiration and trepidation, I reached into my pocket and took out the vial that held the spirit of Carson's mom. I was taking a huge risk—losing an innocent soul to the Jackal in an attempt to save a blackened one. And one just slightly gray one, if you counted Carson's.

Everything relied on my timing and my own sagging strength. I dropped the glass to the floor and crushed it with my heel.

Helena! Her name burst into my mind as her spirit burst from the prison, bright and blinding.

The Veil appeared with a waiting swiftness. It rang with a pure, true note in the middle of the discord. To me and the spirits—my spirits—it sang a welcome.

To the Jackal, it was a warning. He whirled to face me, and the curtain that shimmered open between us. He lost his grip on Alexis, and her racked soul stretched and twisted on its way through the portal, her tortured screams cut off as the surface tension between worlds rippled in her wake.

"You can't," said the Jackal, anticipating my plan. "Not without sending your young man through, too. We are *bound*."

"*Help him*," said the shade—no, the soul—that had taken Mom's place beside me. Helena pled, "How can I help you help my son?"

"Just hold tight," I murmured, and shored up my resolve—or at least my bravado. To the Jackal I called, "I unbound you before. I can do it again."

I hoped.

"But without my magic," crooned the Jackal, "he'll die from his bullet wound." He held up bloody fingers and tsked. "I think it may have gotten his lung."

This was a chance I had to take. I would gladly risk my life or my soul in place of any of these people. But I couldn't. I had to do what I did best—talk big, and pray I didn't screw this up.

"Enough chitchat," I said. "Let's dance."

I let my psyche slip away from my physical form, a shade of my own self. Unconfined by distance, I grabbed at the jackal mark on Carson's back, the spot where the two were knit together. The threads had tightened, and somehow I had to unstitch them without unraveling the half that I cared about.

The more the Jackal struggled, the more blood ran down Carson's chest. The Veil hummed and shimmered with infinite patience as I picked at the tight snarls of the binding, but the longer it took, the paler and weaker the living body became, so weak I worried Carson's soul would make the trip, too.

I needed to rip the Jackal off like a Band-Aid and get him through the Veil. My psyche was strong, but I needed force and inertia. I needed the weight of a soul.

Carson's mom was no more than a translucent vision, and no less than everything that made her human. "You wanted to help? It's risky."

"He's my *son*. This is no risk." Then she laughed. It was a beautiful sound, of someone used to laughing. "It beats the purgatory of Devlin Maguire's office for eternity."

I smiled in spite of myself and held out the threads of the Jackal's binding to her. She took them, smiled back—a devilish smile—and ran for the Veil, painting the air with light as she leapt through.

The Jackal gave an angry shout as he was yanked toward the curtain of eternity, scrabbling to hold on to this world with psychic tooth and claw. At the tipping point, he began sliding toward the Veil without my help. But he was taking Carson's spirit, unconscious and unable to fight, with him.

"If I go," sounded the Jackal over an intangible roar of wind, "he goes, too."

"You don't get to say who stays and who goes, you son of a bitch."

Neither did I, but I knew how to fight for a spirit. As the last thread of binding pulled loose, I grabbed Carson, body and soul, and anchored us in the here and now. But he was so heavy, and all of eternity yawned before me.

The open Veil offered tantalizing glimpses outside the walls of time and space. It awed but didn't frighten me. Maybe it should have. I was so small and eternity pulled at the fragile bond of my body. I was an atom and a star, an infinitesimal speck of identity suspended before the gravity well of fathomless eons of souls.

Daisy . . . A woman's lullaby voice from beyond, chiding me gently. *The job is done. Let the Veil close.*

"Daisy!" A guy's voice. A young man. Naming me and calling me back. "You did it. It's over . . . and we need your help with your relatives."

I sat up, unable to remember lying down. But I had, in a position that strongly indicated that Taylor had caught me when I collapsed and held me safely until I came to.

The shade of the T. rex was gone, and when I looked at the skeleton, the only hint of her adventures was a fading green glow in the sockets of her skull. The color was all Goodnight, but the wink—there was no mistaking it for anything else—I was sure that belonged to Sue.

"What relatives?" I asked, seeing no other remnants. I would be sad that Mom hadn't said goodbye, except we didn't need to.

Then I heard them, the unmistakable rallying shouts of Goodnights on the march, coming from outside and demanding to be let in. The museum doors stood open and the hall was flooded with cops, armed response officers, museum officials, and paramedics—

Carson. They surrounded him. I'd been holding on to him—no, that was just with my psyche. Now all I could see were his shoes. I started to get up, but Taylor's hand on my shoulder kept me where I was. "He's fine," Taylor assured me. "The fuss is because they can't figure out *why* he's fine."

"Oh." I took a moment to look around. What a mess, with mummy dust and toppled totem poles and the museum store looking like it had had a retail explosion. "Did you See anything?" I asked Taylor, meaning the big battle.

"Besides the big dinosaur rampage? Not really. The temperature dropped about fifty degrees and you said 'Basingstoke' and collapsed." He pointed at his eyes. "Serious REM going on, though."

"Great. Phin will want to hook me up to brain electrodes next time."

Jeez, I hoped there wasn't a next time.

Taylor ducked his head to catch my gaze, studying my face and heaven only knew what was written there. "Are you okay?" he asked gently, and he wasn't talking about three days' worth of psychic backlash headache that I could feel looming like a pain tsunami.

Blushing made me feel disloyal to Carson. Which was stupid, because wanting to go over to Carson made me feel disloyal to Taylor, who had *never* lied to me, even by omission... and who had killed his first person today.

For me.

"Are *you* okay?" I asked.

"I'm fine," he said.

I allowed myself a smile. "You keep saying that word. I don't think it means what you think it means."

He couldn't—quite—let himself laugh. Instead, he looked over my shoulder. "You'd better slide in there and say what you've got to say while you've got the chance."

That sounded very dire, but I realized he didn't necessarily mean life or death. Police swarmed the place, and I saw Gerard waiting like a middle-aged vulture, and any minute now my family was going to storm the barricade and drag me home to Texas tied to their broomsticks.

Taylor got to his feet and gave me a hand up. I was shakier than I liked to admit, and he squeezed my hand before letting go and flashing his badge so the crowd around Carson would let me through.

He looked awful. The blood loss had made his old bruises appear even more livid, and his new ones were watercolor blotches over just about every inch of him. And that was only the inches that were showing.

When he saw me, he winced. And I hadn't even said anything yet.

"So…," I started. What do you say to a guy who unwittingly uses you to get a magical artifact ahead of a secret organization that he lies about not knowing, and maybe breaks a little bit of your heart, even though you've only known each other a couple of really intense days, right before he jumps in front of a bullet for you.

I mean, what do you *say*?

You say nothing. Because just then, Agent Gerard arrived, and wouldn't be put off. "Christopher Carson Maguire, you are under arrest—"

"Christopher Carson?" I interrupted. "Your name is Kit Carson?"

"*You*," said Gerard, aiming his laser stare at me. "I'll get to you in a minute, Peanut."

"No you won't," Carson said, in his most steely voice ever. "She didn't do anything. And if you want all the information I have on Maguire Enterprises, all their holdings and financial dealings, you'd better remember that."

Maybe "I'm not a nice guy" really *was* the biggest lie he ever told me.

38

THE JUDGE'S GAVEL fell, and Carson was off the hook for everything but the motorcycle theft, since two FBI agents had actually seen him do it. Some of that might have been luck, or extenuating circumstance, or even a lot of payoffs—like two car owners and some museum boards—or the fact that when it came right down to it, no one could really explain what happened at the Field Museum that day.

And of course, Carson had all the dirt on his father's criminal activities. Not just a whale, but a whale of a whale with a really big headline takedown. The making of a DA's career. I wasn't in on the details, but I bet they were happy to work with Carson and his high-priced lawyer.

At the verdict, the courtroom erupted in camera flashes and reporters calling out questions. From a few rows back, I watched Carson stand and shake his lawyer's hand. He was looking a lot better than the last time I'd seen him. Which, really, was not a stretch. It had been two months, and I'd only seen his picture on news websites until I returned to Chicago with Agent Taylor to testify at the hearing.

My cousin Amy, who'd come from Texas for moral support, asked, "Ready to get out of here? Or do you want to say hi?"

"He knows I'm here. Trust me. If he wants to talk to me, he'll find me."

She gazed at me for a long moment, ignoring all the people trying to get past us in the busy courtroom gallery. "You know, guys are weird. Sometimes, when they think they've offended you—because they have—they don't know how to come talk to you, because they think you don't want them to, and they've been raised to respect when a girl doesn't want them around."

I took that advice for what it was worth. "Sorry, Amaryllis. You're not exactly the expert on smooth-sailing romance."

She frowned in equal parts annoyance and embarrassment. "Well. Things sometimes work out for the best in spite of our best efforts to screw them up."

The crowd was getting to be too much for me. Because you know who has a lot of ghost baggage hanging around them? People who spend time in courthouses. "Let's get out of here."

We grabbed our things and headed out to the hall. Winter involves a lot more *stuff* in Chicago than it does in Texas. Coats, hats, scarves, gloves. I don't even own half that gear.

A couple of reporters waved recorders at me, asking questions, but I'd gotten good at ignoring them, and Amy had always been good at spin-doctoring the weird parts of Goodnight life without actually lying. She'd helped both Taylor and me prepare our testimony, because we *didn't* want to lie and we *couldn't* tell the weird parts. Not even the Goodnight charm could handle faux demigods, real mummies, and spirit dinosaurs.

Agent Taylor was down the hall, talking to the judge, who'd ditched his robe for shirtsleeves in the overheated courthouse. He waved me over, and I approached warily, worried we'd been caught out in the spin-doctoring, but it seemed His Honor was just being nice.

"I wanted to thank you for your help with this case, young lady." The judge held out his hand and shook mine heartily when I took it. "It sounded like Carson got tangled up in things way beyond his control."

"We both did," I said, the rote response.

The judge started rolling down his sleeves. "Well, I'd better get back to work. Thank you again, Agent Taylor. And you, Miss Goodnight."

An unexpected glimpse of black distracted me, and Taylor had to nudge me to respond. "You're welcome, Your Honor."

The judge went back to his chambers, or wherever, and Taylor and I began strolling down the hall, to where Amy waited. "What bee got in your bonnet?" he asked.

"What bee in my . . . What are you, ninety?" I glanced over my shoulder, but the judge had disappeared. "He had a tattoo on his arm."

"Well, yeah. Lots of people have tattoos, Daisy. Don't get weird."

I snorted. "Too late. So, when can I start working murders again?"

"Anytime. I'm back on duty, and you're cleared of everything. In fact, that was why I was talking to the judge. To make sure there are no surprises here in Illinois. You're good to go, Jailbait."

"In two more weeks, you'll have to stop calling me that, *Jack*."

"In two more weeks, I'll still be too old for you."

I stared at him, stunned that he'd actually *said it*. Okay, he'd said it before, which was how the whole jailbait thing started. But this time, he said it like he was reminding both of us. And I wasn't sure why it made a difference, but it did. I liked knowing it was safe to have a crush on him. But maybe not *too* safe.

With a careless shrug, I started walking again. "It doesn't matter. We could never date anyway. Doesn't the FBI have rules against partners dating? Even if I am just an unpaid consultant."

"I'd certainly never want to date Gerard, so I never asked."

We reached Amy, who was pretending to check her text messages, or maybe really was reading them, but also keeping an eye down the hall, where Carson was talking to his lawyer and his aunt.

Talking to them, and sliding glances my way.

"When he breaks free of them," said Amy from the corner of

her mouth, "go over there. Have pity on the guy and let him say what he has to say."

I didn't have to go over. When Carson wrapped up his conversation, he headed toward me. I looked around for an escape route, but Amy grabbed my arm and made me stay until Carson reached us.

He nodded to Taylor and to Amy. Then to me he said, "Hey, Daisy."

"Hi, um, is it Chris? Christopher?"

"It's still Carson."

"So you're going for the one-name celebrity thing?"

He frowned. "I *was* going for the 'come over and see how you're doing' thing."

"Oh." I folded my arms and wished I knew what to do with my hands other than flap them around nervously while I talked. "Sorry."

The four of us stood there awkwardly until Amy turned to Taylor and said, "Is there a place to get a cup of tea around here?" She blew on her hands. "Even my insides are cold. We're a long way from Texas."

Taylor looked reluctant to leave us, but Amy was sort of a force to be reckoned with when she got going. Then they were gone and Carson and I were standing in the hall on our lonesome. Well, as lonesome as you can be in a really busy hallway full of reporters and stuff.

"Do you want to walk for a bit?" Carson asked. "I can guess where your cousin and Taylor are going. We can walk that way and you can join them."

I couldn't think of a reason to say no, and there were several reasons to say yes. Just because *closure* is a pop-psychology cliché doesn't mean it's not true. My talent with the dead was sort of all about closure.

We walked all the way to the front doors in silence, and then he helped me with my coat, also in silence, and then we stepped outside, where a bunch of reporters nearly went into raptures when they saw us together. Then *I* stayed silent, and Carson said, "No comment, no comment," as we shouldered through the crowd.

Which was how I found out Carson had a bodyguard. He stopped the guy from following us down the street.

"He's just for times like this," Carson explained. "The rest of my days are very normal."

"Uh-huh."

We walked for a few steps, and he said, "You look great in that suit."

"I hate it. It looks like something a sexy TV lawyer would wear."

"Which is probably why I like it."

I turned to him, skipping to the entrée in this three-course dinner of awkward. "This is crazy. Why are we talking about my clothes? Why are we here at all? Do we have anything to talk about with no mummies rising or dinosaurs stepping on us? With no one trying to hijack or kill us—?"

I clapped my hand over my mouth, because that was tactless, even for me. His father was going to jail for a very long time, and his half sister was dead, which deserved respect even if she was a homicidal nut job. Not that I would put it that way to Carson.

"We're talking," he said, in that composed voice he used when he wasn't feeling very composed at all, "because I want to see you." He cleared his throat. "Like, socially."

I folded my arms. "How is that going to work, Chicago and Texas? Do you have some frequent-flier miles to burn through?"

"Well, you're off from school for the winter break, right? Do you have a passport? The Cayman Islands..."

"Oh. My. God. Just... no." I started walking again, at a good clip, thanks to my long legs and a tailwind. The Windy City for sure. "I'm not going to the freaking Cayman Islands with you. Why would you even want to?"

He caught my elbow and drew me to a stop. "Because I want to *find out* if we have anything to talk about when not..." He tightened his jaw, then went on. "When not all those things you said."

I folded my arms and studied him. There was no doubt he was sincere. "Why?"

"Because I like you. I like the way we fit."

"Carson, you raised the dead. And that was before you were possessed."

"Only once. And you put them back down again. It sounds like we're a great team."

"That's why you want to see me? Because we'd make a good crime-fighting team? I already *have* that."

He gave me a look. A we're-standing-on-a-busy-sidewalk-

382

and-people-are-taking-our-picture-but-if-we-weren't-I-would-let-you-know-exactly-why-what-you-just-said-is-stupid look.

And suddenly Chicago didn't seem so cold after all.

"Okay," I said. "This is how it's going to be. If you want to see me, you come down to Texas for the holidays. You spend them on the Goodnight farm with all my family, which contains several very intimidating chaperones. *Much* better chaperones than your aunt."

He blinked. And maybe paled a little. "All your family? Can't we just go on a date? I promise not to pick you up in a Corvette."

"You can pick me up in a not-a-Corvette on the twenty-third. But the next two days..." I chewed my lip for a second, analyzing this impulse. "You need to see how a real family works, Carson."

He thought about it until my nose started to run in the cold. "That sounds a lot like taking my medicine."

"Dude!" I threw my hands in the air. "Do you want to get to know me, or do you just want a holiday hookup?"

"Why is this an either-or question?"

I made a disgusted sound and started walking again. Carson caught my arm before I'd gone more than two steps. "Hey, I'm sorry. It's just ... you've got a *lot* of family. Can't I start small? With a cousin or something?"

I thought about it, not for as long as he did. Because I was freezing. "My cousin is in that coffee shop. Let's start with her."

After only a microscopic hesitation, he slid his hand down to link with mine. "Do I have to bring presents for *all* your family?"

"They're not going to approve of you if you're cheap."

"Then I'll have to come to Texas early so you can help me shop."

"You can mail-order. I'd rather raise another dinosaur than go to the mall at Christmas."

We walked along, hand in hand, like the normal couple we were not, and never would be, because we weren't normal. My phone buzzed in my coat pocket with a text from Taylor.

What do you hear?

I thought about it. I liked not normal. Maybe I could handle being a not-normal couple.

I slipped off my glove and texted my answer with one hand while Carson and I bantered, and he held the other.

Nothing but the rain.

AUTHOR'S NOTE

I don't usually like to use specific places in my books because (a) it constrains me to what's actually there and (b) I tend to destroy them. But I made an exception for this book, mostly because of Sue. And how could I not use places so full of real, cool stuff?

Things that are real: the Oriental Institute, its pharaoh statue and reading room; the Field Museum with its twenty-three mummies, Great Hall, and three man-eating lions; the St. Louis Art Museum and the *Little Dancer* Degas bronze and room of Egyptian art.

And of course, Sue the T. rex is real. I couldn't make that up. You can even follow her on Twitter @SUEtheTrex.

Things that are not real: pretty much everything else. I tried to keep to the true layouts and geography, but the St. Louis museum in particular got a rearrange (and has no Pompeii art or exhibit).

I love museums, and the Field Museum is awesome. You can actually watch the lab geeks work in the DNA and fossil labs. Sorry I made such a mess of the place, guys.

ACKNOWLEDGMENTS

I must thank, as always, my marvelous agent, Lucienne Diver, of the Knight Agency, and my editor, Krista Marino. This book went through a lot, because I went through a lot while I was writing it. They were both patient, but not so patient they didn't push me to my best writing. Thanks also to all the staff at Random House.

Love and appreciation to the IHOP Musketeers, aka the Ninja Turtles, for listening, laughing, and butt-kicking as necessary. To Jenny Martin, Carson's biggest fan, and my favorite writing buddy. To Kate Cornell, for asking me just the right questions to help me sort out the rough spots. To Cheryl Smyth, my magical sounding board. Yes, C, we need to work on that Goodnight family tree.

As always, love and gratitude for the support of my family and friends. It's been a crazier ride than normal, and I couldn't have made it without you.

And finally, to my readers, and to the bloggers, teachers, and librarians, just for being awesome.

ROSEMARY CLEMENT-MOORE is the author of *Brimstone, Highway to Hell, The Splendor Falls,* and *Texas Gothic.* She grew up on a ranch in south Texas and now lives and writes in Arlington, Texas. You can visit her at readrosemary.com.